ICE TONGUE!

I closed off all surmises, everything but my driving will. . . . In my sight the sword appeared to grow, no longer fitting the hand of any true man—rather such a weapon as only a giant might swing. And it began to move . . .

ICE TONGUE!

I put into that silent call the full strength I could summon. The Dark One still balanced his wand as a spear . . .

ICE TONGUE!

The sword gave a kind of jerk, its point rising through the glowing crystal. . . . There was a bolt of force no one could see, but which struck straight into the mind my efforts had left wide open. I had a single instant to think that this was death—then there was nothing at all.

TREY OF SWORDS

WITCH WORLD Books by Andre Norton

WITCH WORLD

WEB OF THE WITCH WORLD

THREE AGAINST THE WITCH WORLD

WARLOCK OF THE WITCH WORLD

SORCERESS OF THE WITCH WORLD

THE YEAR OF THE UNICORN

TREY OF SWORDS

All from
ACE Books

TREY OF SWORDS

by

Andre Norton

ace books
A Division of Charter Communications Inc.
A GROSSET & DUNLAP COMPANY
360 Park Avenue South
New York, New York 10010

An ACE Book

Cover art by Charles Mikolaycak

First Ace printing: July 1978

Contents

I
Sword of Ice

1

My mother was of the Old Race, those hunted out of Karsten when Duke Yivan put to the Outlaws' Horn all of a blood far more ancient than his, upstart mercenary that he was, dabbler in forbidden things, one who companied with the unspeakable Kolders.

Of a heritage older than Karsten's naming, all my mother brought into Estcarp when she fled death was herself and a tail of three fighting men from her father's lordship. Those she sent to join the Borderers who served under the Outworlder Lord Simon Tregarth, to hold back the evil which had come upon our world. She herself took refuge with a distant kinswoman, the Lady Chriswitha. And later she wed, not with a man of her own people, but with a Sulcarman, thus divorcing herself abruptly from her kind.

But he was slain in one of the forays against the southern ports. And, since she felt no home-love among his people, she returned to her own kin, bearing in her body a child conceived during her short wed-time. Also within her the need for life dimmed, so that when I was born ahead of the proper day, she went out from this life as goes a candle blown by an impatient breath.

The Lady Chriswitha took me, even keeping me though she had married another lord fled from the south, Hervon. His family had vanished during the horning, but he was a man of war learning and wrought well along the Border, rising to his own command. And he had two daughters and a son, Imhar. This Imhar was my senior in age by two years; a strong, healthy boy who took readily to the uncertain world of alarms and war in which we were bred.

With me it was not so. From my birthing I was a weakling and needed much care, given to many small illnesses so that I was ever a concern and a source of impatience to all but my lady, this impatience being made plain to me as soon as I was old enough to be aware of those about me. Though I strove to match Imhar, there was never any chance during our boyhood that I might. A sword fitted into his hand as if he were born carrying that blade, and he used it as if it were an extension of himself, with a skill precise and beautiful to watch.

He rode fearlessly, and was out on patrol before he could count barely the years of his youthful training. And Lord Hervon took pride rightfully in his heir, a youth who had all the attributes necessary to make his way in perilous times.

I trained with sword and with dart gun—the weight of the war ax was ever too much for my arm. Among the dark Old Race, I was a stranger in more than my lack of physical strength, for I had the fair skin, the light hair of the Sulcars—but unfortunately, neither the height nor the fine strong body of that people.

Though I tried so hard to match Imhar, in my heart I longed for something else. Not the sea of my father's people, which might have been natural enough, but rather learning—the forgotten learning which had once been a part of our past.

It is true that no male could possess the Power, or so the Wise Women, those Witches who ruled in Estcarp, proclaimed. But there were old legends, fragments of which I heard from time to time and treasured in my memory, that this was not always so. That once men had also walked that road, and to some purpose.

I could read well enough, and I hunted out all I could that pertained to this age-dimmed past. Though I never spoke of such to those about me—for they would have deemed me stricken in wits, perhaps even a danger to the household should the Witches learn of my heresy.

In the year I belted on my own sword and took to riding with the Border Guard, Karsten loosed against us the greatest threat of all. The Kolders were gone, Lord Simon and his lady having ventured overseas and closed the World Gate through which that horror had come. Yivan, lord in the south, had been a part of the Kolder menace and had died of it. Then, for some time, there had been chaos across all of Karsten, as lord fought against lord for the leadership.

At last Ragan of Cleen triumphed. And, to unite his people, proclaimed a crusade against the Witches. For it is always in such straits a shrewd move to find an enemy outside the borders against which all may march, taking their minds away from wounds and losses nearer home.

So there came a great hosting, but not of our swords, rather of the Power. For the Witches united for a single night and day, summoning such strength as they could call. And then they aimed this southward and the land itself obeyed their commands. Mountains moved, the very earth twisted and rent this way and that. Accordingly they themselves paid a great price, for many of their number perished, being used to channel that Power until it burned out their lives

Lest chaos fall upon us as it had on Karsten when Yivan was slain, Koris of Gorm took command in the land and the rule passed then from the Council to him.

Lord Simon and the Lady Jealithe had been lost long since in a quest to the northern seas, and there was no other war leader great enough to command the respect and loyalty of Estcarp.

But there came a strange tale, passing from manor to holding, holding to manor, that the children of the House of Tregarth had fled the land under the great anger of the Witches and that they were now outlawed, to be given no aid by any, lest those be condemned also into the state where all men's hands were lawfully raised to pull them down.

It was whispered that the known "Power" which Lord Simon had had and used was in his sons also. And that they had conspired, against all rightful custom, to aid their sister out of the House of the Witches where she trained. There was a very strange thing about them, unknown elsewhere in the world; the three had been born at one birthing! Thus, they were very close.

I speak of these three because they caused the changing of my life, and the lives of all who dwelt in Lord Hervon's household. And I, myself, was eager to hear all I could of the young lords who, as their father before them, differed from our kind.

Karsten being no longer to be feared, Lord Hervon had set about realizing his own dream for the future. During his riding up and down the land in his hosting, he had found a place which seemed to him a fair setting for a manor. And none would gainsay his claim as it lay well to the east, in a section of the country which had long been forsaken and half forgotten.

Thus, we set out for this place to build anew in a peace which still seemed strange and which we still doubted, so men went armed and we kept sentries about. There were

4

fifty of us, mainly men—though the Lady Chriswitha had five women in her household and she had also her daughters, her sisters, and their husbands, as well as a child born two years after me to her younger sister, who died thereafter.

Now I must speak of Crytha—yet that is difficult. For from the time I looked down into her cradle on the hearthside, there was something which tied me to her, in spite of all reason. No kin-tie lay between us, nor could any. For by the ancient custom of our people, she must wed Imhar when the time was right, thus unifying the lordship Hervon was determined to found.

She was truly of the Old Race, dark and slender. And to my eyes, there was always something a little remote about her, as if she sometimes said, or heard, that which was not shared by those about her.

Because of my weakly boyhood, I was closer in companionship with Crytha than Imhar, and she began to turn to me in little things, asking that I aid her in nursing a wing-broken bird and the like. For it was apparent from her earliest years that she had a gift of healcraft.

That her talents went farther than that I learned when I was near the age to ride with the Borderers (having gained strength to the point that I could call myself a fighter, if not an outstanding one). I had come upon her unawares by the brook which ran near the farm-garth which, at that time, the Lady Chriswitha called home.

Crytha sat very still in the grass, which there grew nearly as high as the top of her head. Her eyes were closed as if she slept, but she moved her hands gently back and forth. I watched her, puzzled, and then saw, with sick horror rising in me, there coiled in the grass a snake perhaps as long as my sword arm. Its head was raised and swayed, following the command of Crytha's hand. I would have drawn steel and slain the thing, but I found I could not move.

At length she clapped her hands and opened her eyes. The snake dropped its head to the ground, disappearing into the grass as if it had been a hallucination.

"No fear, Yonan." She did not turn her head to look at me, yet she knew that I was there. And as she spoke, that compulsion on me vanished, as had the snake. I took two strides to her side, my anger rising to match the fear that had held me.

"What do you do?" I demanded.

She looked up at me. "Come sit." She beckoned. "Should I explain myself to a mountain whose eyes I cannot meet without a crick in my poor neck?"

I gingerly surveyed the grass, longing to rake through it with my sword that I might not drop upon her late companion—with dire results for both of us. And then I settled down.

"It is a part of healcraft—I think." But her voice sounded a little puzzled. "They do not fear me, the winged ones, the furred ones, and today I have proved that even the scaled ones can be reached. I think we close our minds too often, or fasten them on such as this"—she leaned forward a little to touch a single finger tip to my sheathed sword—"so that we cannot hear much of what lies about us—the good of the wide world."

I drew a deep breath, the anger seeping from me. For some inner sense told me that Crytha knew what she was doing, even as I knew the swing of steel.

"Yonan, remember the old tales you used to tell me?"

For it was with Crytha alone that I had shared my scraps of legend and ancient song.

"In that world, man had Powers—"

"There are Powers in Estcarp," I pointed out. And then a new fear rose in me. The Witches were avid recruits to their number. So far they had not drawn upon the refugees from Karsten, unless some girl child showed unusual skills. Crytha—Crytha must not vanish behind their gray walls, lay aside all that life made good in return for power.

"I am no Witch," she said softly. "And, Yonan, with you alone I share what I know. Because you understand that freedom is more than Power. Of that one can become too fond."

I caught her wrist in a firm grip and held it, also drawing her gaze squarely to meet my own eyes.

"Swear not to try that again—not with any scaled one!"

She smiled. "I do not swear any oaths, Yonan; that is not my way. This much I shall promise you, that I will take no risks."

With that I had to be content, though I was seldom content in my mind when I thought of what she might be tempted to do. And we did not speak of this again. For shortly after, I joined the Borderers and we saw each other very seldom indeed.

But when we went to the east and set up the new Manor hall, it was different. Crytha was of hand-fasting age. It would not be long until Imhar could claim her. And the thought of that was a dark draft of sorrow for me. So I tried not to be in her company, for already I knew my own emotions, which must be rigidly schooled and locked away.

It was before we had the hall complete that the stranger came.

He walked in from the hills, one of our sentries at his

back, and he gave to Lord Hervon the proper guesting greeting. Yet there was about him a strangeness we all felt.

Young he was, and plainly of the Old Race. Yet his eyes were dark blue, not gray. And he held himself proudly as one who had the right to greet named warriors on an equal ground.

He said he was a man under a geas. But later he revealed that he was an outlaw—one of the Tregarth sons—and that he came recruiting into the lowlands from the long-lost land to the east—Escore—from which, he said, our race had sprung in the very early beginnings.

Lord Hervon saw danger in him, and to this point of view he was urged by Godgar, his marshal. So it was judged he be delivered up to the Council's guard, lest we be deemed outlaws in turn.

But after he rode away with Godgar, there grew unrest and uneasiness among us. I dreamed and so did others, for they spoke aloud of those dreams. And we went no more to cut wood for the building, but paced restlessly about, looking toward the mountains which rose eastward. In us there was a pulling, a need. . . .

Then Godgar returned with his men and he told a story hardly to be believed, yet we knew in this haunted land many strange things came to pass. There had been a vast company of birds and beasts which had gathered, stopping their journey to the west. And, guarded by those furred and feathered ones, Kyllan Tregarth had started back to the mountains. But that company had let Godgar and his men also return to us unharmed.

It was then that the Lady Chriswitha arose and spoke to all our company.

"It is laid upon us to believe this message. Can anyone beneath this hall roof deny that in him or her now there does lie the desire to ride? I spoke apart with Kyllan Tregarth—in him there was truth. I think we are summoned to his journey and it is one we cannot gainsay.''

As she so put it into words, my uneasiness was gone; rather there arose in me an eagerness to be on the way, as if before me lay some great and splendid adventure. And glancing about I saw signs on the faces of the others that in this we were agreed.

Thus, gathering what gear we should need for such a journey, not knowing into what we rode, we went forth from the Manor we had thought to make our home, heading into a wilderness in which might lurk worse danger than ever came out of Karsten or Kolder.

2

Thus, we came into Escore, a land long ago wracked by the magic of those adepts who had believed themselves above the laws of man and nature. In an uneasy peace, it had lain for generations keeping a trembling balance between the forces of Light and those of the Dark. The adepts were gone—some had perished in wild quarrels with their fellows which had left the land blasted and shadowed. Others had wrought gates into other times and worlds and, possessed by curiosity—or greed for power—had departed through those.

Behind, the vanished Great Ones had left a residue of all their trafficking in forbidden things. They had created, by mutation, life forms different from humankind. Some of these were close enough to man to allow kinship of a sort. Others were of the Dark and harried the country at their will.

Before the Old Race had claimed such power, there had been another people in the land; not human, but appearing so. These had a deeper tie with the earth itself than any man could have, for they did not strive to rend or alter it as is the custom of my kind; rather did they live with it, yielding to the rhythms of the seasons, the life which the soil nourished and sustained.

These were the People of Green Silences. When the doom wrought by the adepts came upon the land, they withdrew to a waste yet farther east, taking with them or drawing to them certain of the creatures which the adepts had bred. And there they dwelt, holding well aloof from all others.

But there were remnants of the Old Race who were not seekers after forbidden knowledge. And those had journeyed westward, preyed upon by things of the Shadow, until they reached Estcarp and Karsten. There, even as the Witches had done to defeat Ragan, those among them possessing the Power had wrought a mighty earthshaking, walling out their ancient homeland. So strong was the geas they then laid upon men that we could not even think of the east—it dropped from our memories. Until the lords of the House of Tregarth and their sister, being of half blood and so immune to this veiling, dared return.

Our journey was not an easy one. The land itself put many barriers in our way. And also, though we were met by those Kyllan had aroused to wish us well, we were dogged by creatures of the Dark, so that we won to the Green Valley as pursued as we had been in the flight from Karsten a generation earlier.

But the Valley was a haven of safety—having at its entrance special deep-set runes and signs carved. And none that were not free of any dealing with the Shadow could pass those and live.

The houses of the Green People were strange and yet very pleasing to the eye, for they were not wrought by man from wood and stone, but rather grown, tree and bushes twined together to form walls as deep as those of any Border keep. And their roofing was of the brilliant green feathers shed in season by those birds which obeyed the Lady Dahaun.

She was of our most ancient legend—the forest woman who could call upon a plant to flower or fruit, and it would straightaway do as she desired. Yet, as all her people, she was alien. For she was never the same in men's eyes, changing ever from one moment to the next. So that she might at one breath have the ruddy, sun-tipped hair of a Sulcarwoman, and the next the black locks and ivory skin of the Old Race.

Her co-ruler here was Ethutur, and all which remained steady about him also were the small ivory horns which arose from the curls of hair above his forehead. Yet his shifts of feature and color were not as startling as those of Dahuan.

Under Lord Hervon's orders, we pitched tents in the Valley for our own abode. For, though it might be chill and coming into winter without the rock walls of this stronghold, within lay the mellowness of late summer.

It would seem that here legends came to life, for we saw flying, pacing, sporting, strange creatures which had long been thought by us to be out of imagination—wrought by ancient songsmiths. There were the Flannan—very small, yet formed enough like men to seem some far-off kinsman. They were winged and sometimes danced in the air for seeming sheer delight that they lived. And there were also the Renthan—large as horses, but far different, for they had tails like brushes of fluff clapped tight to their haunches; on their foreheads, single horns curved in gleaming red arcs.

These had borne us from the mountains, but they were not in any way ruled by their riders, being proudly intelligent and allies, not servants, for the Valley.

There were also the Lizard people—and of those I learned much. For I made my first friend among their number. That came about because of my own private heartache.

Crytha had come into paradise, or so she thought. She blossomed from a thin, quiet half-child, half-maid into a person strange to me. And she ever followed Dahaun, eager to learn what the lady would teach.

Imhar was constantly at the councils of the warriors, not always on the fringe as was fitting for one of his youth. He lapped up all the knowledge of war as a house mog-cat will lap at fresh milk.

For we had come into a Valley which was peace, but which was only a small cupping of that. Around us Escore boiled and seethed. Ethutur himself rode out as war herald with the Lord Kemoc Tregarth to visit the Krogan, who were water dwellers. And other heralds went forth to arouse what help would come at the rising of the banner.

There was a shaping of arms at the forge, a testing of mail, and all that stir which had been so long our portion in Estcarp. Save that now we were pitted not against men but against an unholy life totally alien to ours.

Fight I would when the time came, but in me there was a feeling of loneliness. For in all company, I had not one I could call rightly shield brother or cup mate. And Crytha was seldom in sight.

It was the day of the storm which began the true tale of

Yonan, as if up to that time I had been a thing only half finished, rough-hewn, and only partly useful.

I had gone with a detachment of Lord Hervon's swordsmen, with one of the Green People as a guide, climbing up into the rocky walls which were our defense, that we might look out beyond and see what lay there, also select for the future those places from which we could best meet any attack. It had been a bright day when we began that climb, but now there were gathering clouds, and Yagath, who was our leader, eyed those with concern, saying we must return before the worst of the wind broke upon us.

The clouds (or were they of the Shadow and no true work of nature?) rolled in so fast that we hurried indeed. But it chanced I was the last in line, and, as the wind came down upon us with a roar to drown any other sound, my foot slipped. Before I could regain my balance, I slid forward, my nails breaking, my finger tips scraped raw by rock I fought to hold.

Now the dark and the wind dropped a curtain to cut me away from everything but the rock pocket into which the force of my descent had jammed my body. My mail had not served to save me from painful bruising; perhaps it had but added to that. And water poured down upon me, as if someone on the surface of the cliff above emptied one pail after another into my cramped resting place.

I pushed with all my strength and so got farther back into this temporary prison, where a rock poised above took some of the wind and rain off me. Later, I thought, I could climb, but dared not try it yet in that rush which was becoming a stream cascading down the wall to my right.

There were fierce slashes of lightning across the small

portion of the sky which I could see, reminding me of the most effective weapons of the Green People—their force whips. Then came a fearful and deafening crash close by, a queer smell which made me think that lightning had indeed struck, and not too far away.

The rush of water carried with it small stones, and it did not drain fast from the crevice I occupied, though that had an open end facing outward from the Valley. So the flood lapped about my knees, and then touched my thighs. I squirmed, trying to reach a higher portion in which to crouch, but there was none.

While the drumming of the rain, the heavy boom of thunder never ended.

I was aware now, as I turned and strove to find a better shelter, that my right ankle gave out sharp thrusts of pain, enough once or twice to make me giddy. So I subsided at last, imprisoned until the storm might pass.

It was during one of those vivid flashes of lightning that I first saw an answering glint of light from the wall to my right. For a moment or two, that meant nothing, save there must be something there which reflected the flashes. Then I wriggled a little, to free my shoulder better, so I might feel along the wall.

My abraded finger tips flinched from the rough stone, then they slid onto something smooth; not only smooth, but in a way oddly cool and pleasant. In the dark, I explored my find. It seemed to be a rod of some sort, extending outward perhaps the length of my thumb and only a little larger than that digit in size. I tried to pull at it, and it seemed that it was a little loose but did not yield to the small amount of strength I could exert in my cramped position.

Yet there was something about my unseen find which

kept my fingers seeking it out, touching it. That it was part of the natural rock, I doubted. It was too smooth, more like a piece of metal or crystal which had been purposefully worked. Yet the way it protruded from the native rock, with no break in that to hold it (as I was able to discover by touch), argued it could not be man-made.

The fury of the storm continued. From my constrained perch I looked out at the world beyond the valley, but the darkness kept me from seeing anything. Save here and there some glow close to ground, marking, I was sure from all I had heard, a place where a remnant of the Power force still burned. For these we had seen in our journey from the mountains, such being called to our attention. If the glow was blue that signified a point of safety where a man might shelter. But a sickly dull white, or a green, or worst of all a red shot with black—those signaled traps for our kind.

The storm cleared after what seemed to me a very long time. Now the water drained from the crevice. And the lightning no longer was laid whipwise over the hills. I edged forward from under the rock ledge which had been my shelter and tried to straighten up. My wet limbs, my wracked ankle, made such movement painful. I could feel rough outcrops to climb, but could I put enough weight on my ankle to try that?

Then I froze. There was a sound, not of rain nor thunder—more like a skittering across the rock above me. Could one of the Dark creatures have found its way up during the cover of the flood, was it now waiting to attack me?

There came a light, a glow. By it I saw the pointed, tooth-rimmed snout of one of the Lizard folk. And then his forefeet, so much like slender, fingered hands, came into view. The light descended slowly toward me so I saw that it issued from a stone held in a mesh of delicate wire fastened on a slender cord.

The Lizard folk, like the other nonhumans, communicated by thought. But I had none of the mind touch which Crytha had so nurtured. I reached my hand and caught the caged stone. By that I could see my ankle. The boot was very tight and the leg above it swollen. I had given it a bad twist and it was plain I dare not put any weight on that.

With gestures, I tried to make my dilemma plain to my rescuer. He stared at me with jewel-bright eyes, then in a breath he was gone. For help, I hoped. Though I now began to dread that, too. My ineptness had long been a matter of rough badinage among Hervon's men. Here, on my first wall patrol, I had managed to make the worst possible showing.

With the Lizard gone, curiosity led me to duck back under the ledge and survey what I had found in the wall. When I advanced my dull light, there awoke a brilliant fire which was dazzling.

The thing was a rod right enough, fashioned of some kind of crystal which drew light. And it glowed with a bluish sheen. Yes, it projected directly out of the rock itself, but there was no mistaking that it was the product of some intelligence. Even though to find it so encased in solid rock was surprising.

I closed my other hand around it and tugged with all my might. The rod gave only a fraction. It was plain that to free it entirely, one must break the rock in which it hung. But that I would do! I must do! As the geas which had been laid on us all to bring us into Escore, I knew now that some force outside my own imagining was driving me to do this. That my find was important—that I would have sworn oath to.

Now I turned quickly—there was a further noise over-head and the Lizard man came clambering down the wall with ease. To him, this stone was an open stairway. He carried a rope coiled about one shoulder, and when he reached the bottom he made signs that I was to tie one end about me.

Thus, I found in the storm both my destiny in this long-shadowed land, and a friend—for Tsali was indeed a friend such as one could trust his life and more than his life upon.

3

So I was pent in the Valley for a time. But the Lady Dahaun had shared her knowledge with Crytha, who brought to me a basin of bubbling red mud. This she used to make a casing for my ankle once my boot was cut away. And as its heat enclosed my flesh, the pain faded and I slept.

My dreams had never been real, nor of the kind one might name true sendings of the Power—such as favored ones of our Race have from time to time had as warnings. But this time I strode through a land which was as real as if I were waking. And in my hand I carried a sword—one fitted into my palm as firmly as if it were an extension of my own body, so that in my dream I could not imagine my life without that to hand.

Yet there was on me a great sorrow and fear, not for myself but for others. And as I went, I wept silently for a loss I could not remember and yet which was very great, weighing upon me heavier than any scout's pack. I saw that the mail I wore was broken in places and rusted by stains. While my left hand was pressed against my side, the fingers bloodied. Pain gnawed under that pressure, a pain I fought against. For there was that my body must aid me to do before I yielded to death.

Immutably death drove me; I knew that for the truth. All behind me was lost to the Shadow, save what I carried. In my dreaming mind, I knew that this sword must not fall to those who now sniffed my trail.

But I wavered, the burden of pain nigh bearing me to the ground. While that which lay before me shimmered in my sight. Time raced for me, with it my life, oozing in sluggish drops from my side. Yet my will did not yield to either time or my failing body.

The ground under my stumbling feet rose steadily, so that for all my determination, my pace slowed. Still I kept onward. Now there arose a mist before me. My lips shaped words I could not understand. Yet I knew that once I had known such and they had been to me weapons near as potent as the sword.

Perhaps it was the Power of the words which carried me past the limit of human endurance. My breath came in gasps; I could no longer master the pain eating at me, but my will still held.

I faltered at last to a halt, teetering on the lip of a drop. The mists rose from below, and I knew, in a part of my fast-dulling mind, that these were born out of what lay below—raw rock churned and set to a boil as if it were water, molten. Into this I hurled the sword. With it went out of me that strength which had kept me on my feet, brought me from the stricken field where the Shadow had triumphed.

As I crumpled to earth, knowing that now I could meet death, and did it willingly enough, I awoke. I was sweating and my hand was fast pressed to my side. I looked down, expecting still to see the blood dripping down the shattered mail. But instead my skin was smooth, unbroken. And I knew it had been a dream.

I had not been Yonan then—no. Nor could I have put name to the man I had been in that time. But I carried with me from that dream of death one thought—that which I had found embedded in the rock on the heights was of the sword. To my hand had it once well fitted; so would it again.

However there was also in me a need to keep this secret; the reason for that I did not know. I endured Imhar's jeering at my ineptness. But, when Crytha came to inspect the casing on my ankle, I asked her concerning the Lizard man who had found me.

It was she who told me his name—Tsali—and that he was one of the scouts of the heights. I envied her her gift of communication with those other life forms and asked her to give him my thanks. But I was surprised when later that day he padded into the small shelter where I lay and squatted down beside me, watching me with his jewel-like eyes.

He stood perhaps near my shoulder in height, being large for his species. And as he squatted now on hind limbs, limber tail outthrust as a balance behind, he slipped from one wrist a cord on which white and red earth-colored beads were interstrung, counting these through his slender fingers as if he gathered something from the touch alone. I had seen his people do this before and heard some remark about it among our men—that so the Lizard folk apparently kept records among themselves.

I stared at his crested head and longed to speak—though I knew that the words I would mouth, even in the old tongue, would have no meaning. Only those of the Green People could speak mind to mind with all who shared the Light with them, against the Shadow.

Suddenly, Tsali wrapped his beads once more about his wrist and, from a pouch at the belt (which was the only thing he wore over his rainbow scaled body), he brought a piece of thin, smoothed stone about the size of my flattened palm. On this were carved lines of runes, the first interfilled with flakes of gold so that they were clearly visible, the second row with red, the last with ominous black.

I had seen such before. These were for foretelling and were used by Wise Women who had not enough of the Power to become full Witches. Yet, as Tsali held this up before my eyes, I believed that these runes were different in part.

With the plaque still in one hand, the Lizard man reached out his other to catch at my right wrist before I knew what he would do. Holding my hand with his, he raised it until my fingers slipped over the smoothness of the stone, felt the twists and turns of the deeply graven markings. Oddly enough, the stone was not cold as I thought it would be; rather warm, as if it had rested near a fire for a space.

Under my flesh the symbols brightened and grew more distinct. First, the gold, then the red, and at length, the black. Yet my flesh shrank from the last of those rows, for I well knew, even little learned in the Power that I was, that these last were signs of ill omen and despair.

Tsali had watched as the runes came to life and faded in turn, and there was about his scaled body growing tension.

For it seemed that if I could not read what I brought to brighter sparking there, he could. When at length I had pointed out the last of those symbols he took the plaque and once more stowed it away. Yet he did not leave me.

Rather he leaned forward, his eyes focused on me in such a steady stare as compelled a like answer from me. Slowly, very slowly there came a faint stirring in my mind. At first that started me into flinching away from him, my astonishment so great that I could not believe that this was more than my imagination.

It was not clear mind speech between us, I was too lacking in skill to handle such as that. Rather, I could sense only a query of sorts. And that had to do with something from the far past—

But there was nothing in my past which was of note, which would send Tsali so delving into my mind. I was, perhaps, the least of the House of Hervon, and not even of the full blood of the Old Race. Or—what was I?

For one giddy moment, I seemed to whirl back into that dream when I walked to my death in order to preserve something (or destroy it); something greater than myself, yet which had been mine. And I found that even waking I remembered now in detail that climb to the lip of the cup, the loss of the sword which had been so wholly a part of me.

But that was only a dream—not of the here and now. I was not that stranger, death-stricken from an unknown battle. I was Yonan, the half-blood, the weakling—

I was—both!

How I knew this now—that I could not explain. I had heard of beliefs held by some Outlanders that, though an adept can live many lifetimes in length during his space allowed in this world, other and lesser men return, to be born again, if some task they have been set is ill done, so that they may once more choose and act. It is hoped this time for the better.

Was the inner me such a one? Had the dream been not fantasy but a far-off truth? Who could prove it yes or no? Only my dying walk was as real to me now as if I had indeed been a part of it—yesterday—or last night when I had thought I wandered in a dream.

Now I knew that I must prove that to myself. For that proof there was only one action—I must return to the cliff top, seek out that which was prisoned in the stone, and bring it forth. If I saw it, if I held it once more in my hand, then—then perhaps that knowledge that it had been mine, was meant to be mine, would come again.

There sounded a hissing from Tsali. Slight as it was, it broke my concentration. He was still watching me, but not with that compelling intensity. Now he nodded, his crest head moving gravely up and down. And I knew that, if I could not read his thought, save in the faintest degree, mine had been far more clear to him.

I spoke, though I did not know if his alien ears could pick up and sort out the sounds I made into an intelligible pattern.

"I must go back—"

It would seem that he understood. For once more he nodded solemnly. And that nod had something of a promise in it, as if he intended that I must do just what I desired.

Now I was impatient for the healing of my ankle and pestered Crytha to be loose from the heavy cast of mud. Until she at last broke that and freed me. I could feel no pain, there was no swelling, no mark. And when I got to my feet, I felt nothing save what was normal.

But time to do what I wished, that was a different thing.

I could not walk away from the drilling, the constant honing of our small force into a weapon for defense. Oddly enough, I had in me the strong belief that I must not share with any—save Tsali—the story of my find. So that it was after three full days of frustration and impatience that I slipped away at dawn, to once more climb the cliffs. But before I reached the first handholds, the Lizard warrior appeared out of nowhere, flashing past me up the rough stone with an agility no man possessed.

It was good that Tsali had joined me. For once aloft, I could pick out no landmark; I did not know in which direction to begin my search for the crevice into which I had so unexpectedly fallen. But it was plain Tsali did, for looking up to me and then bearing right, he made clear that he could guide me.

In the day, with no storm clouds about, the rugged heights of the Valley were very visible. There were many crevices in these peaks and they looked much alike. However, Tsali had come to a halt by one, and with a full swing of his arm, beckoned me on.

I got to my knees, peered down into the gash in the rock. From here I could see nothing. My find must lie farther back, under the half-shadow of the roof rock. To my belt I had fastened a small hammer which I had selected secretly from among the smith's tools, with it a sharp-bladed chisel. Though both were metal, I did not know how they would cut this rock.

With care I crawled down into the cut, Tsali lying belly down now on the lip of the crevice watching me with steadfast eyes. I might have missed what I sought, for it was near the color of the rock which held it. But the fact that it protruded was my aid.

Though the rod had the feel of crystal, it was opaque,

gray—like any jutting knob about. How then had the lightning revealed it with a glimmer? I fitted my finger to it. Yes, it moved, but a very little. I could see, peering close, that there was a line separating it a little from the rock which enclosed it.

Delicately as I could, for I feared to break it, I began to work with chisel and hammer, tapping slowly, with care. Parts of the rock dropped away in very small and hard-won chips.

But I schooled my patience and worked with a care I have never used in any act before. It was needful that I do this—that filled my mind, possessed me fully. I was not aware of the sun which blazed down, to make the crevice a caldron of glowing heat so that I doffed first mail shirt, then underjerkin of padded leather, and worked with my skin reddening in the force of that beam.

My hands began to shake and I leaned back against the wall of the crevice, suddenly afraid that, with some off-center blow, I might shatter what I sought. There was a hissing from above. I looked up and Tsali held down to me a bottle fashioned of the tough valley gourds.

Working out the stopper, I drank thankfully. My shoulders ached—but when I looked at the stone where I worked, my spirit was as renewed as my throat from that drink. It was indeed a sword hilt I had so painfully uncovered. I had it free now down to the cross hilt. But it would take hours more to manage the blade—if I ever could. How had any metal lasted through the heat generated by the molten rock into which my dream self had hurled this?

I put out my hand, curved my fingers, and grasped the hilt. That which I had felt in the dream once more flooded into me. This was *mine!* Never before had I felt so strong an impression of ownership, as if some object had been fashioned only for my own handling, to be held jealously from all others.

My grasp tightened. Without being truly aware of what I did, I pulled the hilt toward me. There was a moment of resistance, and then it came loose with such a snap that I overbalanced and fell back against the other wall of the crevice.

But—what I held was only the hilt. No blade projected, strong and keen-edged, beyond it!

My disappointment was so vast that for a second or two I could have wailed as might any child. It was mine—but what it had been was gone, lost in time and boiling rock, even as I had feared.

Still, I could not toss it from me. My fingers curled and held as if now their will was apart from mine, or else they were commanded by a part of me I did not know nor understand.

I held my find farther into the sun. Perhaps one of the valleysmiths could reset it to a blade. It was not a treasure in itself that I could see. In color, the crystal of the pommel was gray, yet in the sun I caught a faint rippling of inner light. It had been worked with a carving like a scrawl of runes, perhaps to keep it from turning in the hand. However, those were so worn they were now but a pitted pattern of unreadable lines. The crossbar was of the same crystal-like material. Yet I was sure this was no crystal nor quartz of which I had knowledge.

I sighed. When I shrugged on my jerkin again, I stowed my find against my skin. A useless thing—still—there was something—

Was it a scrap of before memory which stirred deep, deep in my mind? I could not catch it. I only knew that what I held had once been as needful as life to me and that it had come once more into my hand for a purpose.

4

In the days which followed I was tempted often to take the hilt to the smith and see if it could be fitted to any blade he had worked. Yet each time that thought came to me, I found that I could not do this. No, there had been only one blade which would fit. And time had taken that. So my find must remain useless.

But I discovered that when I slept, for some reason, I brought the hilt out (always in the dark and in secret) to hold in my hand. Did I wish to use it as a key to unlock the past? Perhaps. Though another part of me did not desire that either. Still I kept it ever with me.

Perhaps it carried with it some good fortune for a warrior. Or else growing older, and living under the sky of the Green Valley and its healing, brought about a slow change in me. I became more apt as a swordsman—once even disarming Imhar in practice. And that not by chance, for it was ever his way to make me seem awkward and without skill.

Sometimes I believed that had my secret been whole I could have confronted any man in our company and not come out the worse, battle-trained veterans as most of them were.

We of Hervon's House were not the only people to be drawn over-mountain into Escore. Others followed in time. Then we, with the Green People, went forth (for the

Lady Dahaun had always knowledge, carried by her messenger birds, of those winning across the mountains.)

This land was awake, and evil paced it, save those few places guarded by remnants of the Power. Thus were we ever on guard when we ventured on an assay. It was during one such, at night, though our people encamped by a place of Light, that the Thas attacked us.

These live underground, seldom seeking the upper world, then only at night or on days well clouded. Though they had not first been reckoned among the followers of the Shadow, in these hours they listened to the call of the Dark Ones, thus becoming our enemies. During the night attack they were defeated only by an outgush of water which was brought about by Lord Kemoc and Godgar of our own troop. However, Lord Kemoc was grievously wounded and, on our riding, he was swept from us in a flood of the same water which had earlier saved us.

His loss was counted a sore one. For, though a man, he has studied the ancient records at Lormt. And it was a fact that he had called forth a summons and had been *answered* by one of the Great Old Ones, even though those had all been deemed gone from Escore. His sister, the Witch Kaththea, withdrew to a place of mysteries, striving there to find some answer as to whether he lived or died. For she believed that he had not departed on the Last Road as yet.

Thus, Crytha became a closer companion to the Lady Dahaun, though she was not trained in witchcraft as had been the Lady Kaththea. So I saw even less of her. This was not a season for wedding, at least that thought heartened me. For Inhar could not claim her at a time when war raged around us.

Twice we had driven off attacks of the Dark Ones. Monstrous forms had circled the valley walls, striven to climb and bring death to all. Those Gray Ones, who are neither man nor wolf, but the worst part of both, came to harry us; other, even more alien things with them. In the sky above wheeled and battled the great Vorgs who answered the summoning of our hosts. But what sometimes fought with them were such creatures even nightmares could not spawn.

I found that Tsali took to accompanying whatever patrol on the heights I was assigned to. It followed that my companionship without words with the Lizard man became more a part of my life. When we were alone (though such times were few) he often let me know by gestures, in very dim impressions I could pick up from his thoughts, that he wanted to look upon the sword hilt. I would bring it forth (it always felt then a part of me), and he would stare at it intently.

Perhaps, I guessed, he knew more of its history, buried in the rock though it had been, than I did. How I longed to speak mind to mind and ask this. Men have their legends—perhaps the Lizard folk also had their tales from an ancient past. Maybe even one about that dying man who had not been Yonan—

I tried very hard to reach out with my thoughts, but it would seem that the talent was denied me. Yet in otherwise I was changing, as I was sure. And what might have happened had not another fate taken hand in my life I cannot fathom.

It was Crytha who brought the end to one part of my life, the beginning of another. For there came a morning when she was missing from her couch in the Lady Dahaun's hall. And the Lady of Green Silences came to Hervon's cluster of tents with a sober face. She held out her hand, on the palm of which lay an image roughly fashioned from clay. Strands of hair had been embedded in its head, a scrap of scarf Crytha favored wrapped about it in a crude robing.

The Lady Chriswitha, looking upon that thing, grew white. Her hands trembled as she reached forth a finger to touch, and yet did not dare. Then there arose such a wrath as I had never seen in her. She spat out:

"We were told that this was a safe land!"

"So was it," the Lady Dahaun returned. "This abomination was not fashioned here. I do not know how it was put within the bed place of your kin-child. I have learned that she went forth at first dawning, telling my people she would seek a bed of Illbane to be harvested as the dew still lay upon it, making it twice as potent for healings. She appeared as always, under no compulsion; though it seems that in this she was certainly moved by another's will."

The Lady Chriswitha looked about us, as if with the eye she could see Crytha's trail. Her lips came firm together as I have seen them upon occasion, as now her fear was under deep control.

"You can follow?"

"We have followed," the Lady Dahaun replied. "But there is an end to her trail up there." She gestured toward the heights which walled in the valley.

"Why—why Crytha? And from whence came that—?" my foster mother then demanded, "She—she must be found!"

"Why Crytha? Because she is who she is—one of budding Power, as yet untrained—at an age when that Power can be used by—others. From whence it came, it has about it the stench of Thas. They possess certain talents which it now seems they are developing to a degree

we have not known. As to the finding, I have tried the
scrying—there is a wall against the far sight—''

I though of the Thas I had seen during our battle with
them, when they had attacked and been driven off by the
gush of water. They were of the earth, smaller than men,
dusky bodies covered with a growth which was tough and
rootlike. As if they had indeed grown and not been born.
To our eyes they were repulsive—like the legendary de-
mons. And to think of Crytha taken by such!

In that moment I forgot I was liegeman to my lord, that I
was a warrior under orders. I moved without thinking to
snatch that crude image from the Lady Dahaun.

''Yonan!'' The Lady Chriswitha stared at me as if I had
suddenly myself taken on the guise of one of those deep
earth dwellers. ''What would you—?''

But I was no longer the Yonan she had fostered, the
weakling who owed life to her care. In that moment, as my
fist clenched around the image, I felt deep within me a stir
which I had known only in my dream. I was someone else
struggling for freedom, someone with more certainty of
purpose than Yonan had ever possessed. I think that I was
no longer a youth of little promise. Instead, two halves of
me came together to make me the stronger in that uniting. I
did not even answer the Lady Chriswitha, for there was a
need tearing at me which I could not control.

''Where on the heights did they lose the trail?'' I turned
to the Lady of Green Silences, speaking to her as I would
to an equal.

I saw her eyes widen as she gazed back at me. For a
moment, she hesitated. As she did, the Lady Chriswitha
broke in:

''Yonan—you cannot—''

I whirled about, forgetting all courtesy. ''This I will do.
Either I bring Crytha back or else I die!''

It was her turn to show an astonishment which overrode even her anger and fear.

"But you—"

I made a gesture of silence as I looked again to the Lady Dahaun.

"Where?" I repeated sharply.

Her eyes searched my face for what seemed to me far too long a time. Then she answered:

"No man can hunt safely through the burrows of the Thas. The earth is theirs; for them, it fights."

"So? I do not believe this, Lady." My left hand lay on my mail-clad breast and I could feel (and I knew I was not dreaming this time) a kind of throb against my body sent forth by the ancient sword hilt.

She bit upon her lower lip. Her right hand arose and in the air she traced some symbol. There was a faint light following that tracing, gone again in an instant. But now Dahaun nodded.

"The risk is yours, warrior. We dare not raid into the Thas' burrows without greater protection than we have now. This act of theirs may be intended not only to gain control of a beginning talent which they hope to warp, but also to drain us of warriors needed for defense."

"One man may go without weakening your defense by much, Lady. With or without your leave will I do this thing."

"It is your choice," she returned gravely. "But this much will I warn you: if the Thas are now governed by one with the Dark Power, there is little a man can do against such. You know nothing of what you may face."

"True. But who knows when he lies down at night what the rising sun will bring tomorrow?" I countered with words which seemed to flow into my mouth by the will of that shadowy other which the touch of the hilt had awakened in me.

There was a hissing, startling us both. Tsali reared up to my left. His bright eyes met mine for a single instant before he looked on to the Lady Dahaun. I knew that between them now passed that communication I could not understand. In my hand, I squeezed tight that ugly thing of clay, hair, and ragged cloth. I knew enough of the way of Power that this dare not be destroyed. For such a destruction might harm the one I would protect. However, it was a tie with her. Just as the sword hilt, now warm against my breast, was a tie with that other, greater self I could only dimly sense as yet.

"Tsali will go with you."

It was my turn to be surprised. Though the Lizard men were of the earth, even as those of the Green Valley, still they are not like the Thas, who hate the sun and are not at ease save in their deep burrows.

"He can be eyes for you, such as no man possesses," Dahaun continued. "And it is his free choice to do this."

Perhaps I should have refused to draw another with me into an unknown governed by the Shadow. But at that moment the part of Yonan which was still uncertain, lacking in confidence, felt a surge of relief at that promise. Alone among the Valley People, Tsali shared my secret. It did not matter that his skin was scaled, mine was smooth; that we could not speak to each other. For he could project, and I could receive, a feeling of rightness about what I must now do.

I shouldered a bag of rations and two water gourds filled to their stopper levels, those stoppers being well pounded in. For arms, I had my sword. I would not take the dart gun, for these had very little ammunition left, and what remained must be for the defense of the Valley. The Lady Dahaun brought me a pouch which I could clip to my belt, holding some of her salves for wounds. But it was with the Lady Chriswitha, Lord Hervon still being absent on a patrol, that I had my final word before I left to face the unknown.

"She is already hand-fasted, Yonan." My foster mother spoke quickly, as if what she had to say made her uneasy and she would have this over.

"That I know."

"If Imhar were here now—"

"He would do as I am doing. But he is not, and I am."

Then she acted as she had not since I was a sickly little lad. She put her hands, one on either side of my face. The throat veil of fine mail which depended from my helm hung loose so that I could feel her touch warm on my cheeks.

"Yonan, Yonan—" She repeated my name as if she must. "What you try—may the Great Flame abide about you, hedge you in. Forgive me my blindness. She is of my own blood, even though there is in her that which is not of my spirit. For she is like the maidens of the other years, having that part in her which we thought had flickered and died, save in Estcarp. There will be·always that in her which no other can possess, nor perhaps even understand. She is my kin, however—"

"And hand-fasted to Imhar," I replied grimly. "My honor is not totally lost, even though I am not of pure blood, my Lady. She will come back, or else I will be dead. But after, I shall make no claims on her. This I swear."

There were tears in her eyes now, though she was not

one who wept easily. And all she answered then was my name—

"Yonan!" But into that one word she put all she could summon to hearten me.

5

I kept the image, tucking it into my belt and making it fast there with a thrice-knotted loop. For such things, even if they are used in the working of evil, are connected with the victims they are used against. It might be that in this rough thing of clay, rag, and hair I could find a guide.

Near midday we climbed the cliffs, following the path of those who had traced Crytha earlier. Tsali took the lead, as ever, his clawed hands and feet far more apt at this business than mine. But I had caught up to him as he paused by a deep cleft in the rock, one into which the sun, burning brightly as it did, could not far penetrate.

I lay belly down on the rock which lipped this, striving to see what lay down below. But there lay a thickness of shadow there through which only part of the rough walls was visible.

While the closer I put my face to the opening, the more I was aware of an odor, fetid and heavy, after the cool clean air of the valley. This carried the half-rotted scent of wood, fast being reduced to slimy sponge by age and water, and with that, hints of other nastiness.

I checked my pack, my weapon, before I swung over that lip, searching for hand and toe holds. The descent was rough enough to offer those in plenty. As I went that smell grew stronger. Tsali had followed me, but more slowly than usual. He wore a cord about his neck, a pouch of netting in which was a jumble of stones. As we went farther into the shadows of that ominous cutting those took fire, to give off a glow of subdued light.

The descent was a long one, far longer than I had judged, and had speculated. And, for all my care, I made what I thought was far too much noise, my boots scraping on the stone as I forced the toes into holds. Time and again I froze, flattened against the wall, listening. Yet never was there anything, save my own breathing, for Tsali made no sound at all.

However there hung about us a subtle warning of danger, the knowledge that we were indeed intruding into enemy territory. So I strove to alert all my senses, bringing to service all that I had learned of scouting.

At last I reached a level surface. With care, I edged around on that, thinking I had merely found a ledge. But Tsali landed lightly on the same perch to my left, and held out his bag of luminous stones. By that dim light we could see that we were indeed at the bottom of a giant slash. A narrow way led both right and left, but Tsali gestured left.

Judging that he must know more of such burrows than I, that then was our choice. Though this was no smooth road, for we scrambled over loose rocks, squeezed by outjutting of the walls. What had been a crevice became a cave. When I stretched back my head to look aloft there was no longer a ribbon of sky to be seen.

Tsali pounced, using his claws to free something from a sharp rock, then held out to me a pinch of fiberlike stuff. From it arose strongly the noxious odor. I touched his find gingerly. The stuff was coarser than any hair I had ever fingered, more like fine roots. I could understand that this marked the passage of one of the Thas who had so scraped free a small portion of his body covering.

Tsali hissed and hurled the discovery from him, his gesture plainly one of scorn. I had not known before his personal feelings concerning the Thas. But with that gesture he made them plain enough. Again I longed for the power to communicate with him.

The roofing of this way dropped abruptly. Water beaded the walls around us, trickled down the stone, to puddle between the loose stones, making hazards. Luckily soon this changed and we crept along, only moisture-sleeked level rock underfoot.

Tsali's light was very limited. We could scarcely see more than a foot or so beyond us, though he held the pouch well out. Then we had to get down to our hands and knees to crawl. I put off my pack, pushing it before me. Still my shoulders brushed the roof of this passage from time to time.

Save for the smell and that tuft of hair, we came across no further signs that this was a way used by the enemy. Perhaps it had recently been opened or explored, in testing for some underground entrance to the Valley. But any such would fail, since the Green People had long ago set about their stronghold such signs of Power as none of those serving the Shadow might cross.

How long we crawled I do not know, but at length that hole gave way to a cavern, one far beyond our reckoning as to size depending upon the feeble light we had. Rows of stalagmites arose like savage fangs, to be matched by stalactites as sharp above. Tsali squatted, his head turning from side to side.

Even my senses, which were far less than his, caught the thick scent which was lying here. The Lizard man closed both hands over his pouch of light stones, shutting off even that small source of illumination. I knew that he so signaled the need for extreme caution.

I listened—so intently that it would seem all the strength of every sense I had was now channeled into one. And there was sound. Part of it I identified as a steady dripping—perhaps from some steady, but small, fall of water.

However from farther away, much muted, came a rhythmic rise and fall of what was neither distinguishable words nor song, but which, I was sure, was not of the cave, rather of those who used it.

There was a very faint gleam to my left, Tsali had dropped one hand from the net bag. Now I felt his clawed fingers close around my wrist. With that hold he gave me a small, meaningful jerk. He wanted us to advance on out into the great blackness of the unknown.

I heard it said that the Lizard people could see above and below the range of men, able to pierce what might be to us full darkness. It would seem that I must now allow my companion to prove the right of that.

Slinging my pack back into place, I arose, Tsali beside me. Step by cautious step, we ventured on. Our path was not straight, for Tsali zigzagged, apparently to avoid the rock formations which would make this a giant maze-trap for anyone as nightblind as I. As we went that other sound grew stronger, taking on the rise and fall of a chant. But if those we hunted were within the bounds of vision they had no light to betray them.

Tsali took another sharp turn to the left. Now I could see a glow, faint, greenish, but still a break in the thick dark of the cavern. Against this the formations made misshapen rods like a grill, sometimes thick enough to veil the gleam altogether.

The chanting continued, growing ever louder—but in

no tongue I knew. Somehow that sound made the skin on my body prickle with that warning which my species feel when they go up against the Shadow. Tsali crept now, dropping his hold on me, since we had the guide of that distant light. And I strove in turn to move as noiselessly as possible.

The unwholesome radiance flourished as we crouched close together to look into a second and smaller cavern. There hunched Thas, unmistakable in their ugliness. I counted at least a dozen. But rising above their misshapen forms was Crytha.

They had half-encircled her, but their low-slung heads were not turned in her direction as if they watched her. Rather they all faced toward a tall standing pillar which glistened in the light cast by stalks of lumpy growths half of the Thas held before them, as might worshippers hold candles at some shrines.

The pillar had a sleek, smooth surface facing Crytha. Now I could see that her eyes were tightly closed. Yet her face was serene, not as someone forced into action by her enemies, rather as one who moved in a dream.

Dimly I could sight something beneath that surface, as if the pillar held a captive or a treasure. The Thas wore no visible weapons. Slowly and carefully I eased my sword from its scabbard, loosed my pack to set that aside. The odds were very high, but it was Crytha who stood there, whom they had somehow claimed to do their bidding. For that she was now engaged in some sorcery demanded by the Shadow I had no doubt at all. I surveyed the stretch of cave between me and that foul company, wondering if a surprise attack might be the answer. The Thas appeared to feel so safe in this hole of theirs that we had found no sentry. And feeling thus secure would not an attack bewilder them for just long enough?

Such odds were very slim indeed, but I could at that moment see no other action to take.

Crytha raised her hands. Though she did not touch the surface of the pillar before which she stood, she made sweeping motions, first up and down, and then back and forth. While those squatting about her continued to chant in their unknown tongue. I readied myself for a leap which I hoped would take me to the girl's side. If I could then break whatever spell they had laid upon her—

Tsali hissed. Something brushed my shoulder. I whirled. Out of the darkness behind us streamed long cords like misshapen roots. Before I understood our peril, one coiled about my ankles, to give a vicious jerk and throw me to the ground. I raised my sword in a slash meant to free myself from that bond.

The metal struck true enough, only to rebound from a surface on which no cut was visible. Even as I tried to swing again, another of those root cords snapped tight about my wrist in spite of my struggles.

Within a space of a few breaths I was both disarmed and helpless. But Tsali was still on his feet. It appeared that the cords disliked those gleaming stones which provided us with light. They feinted and tried to strike, but the Lizard man's lightning-fast weaving of the pouch kept them at bay. At length he made a leap far to the left and was gone, leaving me a prisoner.

There had been no halt in the chanting behind me. Nor, to my complete surprise, did any Thas now advance out of the dark to make sure of me. Only the cords still tightened on my body until I was totally immobile. Now I could see both ends of those, as if they had not been used as weapons, but were in some way living entities acting on their own. Yet all I saw or felt were like long unbreakable roots.

They also had an evil smell, which arose about me stiflingly. I choked and coughed, my eyes filled with tears as do those caught in acrid smoke. So the Thas had their sentries after all, such as I had never heard of. I hoped that Tsali had escaped. On him alone could I depend for help. Or would I die, smothered by this horrible stench? My head whirled dizzily as I slipped into blackness.

There were no real dreams. Rather somewhere—a long way off—a name was called. It was not a name that I knew, yet it belonged to me. And the call became more insistent.

I stirred; that calling would not be stilled. Now I opened my eyes. There was a smell of rottenness, but not strong enough to choke me senseless as before. To my right showed a faint light. I tried to turn toward that. Something about me resisted and then broke; another puff of foul odor struck into my face like a blow, so I gasped and nearly lapsed once more into unconsciousness.

The light was above me. I swung my head farther. I lay at the foot of a pillar of—ice! The cold issuing from it was biting. But the front of the column was smooth as glass. And within—within that stood a body!

It was man-shaped, man-sized as far as I could judge. Only the face was hidden in a strange way by three diamond-shaped pieces of a gleaming metal fastened together by chains of the same substance. Two covered the eyes, the third masked the mouth, leaving only the nose and a bit of cheek on either side visible.

The head was crowned by an elaborate war helm from which a crest in the form of a jewel-eyed dragon looked down at me. And the body wore mail. While the hands were clasped on the haft of a great double-sided ax.

I levered myself up, more puffs of stench answering

every moment. When I gazed down along my own body I saw that black and rotted cords were falling away. Apparently the rootlike sentries of the Thas had not too long lives. Also they had dragged me within their shrine, for I was sure this was the pillar before which they had chanted. Therefore—how soon would they return? Or had they believed me dead and so laid me here as an offering for the pillared one?

Action, not guessing, was what I needed. I pushed back from the freezing chill of the pillar and got stiffly to my feet. Perhaps I could break off part of one of the stony growths in the outer cavern, use that for a weapon. I looked longingly at the ax embedded in the ice. That was of no use to him who now held it, and perhaps far too heavy for me even if I had it to hand, but it was the only arm in sight.

I saw now that the column was not the only ice formed in this chamber. Beyond the pillar, to my right, long icicles, thicker than my wrist, depended from the roof. Some of them had sharp enough points—for weapons? I almost laughed at that idea, certainly that of a crazed man. Those would shatter at a touch—

"Tolar!"

I turned my head. Who had called that name? It was the same as had sounded through the darkness to draw me back to life again. I—I was Yonan! Yet something in me responded.

Hardly knowing what I did, I loosened the lacing of my mail shirt until I could grope beneath it, close my hand about the sword hilt, bring it forth. Here in the darkness —it glowed! The gray-white of the dull crystal came to life as strong inner fires blazed within it.

If I only had a blade!

A blade—!

My eyes went, I did not know why, save as if something so compelled them, to those long icicles which hung from the roof. And to them I went, though I knew this did not make sense. Still I selected one of those sharp points of ice, the length of a sword blade. Then I exerted force enough to break it free.

The ice snapped off cleanly as if cut. Still moving under a command I did not understand, I fitted the hilt to it. There was a burst of light which blinded me for a moment.

I might still be dreaming, or I might be indeed mad, but that which I held now was no thing of metal or ice, but a sword, perfect and balanced. It had now been called out of time itself to exist again for the sake of the Light.

6

Now I returned to that prisoner in the block of ice. Surely he was a dead man. Still an uneasiness lingered in me as I studied him, as if, should I walk away and leave him so pent there, I would indeed be deserting a battle comrade.

I approached closer to the pillar, kicking aside the shriveled remains of the root bonds which were rotting away. There was a deep silence around me. Except in my own mind, where, very faint and faraway, sounded once more that name:

"Tolar!"

In my hand the new-knit sword did not cease to radiate light, though not with the full brilliance it had given off when I joined ice to metal. But enough to provide a torch far more effective than those stones of Tsali's, and I wondered if its gleam could betray me. Yet I could not put it aside in this place of dark mystery.

Crytha—Tsali—where were they? How could I track them through this maze? With no mind touch I would be lost as any talentless beast, unless I could gain some clue.

The smell of the Thas remained, but I could see no tracks. For underfoot was bare rock holding no print.

And my eyes were continually drawn back to that inert figure in the pillar, as if some deep compulsion tied me here—to it—rather than releasing me to the quest for the freeing of Crytha. Against my will I advanced toward the chill of that frozen column. Cold radiated from it, even as the light did from my strangely forged weapon. Yet the grip of that in my hand was warm, reassuring.

Who was this prisoner? How had he come to stand so in Thas territory? Plainly, from what I could see, he had no physical kinship with the squat, ill-formed earth people. Was he their god? Or some ancient prisoner they had so set to mock and gloat over at intervals? Why had they brought Crytha here to perform so oddly?

Questions for which I had no answers. But, almost without conscious thought, I reached with sword point, to touch the surface of the frozen prison. As I did that, I was seized as tightly as the root things had bound me. No longer was it my will which moved me. No, another force overrode all which was Yonan.

I raised the sword, to bring it down against that pillar. One unyielding surface met another, jarring muscles along my side and shoulder. Yet I could not stop myself aiming such another blow, and a third; without any effect on either blade or pillar which I could perceive. I could not move away, held as a man in a geas, pledged to beat away at this column of ice, fruitlessly, while my body ached in answer each time the sword thudded home against the unbreakable.

Or was it breakable?

I could not be sure. Had a small network of cracks begun to spread outward from that point I had been crashing my blade against? This was the height of folly, to so fight to uncover the body of the long dead. My brain might know that well, but what moved my arm did not accept such logic.

Nine times I struck at the ice pillar. Then my arm fell to my side, so wearied by that useless labor that I could not summon strength for another blow. But—

The cracks I thought I had imagined—were there! Even as I stared, they widened, reached farther across the surface, deeper, farther—a piece of ice as large as my sweating hand flaked away, to hit the rock below with a sharp tinkle. Then another and another joined that!

I could no longer see the man within, for the cracks were so many that they starred and concealed all beyond the surface. More and more bits of ice fell out. With them came a rush of air so cold I might have faced the worst breath of the Ice Dragon. I stumbled back, enough wit and control left in me to flee the range of that blast.

Now the shattered ice flaked quickly, fell in jagged lumps. There was nothing between me and the body. While always the sword blade pulsed with light showing the stranger.

"Tolar—so long—so long—"

I would have cried out, but my tongue, my lips, my throat, could shape no real sound. Those words had not been spoken aloud, rather they broke into my mind as a great cry holding a note of triumph.

''Tolar—aid—''

There was no longer a greeting, rather a plea. And I knew whence it had come, from that body which had been locked in ice. I moved jerkily, again as if another mind and will, roused from some unknown depth within me, was ordering my limbs—pushing that identity which was Yonan into some side pocket where its desires could not interfere.

I stooped stiffly, laid my ice sword upon the rock, and then I went forward. No longer to meet a freezing blast (perhaps that had been dissipated upon the opening of the crypt) but to reach for the shoulders of the body within.

His mail was ice-cold, the flesh beneath it seemed rocklike. But I tugged and pulled, until the masked man fell forward, near bearing me down also by the weight of his body. He was utterly stiff, as if completely frozen as the ice which had encased him.

I tugged and pulled until I had him stretched on his back, his hands still tight gripping his battle ax, his hidden face turned upward. Then I knelt beside him, wondering what I must do now. It seemed to me that no natural man could have survived that cold. But there had been adepts and men of Power in plenty in Escore in the old days. And it could have been that such as they were able to stave off death in ways we ourselves had lost record of during the years of our exile.

To warm his flesh—I had no fire here and I did not see how I could get him to the surface. Or if I wanted to! For we had been warned often by the Green People that many of those who remained outside their own Valley were more apt to be of the Shadow than of the Light. Perhaps this was some Dark lord who had fallen afoul of one of his own kind and ended so because his knowledge of the Power was less than that of his enemy. If so—we wanted none like him loosed, and what I had already done, under that strange compulsion, was to aid evil.

I peered down at him, holding out the sword, that its light, close to his body, might give me a clearer view. He was human in form as far as I could see. Which meant little enough, as the adepts had once been human, and there were also evil things which could weave hallucinations to cloud their true forms.

The helm and the mail he wore were different from any I had seen. And the ax, with its keen-edged double head, was no weapon I knew. While those odd diamond pieces veiled his face too closely for me to judge what might lie beneath.

Now that command of my will which had brought me to free him ceased. No voice cried "Tolar" in my mind. I was again Yonan, myself. And any decision would be mine alone.

Above all I wanted to leave him here—to go out hunting Crytha. Still—

Among fighting men there are certain laws of honor by which we are bound, whether we desire it or not. If this captive was alive, if he was of the Light—then I could not leave him to the Thas again. But what was he—friend or bitter foe?

I laid down the sword, not again on the rock, but across his breast, so that the metal of its new blade rested partly on his ax. My fingers went to those chains which held in place his mask. For it seemed to me that I must look upon his real face before I made my choice.

The chains looked frail enough, until I took them into my fingers, lifting them a little from the icy flesh against which they lay. I tugged at those which lay across the temples beneath the shadow of that dragon-crowned helm. Suddenly they gave so I was able to pull them up and away from the cold face. A second pull loosened that of the chin fastening, and I threw the whole from me.

I had so bared a human face with no distortion of evil I could detect. But then such evil can lie inwardly, too. He seemed ageless, as are all the Old Race after they reach maturity until just before their long lives come to an end, unless they fall by accident or battle.

Then—

The eyes opened!

Their stare caught and held me, my hand half out for the hilt of my sword. A very faint frown of puzzlement drew between the dark brows of that face.

"Tolar?"

Once more that name. Only now it was shaped by those lips slowly losing the blue of cold.

"I am Yonan!" I returned fiercely. No more tricks would this one play with me. I was who I was. Not a dying man in a dream—a body answering to a spirit it did not know.

His frown deepened. I felt then, and cried out, at a swift stab into my mind. He read me ruthlessly as I writhed, unable to look away. He was—

"Uruk—" He supplied a name. Then waited, his eyes searching mine, as if he expected some answer out of my memory.

I snatched the sword, drew away from him. It seemed to me at that moment that I had indeed brought to life one of the enemy. Yet I could not kill him, helpless as he was now.

"I am not—of the Shadow." His voice was husky, hoarse, like metal rusted from long disuse. "I am Uruk of the Ax. Has it been so long then that even my name is now forgot?"

"It is," I returned flatly. "I found you there." I gestured with my left hand to the pillar, keeping the sword ready in my right. ''With the Thas yammering before you—''

''The Thas!'' He strove to lift his head, the upper part of his body, but he struggled like a beetle thrown upon its back, unable to right itself again. ''And what of the Banners of Erk, the Force of Klingheld, the battle—yes, the battle!''

I continued to shake my head at each name. ''You have been long here, you who call yourself Uruk. I know of no Erk, nor Klingheld. Though we fight the Dark Ones who move freely in this Escore. We are allied with the People of Green Silences and others—with more than half the country at our throats—if they can be reached!''

There was a skittering sound, bringing me instantly around, my sword ready. And it appeared that my wariness gave that weapon power, for its blade blazed the higher. But he who spun into the open in a great leap was Tsali, hugging his net of stones still to his scaled breast.

He looked to me and then to Uruk. And it was upon Uruk he advanced. Though his mouth was open and I saw the play of his ribbon tongue, he did not hiss.

While Uruk rose now so that he supported himself on his elbows, though that action followed visible effort. Now he watched the Lizard man with the same searching stare which he had first used on me. I believed that they were in that silent communication and I was again angry that I lacked the talent. My boots crunched on the splinters of ice which had fallen from the pillar as I shifted closer to them.

Uruk broke that communion of gaze. ''I understand —in part. It has been very long, and the world I know has gone. But—'' The frown of puzzlement still ridged his forehead. ''Tolar—Tolar I reached. Only he could wield the ice sword. Yet I see it in your hand and you say you are not Tolar?'' He made a question rather than a statement.

''I am not ~~Tolar~~,'' I returned firmly. ''The hilt of the sword I found set in a rock; by chance alone I found it. Here the Thas had taken my weapon. After, by some sorcery, I was moved to break off one of those icicles. And when I set it against the hilt—it became a full sword. I have none of the Talent, nor do I understand why this thing happened.''

''That blade would not have come to your hand, nor would you have had the power to mend it,'' he answered slowly, ''if some of that which was Tolar's Power had not passed to you. That is Ice Tongue—it serves but one man and it comes to him of its own choice. Also, it is said to carry with it some small memory of him who held it last. Or perhaps the speculations of the White Brethren may hold a germ of truth in them—that a man who has not completed his task in this world is reborn that he may do so. If it came to you—then you are the one meant to bear it in this life, no matter who you are.''

Tsali had laid aside his bag of light stones, was snapping open a second pouch he had at his belt. From this he took another round object. Holding that between two claws, he began passing it down Uruk's body from the dragon helm on the man's head to the boots on his feet. From the new stone there diffused a pinkish mist to settle down upon the body he treated, sinking into the other's white, chilled flesh.

Now Uruk sat up.

''You spoke of the Thas,'' he said to me, and the grating hoarseness was gone from his voice. ''Thas I would meet again. And I believe that you also have a purpose in hunting them—''

Crytha!

I took even tighter hold on the blade this man from the past had called Ice Tongue.

"I do," I said quietly, but with a purpose enough to make those two words both promise and threat.

7

Our new companion moved jerkily at first, as if the long period since he last strode by his own will had near locked his joints. But, as we went, he stepped out more nimbly. And I saw that he turned his head from side to side, his eyes under that dragon-crowned helm alert to the dark which so pressed in upon us. Only the bared blade of Ice Tongue and the stones Tsali carried fought against that.

Once more I must trust the Lizard man as a guide, for he beckoned to us and then wove a pattern back and forth among those fangs of stalagmites, seeming entirely sure of where he went. I hoped that, having escaped the menace of the root bindings, he had followed Crytha and the party which held her when they had left me in the ice cave.

Uruk did not speak, nor did I, for I thought perhaps any sound might carry here, alerting those we sought. But I saw as I went that he began to swing the ax, first with his right hand and then the left, as if with that weapon he was equally dexterous in each hand.

The great ax of Volt which had come to Koris of Gorm—or rather he had taken it without harm from the body of Volt himself; a body which had vanished into dust once the ax was in Koris' hold—that was the only war ax I had knowledge of. It was not a weapon favored by either the Sulcarmen or the Old Race—at least within memorable time. But there was such utter confidence in this Uruk as he exercised that I was sure it had been for him the prime arm, more so than any sword or dart gun.

Questions seethed inside me. Who was Uruk, how came he to be encased in his ice prison? What part had he played during the final days of the chaos which had engulfed Escore after the adepts had enacted their irresponsible and savage games with the Power? He might be an adept himself, yet somehow I thought not. Though that he had something of the Power within him I did not doubt.

We came out of the great cavern into another one of the runs which formed the runs of the Thas. Here the smell of them was heavy. I saw the ax in my companion's hand rise, his survey of what lay about us grow even more intense.

Tsali beckoned again, bringing us into the passage. Luckily this was not one in which we had to crawl. But it was confined enough so that only one at a time could walk it. The Lizard man went first and then Uruk gave me a nod as might a commander in the field do to a subordinate officer. With a gesture at my still-shining blade, he indicated that its light made my position in the van necessary.

The passage took several sharp turns. Where we might at present be in relation to the upper world, I could no longer even begin to guess. Once we had to edge across a finger of stone laid to bridge a dark crevice. Then I believe I could hear, far below, the gurgle of water.

Suddenly Tsali stopped. While Uruk's hand fell upon my shoulder in noiseless warning. But, dull as my hearing might be in comparison to that of the Lizard man, I could catch the sound, just as I could see a grayness. As if the passage we now followed opened into a larger and lighted space—though that light must be a very dim one indeed.

Tsali gestured once more. From here we must advance with the greatest of caution. He himself dropped to all fours, as the Lizard men seldom traveled while in the presence of humans, to scuttle on. I gripped the blade of Ice Tongue between my teeth and crept on hands and knees toward that light.

Moments later we reached the entrance to the tunnel. What lay beyond us must have once been a cave large beyond any measure I knew. But long ago there had come a break in the roof which arched over our heads, a wide crack far above any hope of reaching. And it was that break, very small in comparison with the roof itself, which emitted a light born of an exceedingly cloudy day, or of beginning twilight. So that it did very little to illumine what lay below.

This was a city—or at least a town—laid out by precise patterning. Narrow lanes running between crude buildings made by fitting rocks together into misshapen walls. These were perhaps as high as a tall man might reach, were he to stand on tiptoe. And the structures had no roofs nor windows, only a single door opening at floor level.

The Thas were here—in their boxes of houses, scattered through the narrow streets. There appeared to be a great deal of activity, centering on a round-walled building near the center of that collection of roofless huts. I heard a sharp, indrawn breath beside me and turned my head a fraction. Uruk, stretched nearly flat, but with both hands clasped about the haft of his ax, stared down into the teeming life of the Thas village, and his expression was certainly not one of curiosity nor of peace, but of a cold and determined resolve.

"They will have the girl," he said in the faintest of whispers, "in the chief's tower. Whether we can reach her or not—"

The chief's tower must be that edifice centrally placed. Though in the outside world I would not have named it "tower," since it stood perhaps only a little above my own height. I was more interested at the moment in those dwellings closer to where we lay.

Stones had been piled to erect those walls, yes. But I could see, by straining my sight to the uppermost, that even though those rocks had not been mortised into place by any form of binder, they seemed to stand secure. And I remembered far back in my childhood watching a master mason lay such a dry stone wall, choosing with an almost uncanny skill just the right stone to lie next and next.

Those "streets" which wound so untidily through the settlement offered numerous possibilities for ambush. To fight on the level of the Thas, when perhaps they had more surprises such as the root ropes, would be complete folly.

Instead, I began to mark a way from one wall to another in as straight a line as I could to where Crytha must be. To climb the first wall (which was rough enough to allow hand and foot holds in plenty) and then, using all one's care, to leap to the next and the next was possible. There was only one place where that leap would force a man to extend himself, and that lay at the open space surrounding the "tower" itself.

The Thas were smaller than men. Perhaps their tallest warrior might barely top my own shoulder. But they were numerous enough to drag a man down—unless he could, travel from one house wall top to another across their hidden city. And when a man is desperate, there sometimes comes a confidence which he never before believed he had.

Swiftly, I explained what I believed might be done. I spoke directly to Uruk, since I was sure that he could mind-contact Tsali far better than my clumsy gestures.

The Lizard man hissed. But he made fast about his neck his bag of light stones.

I hated to leave Ice Tongue out of my hand, but I would need both of those to make such a try. So I sheathed the sword. Much of the radiance was shut off. But the hilt still showed inner, rolling stripes of alive color.

Uruk fastened his ax in such a way (he tried it twice to make sure it was positioned just right for emergencies) so that he could seize it from over one shoulder from where it rested upon his back. Having made such preparation we wriggled down the slope, going to earth time and time again, until we were behind the first of the box houses I had marked.

I could hear the guttural speech of the Thas, but not near to hand. And, although I had come to grief on the heights of the Valley during the storm, I believed that this I had to do. I pushed all thought of failure out of my mind.

The climb was as easy as I guessed and, only moments later, I reached the top of the wall. Luckily that was wide enough to give me good foot room. Tsali flashed up and past me, rounding a corner, leaping with the grace and ease of his heritage to the next wall. There was no one in the single room below, but that did not mean that we would be so lucky a second or a third time. It needed only one Thas to look aloft and spy us and then—

Resolutely, I shut such mischance out of my mind, followed Tsali. My leap was not easy or graceful as his but I landed true, to hurry in the wake of the Lizard man. Nor did I look behind to see if Uruk had followed, though once or twice I heard him expel his breath in a short grunt.

We were three-fourths of our way toward the goal of the ''tower'' when we were spotted at last by one of the dwellers in a house we used so unceremoniously as a steppingstone. A shrill cry made me flinch, but I had not really believed we could win across the town without a sighting. And I thought we continued to have a chance —unless the enemy was equipped with more of those noxious roots.

Tsali had already made the next leap; I again followed. But the discovery must have shaken me more than I knew, for I teetered on the stone and had to drop and hold on lest I fall into the room below.

Now I heard cries echoed along the streets, and those I must close my ears to, concentrating only on winning to where Crytha might be. I had reached the last house. Before me was the space which I was not sure I could cross aloft. I saw Tsali sail out, alight on the tower wall, but such a leap was beyond my powers.

As I hesitated, Uruk drew up beside me. "Too far," he echoed my own thoughts aloud.

Below the Thas poured from every crooked way, massing about the doorway to the tower. There was nothing left but to fight our way through. I drew Ice Tongue. And, as if the strange blade recognized our peril and would hearten us to face it, the sword length blazed brilliantly.

From the Thas, there arose a wailing. I did not wait to see what weapon awaited me now. Instead, I leaped directly into the crowded space. At least one body was borne down by my weight, but I kept my footing. Now I waved overhead the blazing sword. It made a humming sound, nor did the light of its blade dim.

Thas cowered away from me, crying out, raising hands to shade their eyes. Then Uruk drew level with me, ax ready in hand. His appearance was a greater blow for the earth men. They fought, yes. Some died, by sword, by ax, but it would seem that the sight of our two weapons, or perhaps us also, had weakened their morale. I heard Uruk chanting as he swung the ax, though the words I could not understand. In that moment, another flash came out of that dream-life. Surely we had fought so before. And Ice Tongue, that was born of water, could tear away the earth.

We pushed our way to the door of the tower. As we reached it, Tsali edged forth from its interior, walking backward. His eyes were fixed on Crytha behind. He drew her as he might lead a horse forced to obey by pressure on the reins.

Her face was without expression, her eyes were still closed as if she slept. Uruk edged beside her. Before I could move or protest, his arm encircled her slight form; he raised her across his shoulder, leaving his right arm free to wield the ax, while the girl lay as limp as the dead in his grasp.

Now Tsali joined the battle. From his belt pouch, he scooped handfuls of powder which he hurled into the faces of those Thas who ringed us around. They cried out, then hands dropped clubs and spears, to cover their eyes as if blinded.

We could not take to the wall tops again, and the largest body of the Thas stood between us and that passage by which we had come. Uruk assumed command now.

"This way." His order was confident, as if he knew exactly what he did. Because I could offer nothing better, I had to go with him.

We retreated, doggedly, not down a lane—but into the tower itself, which to me was arrogant folly. But Uruk, still holding Crytha and the ax, while Tsali and I stood ready to defend the door, looked about him as might a man who knew very well what he should do.

"At least *this* has not changed," he said. "Hold the door, Tolar—I do not think they have found the below way after all."

He laid Crytha on the rock floor, to give a mighty shove with his shoulder against a low table which occupied the middle of the room. When that did not move, he raised his ax, to bring it down with a force I could almost feel. Under the blade, the table split, cracked into pieces, which he kicked aside impatiently.

Then I heard hissing from Tsali and swung around to bare the sword at gathering Thas. They had brought pieces of rock which they held like shields to hide their eyes while behind those they advanced grimly.

"Come!" Tsali remained to throw a last handful of his potent dust into the air. That formed a small cloud, moved out over the Thas, and sifted down. By so we gained a short breathing space. Where the table had stood there was revealed a rectangle of dark. Uruk, with Crytha once more over his shoulder, dropped waist-deep into it.

"Hurry!"

I sped with Tsali to that opening and we crowded through, though my feet must have been very close to Uruk's fingers. The descent was not long. Our stones and the sword gave us light enough to see that we stood in another way leading into the dark.

"Take her—" I had barely time enough to catch Crytha, steady her against me. Uruk reclimbed that stair to jerk down the trap door. I heard the pounding of his ax and saw that he was jamming into place bars I thought nothing might break.

"So—" I heard him laugh through the gloom. "It would seem that a man never really forgets what he needs to know. Now, Tolar who is Yonan." He descended the ladder again. "We walk ways which were old before the Thas came to play vermin in these hills. And I believe we can walk them safely. Shall we go?"

Though Crytha remained in her trancelike state, Tsali could control her in part. So, as we threaded through very ancient corridors which time itself must have forgotten, she walked on her own two feet. Also, the longer we journeyed so, the more she came back to life. When, at last, we came to the end of a final, long passage and Uruk pressed his hands here and there on the wall, she was near awake, knowing me and Tsali, though she seemed uneasy with Uruk.

The stone which barred our way slipped aside with a harsh grating, letting us out into the world above. I looked around, searching for a familiar landmark. And sighted one such directly above. We were again on the mountain wall of the Green Valley. Once back there, the Lady Dahaun could surely bring about the complete healing of Crytha.

Uruk tossed his ax into the air, caught it by the haft.

"It is good to be alive—again," he said.

My fingers caressed the hilt of Ice Tongue. "It is good to be alive," I agreed. I still did not know what kind of ally I had unwittingly brought into our ranks, but that he was a friend I no longer doubted. No more than I doubted that I could face battle as readily as any of my kin. And with such a sword—what might a man live to do? A confidence I had never before known swelled within me.

II
Sword of Lost Battles

1

In the morning light there seemed no shadow able to threaten this land. Below, the cup of the Green Valley lay alive under the touch of the sun with something akin to the glint of a great jewel. While for the four of us on the heights—or at least to three of our company—this held all the promise of welcome and safety we believe possible in this badly riven and disturbed country.

I reached out to Crytha, forgetting at that moment I had no right to claim more of her than common comradeship, or at the most, such affection as she might hold in her heart for a brother. For she was already promised to Imhar, son to my foster lord, Hervon. I was only Yonan, near the least of his household liegemen; though at my birth his lady had opened her heart and arms to me.

But Crytha's arms hung at her side. She did not look toward me. Rather she stood with her teeth set upon her lower lip, blinking her eyes slowly, as might one awakening after a puzzling dream. That she had been completely ensorceled by the Thas, who had stolen her for purposes of their own because she possessed in part some of the Talent of the Power, that I had known from the moment I had seen her with those deep-earth dwellers in my quest for her freedom. In my belt pouch I could, if I would, still find that lumpy figure of clay, hair, and rag which had lain secretly in her bed to draw her to their purposes.

It was Tsali, the Lizard man, who had used the mind touch to control her as we fought our way clear of the

Thas. But during the last part of our journey it had appeared she was regaining her full senses. Though to us so far she had not spoken.

Now I dared to break the silence between us:

"Crytha?"

Very slowly her head turned, allowing her eyes to meet mine. But her stare awakened fear in me, there being no depths in that gaze. She still looked inward, I guessed, not outward, and that by her free choice.

"Crytha!" I repeated with an urgency which I hoped would reach her ear as I could not myself reach her by thought.

Now something did stir deep in her eyes. The frown of a puzzled child ridged her forehead. She shook her head as if to banish so the sound of her name as I had uttered it. Then she spoke, hardly above a whisper:

"Tolar—"

"No!" I flung up my sword hand between us. That name haunted me, come out of a dead dream, out of the past. Just as I had felt a stranger move within my mind, take command of my body, when I had brought to being again the uncanny sword which now rode on my hip, seemingly whether I willed it so or no. Such a strange sword, newly forged by some Power from a hilt once bound in a rock centuries old, and a length of ice I had broken free from a cave wall. Yet it fitted my hand as if it had been fashioned only for me.

"I am *Yonan!*" I near shouted that.

She gave a whimper, and shrank back from me. Tsali, in one of his flickers of speed, pushed between us, hissing at me. The fourth of our company spoke first.

He had lagged behind as we came to the inner rim of the Valley wall, as if reluctant to take our path, and yet, because he knew no other, he was drawn to us.

Uruk—and who was Uruk? He had been a prisoner of the Thas, set for what must have been generations of time (as we mortals knew it) within the heart of an ice pillar in one of their innermost caverns. It was my strange sword, which he himself had named "Ice Tongue," that had freed him when that stranger battling for recognition within me had forced my attack against the pillar with the blade. And he had also called me "Tolar."

He stood now, studying me from beneath the shadow of his helm on which hunched the jewel-eyed dragon of his crest, his great ax resting head down upon the rock, but still gripped by both his hands. My uneasiness again awoke as I stared defiantly back. He must have been an ancient enemy of the Thas, yes. But that did not necessarily mean, in these days of war, that the enemy of an enemy was a friend or an ally. And of Uruk, in truth, I knew very little.

"She has been far under the Shadow," he said. "Perhaps she so gained a clearer sight than most—

"I am Yonan," I said grimly. Now I jerked Ice Tongue from my scabbard, and I would have hurled the blade from me. But I could not.

"You hold Ice Tongue," Uruk said. "Having been born again, it carries its own geas. And that has been transferred to you—whoever you may be or how you name yourself. It is one of the Four Great Weapons, and so it chooses its own master."

With my other hand I fought to unflex my fingers, break the hold they kept upon the crystal hilt, which was no longer clouded, as it had been when first I found it, but rather shone with that sparkling of light which had fired up in it when the blade had been once more fitted to the grip. But I knew within me that there was no use in what I tried; I was not the master, but rather the servant of what I carried. And, unless I could learn the mastery I lacked, then I would—

I saw Uruk nodding and knew that he could read my thoughts, as could any wielder of the Power.

"Time is a serpent, coiled and recoiled upon itself many times over. It can be that a man may, by some chance or geas, slip from that one coil which is his own, into another. If this happens he can only accept—for there is no return."

"Tolar out of HaHarc—" Crytha was nodding too, as if she had the answer to some puzzle at last.

HaHarc? That was a tumbled ruin which lay beyond the Valley, a place so eroded by time (and perhaps beaten by the Shadow) that no living man could make sure which was house, which was road, if he passed among its shattered blocks.

Men said that the hills themselves had danced when it fell; but that they danced to a piping out of the dark. Even the legend concerning it now was a very tattered one.

"I am Yonan!" I slammed Ice Tongue back into my sheath. "HaHarc is long dead, and those who lived there are forgotten by man and monster alike."

"So HaHarc is gone," Uruk spoke musingly. He no longer watched me so closely; rather he looked into the Valley lying below us. "And this is your stronghold, Tolar-turned-Yonan?"

"It is the stronghold of the People of Green Silences, their allies, and we who come over-mountain."

"Those are they who now come then?" He freed one hand from the hilt of his ax, to make a slight gesture downward. And I saw that a party was indeed climbing the rock wall toward us.

Crytha gave a sudden little sigh and sat down, as if her

legs could bear her no farther. And Tsali flashed away, down to meet those climbers. When I would have moved to follow him that I might speed help for Crytha, I discovered I could not go any nearer to the drop than where I still stood.

In me there was a rise of fear. The valley was guarded, not only by the valor of those within its walls, but by most ancient and strongest signs of the Power. If any carried on him the brand of the Shadow, he dared not cross its lip, unless he was an adept of the Dark.

Which I was not—not of the Shadow! Unless—I looked at Uruk and my lips flattened against my teeth. I had freed this man against my will, but I had done so. Was he of the Dark, such an act would have besmirched me also.

''You—!''

He did not give me time to add to that threat, or accusation. In answer he strode past me, lowering himself a little over the rock rim, only to return and bend over Crytha, lifting her gently to lean against him, where I was helpless to move.

Fear and rage warred in me. It was plain then that the danger to those of the Valley lay not in Uruk—but somehow in me—or in the sword! Yet the hilt of that I had dug out of the very rock of its walls, and that had companied me down into the heart of our defense, meeting then with no barrier. Save that I had dreamed thereafter, horribly, of how it had come to an end and me—or someone who had once been me—with it.

Now I set, with trembling fingers, to the unlatching of the buckle of my sword belt. I could try once more to rid me of this encumbrance, this threat to the Yonan who was. Perhaps if I did not touch the sword itself I could succeed.

And it would seem that in that speculation I was right,

for when sword and belt fell from me, I could step over them to the same cliff edge as Uruk had done. But I heard his voice from behind me:

"No man can so easily set aside the fate laid upon him!"

"So," I snarled like a snow cat, my anger blazing high as I had seldom felt it before. "We shall see!"

I would kick this sword, send it flying back, away from this place. The rock broke in many crevices; let it fall into one such and be buried, even as the hilt had been hidden before.

But, before I could move, those from below reached us. The Lady Dahaun moved quickly, nearly as swiftly as Tsali, and she was the first to reach us. Behind her came Lord Kyllan and with him, Imhar, and three others—two of the Green People, one of our own men.

Crytha pulled away from Uruk with a weak cry of joy, such as I would have given the pain of a wound to hear had it been uttered for me. She fled into the open arms of the Lady Dahaun; there she wept with sobs which tore at her young body.

The Lady Dahaun whispered gently and that sobbing ceased. But Lord Kyllan, with Imhar at his shoulder, moved forward to face Uruk and me. And it was to my companion that they looked the first, their glances flitting quickly by me.

Uruk was smiling, a small smile which lifted lips alone and did not reach his watchful eyes. I saw that Lord Kyllan was as much on guard in his own way. But Imhar scowled. However, neither was the first to break silence—it was as if they were not quite sure which words to choose at this moment.

It was Uruk who spoke, and not to them, but directly to the Lady Dahaun.

He swung up his ax, holding its double blade at the level of his breast in what was plainly a salute.

"Hail, Lady of the Green Silences—Merhart that was!"

Still holding Crytha close to her, she raised her head to stare at him as if she would reach his every thought.

"It has been long since *that* name passed the lips of any being—"

"So I have guessed, Lady. But it has been long since I was able to walk this earth. Whether you be in truth she who bore that name, or one come later of her bloodline, still you must know me."

She nodded gravely. "Uruk of the Ax. But the years fled past have been very many."

He shrugged. "To me they were a dream. I was captive to Targi—one of his choicer jests, or so he thought it. I have even been a god—to the Thas—if one can conceive of the Thas wishing a god to bow to. But I would guess that even this long toll of years you speak of has not yet resolved our warring."

"That is so. For a while we dwelt in the waste, to allow the Shadow to grow dim, rent by its own many furies. Most of the Great Ones are gone. But what some of them left spots the land now as diseased fungi will spot once solid wood. And the war sword has gone forth to raise us again."

Uruk laughed. "Then it would seem that I have been roused in time. Uruk of the Ax never refused battle."

Lord Kyllan broke in then, and I believed he still looked at Uruk with small favor and more suspicion.

"This man is truly of our belief, Dahaun?"

"He is a legend," she replied. "And legends grow—"

"Out of proportion in truth," Uruk broke in to end her answer. "Yes, Lord, I am not of the Shadow. Once I was master of a city; I led a province of this land into battle. What I am now is a single pair of arms, a head with some old skills of war hidden among my thoughts, and this.'' He lifted the ax a fraction higher. ''It is one of the Four Weapons. And,'' now he swung a fraction, pointing with his chin at me, ''there stands he who can hold another —Ice Tongue has been reborn in his hands!''

I heard the Lady Dahaun draw a swift breath. She looked from me to the sword and belt I had shed, and then back to me again. There was a little wonder in her eyes, which speedily became measurement.

''The Sword of Lost Battles—'' she said.

''Yes. And this young lord has just discovered the first of its secrets—that it cannot pass your protection runes.''

''I will not have it!'' I cried out and would have kicked it far from me as I had planned to do. But the Lady Dahaun shook her head slowly.

''You can leave it here,'' she said, ''yet it will not leave you. Each of the Four Weapons chooses but one owner, in time to become one with that man. But this one has an ill geas on it. It was meant to serve the Light, but there was a flaw in its forging. It brings ill to him who carries it—to the cause in which it is carried. Yet it is not of the Shadow as we know and hates all of the Dark.''

''Yes,'' Uruk added, ''until it be returned to its source it is ill-fated. But who says that the time of return may not come now?''

I shook my head and moved away from the sword determinedly. ''Let it lie then. We need no ill luck. And I am no time master to meddle with the Power or the past. Let it lie and rust into nothingness where it is.''

And I thrust my right hand into my armpit and held it there, for at that moment my very flesh rebelled against me and my fingers would go forth against my will to pick up once more that ill-omened blade.

2

The fire danced high, its light touching now on this face among our company, now that. For there had been a gathering of all those of authority, both small and large, within the Valley. The Lady Dahaun and Lord Ethutur of the Green People, Lord Kyllan and Lord Hervon from over-mountain, he who led the Renthans, and Verlong, the winged, also the chief of the Lizard men. And together with them had come their chief warriors, spreading fan-wise back into a dark where the flame light did not reach. Among the first rank sat Uruk, his ax across his knees, with never one hand nor the other far from it.

Between her fingers, the Lady Dahaun held that figure of clay and hair and rag which had drawn Crytha from our protection to the Thas. And the eyes in that company fastened on what she held.

"It would seem," Ethutur broke the small silence which had lain for a space on us, "that our protection is not as secure as we believed it. For such a thing could not have come into this place otherwise."

I clasped my hands tightly before me. My right palm itched; the fingers kept cramping as if they would hold something. In me a hunger gnawed, a hunger I must fight with all my strength. For I had done as I had sworn. Ice Tongue lay where I had dropped it on the heights above and I would have no regrets—no regrets!

"This," the Lady Dahaun balanced the ugly talisman

69

on one palm, "was not fashioned beyond our walls, but within them."

At that saying, our uneasy glances swept from face to face around our circle. Would she tell us now that among us was a traitor? Yet how could that be? Who had enough strength of the Dark Power to pass the barriers so often renewed and set to our defense?

"The clay," she continued, "is of the brookside; this hair is from the head of Crytha, as is this also hers." She flicked with one finger tip the rag twisted around the image.

"Who—" Lord Kyllan's hand was on his sword hilt. His face, young-seeming as it was, was grim and set as if he looked ahead to some battle wherein he might go down to defeat.

"Crytha." Her answer came so quietly that it took me two or three breaths of time to understand. And then I would have protested, but before me was Lord Hervon.

"Why, Lady, would she fashion a trap in which to entangle herself? This is not sense, but folly!"

"*She* did not fashion it, my lord, not knowingly. But this maiden of your house has more talent within her than we realized. Untrained, the Power can harm as well as aid. She had drawn upon what lies within her eagerly, as a man drinks at a pool of clear water when thirst torments him, foreseeing no evil in her acts since all she desired was for good. She is a born healer of great promise. But no talent is single in one, and where Power opens the door and there are no safeguards, then there can creep in that which we fear most.

"Those safeguards we have set to make invulnerable this Valley work against physical invasion. But some subtle brain has devised a way of reaching out along a level of mind which is not guarded, which cannot be detected, except by the training which those of the Talent use as their shields.

"Such a questing thought will not trouble us who are so shielded. But it can influence—and without their knowledge or understanding—those who have not such shields. Fear not, now that this evil has so revealed itself it cannot use her again as a tool in its hand. Uruk"—she spoke directly to him—"who holds the Thas within his hand?"

He did not answer at once. And when he did, he spoke musingly as if he himself faced some riddle.

"Lady, you say I am but legend in this new world of yours. I lived in another time and a different Escore. My enemy there was Targi. The Thas paid him some liegeship—enough to let him use their burrows for my prison. But Targi—" He shook his head slowly now. "I have not sniffed out any of his mischief since I was freed. If he lives—" He slapped his hand flat down upon the head of the ax. "I would know it! We are too bound in enmity for me not to do so."

"Targi was slain in Emnin." The words came from my lips, but they were not mine. I saw all those in the company turn their eyes, startled, toward me. "It was the Lost Battle." That which was not Yonan continued. "Lost for the Banners of Eft, for the Fellowship of HaHarc. Yet the Shadow was also driven back; no side could claim victory on that day."

My sword hand flew to my lips, covering them. I was shaken by this sudden arousal of that *other*. And was well aware that those on either side of me withdrew a little as if I were revealed as an unclean enemy. Yet I had thrown away Ice Tongue—I was *Yonan*!

I saw that Ethutur regarded me with a frown. His lips

moved as if he would speak, but the Lady Dahaun checked him with a gesture. Then she raised her hand and traced in the air certain symbols. As green fire they blazed, and then the green became blue. While it seemed to me that I whirled giddily across the fire between us, that all which was me hung in midair, naked and defenseless before those signs of her witchery.

"Who are you?" I saw her lips move to shape the words, but they sounded very faint and far away. Some mighty chasm now stretched between us.

I struggled. Yonan—I was Yonan! But I heard my own voice answer in the same thin and faded tone of far distance.

"Tolar—Tolar of Ice Tongue."

"And what would you here, Tolar?" came her second question.

"The past must be erased, the evil geas broken."

"And this is your will, Tolar?"

"I have no will in this. It is a geas which has been laid upon me, that my failure be redressed and time rewoven."

I—or that substance which was part of me—no longer hung before the Lady of Green Silences. Rather I was back once more in my own body. But I no longer sat among the people of Hervon. Rather, I had moved into the open, so that the breath of the flame nearly scorched my boots. I knew, bitterly, that he whom I had fought so hard to destroy was now fully awake within me. I had no longer a place here, but must be about some strange and terrifying quest which held little contact with the world I had always known.

"I must return." My lips felt stiff. In spite of the heat of the fire I was chilled, as I had been when I had hacked open the ice pillar of the Thas to free Uruk. And in me at that moment there arose the conviction that I went to death itself, yet I could not prevail otherwise against the compulsion which moved me.

Uruk arose. "This hosting is mine, also. For though the craft of Targi prevented my fighting aforetime, it shall not now. Lady"—once more he saluted Dahaun with the ax—"we go into the dark; think of us with fair wishing, for our path will be very strange and the dangers along it such as few men have ever experienced."

"Boy—" I was aware Lord Hervon was beside me, his hand grasping my sword arm. There was a growing pain in my right hand, a pain which would never leave me until once more I clasped Ice Tongue and carried through what that uncanny sword, and this stranger within me, wished. "Yonan—what will you do?"

I sensed concern in his tone. And that part of me which was still the youth he knew gathered a measure of courage from his thought of me. But so small a part of my person was now Yonan it might have been that a stranger spoke those words.

"My Lord." I gave him full courtesy; to me he now seemed as far away as our voices had earlier sounded. "I go where I must go, do what must be done. For I am what Ice Tongue has made me, and it I shall serve until once more comes the end. Perhaps this time"—small hope struggled within me—"the end will be a better one." Yet memory overclouded that hope, as I knew again the sharp pains of my wounded body as I had dragged myself to that place into which I might fling the sword, lest evil find it and turn it to a still greater danger.

His hand fell from my arm. While that company moved out and back, leaving a path into the dark, away from the cheer of the fire. Down that steadily darkening way I walked, and shoulder to shoulder with me, Uruk. While within me something was stricken and began to die. When it was truly dead I would be a man without hope, with only the geas left to move me on.

Though it was dark my hands and feet seemed to find for themselves the way to climb the cliffs. And I went upward with greater speed and ease than I had ever gone before. Dimly I heard the movements of Uruk to my right. I felt no comfort in his company, he was too much a part of this thing which held me prisoner—which was killing Yonan as surely as if it tore open his breast to slit his heart.

When we reached the top of that way I saw the light and it drew me. The sword I had discarded had a torchlike hilt. I stooped and picked up the belt, buckling it once more about me. Then I fingered the grip, to find it warm, not chill as normal crystal.

For the first time since we had left the fire, Uruk spoke. He did not make a question of that word, it was rather as if he affirmed a resolve.

"HaHarc."

"HaHarc," I echoed in agreement. As yet that stranger (he whom they called Tolar) was not in full control of my mind, only of my will and body. I did not have his memories—except in fleeting, time-broken pictures. But when Uruk had uttered that name, then I knew it for our goal.

But we were not to reach those near-forgotten ruins unchallenged. For, as we made our way down the opposite wall of the mountain encirclement, my skin seemed to prickle between my shoulders; I found myself sniffing the air, listening. Evil was abroad in the night—and the menace it exuded was strong enough to awake every instinct of caution. I could not throw away my life, rather must I live for the veiled purpose to be demanded of me.

It seemed that my hearing was keener, that I had other and new senses which brought me strong intimations of danger waiting below. And in the moment there flashed into my mind words—a thought not my own—

"Those of the Shadow move—"

But I had none of the Talent; how could I have caught this warning? No, *Yonan* had no Talent, but what did I know of the gifts and strengths of Tolar?

A rising puff of wind carried to us a thick stench. Not Thas, no—Gray Ones. Those runners on evil roads who were neither man nor beast, but the worst of each wedded into one. I paused in my descent to listen.

A faint scratching at the rock—not directly below but farther to my right. I peered down into a well of blackness. Then I saw the pallid blink of eyes which had a vile radiance of their own as they were raised to mine.

"Move to the left." Once more that mental message came clearly. "There is a ledge. I already stand upon it."

The Gray Ones made no sound. I set myself to exploring handholds to my left. There were enough to give me easy passage. Only moments later my feet found a firm surface and I could let go of those holds, turn to face outward.

"They are not silent hunters usually," my companion continued his soundless communication. "There are but five." He mentioned that as if five of the Gray Ones meant nothing at all to armed men. At that I wondered, fleetingly.

I saw the betraying eyes below. They moved steadily along what must be the base of the cliff, perhaps the height of a man—a little more—until they were again beneath us. I drew Ice Tongue.

It was as if I had suddenly produced a torch, limited though that illumination was. And in my hand, the sword itself gave forth a sound so strange that had not my fingers clung to it willessly I might have dropped it.

The songsmiths who tell and retell our legends, keeping alive so much which is long since gone otherwise from the world of men, speak at times of "singing swords," marvelous blades which give forth a shrill song when they are battle-ready. But Ice Tongue—snarled! There was no other word to describe the sound it made.

And its snarl was echoed from below. A dark bulk sprang up toward us. Not a Gray One, for it showed no lighted eye discs.

Uruk moved and, in the light of my blade, I saw his ax descend into that black mass, heard a horrible howling as the creature, whatever it might be, fell back and away. Now the Gray Ones leaped up, as if maddened into stupidity by the wounding of their battle comrade. For our position above them gave us a superiority which no sane creature would have ignored.

Again Ice Tongue snarled as I cut down at a misshapen head, felt flesh give, bone shatter. They leaped to reach us as if they were frenzied, compelled to attack in spite of the fact that we could so well deal with them from where we stood.

Thus in the dark we slew and slew again. Screams and whimpers arose from below us. But we twain voiced no war cries. Nor did Ice Tongue "speak" by my will or training, but as if it, itself, had such a hatred for those below that it must vent that in force.

At length, Uruk's thought came to me, "Enough. They are dead."

I leaned on the bared sword, searching for any telltale flash of luminous eye, listening for any sound. But the night was now both black and still. I felt myself weary, drained, as if Ice Tongue had drawn upon my very spirit.

"We must move," Uruk added. And in me, too, a feeling of urgency warred with that weariness. "Those here have their masters, who will soon know that they are dead."

We followed the ledge on for a little and found at length that it narrowed so that we must descend once more. And, when, at last, the ground was under our feet, Uruk turned sharply away from the scene of our struggle.

"HaHarc—" he said. "We are not yet masters of time."

What he meant I did not yet guess, but I wiped Ice Tongue on a rough clump of grass and followed him, though I kept that blade bare and ready as I tramped along.

3

Though there was no moon and the stars were very far away, affording no light at all, yet we two strode through the night even as we had left the fire in the Valley, shoulder to shoulder. We might well be following some torch-illumined path. In me there was a certainty as if my mind saw instead of my eyes. Yet another part of me was ever on sentry duty against what might slink behind on our trail.

I had been tired when we had returned from the venture in the burrows of the Thas. My rest had been but a short one before we had been summoned to that council. Yet now I had no feeling of fatigue, only a burning desire to get ahead with what must be done. Though the nature of that act, whatever it might be, was still hidden from me.

Uruk did not break the silence between us, with either

thought or speech. The Lady Dahaun had called him legend, but she had accepted him at once, which meant he was not of the Shadow. And he had known Tolar—yet I was afraid to try to recall any early tie between us. Yonan still flickered faintly within me, his fear enough to impose this last desperate restraint.

If evil did sniff behind us that night, it kept its distance well. Perhaps the slaughter we had wrought at the base of the cliff made the enemy wary. Or maybe they would entice us on in our folly well away from the Valley so that we would be easy meat for them. Dully, I wondered which of these guesses was nearest to the truth as I went, ever on guard.

That wan light of gray which is the first awakening of the morning rendered visible a wild, churned land. Some chaotic movement of the earth had had its way here. Uruk slowed. I saw his helmed head move right to left and back again, as if he sought a sign which was missing.

Now we must weave a path through a choking of brush and shrub which grew up about tumbles of dark blocks of stone. Still, when I surveyed this with half-closed, measuring eyes, I could see patterns—as if buildings of mist and fog spiraled upward from those battered remains, and roads opened for us.

Uruk paused. When I looked at him I saw his face set, his mouth grim-lipped. He searched the ruins ahead with a fierce, compelling stare as if he would tear out of them by the force of his will alone some mighty secret.

"HaHarc—" He did not use the mind touch, rather spoke aloud as if he could not quite believe in what he saw. Then he swung the ax, and there was rage in that swing as he brought the weapon down, to decapitate a thin bush. He might have been striking out against all the past with that useless blow.

For a long moment he stood, the withered leaves and branches he had cut still lying on the ground, the blade which had severed them pressing their wreckage into a drift of soil. Then he shook his head. Once more he stared about him intently and I sensed that he sought some landmark which was very needful for whatever he was to do here. But my battle with that other within me had begun once again, and I felt suddenly drained of strength, of any care concerning what might lie ahead.

Uruk moved forward, but hesitantly, not with the swift purpose he had shown before. It could be that, fronted by these ruins, he had lost some landmark which he needed. Still we wove a way among blocks, pushing through the growth, though now I followed behind him.

The valley which had held HaHarc was narrow at its entrance. I could mark in the growing light that it had been closed here by a wall or fortification running from one side of the heights to the other. Though the stones of that building were so cast about that it would appear the land itself had shaken off that bondage, as indeed it must have done.

Past that point, the way before us widened and those structures which had been divorced from the walls showed taller, less tumbled. The stone was darkly weathered. Still here and there, even in the gray of early dawn, I could sight remnants of carving. Sometimes I had to close my eyes for a breath or two because I could also see the mist curdle, raise, bring back ghostly shadows of what must have been.

We stumbled upon a street, still paved, though drifted with soil which had given rootage to grass, some small bushes. This ran straight into the heart of the destroyed fortress city. For I knew without being told that before its destruction HaHarc had indeed been both. Like the Green

Valley, in its day it had stood as a stout oasis of safety against the Shadow.

On Uruk tramped, now facing straight ahead, as if he had at last found the landmark he sought. Thus we came at length upon an open space where the ruins walled in a circling of stone blocks, tilted and fissured now. At regular intervals about this had been set up, on the inner side of that circle, monoliths, carved with runes, headed by time-eroded heads; some of men and some of beasts, strange, and yet menacing—but in their way no more menacing than those creatures of intelligence who comraded the People of Green Silences.

Some had fallen outward, to shatter on the pavement. But others leaned this way or that, still on their bases. And two or three stood firmly upright. Within the guardianship of these there was another building, which, in spite of its now much broken and fallen walls, I think had been tower-tall. And the stone of its making was different from that I had seen elsewhere in the ruins—for it was that dull blue which marked those islands of safety throughout Escore, the blue we had been taught to watch for during any foraying as a possible place of defense.

Once more Uruk stopped, this time facing a gateway in the tower. Had there ever been any barrier of a door there, that was long since gone. I could see through the opening into a dim chamber, wherein blocks fallen from the higher stories were piled untidily.

''Tower of Iuchar—'' Again he spoke aloud and his voice, though he had not raised it, echoed oddly back. ''Iuchar, Iuchar.''

My other memory struggled for freedom. Iuchar—I had known—

A man—tall as Uruk—yet not one I had seen in the

body, no. Rather he was—what? A ghost which could be summoned at will to hearten people, who in the later days of HaHarc needed strongly some such symbol to reassure them in a war they sensed was already near lost? Iuchar of HaHarc. Once he had lived—for very long had he been dead—dead!

I denied Iuchar, for all his tower. Uruk, leaning a little on his ax, turned his head toward me. I saw his eyes beneath the rim of his dragon-crested helm. They held a somber anger.

"Iuchar—" he repeated the name once more, to be echoed. He might so have been uttering a warning to me.

Then he raised the ax in formal salute to that travesty of a tower. And I found myself willed by that other to draw Ice Tongue also, and give with it a gesture toward the open doorway.

Uruk went forward, and I followed. We passed beneath that wide portal. And I saw on the walls without the traces of flame, as if Iuchar's tower had once been the heart of some great conflagration. But within—

I halted just beyond the portal. In my hands Ice Tongue blazed, and there was an answering fire running along the double blades of Uruk's ax. There was an energy in this place, a flow of some kind of Power which made the skin tingle, the mind wince and try to escape its probing. However badly time and disaster had treated HaHarc, in this, its very heart, the Light held, fiercely demanding. Bringing with it a fear which was not born of the Shadow, but rather a foretaste of some great demand upon courage and spirit, from which he who was merely human must flinch.

But there was no evading that demand. My hands shook and Ice Tongue quivered from that shaking. But I did not drop the sword, that I could not have done. Uruk had moved on until he stood in the very center of that circular chamber, and now he turned and beckoned to me.

Unhappily, but realizing that I could not resist what had lain here so long waiting, I took three or four long strides to join him. No earth had drifted here, the stone under our boots was clean; for those rocks which had fallen from above lay close to the walls. It might have been that the force which clung here determined to keep the core of its hold clear. Now I saw that the pavement was crossed and recrossed by lines, into which some dust had shifted, so that the pattern they fashioned was not to be too clearly defined.

Uruk took his ax, and, going down on one knee, he used one of the blades with infinite care, scraping away that shifting of ancient dust, to make plain that we stood within a star. While again moved by the stirring of that other will which had become an inner part of me, I used the tip of Ice Tongue in a like manner, bringing into clarity certain runes and symbols, all different, which had been wrought near each of the points of that star. Two I recognized; those the Valley used for its safeguarding; the others—I could have opened Tolar's memory perhaps, but stubbornly I resisted.

While always about us, pressing in upon mind and will, was that sense of waiting Power. Had any of it drained during the ages of HaHarc's loss? It did not seem so to me. Rather I thought that it had stored energy, waiting impatiently for the release we were bringing, if unwillingly on my part.

His task done, Uruk arose and gestured again to me. "The fires—"

I knew what he meant, though the logic of Yonan

denied that this could be done—even while the sword of Tolar moved to do it.

I passed slowly around within the star, reaching out with Ice Tongue. And with that ice-turned-uncanny-metal I touched the tip of each point of the star set in the rock. From that touch sprouted fire—a fire unfed by any lamp, or even any fuel, burning upward unnaturally out of the blue rock itself.

Then Uruk raised the ax high and his voice boomed as might the gong in one of the shrines tended by the Witches. I did not understand the words he intoned, I do not think perhaps that even that long-ago Tolar would have known them. To each adept his own mystery, and I was certain that Tolar had never been one of the Great Ones of Escore.

If Uruk was (but somehow that I doubted also), at least he had given no other sign of such. But that he could summon *something* here I had no doubt.

From those points of flame my own sword had awakened into being there now spread a haze—sideways—though the flames of blue still arose pillarwise toward the broken roof above us. And that haze thickened.

As Uruk's voice rose, fell, rose again, the wall of mist grew thicker. I sensed that out of our sight, hidden behind that, presences were assembling—coming and going—uniting in some action which Uruk demanded of them. I kept Ice Tongue bared and ready in my hand, though the Tolar part of me felt secure. Excitement was hot along my veins, quickened my breathing.

The mist had risen to fill the chamber save within the star where we stood. My head felt giddy. I had to tense my body to remain standing; for I had an odd idea that outside the mist the whole world wheeled about and about in a mad dance no human would dare to see, or seeing, believe in.

Uruk's chanting grew softer once again. He dropped the ax, head down, against the floor, leaned on its haft as if he needed some support. His whole body suggested such strain, a draining of energy, that, without thinking, I took a step which brought me to his side, so that I could set my left arm around his shoulders. And he suffered my aid as if he needed it at that moment.

His words came in a hoarse, strained voice, and finally they died away to silence. I saw that his eyes were closed. Sweat ran in runnels down his cheeks to drip from his jaw line. He wavered, so I exerted more strength to keep him on his feet, sensing that this must be done.

The fires on the star points flickered lower, drawing in that mist, in some way consuming it. There were tatters in the fog now, holes through which a man could see. But I did not sight the fallen blocks, the same chamber in which we had entered. Now the floor was clear, and there was other light beyond our flames, flowing from lamps set in niches. Between those lamps strips of tapestry hung, the colors muted perhaps, but still visible enough, blue, green, a metallic golden yellow, with a glitter, as if the real precious metal had been drawn out into thread to be so woven.

Then the star fires flashed out as if a giant's breath had blown them altogether. We were left in the glow of the lamps, while beyond the open doorway shone the brightness of the sun. I saw near that door a table and on it a flagon and goblets.

Steadying Uruk, who walked as if he were nearly spent, I brought him to that table. Laying Ice Tongue on its surface, I used my free hand to pour pale liquid from the flagon into one of the cups, then held that to my companion's lips. His face was drawn, his eyes were closed. But he gulped at what I offered as if he needed that to retain life within him.

And as he drank I heard sounds—voices, the hum of a town. I looked over Uruk's shoulder. As the room had changed, so had HaHarc. My hands shook as I realized what must have happened. We were—*back!*

No!

Tolar memory no longer warred with Yonan, but with its own self. I could not—I could not live this again! The pain from my first dream shot through my body as I remembered, only too vividly, what the past had held then, and now it had returned to face me—*no!*

4

There was no brightness in this day. Dusky clouds covered in part the sky, while from the ground mist curled like smoke from uncountable campfires. Thick and evil was that mist, eye could not pierce its billows, nor could any mind send exploring thought through it. Thus we knew it was born of wizardry and what it held was truly the enemy.

I stood with Uruk, with others who wore battle mail and helms fantastically crowned by this and that legendary creature. To most of them the self I once was could give names, yet we did not speak one with the other. Our silence was as thick as the mist below on the plain.

Uruk shifted his weight. I could guess what was in his

mind, for memory had returned to me full force—Tolar memory. But that was also a memory which stretched into the future. This was the Lost Battle. Though I could not see them, I could count over in that memory the names —and species—who gathered within the mist below.

What task lay upon Uruk and me now was something which I believed no man, nor adept, had tried before. Could we, knowing what we did, alter the past? Or would we be slaves to it—marched on to face once more the same fates which had overtaken the men of HaHarc in the long ago?

Though I had searched my small gleaming of legendary lore, I had never chanced upon any tale of time travel, of the ability to so alter what had been. And if we were so fortunate—what would be the result? Would HaHarc later fall to some other Power from the Dark?

Time—what was time? A measurement we ourselves forced upon the world, counting first by light and dark, then perhaps by the building of cities, the reigns of notable lords. Time now stood still as we drew our battle line and watched the forward creep of the fog.

"Be ready." Uruk's half-whisper reached my ears only because we stood shoulder to shoulder. It was coming —my skin crawled, my body tensed—the first of our chances to fight memory reached out to us. My mouth seemed overfull with saliva. I swallowed and swallowed again.

If we were not the puppets of time—then—

There was a sudden swirl in the mist. A dark figure strode through its curtain. Manlike, it stood erect. But it was not human.

"Targi's familiar—" Uruk's ax lifted slowly, very slowly.

Memory supplied what was going to happen now. In the

before Uruk had met that creature, slain it—and then the fog had taken him. I watched, waiting for the pattern to grip him now. I saw him sway, as if some force pulled at him strongly.

"No!" His voice was as loud as a battle cry. "I play not this game the second time!"

I heard the men about us stir, mutter, and knew that stares of astonishment were aimed at him. For them there was no coil in time; this happened in the here and now, not in the distant past.

The thing which was Targi's servant was fully in the open. It was thick-bodied, wearing no mail, covered only by a wiry pelt of coarse, tangled hair. Its head was both feline and apeish in contour, and it snarled, its lips curling back to show tusks. Its great paws were clawed, and in one it carried a short spear with long, serrated metal for a head.

Those with us still looked to Uruk. We could all catch the challenge now. The thing below did not issue that. It was only a vessel which carried Targi's hate. Its legs were bowed as if by the great weight of the barrel of its body, and it rocked a little from side to side as it came.

No, the challenge shot into our minds, as a burning fury of battle lust and red hate. I saw men surge forward, ready to break our line on the heights, drawn by that defiance in a way they could not control. So had it happened before—

But Uruk did not stir. He must be using all his own Power—for still he wavered forward a step or two jerkily. On him was that challenge centering. Once he had answered it, not realizing then what it meant.

"No!" The word broke again from between his teeth. His eyes were aflame by the rage aroused in him, rage which perhaps (even knowing to what fate it would deliver him) he could not long continue to control.

If Uruk went to meet that thing it would die—but we

would also lose our small advantage bought of memory. This was the first test set the twain of us.

And if Uruk did not go? Two men were already running downslope, heading to answer that overwhelming challenge. While those about and behind us were muttering, watching Uruk with unbelieving eyes. They might all break, dash forward into that mist. Only Uruk could hold them from such folly. But—

I was running. Without taking any straight thought, I headed for the beast, whose ears went flat like those of an angry cat. Spittle flecked about its fangs. Ice Tongue swung free in my hand, and again I heard the snarl which was its own battle cry. As I neared Targi's servant, fear was a weight on me. The hairy thing towered well above me in height; that weapon it was swinging up might shatter the sword I held if blade met blade—of that I was sure.

There were more dark forms breaking through the curtain of the mist. I heard a human voice scream, but I dared not look save at the monster before me. Tolar had not done this before. In so little might I indeed disjoint the flow of the past.

I did not think, it was rather that something outside myself commanded my body. The thing lumbered on, its awkward-seeming pace much swifter than I had guessed. I dropped to one knee. Ice Tongue slipped through my hand even as the full force of that hate which moved the enemy switched from Uruk at last, to beat at me, an unseen weapon worse than any forged steel.

Did I cry out my horror and fear when that mind thrust struck me? This is one memory I cannot search and find. But I used my sword, not as I would have in decent and honorable open battle. Instead I hurled it as one might a throwing knife.

It was not balanced for such work, yet the impetus of my throw carried it true to target. I saw the point of the flaming blade strike into the creature's swaying paunch, not biting deep enough perhaps to count, but cutting skin and flesh.

The shaggy thing paused, staring down at the sword piercing into its body. Its left hand caught at the blade. Then it threw back its head and howled, its red eyes coals of sullen fire. I felt its pain—but my own spirit leaped. It could not bear to touch that blade. The Power which had wrought Ice Tongue was utterly enemy to any of the Shadow.

Now the monster swung its weapon, not to reach me as yet, but to batter at the sword. One of those serrated edges caught at the hilt and jerked it free from the thing's body. Ice Tongue whirled away to my left.

I threw myself, with such force that my body skidded along the ground, the tough grass sleeked by tendrils of escaping mist aiding me. But just as I reached the blade, put out my hand to close about the hilt, a great clawed foot stamped down upon my wrist. The weight of the beast towering over me, the stench of its body, near laid me open to panic. So—if I did not die in one way from the Lost Battle, I would in another. We might not alter that final reckoning, even if we turned back time.

Straining to turn my head, I endeavored to make myself face death as it came by the hands of Targi's servant. There was shouting around us, yet I was not aware of any other caught in that struggle. My world had narrowed to the hulking shape hunched over me. Blood dribbled from the gaping wound in its belly. It tossed away its weapon. One hand strove to close that wound; the other, claws ready to pierce me, mail and flesh alike, descended to tear me apart. I fought madly against that pressing weight on my wrist. Then some saving sense took command. Instead of struggling I went down limp, as if easy meat for this nightmare.

Only my left hand caught at Ice Tongue. I had time for a single act. In my fingers the blade cut at my palm; still I had no choice. I pushed up a little to stab at that descending paw.

Perhaps the force of the blow the creature aimed at me added to the success of my desperate defense. For the point impaled the paw even as it had cut the paunch.

The thing squawked, jerked up its paw, drawing by so the cutting edge of the sword grievously cut my palm. I could not hold on. So I had to watch helplessly as, with a shake of the fist, it again freed itself from Ice Tongue, sending the sword flying out of my sight.

Now it raised its other great foot, the one it balanced upon grinding my wrist into the ground so that the pain made me dizzy. I knew what the thing planned to do. One mighty stamp with that other foot and I would be as smashed as an insect under a boot sole.

I had no defense. I could not even see well, since the pain from my pinned wrist and lower arm drew a red haze between me and that very certain death. Yet the smashing blow I expected did not fall. Instead the beast reeled away, back from me. I heard it give a grunting howl and its body crashed not too far away, blood pumping from a huge wound in its throat. For its deformed head had been almost, but not quite, severed from its neck.

''No!'' In spite of the wave of pain from my wrist and the other hand which streamed blood, I held on to consciousness. There was no mistaking the swing of that ax. To save my life (or perhaps because the ancient compulsion had indeed been greater than he could withstand) Uruk had followed the pattern of the past—he had killed Targi's servant.

I saw him go into a half crouch, his ax once more at ready. Somehow I levered myself up on the elbow of my injured forearm, though each movement was like a stab into my shrinking flesh. Ice Tongue—?

Then I saw something else—something which whirled out of the mist. I found voice enough to warn:

"Behind you!"

Uruk whirled with a skill born from long hours of training. His ax was up as he turned. Something dark, ropelike, hit the blade of that, dropped limply away again, severed. But it was only the first of such attacks. He ducked and struck, ducked and struck again and again. Then, in backward stumble to elude a larger one of those flying cords, he tripped against the body of Targi's servant. Before he could right himself one of the cords snapped home about his arms, drawing them together though he fought in vain to get ax blade against them.

I knew those living ropes—Thas' work! Now I got to my knees, holding my broken wrist tight against my body. My other hand was sticky with my own blood—to move it or my fingers was torment. But—

Just beyond where Uruk struggled and fought for liberty, I saw something else. Ice Tongue was standing, point into the ground. Its hilt was a light to guide me. Somehow I tottered to my feet, skirted the severed root which still wriggled, reached the sword. I could not close either hand about its hilt. Giddy, I went once more to my knees, leaned closer to the shining blade. My mouth gaped wide. I bent my head sideways and caught the hilt between my jaws.

It took effort to work it free of the soil. Then I had it. Uruk—I turned around. He was now completely prisoner; even the severed ends of roots crept to weave their lengths about him though he struggled and heaved.

I did not have strength to get to my feet again. Rather, on my knees, I crossed the space between us.

"Your hands—" I aimed the thought at him.

I saw his eyes go wide as they found me. He lay still as I moved toward him. The mist had not parted, but we could hear shouts, screams, and the sound of weapon against weapon. In spite of all our plans and hopes, the men of HaHarc *had* been drawn into Targi's chosen battlefield. Uruk free might make the difference; his orders they would follow.

I reached his side. The hilt of Ice Tongue wavered in my mouth. Any blow I could deliver with it would have little force. I now possessed only one small hope. Targi's creature had not been able to touch it; might it then have the same effect on the living ropes?

Bending my head, I pressed the point of the blade into the root which had so ensnared Uruk's arms. I had no strength, the point would not penetrate—my gamble had no hope—

But—

The root under the point of the sword wiggled, strove to elude that touch, light as it was. I fought grimly to bring all the pressure I could bear on it at that point. Suddenly, as if the metal had sawn through tough hide to reach a core no tougher than mud, the point sank in.

Like the living thing I more than half believed it was, the root snapped loose from its hold on Uruk's wrist to strike upward at my shoulder and caught. I could no longer hold Ice Tongue. The sword fell from my mouth. In its falling it clanged against the head of Uruk's ax. Now the ax blazed under that touch as the sword had upon occasion.

As I slumped forward, the roots writhed away from that blaze, reaching instead for me, clinging and squeezing, where they clung, with a kind of vindictive anger. But I saw Uruk swing the ax once more, slicing through what was left of his bonds.

Just as he won to his feet, had half turned toward me, the fog gave up another form and with it smaller things I knew of old. Thas! While he about whom those clustered—

I heard Uruk's cry:

"Targi!"

5

As his dead servant, this Lord of the Dark towered above the smaller Thas. He was a figure brought out of some tomb—his dark mail dull, bedewed by the condensing mist. But his head was bare, and he carried no weapon save a slender black rod, topped by the bleached-bone skull of some small animal. His skin was a pallid white, showing the more so because of the darkness of his mail. And his hair, which grew in a brush like the mane of a Renthan, was brilliantly red. Tongues of fire might so appear to rise from his long skull, for that hair bristled erect.

Nor was his face entirely human. It bore no expression now—only the eyes were alive And in them boiled such a fury as no man could show. Uruk was on his feet, his ax ablaze as I had seen Ice Tongue. That blade lay on the ground. I saw a Thas dart to seize it, leap backward again with a guttural cry. I held on to consciousness with all my strength.

"Well met." Uruk's voice did not soar to a shout, yet it carried even through the din of the mist-shrouded valley. "This match of ours is long overdue, Targi."

There was no answer from the sorcerer, nor did the deadness of his bleached face show life. But he paused and I saw his eyes go from Uruk to the ax.

"You are a dead man." The words burst in my mind, coldly, shaped without emotion behind them, formed with such a vast self-confidence as struck at the beginning hope which had sprung in me. For by this much had we altered the past—Uruk was not prisoner to the commander of the Thas.

I then saw Uruk laugh, though I could not hear the sound of his laughter. The two of them had forgotten me. Hugging still my broken wrist against me, I strove to pull myself up. There was a flick across my body. One of the root cords looped there. I plucked at it feebly with my wounded hand. Then the Thas closed in, though they did not drag me from the field. Rather stood about me, watching their master and Uruk.

One of them gave a coughing grunt and fell. I saw the end of a dart between his shoulders. Then the others scattered, or threw themselves to the ground, striving thus to present the smallest of targets. I saw a Gray One lope from the mist. He stood watching for a moment, his tongue lolling from his fanged jaws. Then he sheered away. It would seem that Targi was to be left to his own actions.

The black wand wove a pattern in the air between the Dark One and Uruk. But the latter raised his ax and slashed down, his target not yet the man, nor even the wand. Rather that weapon was used to cut through the air whereon reddish symbols shown. As the ax passed, they did break into wisps of mist, blood-dyed in color.

I could have cried out at what filled my mind—syllables roared there. It was as if my thoughts were shattered before I could shape them, dashed and broken. Targi —what man could stand so to the spells Targi could command?

There was one—Tolar was of this time, he had been shaped by the knowledge of such as Targi. But—Yonan had not. And—

I was Yonan!

Deep I reached, fighting against the pain of both body and mind, seeking that other who knew not Targi, nor HaHarc, nor this world. Yonan who had none of the talent—could I hide behind his very lack, that lack which I had half resented all my life, at this moment?

My head was a battlefield. The will of the sorcerer might be aimed principally at Uruk, but some of his compulsion spilled into my mind, churned and obscured my thoughts. I concentrated, first on pain, summoning the pain of my hand, my wrist, to dwell upon it, surrender to it. While behind my embrace of that pain of body, I sought for Yonan.

He was buried—as near death as any personality might approach before the final flickering out of identity. I *was* Yonan! And over Yonan men long dead had no dominion, no matter how potent their talent might be. I was Yonan!

My pain I cherished, used it as a barrier while I sought to nourish into life that small spark from the far future.

"Yonan!" So did I call upon my other self.

Targi raised his wand, pointed it at Uruk. In spite of my own efforts I could sense, through every nerve in my battered body, even through the mind I sought to fortify against his sorcery, how he was drawing Power to him. It was almost visible to the eye, that Power.

Still Uruk swung the ax back and forth before him, touching nothing tangible. It might be that in that ceaseless swing he erected some barrier against the other's attack. And, slowly, he moved forward.

I felt Thas' crooked hands on me, drawing my bound body to one side, as they kept well away from the space between those two. The forces there might well be lethal to lesser beings. I was Yonan—momentarily I had been diverted from my own quest within. No, I dared not relax my poor protection again. Waves of that force had lapped against me, bringing a black despair so great that, had I been free and Ice Tongue within my reach, I would have turned its blade upon myself. Who can stand against such as Targi's assured thought? Master of Power that he was, who else could put himself forward as an enemy?

The very body in the dull black mail seemed to swell, to grow. The eyes of Targi were twin flaming suns under the still-clouded sky. And this man who would front him —who was he to challenge the strength of Targi! That demand burst redly in my mind.

"Who am I, Targi? I am what you yourself made me." Uruk spoke aloud, as if he would not touch minds with the sorcerer. In that way instinct told me danger did indeed lie. "To each evil, Targi, there is an answer. It would seem that we are so paired." Once more his ax swung.

Now the Dark One no longer painted his blood runes on the open air. He drew the wand between the fingers of his left hand. And I saw, yes, in truth I saw it—unless it was some ensorcelment which touched and held my mind —that the skull which crowned it opened its fleshless jaws and from that issued a shrill keening.

The pain I had called upon for my defense became at that moment my bane. It arose in a red agony, pulsing in answer to the keening of the skull. And I saw the Thas cower on the ground, their gnarled hands, which looked so much like twisted twigs, tight held over their ears.

Did Uruk's swing of ax slow? I could not be sure. Now Targi balanced the wand as a man balances a light throwing spear. Even the Tolar part of me did not know what would happen should that weapon of the Shadow strike Uruk. But that it would be more potent than any steel —that I could guess.

Ice Tongue—I glanced at the sword, which lay with its glittering blade belying the grayness of the day and the fog. It was far from me now as if it did indeed abide in another age.

Ice Tongue obeyed but one master—had not Uruk said that once? How well did it obey? Dared I—dared I let Yonan retreat from part mastery within me? I believed that now Targi's awareness was centered on Uruk; I had only to fear the side lash of the power he might use against the axman. Tolar—and Ice Tongue. Oddly enough I had not tried to explore before what that stranger within me knew of his forceful weapon. I did not know—

No, that was false! Tolar leapt into command within my memory. Ice Tongue—one of the Four—it became part of him who took it—but only if he were the one to whom it would answer. There were things about the sword which even Tolar had only heard rumored.

Taking a great chance, I fought against the wall of pain I

had so carefully erected as my defense. I opened wide once more the door for Tolar.

Though the Thas squatted about me and I was surely their prisoner, my mind was not bound. I willed my attention only at the sword.

Ice Tongue! Of my desire and need I feverishly wove a cord as strong and supple as the root ropes. I was not even aware at that moment that what I would do was utterly beyond any knowledge of Yonan's, even of Tolar's. In the world where I lay now existed only two things—Ice Tongue and my will.

I had heard much spoken of the disciplines those who wield the Power must set upon themselves, of the years they must work to bring into their hands the reins of illusion and ensorcelment. Yet they were then able, by pouring energy into the right channel, to make the earth itself obey them—even though they might die, burned out, in the doing of it.

Ice Tongue—

Was indeed that blade blazing brighter, glowing like a narrow stream of fire in the grass trampled down by our struggle? I closed off all surmises, everything but my driving will. It was like shutting all the doors along a corridor, so that one's mind dwelt only upon what lay at the far end.

Ice Tongue—

In my sight the sword appeared to grow, no longer fitting the hand of any true man—rather such a weapon as only a giant might swing. And it began to move—

For a moment a small tinge of triumph broke my concentration; I was quick to wall that off. All which lay within me, which I called "will," "desire," "determination," must be focused on what I would do.

Ice Tongue! I put into that silent call the full strength I could summon, sending forth that order silently but still as strong with any Talent Tolar might possess.

The blade slid forward, as if indeed my thought was a cord or one of the root ropes looped about its hilt.

It came between Uruk and Targi. The Dark One still balanced his wand as a spear, but he had not yet thrown it. Or did he need to throw it; was he rather aiming its full energy? Uruk was forced back one step and then a second.

Ice Tongue!

I put into my unvoiced command the last distillation of all I had called upon, that faculty I had not even known I possessed until I put it to this final test.

The sword gave a kind of jerk, its point rising though the glowing crystal of the hilt still rested on the ground. It arose so—and fell again as the energy drained out of me far too swiftly. But it fell toward Targi, striking across his foot.

There was a bolt of force no one could see, but which struck straight into the mind my efforts had left wide open. I had a single instant to think that this was death—then there was nothing at all.

But if death were nothingness it did not claim me. For pain sought me out first, and I could not set that aside. It filled me with a deep torment. Then I became aware of a touch on my forehead between my eyes. At first that touch, light as it was (though it was firm enough), added to my pain, which throbbed and beat, making of me a cringing animal who had no hiding place.

Then, from that touch, there spread a coolness, a dampening of the fires of my agony. Little by little pain subsided, though it left me apprehensive even as it went for fear that raging torment would be unleashed again. But the coolness which came now was like rain on long-dried soil, soaking in, strengthening me.

I opened my eyes.

Above me was a sky still drably gray. But hanging over me was a face which my dulled, exhausted mind could remember.

"Uruk?"

I must have shaped his name with my stiff lips, but he read it, and some of the frown which the rim of his helm nearly hid smoothed out.

Memory came limping back. I shaped a second name:

"Targi?" Only to see the frown once more return.

"We were cheated in so much—he lives," he said aloud, as if mind touch was somehow not to be used. I thought I could guess why—my brain felt bruised, shaken. Perhaps it was as wounded as my body had been and to have entered it would have driven me mad.

"Where—?"

"He wrought an illusion in the end and escaped in it. But there is no safety with Targi free."

"The Lost Battle—?" Memory again stirred and somehow hurt, so I winced.

"We changed that. When Targi fled, those who followed him did also."

"But before he did die." My memories were mixed. When I tried to think clearly, to sort one from the other, the process made me giddy and ill.

"Not this time. In so much we altered time, comrade. But whether for the better after all"—Uruk shrugged—"how can we tell? This much I know, Targi must be our meat."

"Why—?" I found it too hard to voice my question.

But he must have read it even in the chaos which now mixed memory with memory.

"Why did he go? That was your doing, Tolar. Your sword upon his foot disturbed his spell casting. The Power reflected back on him, as it will when any ensorceling is incomplete. He fled the death he would have drawn on us. But he is master enough to win sometime and build therein his own spell. We can only now be hounds on his trail."

I closed my eyes. At that moment I could command neither my body nor my shrinking mind. I wanted only darkness once again, and some mercy gave it to me.

6

My wrist was stiff-set, with a splint to keep it so; my other hand had been treated with the healing mud to which both man and animal turned when there was need. Ice Tongue was sheathed at my side. But we were still in the past, the Valley of HaHarc behind us—the open countryside before. And if the clouds were gone, and the sun shone there, yet it still seemed that there was a shadow between us and its warmth and encouragement.

Tolar had no more memory to lend me now. For we had changed the course of action—I had *not* lurched, death-smitten, from that fog of Targi's brewing to destroy my blade and die hopeless and helpless among the rocks. Nor could I now have much in Yonan to call upon either. Though I had tried with all my determination to learn the ways of war, yet here and now I was like a green youth who had never ridden on his first hosting.

A little apart stood Uruk, leaning on his ax. And though he stared straight into the day, I thought that he saw nothing of what lay before us; rather his mind moved in another fashion—questing—

There had been those of HaHarc who had volunteered to back us; still that Uruk utterly refused. It would seem that the hunting of Targi lay upon the twain of us alone.

"He will go to the Thas." Uruk spoke for the first time, that unseeing stare not breaking. "He will seek his heart—"

"His heart?" I echoed. For in these moments of supreme effort when I had commanded Ice Tongue I believed I had burned out of me most of Tolar memory —even as the Witches of Estcarp burned away their controls when they set the southern mountains to shivering down on Karsten invaders.

Uruk blinked, the masklike brooding left his features. "His heart—that part of him which is his talisman and the core of his strength. He would not risk that in battle, not even with us, whom he deemed so much the lesser. But if he would replenish his Power, then he must seek it to re-energize what he has exhausted."

"To the Thas? We seek them underground?"

Uruk blinked for the third time. "Where else? And we march into a trap if we do so. He will expect our coming, lay his own ambushes, and dispose of his forces to defeat us. Already he has spun a maze through which no thought can penetrate for our sure guide. And he will strive to take us—by body, or by that part of us he wishes the most to control—our minds. This is a wager of high Forces, comrade. The result may fall as easily against us as in our favor—perhaps even the former is more likely.

"Before when his body died," Uruk mused, "his inner essence was helplessly pent where he had concealed it. I remember." The ax shifted a little in his hands. "Why think you he had me kept living in that pillar? He needed a body—but somehow the Thas failed him in that ploy. Perhaps that was why they took your Valley maid, sensing in her some hint of talent which might accomplish what they themselves could not do."

I recalled vividly that scene Tsali and I had witnessed in the cave where Crytha, completely under some spell, had confronted the pillar which had imprisoned Uruk. That—had *that* been a part of the attempt at transference Uruk now spoke of frankly?

Now, too, I thought of those roots which were obedient to the men of deep earth, of the darkness of their burrows, of the fact that we possessed no guide. On the other side of the scale lay even heavier my conviction that Uruk was entirely right—we must destroy this Targi in one time or the other. And it would seem that fate itself had decided it would be in the past.

My bandaged wrist—I could still hold Ice Tongue in my newly healed hand, but I was not ambidextrous in battle. And in any sudden attack I would doubtless prove a hindrance. Still the sword itself, as I had had good proof, was a potent against the Thas.

"When do we go? And where?" My voice sounded weary in my own ears. Yonan, who knew so little and in his life had lacked so much confidence in himself, asked that.

"We go now," Uruk returned. "And Ice Tongue can sniff out the door to any Thas burrow for us. It is in my mind they core these hills now, perhaps striving to weaken the very walls of the earth beneath in order to bring an end to HaHarc."

There was more than a ring of truth in that. I thought fleetingly of the old legend that someone—or *something*—had piped and HaHarc's walls had tumbled in answer. If there existed a honeycomb of tunnels running beneath those upper walls, such might indeed have come to pass.

So we went forth from the place where the mist had hidden the valley of the battle. The bodies of our own slain had already been gathered, laid on a pyre of honor, and reduced to clean ashes.

The Dark Ones had been also so dealt with—but with no honor paid them. For all men knew that some of the Dark Lords could reanimate the dead, though no spirit returned to bide behind their empty eyes. Rather the raised dead were clumsy tools, difficult to use, for they must be eternally held to any task set them.

Gray Ones, monsters—and some were men, so like those I had known all my life that meeting them I might not have realized they had sold themselves to the Great Dark.

Though the bodies were gone there was a litter of weapons still to be garnered, and a squad of men of HaHarc was about the harvesting of those. Those, as they moved, looked straightly at us, but none questioned where we went nor what we would do.

There were tracks cutting the soil, some left by hooves, others by the clawed, half-human feet of the Gray Ones. Also there were trenches, slimed within, smelling vilely, as if what had impressed those upon the once clean earth had crawled upon their bellies after the fashion of giant slugs.

It was only for a short space that Uruk followed this plain trail of those who had fled the battleground. He was heading, I was sure, for a line of hillocks, very small beside the ranges which protected the valley behind us, yet heaped high enough to form landmarks.

And one, I noted under this weak and wayward sun, had three tall stones planted on it, seeming like the bolls of trees whose branches had long ago been riven away by some storm wind. These were not of that sleek blue stone which marked the "safe" islands. Rather the stone was strange to the eye, being much pitted and of a rusty red.

I found I had a dislike for those stones, and the closer we advanced to them, the more my uneasiness and distaste grew. Now I swallowed, as does one who strives to conquer nausea. Ice Tongue, which I had drawn and carried awkwardly in my left hand, still gave forth a light discernible even in the sunlight. Now, through my grip on its hilt, there spread in me a kind of warning.

"Where—?" I dared to break the silence between us. But Uruk neither glanced at me nor spoke. His strides were deliberately measured. Yet there was no hesitation as he climbed the hillock toward those ominous pillars.

Ice Tongue moved in my hold. The point dipped as I climbed, trying to keep up with the axman. I have seen the Wise Women locate water, or things of metal long underground, how their rods then turn in their hands without their willing, pointing to the proper spot in the earth.

So it seemed that this sword out of time now acted in a like manner. I would not have had the strength to force it up and away from the earth which lay at the foot of the red pillars. Uruk was right again; in such a way the Sword of Lost Battles was our guide.

I noticed that Uruk passed the first of the pillars with care as if he wished no part of him or his clothing or armor to touch its forbidding surface. By the second stone he stopped. Ice Tongue pointed in my own grip at the ground beneath my boots. I had to struggle with the blade to keep that hold, for it fought as if the metal had a will of its own and would bury its point into that spot of earth.

Uruk's lips curved in were more a snarl than a smile. "Did I not say so?" he asked. "We have found what we have sought, the door to a burrow. But I think such doors are not for the wary. It would be best we choose our own entrance to Targi's runways. Do you try to trace if it runs beyond this point."

I fought with the sword, finally forcing it away from that point where it seemed to wish to bury itself. Uruk edged by the first of the three pillars, seeking the opposite downward side of the slope. Now he stepped back to let me take the lead.

The sword continued to point earthward, and Uruk uttered a sound close to a harsh laughter.

"So goes it then." He glanced back, measuring the distance from that last pillar. And then he gave a swift nod, as if answering some question of his own which he had not voiced aloud. Raising the ax, he aimed a blow, one with all the weight of his trained strength behind it, at the slope of the hillock.

The metal edge of one head bit deep, gashing the turf, throwing clods of it broadcast. A second and a third time Uruk sent the ax against the hillside. The fourth time it broke through in a small place, loose earth shifting into the hole he had so uncovered.

It took very little more ax work to clear a space so that I could lie belly down and lower Ice Tongue slowly into that opening. The sun did little to pierce the hole, but the gleam of the blade showed that this was perhaps not a cavern, but rather a tunnel in the earth, large enough for us to force a way through.

With a deep breath, walling swiftly from my mind all

the warnings lest I not be able to go at all, I set Ice Tongue between my teeth and wriggled through, landing in a confined space which carried the heavy reek of Thas in its stale air. Though there was no sign of any lurking earth dweller. Swiftly I moved farther down the passage to give Uruk room enough to follow me.

The passage had been shored up here and there by heavy roots deeply embedded in the earth, and rough-sided bits of stone rammed in to aid that precaution, as if this was a runway which it was important for the earth people to keep open.

"Paugh!" Uruk spat. "This stink is foul."

We found that the passage had not been constructed with such visitors as us in mind. For it was necessary to move ahead stooping, our bowed shoulders now and then rubbing against the roof, bringing down ominous trickles of earth I tried not to think about. Here Uruk took the lead once more as if he knew exactly where we were headed.

As we moved away from the hole our only light came from Ice Tongue. I raised it high so that its wan glitter might shine over my companion's shoulder. The earth under our feet was as tightly packed as any long-used game trail, and always the smell of Thas clung.

Within a very short space we came to where the passage ended in a well-like opening. Uruk knelt and felt beneath its crumbling ruin.

"There are climb holes," he told me in a soft whisper. "Shallow, but I think we can wedge toes and fingers into them." Then he slung the ax over his shoulder and warily lowered himself into the dark opening. I kept Ice Tongue between my teeth as I felt I dared not lose the small light it gave us. But I waited until I heard Uruk's soft whisper before I dared swing over and seek those limited holds.

Down, down, down—my jaws ached first, as I kept that

grip on the sword; then the ache spread down my tense body, shoulders, arms, fingers, toes, feet. And still there seemed no end to this descent. I feared I might choke and lose hold on the sword by spewing forth my last meal because of the stench here. But I hung on grimly, limiting my world to two things—keeping Ice Tongue ready and hunting the next and then the next hold.

That descent seemed endless—but perhaps to someone not so tense as we were, it would not have been any great feat. But I was very glad when Uruk's warning reached me and I felt once more a wide and solid surface underfoot.

There was more rock in the walls here, only that rock was crisscrossed with root supports. And the stone on the walls showed signs of having been roughly worked, to the extent of having the worst of the natural protrusions broken away. We no longer had to climb down—but the passage itself sloped more and more, making certain that we were fast going well below the surface of the ground outside.

"Wait!" I had not really needed that command from Uruk. Tolar was not yet totally dead within me, and the sense of an evil presence was so strong that it brought my hand up to hold Ice Tongue at ready for an attack. I saw what glowed ahead—swirling tendrils which reminded me of that other fog which Targi had used to cloak his force. Save that here light was a part of it and the billows shone with a greenish radiance which made me think of long-buried corruption. While an odor even viler than that of the Thas puffed forth at us.

7

Uruk's laugh startled me, for to my mind those arms of mist were indeed ominous. However, there was comtempt in the sound he made as he watched them thin, reach out for us like tentacles of some sea monster such as the Sulcarmen knew in the far south. And quick on that laughter he began a soft chant.

I *saw* his words. By what feat of sorcery this happened I could not explain. But the words formed blue sparks in this gloom, issuing from his lips as a stream, yet spreading out beyond to gather in a glittering puff cloud of their own. He moved confidently forward and perforce I followed.

Then that glitter of blue sparks touched upon one of the threatening tendrils of mist. There was a flash. The mist whipped back to join a center core which grew opaque, ever darkening, as more and more of the unnamable material was drawn to it.

Now there was no mist, rather a wavering figure which did not appear certain of what concrete form to take. From it issued a feeling of menace, building so quickly that it was like a blow. But if whatever that thing was thought to find us open to such counterattack, it learned quickly that we were not. For though it flung itself to the rocky way under our feet and strove to crawl at us, the blue mist dropped in turn.

"Ha, Targi!" Uruk no longer chanted; now he called as a man will shout a personal challenge to the enemy. "Do you then think me already your plaything? Helm-biter''—for the first time he gave his weapon a name—"is no steel of any man's forging. You should know that."

The mist winked out.

Uruk nodded. "He must be greatly shaken," he said musingly. "Targi is not of the Great Ones, no more than am I. But I would have thought he fancied his hold on the Dark Power stronger." Now his voice sharpened and he demanded of me: "How did he die—in that time we know?"

I dredged up Tolar memory. Targi—had Tolar seen him die? Or only heard it reported before his own grievous wound had driven him from the field? Then the words came to me haltingly, for the pictures in my mind were very dim and far away.

"He died by an ax. They raised an outcry when they found his body—that I remember."

"By an ax," Uruk repeated. "Then—"

I knew what troubled him. If it had been his Helm-biter that had so dealt with Targi, to slay him again might avail us nothing. Unless we could also reach the inner core wherein Targi or what was of the real Targi might find secure refuge.

"He will strive to repeat the pattern," Uruk said, this time as if to himself. "So—"

The way before us was dark. That evil coiling thing of little real substance had vanished. However, we had not lost our wariness, which was well. For now out of the dark again came snaking, some actually crawling upon the rock to better entangle our feet, those root ropes. The ax swung—I need not use the proper hand on Ice Tongue to prick at those reptilian, wriggling lines of dark.

It was butchery there in the half-dark. Neither Thas nor rope could truly face our weapons when we set our backs to the wall of the passage and swung the bright metal to bring death. The sword snarl was that of a wolf eager to be at the throat of its prey. And, while Helm-biter did not give tongue in a like manner, yet the very passage of the double-bladed head through the air made a kind of singing. While the Thas squealed and grunted.

Uruk raised his voice above their clamor. "Make an end now!" he ordered. "Targi used these to buy him time—the time he must not have. He thinks he will be safe in that place he has devised, so we must reach him before he sets a lock to guard his safety."

We came away from the wall in a charge. Uruk roared aloud the old battle cry of HaHarc. The sound of his voice was nearly deafening in that small section, and the blaze of our weapons made them living fire in our hands.

The Thas broke. I knew of old that they were fighters who needed the dark to make them confident. And there were bodies enough, mostly from Uruk's hewing, to discourage them. Whether Targi withdrew the compulsion he had laid upon them to attack we never knew. But at our advance they broke and ran. Some fled ahead down the lefthand section of the passage, some withdrew to the right behind us.

Uruk moved swiftly. He might not trot nor run through this murk, but he made the best pace the cramped quarters and our uncertain footing allowed him. And I kept at his back, though I looked often to make sure that those who had run had not doubled back to follow us.

In my own time, the Thas had envenomed their spears. But those we tramped over, lying still sometimes in hands no longer able to raise them, showed no discoloration of point. In so much were we now favored.

We came to a forking of the passage, then a second, and

a third. Each time Uruk turned right or left with no hesitation. I did not ask, but somehow I believed he knew where he went.

Thus we broke from a side way into one of those caves through which Tsali and I had earlier gone—or if not that, one so much like it no man could tell the difference. The stalagmites shown with crystalline sparkling as Ice Tongue's brilliance caught them. I would have been muddled by the number and variety of these age-long mineral growths, but my companion did not pause, nor search. I saw that Helm-biter swung a fraction in his grasp; perhaps that was acting now as one of those needles the Sulcarmen kept locked within bowls to point a path across the sea.

So we reached at last to another opening in the wall, a crevice I might have overlooked, for it required careful squeezing to get by a large lump of rock into it. Another narrow passage awaited beyond, only the walls of this had certainly been hewn smooth, and I saw here and there a pattern of runes I did not know—save from them seemed to reach a coldness to touch the innermost part of a man, awakening in him uneasiness and despair. Only the warm sword hilt in my scarred hand fought that subtle assault upon my courage.

Uruk slowed his pace. His head was well up, for that passage had not been the cramped size beloved by the Thas. Men, or something much like men, had made it.

"Now—" The word was half a breath he expelled. "Now we win or fail, Tolar-that-was, for we have tracked him as he never believed any man born in the Light could do. And at the bay he will throw against us all his strength—"

He had hardly gotten forth the last word when a blow out of nothingness struck against us both. It sent me reeling unsteadily back, toward that half-concealed entrance. This was as if a giant and all-powerful hand had thumped against my chest, leaving me no defense, hurling me away. I lashed out wildly with Ice Tongue, seeing nothing tangible to so attack but feeling that I must do something or be utterly overborne and rendered helpless.

Uruk was forced back also, but only a step or two. His shoulders were hunched a little, his feet planted apart as if he were determined there would be no more retreat. I tried to copy his stance. More than that, I fought to edge forward again to join him.

The pressure continued. I had not been able to win a palm's-length forward; no, instead I had lost two backward. Anger, dour and sullen, filled me, unlike any I had felt before; Tolar's anger, which had in my touch with him been so tattered by despair. Tolar—once more I turned to that hidden other part of me which the sword had brought to birth.

Uruk *was* moving forward, his action resembling that of a man wading through thick mud. Each step he took was short, but he made it. I rubbed shoulder against the wall where my last retreat had borne me. Now I took the sword into my right hand, put out the left. As I had felt for those holds in the deep well, so did I now lock finger tips into the lines of the runes. Very small was the purchase such holds gave me. But I came forward again, slowly, one hindered step against another, just as Uruk moved.

Perhaps his ancient enemy could not divide that force easily, so that he was not able to fend us both off at the same time. Thus we were winning by small lengths. The throat veil of mail of my helm swung loose, I was breathing heavily, concentrating on my battle along the wall.

Uruk fared better—his steps grew longer. Under the

threatening dragon of his helm crest his eyes were set, glowing.

Thus, through a time which seemed endless, we worked our way along that passage. And the pressure against us seemed never to relax. I was panting, and the beating of my own heart pounded in my ears. On—On—!

Then, even as quickly as the mist had gone, so did this vanish. I went to one knee, overbalanced by that withdrawal which came between one breath and the next. I saw Uruk stagger, but not more than a step.

Holding the ax still before him, he broke into a jogging run, one I was quick to try and match.

We emerged into a place filled with that green-gray radiance I had long known marked a strong center of the Dark Forces. There were no stalagmites here, rather pillars worked into shapes of horror, each a monster or a man, the latter seemingly locked in some unbelievable torment from which not even the end of time might deliver him.

Down the wide center aisle between those pillars, which, after a first glance, I would not look upon—for even seeing them stirred in me a fear I feared I could not suppress—Uruk went directly to the center core of this place.

It was perhaps a temple. But what god or force had been worshiped here, that had been none born from the adoration of my species. Here the pillars formed a circle, and in the center of that was set, on a half-pillar of rusty red, a crystal skull.

At the foot of the pillar lay, in a lank tangle, the man I had seen on the battlefield—Targi. His eyes were wide, staring unseeingly overhead, and his body was flaccid, that of the newly dead.

But in the brain pan of the skull—!

I could not force my gaze away from that swirl of raw colors, colors which hurt one to look upon. They surged, interwove in patterns, and—they had meaning. I need only look so for a little longer and that meaning would be made clear to me. It was the greatest thing I had ever done—I would be privileged beyond any of my kind—I would rule—rule!

I saw Uruk step over the body, raise his ax. Uruk—he would destroy—he—it was he who was the enemy in this place! Kill—Kill—!

Only the fact that my injured wrist would not obey my will made my blow a feeble one. Ice Tongue grated against the mail covering his shoulder. But that was enough to deflect the fall of the ax. It clanged instead against the pillar.

The skull rocked on its perch, as the colors caught within it moved in an even madder interweaving. I had kept grip on my sword, but only barely. That ill-aimed blow had nearly taken it from my hold.

Uruk—he was danger! As long as he lived—as long as he lived—

He had turned those blazing eyes on me.

"Let me in, comrade—" In my mind a powerful voice cried like a burst of pain. "We can finish him—together—"

Uruk's ax swung aloft again. I was no match for him even with Ice Tongue—

"Thrust low!" that other in my mind urged. "There is a weak spot beneath his arm—thrust for his heart! And then—"

"Yonan!"

I tottered, raising my hand to my head, crying out with

the pain which was a torment there. The sword hung heavy
in my hold, its point toward the blocks of rock under our
feet.

"Yonan!" came that call again.

"Thrust—now!" bade that other commanding presence pouring into my mind. Weakly I knew or guessed
what was happening—

I raised the sword and I brought that blade down,
largely by the weight of it alone, since there was very little
strength left in me. Ice Tongue fell square upon the dome
of the skull.

There followed such a torment within my head that I
hurled the sword from me, fell to my knees, clasping my
head on either side and moaning.

I did not see Uruk raise the ax again. But I heard the
clack when one of its edges met the skull, cleaving it,
shattering it, as if it were indeed ancient bone. There was a
wild clamor in my mind—I would go mad—that thing
which had tried to possess me would see to that. Babbling
I sank forward, face down on the pavement, while eye-
aching light swirled about me, closing me in.

But there had been a small part of Yonan unconquered,
a fraction which had retreated into hiding. And now (how
long I was under pressure of Targi's will I shall never
know), that scrap of the one I had once been came out of
hiding, in desperation, I think. I was stiff, cold, yet I was
still alive and Targi no longer held me in his bonds. I
centered what remained of my own will on moving my
hand—to prove mainly that this I could do. Then, aching
in every muscle, I struggled up.

Around me was a very gray light, forbidding, though
only a faint shadow of the threat I had conceived had
earlier hung there. Within reaching distance lay Uruk,

while beyond him, where we had seen the discarded body of Targi—

Had those fragments of brittle bone, those ashes, once really been a man or the semblance of one? Of the crystal skull which had dominated this hall, strove to master us, there was not even a broken shard remaining. But there was something else—there lay the hilt of a sword, a bladeless weapon now as dingy gray as the light around.

I crawled to Uruk. His ax had not suffered the same change; no, it lay intact under his hand. I felt for a pulse at the side of his throat. He still lived. Now I fumbled my water bottle loose from my belt, raised his head to rest against my shoulder, and dribbled the liquid between his teeth. At last he swallowed, coughed, and his eyes opened.

For a moment he stared at me as if I were a stranger to him. Then—

"Tolar—?" but he hesitated over that name.

I shook my head. Putting aside the water bottle, I reached for the sword hilt, to hold it into his line of vision.

"I am Yonan—even as you summoned me."

His lips curved very slightly. "And return you did, to our salvation. Targi, great in sorcery as he was, could not control the yet unborn. So Ice Tongue has left you—for good or ill this time, I wonder?"

Somewhere in me laughter bubbled. "For good, so shall I believe. I am done with ill-omened weapons and ancient battles, either lost or won. The future is what *I* shall make it!"

Then I remembered—were we still in the past? I had only the evidence of what remained of Targi to bolster my hope that we were free of time change.

Uruk must have followed the glance I gave to those

nearly vanished remains; his mind caught my thought. "I think it is *your* time now, Yonan-who-was-more. Targi, at least, is very dead. And the shattering of his power could well have swept us onward once again. If that is true, Escore still has some use for us. Shall we endeavor to prove that?"

The hilt of Ice Tongue was dead. I sensed that never again would it play any part in the schemes and ploys of men. I laid it down on the wide step which supported the pillar on which the skull had been. Targi had striven to use me; he had failed. It was that intangible trophy which I would bear from this struggle; no man save myself would ever see it. I was not Tolar, yet something of him would always remain within me, honing what I was now into a better self, even as a careful warrior hones his blades. I could not deny that—I did not want to. But I *was* Yonan—and somehow I did not want either to deny that or forget it.

Perhaps time had indeed swept us forward as the sea tide will sweep that which it carries. If so, there would be other swords, other battles, and for me a new life into which I must fit myself carefully and with more self-knowledge than many men are given to understand.

"Time was, time is, time will be—" Uruk said—no he did not say it, the words seeped into my mind. And in me there was a sudden heady spark of joy. Tolar I could thank for this—that I had at last that other sense I had always longed to possess. I got to my feet, reached down a hand to aid Uruk.

Time will be—the words sang in my mind, awakening impatience in me. Ice Tongue no longer held me, and all Escore waited!

III
Sword of Shadow

1

Around me the night was very still, yet it seemed that just beyond the range of my sight, the seeking of my ears, there was movement. I pressed the palms of my hands tightly together, breathed deeply and slowly, summoned not only courage, but that strange part of my mind which I had never understood, but which, even in earliest childhood, I realized dimly was there—something which could change all the world for me if I could harness it properly. Only there was no one to teach me that then; I had only faulty instinct to depend upon.

I looked down at those hands so tightly enfolded. I had seen them sticky with clay and—no, I was not going to think of that. For remembering too deeply might open a door—like the one of the ever-to-be-feared Gates of the Old Ones—to that which I sensed prowling out there.

Yet there were those moving close about me now, each and every one willing to raise protection such as the Shadow fears, to wall me around with their own defenses. It was in me that the flaw lay. And how deep or dangerous that flaw might be haunted me waking, was a part of my dreams sleeping, sometimes strong enough to bring me gasping to full consciousness, to lie shivering—wondering what *I* might have done during that time my waking mind was not in command.

In my race many women are so cursed. Most may consider it rather blessed, but I do not. In Estcarp those with Talent are early detected and taken for training, taught all the safeguards one must have when one deals with the Power—even lightly.

But I was born into a time of chaos, my people fleeing over the mountains from Karsten, the few remaining members of a very ancient race which the ruler of that land had outlawed. And even had we been left alone I might never have developed my unexplainable gift—since there were no Witches in Karsten to seek out and train their kind. While the Wise Women who did dwell among us did not meddle with the greater Powers, but the lesser, which have in them only a portion of the Talent.

I was born to the sister of the Lady Chriswitha, who fostered me when my mother died of an illness I think now she willed upon herself, since she could not face a world in which her lord lay dead. They said that at my birthing she turned her face to the wall and would not even look upon me. For it was the fact that in protecting her escape from a band of Karsten over-the-Border raiders my father had died.

But the Lady Chriswitha had a heart which was big enough to open wide its door for me. And I was not her only fosterling in those turbulent days. She had also Yonan, who was half of the Old Race, half Sulcar, the son of her heart-friend. There were also her own children —Imhar, heir to the House, the Lady Dalhis and the Lady Meegan, both of whom were older and wed young to liegemen of Lord Hervon. But I was different—

At first they thought that I had been given only the healing gift. For I could look upon man or beast and somehow see the ill which encompassed them. And with the animals I had kinship, so that in time I could not easily eat meat or wish any hunter well. Though this I kept secret within me.

When the Witches of Estcarp performed their last and greatest feat of battle, making the hills and mountains themselves move by the power of their united wills, and so walling off Karsten, then it seemed that a new and more peaceful life stretched before us. I could remember nothing but days of war—it seemed very strange to face peace.

And I wondered how those like Imhar would live. For he was born to war and knew nothing else, nor cared for it, I was certain. I knew so little of him, though he was to be my lord, thus uniting the kin more solidly together. But I think that meant little to him, and mostly it made uneasiness for me.

Yonan was more friend than Imhar. He came from two races which were born to hold sword and measure steel with enemies—yet he was seemingly a son to neither in that fashion. Doggedly he practiced swordplay, shot at targets with the dart guns, strove to do all which was expected of a man in those years. Yet with me he talked of other things, old legends and strange stories he had heard. He might have been a songsmith perhaps—save that to his clumsy fingers the lap harp was more unlearnable than was the sword. It was as if within him the cleavage of race had somehow marred or lessened the man he had really meant to be.

What would have become of us had we stayed in Estcarp? Sometimes I have wondered a little concerning that. Would I have come to wed with Imhar and perhaps never have known what lay buried within me? Would I have been happier for that ignorance? Sometimes my heart answers yes. But there is another part of me which denies that I could have done this.

However, even as we worked to build the Manor for the

House, a youth came to us from the east. And his story of a need for us struck so deep into our minds that nearly without thought we found ourselves riding not only into the unknown, but into a war which was more grim and black of purpose than all the struggles we had known before.

Thus we came over-mountain into the Valley. And there I was like some plant which is given the soil it needs for full nourishment, sun, and water. For I met the Lady of Green Silences—she who bears many names in our ancient tales, but who in this cycle answers to that of Dahaun. She and her people are not of our race, perhaps even of our species, but they are human-formed. And with those of the Old Race who had not defiled themselves with dealings with the Shadow they held kin-friendships.

When Dahaun and I saw each other for the first time there was between us instant knowledge that we sought the same road. She took me into her household, where I first learned how much there *was* for me to learn, and how little I had been able to give because I lacked such knowledge. I was like one long athirst in a desert waste who is offered a flagon of cool water. But I knew that also as one who thirsted, this I must take slowly, a sip at a time. For the talent too strongly seized may turn upon one.

The Valley was a beleaguered fortress—of the Power against the Shadow. For in this land of Escore there had been much ancient evil wrought by adepts who had set themselves above the rules of the Talent, feasting their crooked spirits on what they could warp nature into doing. And that ancient evil, though perhaps much weakened by time, was now waking, gathering its strength to rage again.

Within the Valley, we were told, safety lay, for it was

guarded by such strong runes of Light that naught which carried the foul mark of the Dark might come. Yet our men (together with those who were not men in form and yet gave liegeship to the Light) patrolled the upper reaches of the heights, beating off attacks that strove to win up sheer rock to come at us.

Then—one morning I awoke and my hands were sticky with clay such as I had seen along the riverbank. And in me there was such an uneasiness that I felt as guilty as one who unbars the door of a keep to let through the enemy. Still also this I could not speak of, not to the Lady Dahaun, nor to my foster mother. But I had that to keep me busy. Yonan had been injured in a fall upon the heights—and might have died save that Tsali of the Lizard folk found him wedged into one of the crevices there.

I was glad that I must tend his ankle, occupy myself in other ways. For, though I had at once washed that clay from my fingers, it seemed to me that I still somehow carried the stain of it on my flesh, and the uneasiness which was part of it lay at the back of my mind where I firmly imprisoned it. Three times I tried to speak, and found that I could not shape the words; and so my unquiet grew, and I used what skills Dahaun had taught me—still there was no suggestion that anything of the Shadow had won through our barriers.

But I was reluctant to sleep that night, wishing even I might be watched by someone—yet this I also found myself unable to ask for.

The dream came as suddenly as if I had passed through a door. And it was as vividly real as awakening, so real that all which lay behind me at this moment seemed more of a dream or vision than where I stood now.

This was a hall—not like those I knew in Estcarp

—unless very ancient Es might hold such. The walls appeared so far away on either side that they were hidden by dusk. But the pillars on either side were tall, and their carvings of strange monsters very clear. A light which was not the warmth of sun, nor that of any lamp, but which seeped greenly-yellow from divers of the pillars themselves, gave me full vision.

There was someone waiting here—someone I must meet—

I did not seem to walk normally as I flitted forward down the well-marked aisle; rather it was as if I were drawn through the air, weightless and without the power to resist. Then the aisle ended in a circular space. And on a pillar which was the center core of that, was a skull—life-sized and carved of what seemed the clearest crystal. Still the brain pan was filled with whirling, dancing light of rainbow colors, one shade eternally fading or deepening into another.

And resting one hand lightly on the base where the skull was placed stood a woman. She had some of the same look of Dahaun's people, for she changed color—her hair flaming near to scarlet, then deepening to brown, and at last to black; her skin one moment ivory, the next sun-browned. Yet I knew that she was not of the Valley.

Power radiated from her as if she aimed that directly at me. And, though her coloring changed so from one moment to the next, her features did not lose their own set expression. Her full lips were curved in a small, secret smile, as if she dwelt exultingly upon some knowledge she would share with no one.

Her body was clothed only by whirls of mist which also writhed and moved, revealing now a crimson-nippled breast, again a smooth thigh, the beginning of a slight curve of belly. There was something utterly wanton in that play of clothing which was faintly disturbing, reached perhaps that part of me which was not here in answer to her sorcery.

"Crytha!" She flung out one hand in a parody of friendly welcome. And her voice echoed in my mind, not in my ears. "Well met, little sister—"

There was that in me which cringed at her careless claim of kinship. I was *not* of her blood—I was not! And perhaps my instant revulsion troubled the spell she had set upon me, for I saw her smile disappear, her eyes on me burn with anger.

"You are what and who I will you!" So quick was she with the leash of ownership. "You will do as I say. Come to me—"

I could not fight that compulsion any more than I could have broken chains which might have been forged about my wrists or limbs. To her I went.

"Look you!" She waved a hand toward the skull with its blaze of inner fire. That was now brighter, harsher, alive!

Without my willing it my hands went forth and touched the temples of the skull, one on either side. Into me swept another will, imperious—overriding the last remnants of what I was. I was given my orders; I knew what must be done.

"So!" the woman laughed. "We have chosen well, eh, Targi—" She spoke to the skull as if it were a living being. "Now you"—contemptuously she looked at me—"go you about your task."

Out from the pillars came scuttling shapes. Thas—the underground people, such as had already tried once to betray us. The leader of that band caught at my hand and I could not draw away. Under his urging I turned to the right.

We went through burrows; how many and where they ran, that I could not tell. All which burned within me, with near the same blaze which the skull had shown, was what I was to do. For it came to me that there were limitations on the woman and the skull. What meant so much to them they could not accomplish because these ways were forbidden them. Perhaps the passage ran somewhere under the cliffs of the Valley and, even deep in the earth, the safety runes had a measure of power. If so, such did not now work in my favor. I could pass this way easily enough, but I could not free myself from the tasks laid upon me.

The rest—it became disjointed, more like the broken episodes of a dream wherein one slides from one bit of action to the next without any logical connection. I remember mouthing words which someone else—either the woman or the skull had locked into my brain. And then—

There was something wrong. I could feel the ensorcelment lock even tighter on me. But beneath that prisoning arose baffled rage. I had not completed my task—there had been unseen interference. The Thas surrounded me, pushed and pulled me along their black burrows. What happened after—I could never piece together.

But there came a time when I knew I moved above earth, I saw faces which I should remember, only the hold on my brain would not yet let me. Then—

Then I came fully awake—or alive—once more. I stood in the open air and around me blew sweet wind, the chill of which I did not mind, because it carried the freshness of the world I knew. And there was Yonan, and with him another who wore strange armor and carried a great double-headed ax. There was also Tsali and then—up

from the depth before us which must make the Valley
—Dahaun came and with her Lord Kyllan, who was
hand-fasted to her—others behind.

I cried out—this must be real—not another dream. But
only when Dahaun took me into her arms was I sure of
that.

2

The barrier against speech no longer held, and I told
Dahaun freely what had been my dream. Though dream, it
seemed, it was not. I *had* been drawn out of the safety of
the Valley—and that by the betrayal of a part of my own
wayward mind. For they showed me a figure wrought of
clay. And set to its rounded head were hairs from my own;
about its form was wrapped a rag which I had once worn.
And this I knew without telling was of the Old Evil. So had
I been reached and worked upon by a greater force than we
had suspected had yet striven to break our boundaries.

When I described the woman who abode with the skull,
Dahaun frowned; still, there was puzzlement in her frown.
She made me stay within her own quarters, taking care
before she left me to use a wand, white and fresh-peeled,
to draw around the cushions on which I rested certain
tokens confined by a circle. And, before she had done, the
need to sleep had so weighted my eyelids that I drifted
away. Though I struggled, for I feared above all to lose my
will and thought and be drawn into dreams.

Dream again I did, and not happily. I was not now
physically a part of that second visit to the hall of pillars

and the skull as I had been the first time. Yet I could see—I could hear.

There was a change in her who had woven that earlier spell, for I was as certain as if oath had been taken that it was the woman who had reached out to draw me to her through the runways of the Thas; I so much under her spell I did not know where I went.

She no longer showed the pride and arrogance which had clothed her better than the mist at our last meeting. And her beauty was marred, as if time had served her ill. But still she was one to be feared and I did not forget that. Though at this time she did not look in my direction nor show any sign that she knew of my presence there.

Rather she stood by the base on which the skull rested and her hands caressed the crystal of its fashioning. Those blazing lights had died, or been muted so that only a near-colorless fogging of the inner part remained.

I saw her mouth and lips move, believed that she chanted or spoke to the thing she fingered. There was a kind of passion in her face which was greater than wrath—although that emotion underlaid the other. I could sense the forces she strove to bend, to break, to control by her will—and her frustration and despair that this she could not do.

Then she stooped to set her lips to the fleshless mouth of the crystal. She did that as I believed a woman would greet a lover, the one who was the center of her life. And her arms went around the pillar so that the ''face'' of that grinning thing pressed tightly against her ruby-tipped breasts. There was something so shameless in that gesture that I felt revulsion. But I could not flee, for that which had drawn me here still held—dream though it was.

She turned her head suddenly, as her eyes sought me. Perhaps she now knew that some portion of me had been drawn once more into her net. I saw exultation blaze high in those eyes.

"So—the spell holds yet, does it, younger sister? I have wrought better than I hoped."

Her hands arose in the air to trace lines I did not understand. Straightaway that which was me was locked fast. Now she came away from the skull, and so vibrant was the Dark Power in her that her hair stirred of itself, arose in a great flaming nebula about her head, more startling than any crown a queen might wear. Her lips were slightly parted, their burning redness like a gathering of blood on her ghostly fair skin.

She came one step and then two; her hands reached out for me, that triumph swelling in her and about her like some robe of ceremony.

"There is yet time—with an able tool—" I think her thought was more her own than sent to me. "Aye, Targi," she glanced back for a breath at the skull, "we are not yet lost!"

But if she had some plan it had failed her. For in that instant the spell broke, the woman and the skull she tended so passionately vanished. I opened my eyes again upon the hall of Dahaun to see the Lady of Green Silences standing at my feet. While over me she shook a handful of near-withered herbs, leaves of which broke off at the vigor of her gestures, shifting down to lie on my body. I sniffed Illbane, that very old cure for the ills of the spirit; with it langlon, the tri-leafed, which clears the senses, recalls a wandering mind.

Only I knew what had happened, and I cowered on my bed of hides and springy dried grasses. Tears which were born both of fear and the sense of my own helplessness filled my eyes, to spill down my cheeks.

Dahaun, though she looked grave enough, reached out

and caught my hand even when I would shrink from her, knowing now that some part of me had been attuned to the Shadow and that I was held by all which had and was most evil in this land.

"You dreamed—" she said, and she did not use mind touch but rather spoke as she would to a small child who awakes terrified from a nightmare.

"She—I was drawn again—" I mumbled. "She can draw me to her will—"

"The same woman—?"

"The same woman, the skull, the place of pillars. It was as it was before."

Dahaun leaned forward, her eyes holding mine locked in a gaze I could not break, for all my feeling of guilt and trouble.

"Think, Crytha, was it *exactly* the same?"

There was some reason for her questioning. I dropped my guard and drew upon memory, so that in my mind hers could see also what I had witnessed. Though I began to fear for her, lest some of the taint sleep with the knowledge, to infect her also.

She sat down cross-legged by my bed place. Crushing the last of the Illbane between her hands, she leaned forward, to touch those now deeply scented fingers to my temples.

"Think—see!" she commanded with assurance.

So I relived in memory, as best I could, what I had seen in the dream.

When I had done she clasped her hands before her.

"Laidan—" She spoke a single name. "And—Targi—"

"Who is Laidan?" I ventured at last.

"One who mixed—or mixes, since it seems that she must still live in some burrow of hiding—the worst of two races within her. Laidan was of the People by her mother's right—her father—" Dahaun shrugged. "There were many tales in the time of her bid to rule as to whom he might be—though he was not one of us. It is most commonly accepted that she was sired by one of the Hill Lords who accepted the rule of the Shadow—willingly. Laidan—and Targi—" she repeated thoughtfully.

"Well, for that combination there may be an answer. Those who went forth last night (*if* they can do as Uruk believes) perhaps can make sure Targi shall no longer be a factor in any campaign. But Laidan they would not have met in that past—for at the battle time she was elsewhere, very much engaged."

"The battle?" To me she spoke in riddles. After a long measuring look at me she did not answer that half-question. Rather she spoke about what seemed the most urgent to me now.

"It would seem that Laidan, and that which she has so long guarded, have set part seal on you, Crytha. How this may be I cannot understand. But the roots of it all may lie in the far past. However—if she can compel you to come to her—even through dreaming—"

I already knew the answer to that, though my body was so cold with an inner fear that it began to shake in vast shudders I could not control.

"Then—then I am a danger to you—an opener of gates—" I said in a low voice which I could not hold steady. I knew what I must add to that, but my lips and tongue would not shape the words. The fear which had seized on me was now in near control. However, if I

133

would threaten a break in the defenses of the Valley—it was very plain that I had no longer a place here. I stared at her dumbly, unable to do what duty pressed on me to do.

Dahaun shook her head slowly. "We are not totally defenseless in Power. But it may be that you shall have to face that you will be a prisoner, little sister—"

I flinched. "That—that is how she named me!" To hear the same words from Dahaun added to my burden of terror and guilt.

"So?" There was a firm line about Dahaun's lips. "So—she moves in that way? There is this you must understand, Crytha, because you have not had the training in control which should have been yours when the talent first manifested itself; it is true that you are left vulnerable to such as Laidan. I do not know what she may have learned during the dusty seasons between the time of the Lost Battle and this hour. But that there are limits on her is also the truth, and you must believe it. She never commanded the Green Silences—" Now there was a proud self-confidence in Dahaun. "It took too long to learn and she was ever impatient and greedy. Last time she took your body to do her bidding. This time—that being well guarded—" she gestured toward the runes on the floor — "she could only summon up your dream self —which is useless to her, for it is of another plain of existence and cannot operate physically. If Yonan and Uruk succeed—" Then she stopped shortly.

"Yonan—what of Yonan?" I was for the moment startled out of my own self-absorption. "Does—does he go to hunt this Laidan?"

Dahaun shook her head. "No, for she will not be where he would venture." She said no more, and with a sick feeling, I understood why. In sleep I could be milked of such information should Laidan again summon me.

"That she shall not do either," Dahaun picked the thought from my mind. "For there are other precautions we shall take. Believe you this, Crytha. There is no reason to feel guilt because you have been caught in this snare. Adepts even, in the past, have been ensorceled by their enemies. Warned as to the nature of the foe, then we can take precautions."

It was thus I became for a time a prisoner of my own people, of those I would not have harmed and yet who could not trust now what I might be forced to do. I lived apart in a smaller house where one of the Lizard women waited upon me, for those of that species could detect, through some faculty of their own, inborn and not to be influenced, any change in me. Also, I was forbidden to use the talent in any way—even for healing—since such a use might open a path of thought between me and she whom Dahaun called Laidan.

Yonan and Uruk—through the days I wondered where they went and to what purpose they had gone. None dared tell me, nor could I ask. But the Lady Chriswitha came to me with a suggestion which might be an answer to my fears for the future.

It was well known that among the Old Race she who married, or she who was bedded by any man (as had sometimes been deliberately done in the old days to Witches who were captured by the enemy), lost their power and talent. Only one exception in all the passing years had been known—and that was the Lady Jealithe. But her lord had been an Outlander, of another race. While he himself (against all nature as we conceived of it) possessed a portion of the Talent. However, even after she proved that the Power had not departed from her when she became a wife, still the Witches of Estcarp would not receive her again among their number and she was looked upon askance.

Thus there was a solution to my future. Let me wed and bed with Imhar and I would no longer be any threat to those in the Valley, since I would lose my Talent. And in my despair I almost seized upon this solution.

For Imhar I had no love. But among my people marriages were always arranged for the good of the kin-clan. Though during the years of exile and war some had come about differently—for I knew that the Lady Chriswitha herself had wed by inclination, since there was no clan elder left in her House to arrange such a match for her. Lord Hervon had already lost his family during the massacres in Karsten and had met with her first to bring some news of kin—escorting my mother to her.

Thus her wedding had been of her own choosing. But those of her daughters had come about in the old way, their husbands being now landless lords who had joined with Lord Hervon among the Borderers and so had agreed to add to the solidity of his House rather than start new ones of their own. I had been hand-fasted to Imhar nearly from my birthing; only the constant war had delayed marriage by cup and flame.

Now, though we were still ringed by danger even more perilous, I need only signify my willingness for marriage and take my place as Imhar's lady, putting aside all hope of ever being once more a wielder of Power.

Imhar was well enough. He was comely, a warrior born, and the heir to Hervon. Only—only in spite of my present fear and hurt I could not give consent. I was worn within me by the need for keeping, or striving to keep, that which was my birthright. I could not say the words my foster mother and aunt wanted—they choked in my throat. I thought that my dear lady would be angry with me and I was prepared to add her anger to the rest of the burden I must bear. But she only voiced the suggestion of what I might do and then, after a moment's silence which I could not break, she added:

"No one is born with the same gifts or talents, dear child. Imhar is his father's son, and in him there is a vast energy which since his boyhood has been centered on the making of war. Dalhis and Meegan were content with what life brought them. They wished for nothing else but home hall and children to be borne from their bodies. But if something else is given us—" She fell silent and sat for a long moment looking at her hands where they lay upon her knees. "We are in a place and time of wonders, child. And we of another generation have not the right to choose for you as has always been done.

"Imhar—" Again she paused and then shook her head as if at her own thoughts. "He has his own talent, and he is happy to use it as he does. If you wish to bide as you are—there shall be no pressure put upon you for any wedding—"

"But I am hand-fasted—" I was bewildered, hardly able to believe that she meant what she said.

"Wait, Crytha." Her words came fast and with emphasis as if to impress their meaning the more upon me. "Wait until you are sure!"

"But I—as I am I may be a danger to you—all of you—even to the Valley."

"Trust the Lady Dahaun—and wait—" She got to her feet a little heavily and I saw with eyes which were a little clearer that, though she showed no signs of age (for the Old Race do not until very near the end of their lives), her face was very tired, as if sleep might come to her pillow at night but true rest fled.

I caught her hand in mine and held it tight.

"Thank you—"

Gently she withdrew her fingers. "I would not see waste," she said. "Dear as you would be as a daughter in my house, I would not see waste."

And, so saying, she went away, leaving me only the weight of time and the conserving of my patience.

3

Though I feared each night to dream again—and eagerly drank the potion Dahaun sent me that perhaps this might not be—it was that very night that once more our defenses were breeched. Perhaps it had taken Laidan so long to build powers of her sorceries that she had not until this hour been able to reach me again.

Sight came to me and hearing, and it was as if somehow I had been blind and deaf all my life to that moment. For there were subtleties open to my senses now which I had never known before. Whether I stood in body or mind in that open I was not sure.

But I shivered in the chill of the wind, smelled the heavy scent of the trees which it scooped up from the Valley to fling outward with a prodigal force. Overhead hung the moon—an old moon, nearly dead and ready to vanish from the sky in order to be reborn in a new cycle.

I raised my hands, looking down along my body. I wore riding dress and my hands were scratched, nails broken, as if I had pulled myself by main force to this place. Now I wanted to turn, look down upon the Valley behind me, wondering (if I were indeed here in body) how I had won to this height.

Then I realized that I was caught in the trap of a geas which did not permit me even to look back—but only forward. So I wavered across the uneven footing of this place, where there were many treacherous cliffs and slides to trap the unwary. Also, I moved with purpose and certainty, though it might not be my purpose or will which drove me on.

And I could well guess whose will had drawn me out of safety and set me on this journey. Twice I tried to break the hold upon my mind and body, but so great and concentrated was that it was as if I beat with bare and blood-stained fists against a door cast of sword steel.

Then, realizing that in this there was not yet any chance for escape, I surrendered to the will of Laidan. I crossed the fissured rock, my feet bringing me unerringly to a cavity in the side of the height. There I stooped to push within a very narrow entrance which was half choked with fallen rubble.

There was no stench of Thas here. If Laidan held rulership over those burrowers, she did not use them now, perhaps believing that my will was so locked by hers that I would do exactly as I was bid and not strive to escape.

Though I was not Witch-trained, I had the example of those of Estcarp always at the back of my mind. To control and force obedience on another demanded a vast concentration, continued, unrelenting. I did not know how close to an adept Laidan might be—and had not the Lady

Dahaun said even the adepts themselves might be ensorceled? Every step I took drained more energy from her who bent me to some task which lay in her desire. I walked haltingly, as slowly as I could, ever seeking, with sharp unexpected darts of mental force, to find some weakness in what held me.

That none had yet been found was no reason for me to embrace despair. Laidan, I believed, had fastened the full of what must be a not inconsiderable talent on me. Sooner or later she would—she *must*—feel the strain of what she did. So I must keep probing, at irregular intervals, ready for any second which might win my freedom.

These underground ways were dark. I was swallowed up by blackness as if the maw of some great beast had engulfed me. But I resolutely held fear at bay. Laidan needed me; she would not waste what she needed. Therefore, even in the dark I did not have yet anything to fear—except the will which held me captive.

Now there was a kind of nibbling at my mind. It did not come, I believed, from what Laidan had laid upon me. She had to hold her manipulation of me too taut to take any such liberties. No, this was like a very vague memory struggling to throw open some door and issue forth.

All of my species have such occurrences of memory we cannot account for—times when we see a stretch of country, a building, when an inner voice swells in instant answer—saying, "This you have seen before." Even when we know that that cannot be possible.

What tugged so persistently at me now must be such a false memory. Or can it be true that we live more than one life, seeking in each to repair the wrongs we have willfully committed earlier? I have heard some of the Old Race discuss this theory upon occasion. But for me heretofore, this life had been enough—the wonder and promise of it filling me always.

But—sometime—somewhere—I had walked these ways. I was so certain of that I thought, black as it was here, I could be sure of the walls rising on either side. And those walls were not bare stone. No—deep cut in them were symbols. So, to prove myself wrong or right, I put out my right hand, confident that I would find my fingers sliding over such stone. And so I did. And the wall was pitted and slashed with deep cutting. Though I did not strive to trace any of the patterns I *knew* were there.

For those patterns were not of my Talent. Around them hung a taint of evil, lessened perhaps a little by the many years they had been wrought here. My flesh recoiled as if I had touched fire, or burning acid, when I found them.

The pavement under my boots was smooth, with no falls of rock nor crevices to provide any barrier. Then—I was brought to a halt.

I sensed a sighing—a disturbance in the air. That which had taken command of my body turned me to the left until both my outstretched hands once more scraped across engraven stone. And I tapped out with one foot, knowing, as surely as if I could see, that here a pit opened in the floor and the only way around it was a narrow ledge which my tapping toe located.

So I set my shoulders against that wall, my hands braced tightly against it, facing outward to the pit. Step by step I squeezed by the trap I could not see. While from the depths came ever that sighing, and with it a stale smell. My journey seemed to take an hour, though it could only have been minutes before I was once more on a wide and solid surface of a corridor.

Now I saved my strength of purpose, no longer making

those attempts to break the power holding me. For that passage shook me greatly, the reason for it lying, I was sure, in the depths of that memory which was not a real memory.

I felt also that the passage now sloped upward—at so gentle a curve that at first I was not aware of it. This became steeper as I went. Finally I knew that my feet unerringly had found a flight of steps and I was climbing. Here the wall to my left was smooth and I ran my hand along it for the sense of support it gave me in the dark.

Up and up—was I inside the heart of some mountain? Though I could not remember any peak of unusual height among those walling in the Valley. No, the true chain mountains lay to the north and the west—those we had come over in our venture into Escore.

My hands arose, at the command of Laidan rather than by my own desire. Flat-palmed, they struck a surface just above my head. And I guessed that I had reached some kind of trap door sealing off this place. I exerted my strength, and not altogether at the bidding of my captor —for I wanted out of this trap.

At first I thought that exit must have been sealed or barred. Then, very slowly and reluctantly, it loosened in its frame. Gray light, thin like the last of any winter twilight, outlined a square on three sides. I arose two more steps that I might set my back to the door and, with a last compelling effort, sent that crashing up and back. Ancient dust puffed into my face, making me cough.

For a moment I hesitated, for what might lie above in waiting I could not guess. Then, because I must, I climbed into the open. There were piles of tumbled stone, even a trace of a wall, as if this hidden way had once issued into the room of a building of size and presence. But if that were so, the way was—

I blinked and blinked again. For a second or two I saw clearly the desolation which had been plain enough still in existence—the fallen blocks like shadows. Then those winked out. Walls arose out of the very earth itself, took on sturdy substance. There was a roof high over my head veiling the sky. The place of the skull—?

No—there were no pillars here and the wall was round. I could have entered the ground floor of some tower. Window slits there were, but those gave little light. Rather that came from torch rods set at intervals on the wall, pulsating with a steady, contained flame.

The opening of the trap door through which I had emerged had pushed aside a tanned, furred rug, into the making of which must have gone more than one snow-cat pelt. And there were stools and benches, much carven, a table nearer to the wall on which sat a bowl of ruddy crystal overflowing with those small red grapes which are the sweetest and the rarest my people knew. Beside that was a flagon of worked metal with the sheen of silver and gold interwoven, which had been fashioned in the form of a traditional dragon—its neck curved upward, its mouth open to emit whatever fluid might fill such a container.

All illusion; my mind gave a quick and, I thought, true answer. Yet when I stooped to touch the wrinkles of the rug, my fingers held the softness of fur. So this illusion could control more than one sense at a time.

I swung around toward the table, determined to test that guess further, but there came a curdling of the air. So strange was that I stared as the atmosphere itself appeared to thicken, form a body. Then I faced Laidan.

She laughed, lifting one hand to brush a strand of flame-bright hair out of her eyes.

"So you are duly surprised, little sister? Well, time can be obedient to the will, even as is space—or the other boundaries men so complacently accept as always unchangeable and fixed. This is Zephar—"

For a moment after she spoke that name her eyes were intent upon me, almost as if she expected I might recognize the word. Then she shrugged.

"It does not greatly matter whether you remember or not. But all this"—she flung her arms wide, the mistlike covering that she had worn before seeming in this setting to be more opaque and more like some normal weaving—"answers readily to my call since I once had the ordering of it. Where memory is the sharpest, there we can beat time itself.

"However, that is of no consequence. You are—"

She seated herself with deliberation on the only true chair in that chamber, one placed at mid-board by the table, its dark high back framing her hair to make those strands appear even brighter.

"Yes, we are in Zephar, younger sister. And in Zephar there is that which even in this crook-coiled time you can do." Now she set her chin upon one fist and planted the elbow of that arm firmly on the table. Though her mouth might still smile easily, her eyes were like bits of ice drawn from the teeth of the Ice Dragon, as from them appeared to spread a chill which grew strong within that tower room.

"You are life-linked with this one you call Yonan—though once he had another name and played the part of a fool—only not well enough. He had his death of his own pretensions, but not in time—"

And the word "time" seemed to echo through the chamber like a gong from a distance, a sound not to be denied.

"Now he would play the fool again," she continued. "But the past must not be reversed, rather it shall be improved upon. You, and through you Yonan (who is nothing but who unfortunately can move to destroy what a lifetime—twenty lifetimes—cannot bring once more into being), must be used. Therefore—younger sister—you shall take a hand and all will be as we wish—"

I found my tongue at last. Perhaps it was the thought that she would make of me a tool to pull Yonan down which brought that croak out of me, rusty-sounding as if I had not given tongue in a score of years.

"As *you* wish—" Had the two of us ever stood and bargained so before? A teasing ghost of memory assaulted me once more. Perhaps not just in this same way, I believed, but we had been opponents long ago. Then I must have known more—much more—

For a second time she laughed. "If you hunt down that very forgotten trail you will not find much at the end of it—save that you failed then even as you will fail now. Believe me"—her eyes were afire or else had put on the diamond brightness ice can sometimes show under the sun—"you will fail. You are even less this time than you were when once before we fronted one another. Yes, you shall give me Yonan and all shall be well. I will make very certain of that. Come!"

She arose, beckoning me. And, as it had been since I had come into consciousness this time among the hills, I was wholly subservient to her will.

She did not even glance back to see if I followed. Rather she went directly to where a stair spiraled around the circular inner wall of this place and climbed quickly, I constrained to follow.

We came so into a second and upper chamber where the ceiling was not so high. Here were shelves and tables holding all manner of basins, beakers, and small boxes. From the ceiling and along the walls dangled bunches of withered vegetation which I thought I recognized as dried herbs. But the center of the chamber had been kept bare of any furniture. And there, set into the floor in various colored stones so that it would ever be permanent and ready to hand, was the pentagram of witchery. On the points of the stars were thick black candles, which had been lighted before, as drippings of evil-looking wax ridged their sides.

Beyond the pentagram was a smaller circle, this bordered by runes which had been drawn on the pavement in black and red. But lying in the middle of that, tightly bound, a gag forced between his wide jaws, was—Tsali! Though how the Lizard man could have been brought here I could not guess.

4

Instinctively my mind reached to touch his. Only my thought send recoiled from an unseen barrier so intricately woven that nothing could pierce it—more of Laidan's sorcery. She had turned her back upon me, and there was contempt in that. She must now have believed me so poor a thing that she no longer even had to exert her power to hold me in control. Rather she was concentrating upon a search along those crowded shelves, taking down here a closed pot of rude workmanship, there a flask in which liquid swirled as if it had life.

I looked into Tsali's eyes and strove, though I could not reach him mind to mind, to make contact. And I saw that he knew me, yet there was that about his gaze which held shock—and—did I read repudiation?

In the beginning I had learned what I knew of my Talent because I could communicate with other life forms—those which are not the lesser (though ignorant men may deem them so because they do not walk, speak, or think after our fashion). The Lizard people, the Renthans, the Vorlungs of the Valley—they had arisen from stock totally unlike our own forefathers, but they were no less than we, only different.

Just as a fish lying in a sun-dappled pool, a pronghorn grazing in a meadow, a snow cat stalking in the upper reaches, have in them all the love of life, a way of thought equal to our own in power even if we cannot understand it.

I have also called to me the scaled ones. And I remembered now, in a small flash, how greatly I had troubled Yonan when he had once found me and a serpent as close-linked as was allowed by our divergent natures.

But all those were clean beasts who had nothing of the rot of the Shadow in them. While here in Escore prowled creatures which to mind-touch would be to open wide a gate through which I, myself, could be invaded. How much did Laidan use those born as a result of ancient meddling on the part of a people grown so decadent that they would tamper with nature to amuse themselves—or to provide servants for further evil?

The Lizard man was clearly an enemy. And that she planned worse for him I did not have to be told. But since she had lifted from me most of the force of her will, leaving only enough to keep me here, I began tentatively to look about me, seeking any weapon, any ally I might find.

This cradle of sorcery had no windows, and the thick stone walls were all shelved. Also, the ceiling over my head was much lower than that of the chamber below. Now I could see that in the corners of that there hung the soft thickness of years of webs, some so heavy with settled dust that they seemed small ragged bits of curtains. And in those webs—I sent out a very small quest of thought.

The mind that I touched was totally alien, the spark of intelligence frightening in its cold avid hunger. I had never tried to summon any of the insect world before. But that I had managed to touch at all was a small triumph. And, apparently, Laidan, in her preoccupation, had not been warned that in so much—or so little—I had begun to evade the geas she had laid upon me.

I located another creeper consciousness, a third. It was very hard to hold to them, for their level of consciousness was so different from my own it was like grasping a cord which was constantly jerked from my fingers, caught again just before it had totally escaped me.

There were huntresses in those dusty webs, cold and deadly. Of our concerns they knew nor cared nothing at all. But they were there. And now I made an effort, concentrating on the largest and what might be the oldest of the webs. Something moved in the hole that was its center. So—I had drawn its inhabitant thus far into the open! I had no plan at all, nothing but a hope which was very dim at that moment. But I put my own talent to the test, summoning those who dwelt above. They seemed to have fared very well, for when they appeared their bodies were bloated with good living—and that in the largest web was larger than my palm.

These were no ordinary spiders. There was poison in their jaws. They could immobilize their prey, enclose it in the web for future eating while it still lived. And their tiny eyes were sparks of evil light.

Laidan had finished her selection of supplies for whatever infamous sorcery she would do here. Now she moved purposefully around the star, setting a second candle beside the first, sprinkling the lines uniting them with powdered herbs—the smell of which was noxious.

I could guess what she intended—that we would be within the barriers she was making very secure, but that Tsali would lie in that wherein should appear whatever being of personified evil she strove now to summon from Beyond. Tsali was meant to furnish the blood-gift to that—

However, she had to release more of her hold on me to concentrate on what she did. Now she muttered words I did not know, keening spells no true Witch would soil tongue with. These must be very exact—for her life would also be forfeit were she to neglect any of the safeguards she now wove here.

The largest of the web dwellers came scuttling to the edge of her noisome dwelling, teetered there, her sparks of eyes seeking the prey which I had set in her mind was not too far away. She launched forth into space, spinning as she came the cord linking her to her dwelling. Now she swung back and forth, her fat body an orange and black dot in the air.

I sensed the creature's dislike of the scents rising from the bruised herbs below. She longed to retreat, but the mental picture of rich feasting I forced upon her held her suspended. A second lurking spider dropped from her dust-coated den—then a third.

"Ah." Laidan arose and rubbed her hands together, freeing them of the last fragment of leaf and stem. "We are ready, little sister. There need only go forth the summons—the sacrifice will be accepted—and you shall be welcomed as one of us—"

"And if I choose not?" I no longer watched the spiders lest Laidan look aloft and see them too.

"You have no choice," she told me. "You have no defense against what I shall call, and it will possess you —for a space. When it withdraws, you shall be its, and then"—she gestured with one hand to indicate all which lay within the room—"you shall learn willingly. There is that in you which shall open doors for us. Think you that we could have summoned you elsewise? And"—now she eyed me oddly—"I think that you even long for this deep within you. You are of our kind, little sister, one who would mold instead of be molded. And that is a truth you cannot deny."

"I am not of the Shadow," I returned stubbornly.

She shrugged. "What is Shadow, what is Light? You have heard only one story, and that told by our enemies. There is much to be learned. Shall we shut doors and lock them upon that learning merely because of some fear of what lies beyond? There is only one true thing to desire —and that is Power! All else is swallowed up by time, broken and forgotten. Nothing within one lasts as long as the will to Power. You shall see, yes, and you shall rejoice in that—that you are one of those into which such Power may be poured, even as winter wine is poured into a waiting flask."

There was something in her words which did find a part of me receptive. Just as I had doubted myself when the Lady Chriswitha had talked with me, so did that doubt grow now in me. I wanted—I wanted to learn what I might do were I to use my talent to the full! I wanted—Power!

Still—another part of me arose to do battle now. Power—it could twist and mar, it could defeat its user, too. It—

The foremost of the spiders hung now above Tsali. I saw the bright eyes in his Lizard skull had moved from me to that dangling creature, marking too her sisters unreeling their threads to descend.

Laidan had come to stand with me within the star. Now she raised a small black wand she had brought from beneath her mist draperies. She pointed it from one candle to the next, and each started aflame with an oily, scarlet light. While she chanted as she moved.

Within me a sickness arose, so I crouched a little, my hands pressed against my middle. Whatever there was of my species which could be aroused by her sorcery was in such revolt that it tore at my body. And my own resolve strengthened.

Even as Laidan summoned that which she would force to obey her, so did I fix my will upon the spiders from above. I still did not know what I might do with them as weapons, but they were all I had. And I had learned enough from the Lady Dahaun to know that in such sorceries the balance was very delicate and easily disturbed. Laidan had enclosed both the circle and the star in which we stood with her precautions, but she had not thought of what might lie overhead.

The candles gave forth what was to me a disgusting

smell. However, I saw Laidan breathing deeply between the words she still mouthed as if, from their scent, she garnered some needful food or energy. Then—

In the circle the air moved. But into that maelstrom there dropped the first spider from aloft. There was a swirling—I saw Laidan start, her chant faltered. A second spider, a third, disappeared into that misty column. Laidan started back—her hand raised to her mouth, for the first time shaken by what she witnessed—or felt—

I might not be as receptive as the sorceress, but I was aware of a vast troubling. Something which had been summoned—it had recoiled; it was angry. And—it was gone!

Laidan gave a cry, her hands arose to her ears as if to shut out some intolerable sound. Though I was aware of nothing, except that withdrawal. Then she, too, vanished—winked out instantly.

The flames of the candles were extinguished, leaving the room in near darkness. I was—free—

In a moment I crossed the star, grabbed from the table a stout-bladed knife and went to Tsali, slashing at his bonds. There was no longer any mental barrier between us. But something else weighed on the spirit in this chamber of the place Laidan had named Zephar.

Tsali stood, his clawed hand closed tightly about my wrist.

"Come—!" He scuttled for the stair, drawing me after him.

There followed a blurring of the walls, of all the things in that room, as if stout stone were melting, flowing away into nothingness. I thought I felt the steps of that stairway crumble and tremble under my weight. And I guess whatever illusion Laidan had set there was now disappearing, and that we might even be either trapped between times or perhaps buried under blocks of stone which the ages between would tumble from their settings.

At last, panting, we stood in the open, with around us only moss-grown and broken stones, a corner of what might once have been an outer wall. Tsali did not relax the hold he had kept on my wrist. His head darted from side to side with a speed my own species could never have equaled as he stood tensely, in such a position of instant alert that I knew that we were far from safe.

"Laidan?" I aimed a single thought at his mind.

"Is not gone—yet—" he confirmed my own fear. "She fled into her own corner of nothingness lest that which she had summoned turn upon her. But there she nurses her hate—which will grow the greater when she learns what has happened elsewhere. And because she has linked with you—then you can furnish her a door through time once more."

"What has happened elsewhere?" I seized upon that part of his warning.

"He whom she would have awakened is at last truly dead. The youth you call Yonan and Uruk of the Ax have wrought their own kind of magic. But in so much will Laidan's hate now be the greater. Though I think she dare not try anything as yet. That recoil of spell drove her too far from us. Only not yet are we finished with her."

He led the way, still keeping hold on me, out of that shell of ancient ruin. Now autumn-withered grass brushed thigh-high about me, near waist-high for him.

"What—why did the spiders—" I began. For though those spinners had done my will and had apparently broken Laidan's sorcery, I did not understand how such a thing could be.

153

"The balance of all spells," Tsali returned, still more than half of his attention given to what lay about us, even though the last of the tumbled blocks now lay behind, "rests very delicately. What Laidan summoned demanded a blood price—and what she had ready for it." He thought-sent matter-of-factly, as if *he* had not been that same price. "But when other life came into it, then it was confused, angry—believing that Laidan had sought to engage its aid with so poor an offering. Those which are truly of the Shadow trust no one. Some spells they are forced to obey, but if any bargain is not kept scrupulously, then they are freed from their obedience. Three spiders did not equal one Tsali—" There was wry humor in that which brought a smile to my own lips in spite of that lowering feeling of being naked of defense in a threatening world which had and did burden me as we went.

"Where are we?" I asked. Was this my own time? And could we win back to the Valley?

"To each question," my companion picked up those thoughts very quickly, "I cannot give full answer. But we must go with all caution. Laidan will have a chance to replenish her powers. When she finds that Targi is no more"—his scaled head shook from side to side—"then she will not be appeased except by a full letting of blood. Since she perhaps cannot get at those who killed that which was Targi, she shall be the more bitter against us—"

"Yonan—Uruk?" I made a new question of their names.

Tsali's answer came as if now more important matters were in his mind.

"Their road is their road—they have done well. It is up to us to keep faith with the Valley. We cannot return while

154

Laidan—'' his thought seemed to flicker there as if he wanted to veil it from me. But, bitterly, I knew what he would have added and so did so myself:

"While Laidan can lay her spell on me." I made no question of that, for I knew that it was the truth and one which I must face with all my strength of body and spirit.

5

We wandered on. Tsali amended his pace somewhat after we had won farther from the ruins. The land was drably brown. Autumn in its last stages had set its imprint here and had emptied the country of all growth, even as frost had drawn subsistence from the grass and weeds, now so dried and sere they rattled faintly in the wind.

There showed the remnants of a road, mainly a block here and there, overcast with drifted soil, or canted upward by the roots of a leafless tree. I stared around, trying to locate some landmark that I could fix on. Though I knew now I could not venture back once more into the Valley—not until I was entirely free of Laidan's influence.

Now I knew hunger and thirst, and I wondered where Tsali would lead us. But I did not ask. Rather I walked as one in a dream, following his urging. Yet inside I sought for what might lie there as a part of my Talent. Against Laidan I had no defense—or so I believed. How long before she dared venture out of hiding, strive to make me again her tool?

Tool?

Somehow my apprehensive thought fastened on that word. Man wrought in two ways, by the vision of his mind (which is not sorcery in itself) and with his hands—or those extensions of his hands which in the dim beginning some thinkers had devised to answer problems they strove to solve.

There were the tools of a landsman—the plow to turn the earth for the receiving of seed, the rake and hoe, the hammer, the saw; others I could not even name. There were, in addition, the tools which I had known—pots one could sling over a fire to withstand heat and cook the food within, the spindle for the making of thread, the needle, the loom—the spoon, if you will, and a short knife, and—

Also, there were other tools—those of war. There was the dart gun—my fingers moved without conscious orders as if to close about one of those weapons, seek its firing button. There were the swords, and lances; men turned more to them in these days when we could no longer fashion the darts. There were shields for defense. And in the Valley, each of the Green People carried at belt one of the force whips which were the children of lightning, tamed and domesticated to their service.

All these were tools—even the mind. But my defeat lay in that I had not been properly taught what might be done with the tool I was born with.

Tsali angled off from the ancient remains of that road, pulling me eastward. I stumbled along at his bidding because I had no other plan to follow.

The day was as ash-gray as the life-sapped grass through which we trode a path. But there were no clouds I could see. Now I caught the sound of running water, and my tongue moved in a mouth which seemed filled with dust. Down an incline which grew even steeper, Tsali pulled me. Only now I was eager in my going for I saw the water, running around rocks and over a stony bed.

I knelt at the stream bank to wash my hands in the flow, which was chill, then made a hollow cup of closely held palms and fingers to raise to my lips. Tsali had gone a little away and crouched to lap with a long tongue. When I had drunk my fill I looked about me with a more conscious gaze. Drink I had had, but there was also the need for food.

Tsali made a sudden lunge with both forelimbs, and arose, water dripping from his scaled skin, a fish wriggling between his claws. He waited until it stilled and flipped it to the ground behind him, then squatted on the bank, his eyes once more intent upon the stream.

Though I had long set my own path of life, that I would not kill a living thing for eating, still now I knew that logic must determine my survival and if Tsali's catch meant life and strength, that I must accept.

But I could not bring myself to touch the dead fish. I could only watch as the Lizard man snaked a second out of its world. He hunted among the drift which bordered the stream, to return with a sharply pointed stick which he used to gut his catch and a stone with which he skinned the bodies.

There was no fire—Tsali would prefer his raw anyway, I knew. I eyed the portion he had set before me with repugnance. But I must live and this was the only food available. I made myself worry loose bits of firm flesh, choke them down. This was no worse than many ordeals a warrior must face. While against Laidan and her world, I had no choice but to go to war.

From overhead came a scream, startling me so I near spit out the last mouthful I had forced between my lips. I looked up to see a bird, its bill opened to voice another such squawk, impudently planing earthward as if to snatch the food from our hands.

In plumage it was almost as dull-gray as the sky. But around its eyes there were circlings of light, blazing red—which gave a momentary impression that it looked upon us through dots of fire. Its like I had not seen before. And, though I immediately alerted my bruised and battered other sense, I found nothing in mind touch save what it appeared to be—a bird of prey, yes, but one which followed its own fierce nature and no order of the Shadow.

Its cries brought another of its kind. However, as they fed upon the offal Tsali had thrown to one side, I experienced once more that far-off stir of what could not be memory (for I would swear I had never seen these birds before), yet—

The flash of their drab feathered wings, the burning scarlet of the mask about their eyes, grew more and more important to me. I found myself on my feet, my hands forming fists pressed tight against my breasts.

"Ninutra—!" I cried that aloud, my voice at that moment rising even above the incessant crying of the birds.

Ninutra? A person—a place—? Under that need to know, I reluctantly opened my mind and sought, deeper, deeper—recklessly. For such delving I had done before only under the control of the Lady Dahaun. And in such a place and time as now I stood, the peril must be very great. But that I brushed aside. I must know!

Ninutra—there was a hazy image forming. I shut my eyes to the sky, the birds, to the world I knew, turned my sight inward. Ninutra—come! I gave order to that fragment of thought—or memory—what was Ninutra?

There was a feeling of giddiness. The mental image

sharpened, I felt breathless, filled with an expectancy in which excitement outweighed, at this moment, both fear and prudence.

A figure—about which held a nebula of flame color to match the patches about the eyes of the birds. If I could only brush away that curtain of brilliant radiance—see the clearer!

Ninutra—a *Power*—not a place. Of the Shadow? What had I then evoked?

No, that built-in warning which Dahaun's teachings had strengthened, did not come to life. Only neither did I feel the confidence I believed would flow about me if I summoned that which was turned to the Light. Could there then be a third force in this rent and warring land, one which stood apart from both the Dark and the Light —followed some path incomprehensible to both?

I fought to clear my mental sight of that image—or Power. But the light clothed it too well. However, slowly there came from it, as water circles outward when one throws a stone into a pool, a feeling of energy which was warm, growing hotter—hotter—

Maybe I cried out. I know that I shrank within me, strove now to will away that image, but I could not. Heat licked at me, but with it no feeling of anger. I sensed that what Ninutra might be was curious, that it stirred out of some deep contemplation of its own because my feeble summons had disturbed it. Was this one of the adepts?

If so, all which had been its human heritage was long since gone. It was pure force of a kind I did not understand, so alien—

Then that image receded from the fore of my mind. With it went some of the heat. Now it was rather as if I looked down a long aisle to see at the far end a form standing. The red glow drew back into its body (I say "it" for there was no sense of sex in this Power, there was little left but a pure force).

As I looked upon it so I was certain that once "*I*" (or the inner part of me), now flawed and long buried perhaps by other lives and ages of time, had once had contact with this Force and it had sometimes answered me. But that was long and long ago and the cord between us had frayed into dust—

I opened my eyes upon the dreary world by the stream. The birds were gone. Tsali squatted on the stones, his jewel eyes on me. I found myself whispering still that name:

"Ninutra—" And then I mind-spoke to my companion. "Tsali—what or who is—was *that* Power?"

His head bobbed, not to me, but as if to the image I had evoked so mistily.

"One of the Great Ones—not born of your blood, nor of mine, nor of any race now living. One of the ones who lingered among us for a space—until those who sought the worst of the Dark arose and tried to summon—"

"But why do I now see this thing?"

"I do not know, Witch maid. Save those birds"—he made a gesture at the sky where I saw the distant wheel of wings—"were once, long and long ago, found in the Place Apart where Ninutra chose to dwell or else maintain some small contact with this world. There were also those there who opened their minds and hearts and at times they spoke of what lay in the future so that even the adepts listened when they were the Mouths of Ninutra."

"Tsali—was I ever such a Mouth?"

He shook his head. "Ask me not riddles, Witch maid. Each race and species has its own legends. Do we live again once we have gone to the cleansing fire? And if we so live, can we remember? I do not know.''

''I saw—Ninutra—'' I answered slowly. ''And—'' I wrapped my arms about myself. ''I was warmed by the Force. I—''

My head came up. Now it was not memory which moved within me, rather a portion of knowledge laid out clear and fresh in my mind, as if there was held in the air before me a scroll fresh from the writing of a keeper of the Deeper Knowledge. I had sought for a long time. And as such a seeker, I had left myself open so that Laidan had been able to enter into that part of me which lay vacant and ready for her sly suggestions. I do not know how my vision had worked upon me in those moments when I had fronted Ninutra, but now some of those empty chambers in my mind were filled.

Tsali stood tall, his crested head erect and swelling in color. I saw those flaps of skin quiver slightly as if his whole body would express emotion.

''Witch maid—what would you now—?''

''I do what must be done,'' I cut across his half-question, half-protest.

Eyeing the bank of the river under our feet, I found what I sought, a length of stick, drift, brittle and bleached, but as straight as the eye could measure it. This I took up, gripping it steadily. And as if it were a brush to lay on paint in the making of a picture, I drew with it in the air that which lay now in my mind. So it must go, and go, and go—

What I had drawn could be seen there. First only as faint lines. Then the color spreading inward from those lines, to give an opaque solidity. It glowed as a coal on a half-dead night fire might glow. I dropped the stick and stood looking at that hung in the empty air, while from my lips came sounds unlike any words, more resembling the harsh calls of those birds which had once nested in Ninutra's dwelling of force and now had come to scavenge in this much later day the results of Tsali's fishing.

Slowly, I put out my hand. In me was the certainty that once my fingers closed firmly on what hung suspended between the Lizard man and myself, I would have pledged my strength to a struggle I could not understand.

The red of that thing was fading, but its appearance of substance grew sharper and more distinct. Why hesitate? I had really known ever since Ninutra had answered me that this was to be done. I closed my hand upon a hard surface, though that was nearly as dull-gray now as the sky above us. Thus, I resolutely drew from the air what a knowledge I did not yet understand had wrought—a sword, which to the eye still seemed vaguely and mistily edged.

"Thus works the will of Ninutra," I said slowly aloud. "For here is the Sword of Shadow—not of the Dark, nor yet of the Light, but which can be born by either belief. Only now do I claim it—and for the Light!"

I swung the miracle blade through the air, as a warrior would test the balance of a new weapon. For that is truly what I did in that moment. It was not as heavy as the steel I had known, nor did it possess a slashing edge or even a sharp point for thrusting. Its threat lay in other directions.

Tsali's thought came to me. "It is done—" I read into those words a heaviness of forelooking.

"It is done," I agreed. "It was for this that I was born—I think. I am now what I must have been fashioned to be. And let Laidan think of what hand she had in such fashioning."

6

The strange sword lost substance slowly even as wisps of mist are banished by the strong sun, though there was no sun over us at that moment. Soon I held—nothing. Still there was now in me the right and learning to call it forth again. I drew a long breath of wonder. My mind—if I could only have a space of peace in which to sort out what had poured without any sequence in my mind. Now I had no guide but my own instinct, that and the sure knowledge that battle lay before me; such a battle as I could not imagine, even though brushed by a Power I had been.

I stared down at my empty hand and I knew that, when I summoned it, that weapon forged in the name of Ninutra would return. But Tsali suddenly looked to our back trail. He hissed as the crest on his head blazed near blood-red.

"Hunters—" his thought reached me in warning.

I was sure that those hunters were not from the Valley, nor perhaps of humankind at all. I sent my own mind questing out, to touch for a bare instant of time, traces of the Dark Ones. Though of what species they were, I dared not probe the deeper to discover.

"They hunt us—" Of that much was I sure.

"They quest for scent; as yet they have not found it," Tsali returned. He flexed his claws and hissed once more.

So—we were hunted. Had Laidan returned to betray us to her evil co-forces, or had our trail been picked up only by chance? The reason for their coming did not matter. It would appear I was not to be given the time I needed to marshal this new awaking of a talent I had never known lay within me.

"Can we seek a hiding place?"

Tsali's head had swung around to a degree no human neck would allow. There were hillocks about us—but the mountain heights lay well behind. And also to those I did not dare to go now. I saw no beacon of blue stone set up anywhere, promising a kind of phantom shelter to those who hated the Dark. We had early been advised that such could be islands of safety in a dubious land.

"Water—" My companion made purposefully for the stream, sliding down the bank to wade out into its slow current.

Of course, the old, old truth—evil of many kinds dared not cross clean running water. I scrambled swiftly after him, felt my boots fill as wavelets set up by my strides lapped in over the tops of that footgear. I held my divided skirt as high as I could, but the hem became sodden quickly. While I discovered the uncertain footing of loose stones slowed me whereas Tsali skittered easily ahead.

My questing sense picked up an emanation as foul to my mind as corruption would be to my nostrils. Yet I had not enough yet to name our pursuers. Now I resolutely did not try to touch again—lest that reveal us in our flight.

The bed of the river was wide but, as we went, the stream grew narrower, a curling ribbon of water as its center, stretches of gravel edging it. Which hinted that there were periodic floods to leave the drift along the way, higher water unknown at this season. Also, it was shallow here and quite clear. I could see the flight of fish and armored things which crawled across the bottom we disturbed by our coming. One thing troubled me greatly

—Tsali had turned his back upon those heights which might or might not wall the Valley. And now I made a decision, reaching out to meet his mind.

"Tsali, warrior of warriors, I have taken a fate upon me which is not your burden. You can return—"

I got no farther. He looked back over his narrow scaled shoulder to hiss at me. And I felt the anger boiling in his mind.

"We go together, Witch girl. Should one of the Brother-Kin of Reto, whose wisdom held even the Great Snake for the space of two heart beats so that it could be truly slain, turn his back on an ancient enemy and say, 'This is no task of mine'?"

"Your pardon, warrior." I could make no other answer. "But there is this—I have accepted the weight of something I do not understand, which may even play me false at the moment we must face our enemies. I would draw no others into what may be a net of ill fate."

"What creature can claim free choice when the Great Ones stir again? Our legends speak little of your Ninutra—whether he was for the Dark or the Light. But I think he was one of those who turned his back upon both and went to a place which he alone mastered. And—"

What he might have added I shall never know but I heard again the squawking cries and saw that over us winged once more those same birds of gray and flame. They whirled and dipped, screeching. And in those moments I began to believe that they were now allied with the evil which trailed behind, scouts sent to make sure we had no chance of escape.

I tried to shut my ears to their clamor, yet they held my attention so well I stumbled on a slime-coated stone and went to my knees, the water shockingly cold as high as my waist. Tsali stood still, as intent upon those winged pests as I had been. Now I saw him rub a clawed finger along the base of his head comb.

He had the attitude of one who listened intently, as if their incessant squawking made excellent sense. I could understand nothing of it; even though in the past I had always before been able to establish contact with any living thing. For, when I cautiously sought mind touch, there was nothing, not even that residue of instinctive cunning which I had worked upon with the spiders in Laidan's sorcery room.

There were—just blanks! I could not even sense a mind barrier at work. And the very fact that these birds were so protected made me uneasy.

Their flying darts came closer; I ducked my head when one screaming bird seemed about to attack my face, my eyes. And I raised my hands over my face in protection.

"Our guides—" Tsali appeared unmoved as they flew so closely about his head that it would seem their wings would brush his crest or his face.

"Guides to where?" I challenged, cowering a little once more as one aimed straight for me.

"Who knows?" The Lizard man shrugged his narrow shoulders. "But if we follow, they will cease this calling, which must ring well down stream by now."

It was a choice between two evils, I knew. No one had ever said that those of the Dark had no cunning. The racket of the birds must indeed alert anyone within perhaps more distance than I wanted to believe.

Tsali already waded toward the righthand bank. Now the birds circled once above his head, flitting on to pay full attention to me. More slowly, because of my waterlogged skirts, I followed him. Then, when my feet were on the bank, their screaming stopped as if cut off. Instead the birds, though they still dipped and fluttered around, mainly before us, were silent.

We were away from the area of the ruins where I had felt stifled and so ill at ease. Before us sloped a meadow. Though the tall grass was dull and near dry, yet here and there a late lingering flower made a scarlet or rust-yellow patch. However, aside from the birds of Ninutra, the field was empty; an emptiness which spread out before us until there stood afar an edging of woodland.

Across that lengthy field we went. Of course in so doing, we left such a trail behind us as the Dark Ones could sniff out with little trouble. But the grayness of the day now lifted a little. I held up my soaked skirt, sitting down once to draw off and empty my boots, which were beginning to show hard usage.

That way through the open was farther than it first looked; rather as if the distant line of trees, through some power, stealthily retreated at each step we advanced. The birds of Ninutra remained silent, but they wheeled and dipped, their movements certainly following a pattern, urging us forward toward the distant wood.

It was very quiet. And then, so faint it was hardly more than a vibration on the air, I heard a howling. That I knew from my days in the Valley for the call of a Gray One —those creatures of the Dark which are neither man nor wolf, but a blasphemous uniting of both. The sound came from downriver, giving me at last a clue to the nature of the enemy.

I had no long knife in my belt, no sword or dart gun. And Tsali's scabbards for knife and sword hung empty, for his captors had despoiled him when they had taken him. I heard him hiss and lift his hands, extend his claws to the greatest extent.

We pushed forward with the best speed we could muster. The Dark Ones who caught any of us in the open had a potent charm against which no magics known could operate. They need only ring us thrice and we would be helpless to escape, fit meat to be pulled down at their desire. If we could reach those ever-beckoning trees, then such ringing would be far harder to accomplish.

It was here that the birds deserted us. Beating well up into the air, they formed a vee of flight and sped straight on toward the wood. Perhaps whatever strange task had been set them was completed.

My dragging skirt tripped me twice, though I held it as high as I could in my hands. Nor did I waste time looking back. For the hunting howl broke again and manifestly nearer. Tsali, unencumbered by clothing, could have flashed away and been out of sight long before I gained the shelter of those trees. But he did not. Instead he stooped swiftly twice, each time arising with a stone caught fast in his claws. No true defense, for all his courage, against what followed us.

I labored on. Hardly was I aware I had reached the trees, so hard set I was, my breath came in great tearing gasps, until I struck one shoulder against a trunk with bruising force. Then I caught at that bark-clad pillar, holding on with a despairing grip lest I fall and be unable to win once more to my feet.

Tsali's hand caught one of mine; he pried to loosen my convulsive hold.

''On!''

He was right, but I was not sure that I was able. There came a third howl from behind, this full-voiced and close, feeding my panic enough to make me let go, stagger ahead with Tsali tugging at me.

I brushed painfully against other trees; my clothing caught on low-growing thorns, tore when I jerked loose from their grasp. On and yet on. Here was only a small gray glimmer of light. These trees, I began to realize, had not lost their leaves—or rather needles, for the refuse under my slipping and sliding feet was composed of brownish needles near as long as my forearm. There was very little undergrowth—even of the thorns—once we had broken through the outer barrier of the wood.

Now I saw the birds once again, settling on branches, only to flutter farther ahead as we made our laborious way in their wake. And there was no sound—no breeze troubled the needles of the trees. Not one squawk issued from a bird throat. My own panting was loud, and that I was not able to control.

I staggered once and nearly fell—reaching out frantically to my right for a huge stone set on end. Only when my fingers dug into the moss which had covered it did I realize that this was no natural pillar but one once embellished by some intelligence. As I clung to that to catch my breath, I could see that this was the first in a line of such pillars which marched on into the depths of the woods. And the carving my fingers had laid bare was that of a bird, its eyes deep pits into which even the moss had not rooted.

Another fragment of that not-memory gave me a moment or so of vision—of the stones of this way unencumbered by any growth, rather gray and splashed with color where the carving on them had been inlaid with paint. I sought the warn-off of Dark-fashioned things, since these were not blue stone. But—no—neither Dark nor Light held here. And I think I then guessed what lay before us—another realm altogether, one in which what concerned those of my blood was immaterial. Was this the place of Ninutra?

Another howl from very close now—the Gray Ones

must be coursing the meadow. I looked about me for some hint of shelter. We could set our backs to this stone, but the outcome would never be in doubt—we would be speedily pulled down—

Or—

Of itself my hand stretched forth into the air, prepared to accept something from the unseen. I opened in my mind the door to that chaotic place into which had been poured all I could not yet understand.

Substance fitted into my palm. I speedily curled my fingers about to hold it firmly. There was the glow— scarlet as if outlined in fresh flowing blood. Once more I had the Shadow Sword.

Now there welled in me something which was not born of my species, which I must fight to hold steady. I looked from the sword to Tsali and spoke what I now knew was the truth.

"This is not yet the place. Let us go!"

From that point, it was I who took the lead along that line of pillars, Ninutra's birds fluttering over my head and a very grisly death, as I well knew, sniffing behind.

7

We fronted a great arch which was a marvel, for I think it had indeed been hewn of a single block of stone so large I did not see how any thereafter could move it to this place or set it upright. This was bare of carving, save at the very top where there was set a face, its eyes well above us to stare down the path we had come. Human in contour it was, but there was a lack of expression, a withdrawal in its gaze, which was not of my kind. Nor could I say whether it was man or woman. Rather the features held elements of both. But what made that image the most notable was, unlike the pillars which had guided us here, it seemed untouched by the years; no marks of erosion lay upon it.

The sword in my hand moved, almost of itself, rising up in formal salute to that carving. I guessed that here was locked part of the essence which had drawn us on.

Behind the arch was only bare earth—or rather sand —silver in color. However, laid out upon that background, in bold patterns, were tracings of other sands to form symbols I did not know. The area was divided into four quarters, each bearing its own range of complicated designs, the division being two narrow paths bisecting it at precise angles.

I went forward down the path which had its opening at the gate. The instant I was passed beneath that portal my flesh tingled, my hair moved as if drawn by energies I had never encountered before. I did not look back to see if Tsali followed; at that moment it was only needful that I reach the exact center of this place.

There was power here surely, such as I had never felt before—even in that chamber where Laidan had woven her abortive spell or in the circles Dahaun used in her own green sorcery.

There are many kinds of magic; the green which is of the earth and growing things and includes in it the healer's craft; the brown which has to do with animals, our younger or unlike brothers we may strive to understand but seldom can; the yellow, the blue, the red, the black. Of most of them I knew a little. But this here was neither of the Dark nor the Light. Its source lay (or had been moved) otherwhere. But what had been left made me feel, as I so moved boldly toward its heart, as if I had flung off all clothing, to bathe myself in a substance neither liquid nor light, possessing elements of each.

I came to the centermost point of that strange sand-covered area, where the four patterns met to form a space only large enough for me to stand and not infringe on any of those squares where lay the symbols. This—this too—I had known!

All my life I had never had a real home—though with the acceptance of my kin I had lived pleasantly and well guarded. Still within me had there always been that longing for somewhere else, something beyond the life I had always known. First I thought I had found it in the Valley when the Lady Dahaun opened my mind to what I might become, should I have the skill and patience to follow the way she pointed.

But this—

I held the sword with both hands, the fingers of one curled about the other. While at that moment I heard —strained to hear—whispers which lay just beyond my distinguishing, so that in my frustration I could have cried aloud in rage and disappointment.

Now I raised my head so that I could look to the sky, that same gray sky which had overhung us from the first. No birds wheeled there, not even a cloud broke its stretch of lowering menace.

And I dared to call aloud—not by the mind touch—

"Great One, I am here!"

It seemed to me that the presence I so eagerly sought could *not* be far away, that any moment I might see before me that form I had mind-visioned so wrapped in mist I could not distinguish its true being. This was the place of Ninutra, of that I was certain. Yet—

There was only silence. Even that murmur of voices, which had so vexed me because I could make nothing of the gabble, ceased. There was some fault in me. If I *had* ever come this way before (and I was sure now that in the far-distant past the *I* who was the inner part of me had done so), then all true memory of that was lost, leaving me now bereft and lessened.

My eyes filled, tears overflowed, to trickle down my cheeks. Because I had somehow been so sure of part of this I had clung to the belief that I knew all—

I dropped my eyes. There would come no answer, no. I was no longer one able to enter into those secrets which drew me so strongly. I glanced at the patterns of the colored sands. Once I had known, now I could push at the buried part in my mind and sense—very faintly—a small part of the meanings of those convolutions and spirals.

In my hand the sword—it was warm, heating. The blade glowed dully red, as if it were indeed steel which had been thrust for a space into flames. More intense grew that heat, yet still I held fast, though I needed to set my teeth fast upon my lower lip to endure. I was only human-kind and not for me was the knowledge I knew was locked within this place.

"Ninutra—" Within my mind I shaped that name, shutting from me the pain in my hands. It felt as if the very flesh was frying from my bones—still I held. For this I had commanded the small Talent I possessed and I would not be robbed of even so poor an answer.

Now in my mind a command rang sharp and clear— "Slay!"

I turned on my small square of path. Tsali had not

followed me into this place—no, he lingered just beyond the great arch.

"Slay!"

One step I took and then a second; the pain in my burning hands could only be cooled by blood—blood running down the blade I held. I had only to strike and that blood would burst forth, to quench the fire which so bitterly punished me for my presumption in invading a shrine not now open to me.

"Slay!"

And at that moment Tsali was gone, rather one of the lean flanked Gray Ones crouched in his place, his wolf's muzzle raised as he gave the call for the pack.

"Slay!"

I was being tricked again. This much I realized as I tottered forward. Then I took a last step, but I fought more valiantly for my mind.

"I pay no blood, Ninutra," I said and tasted the salt of my own blood from my bitten lip. "I deal not in death, but in life!"

As if those words had been a key turned gratingly in some lock long since near rusted into immobility, they brought me freedom. I held the sword and saw the blisters of burns arising on my flesh until the torment was more almost than I could bear—but only almost.

"No blood of mind-friend do I shed, Ninutra!"

There was another long moment of utter silence. Was I even able to communicate with that *Power* which had once been strong here? Or had its essence long since withdrawn, leaving only a residue of what might have formed the baser part of it?

Then—I was free of any pressure. In my hands the hilt of the sword cooled. I did not turn my head to look, but I was certain that that shadow-misted thing I had seen in my own vision was watching me, that I was being weighed one way and then another. I sensed even a very faint surprise, the first trace of emotion which had ruffled the spreading pool of oblique communication in which I was caught.

There was no Gray One at the gate—Tsali stood there, looking back the way we had come, his whole body as tense as one who expected to meet the shock of a battle charge the next moment.

Now I could join him. And I believed that I knew what alarmed him—those who had traced us dared to follow even here. Though in spite of that recent order which I had defied, I still did not believe this was any stronghold of a Dark One.

I glanced at my hands. Those welts of blisters had vanished, and with them the pain. But I still held the sword. In this much had the Presence in this shrine left me armed.

We stood together, Lizard man and girl; Tsali with the rocks he had earlier hunted brought forth from his belt pouch and ready to fling, I with Ninutra's sword. And so they came upon us, but not up the path marked by the stele—rather from the wood itself. As they bounded into the open, the birds of Ninutra screeched and dived at their heads. I saw blood run from a wound which just missed the left eye of the foremost of that stinking band.

Tsali let fly with his rocks. One of the Gray Ones flopped earthward, a great hole in his forehead. Another howled and pawed at his shoulder. But I raised the sword. From its tip there shot a lash of fire as brilliant as any laid by an energy whip. And the Gray Ones pushed back.

Their force parted to let through another, two others.

One was hooded and masked, carrying in hands with unnaturally long nails a whip which he aimed (the lash skillfully snaking out) to entrap my wrist. But I slashed down with the sword and that thing was sliced cleanly through.

His companion laughed, a sound which seemed to infuriate the Gray Ones, for they snarled at her as might dogs who knew her to be their mistress but also hated her.

"So, Handmaiden of one who has long since withdrawn," Laidan spoke aloud. And I knew that, in using her voice, she sought subtly to insult me, perhaps so trick me into some foolish act. "Did you at last remember and come running—to find the Power you sought gone? Did you not recall more—that the Lady of Fire was the first to open her own gate and go elsewhere—?"

I was a little startled. Somehow I had thought of Ninutra (for no reason I could understand) to be one of the Great Ones, yes, but a sorcerer. Adepts had been both women and men. If the inner *I* had served Ninutra in the far past, I did not remember as much as Laidan thought.

"Ninutra is gone," Laidan repeated. "Too many years has her gate been closed. Do you think *your* thin voice can reach between scattered worlds, and even if it did, she would answer? They said of her then that she walked her own way and had none she cherished greatly."

I did not try to answer her jeers. *Something* had answered, or I would not hold the Shadow Sword. Something had reached me when I had stood within that place of multicolored sands. But whether that was only faint lingering of Ninutra's power still able to, in a little, answer those who knew how to call it—who could say?

And was it that same indefinable something which now

put words in my mouth to answer Laidan? I do not know, but I answered without conscious thought.

"You have come seeking me, Laidan. Now you have found me. Let us pledge that this lies between the two of us alone—"

For a moment I thought she would not agree. Still that twisted smile which was a grimace held about her lips.

"*Very* little sister," her voice rang with bitter mockery, "do you presume to challenge *me?*"

"If you wish."

Her smile grew the wider. "Very well." She snapped her fingers and the Gray Ones drew back. But their hot eyes were on us, and I knew well that her hold over them was a thing perhaps I could not count upon continuing for long.

From within her misty clothing she brought forth that black rod she had used in her sorcery, while I took firm grip on the sword. She had never once looked at it, nor seemed to mark that I held any weapon. A small suspicion fluttered in my mind—was it that Laidan actually did *not* see what I had?

She pointed the tip of her weapon at me breast-high. I saw her lips shape words I did not hear but rather felt, vibrating through my whole body as a wrenching pain. I tightened my hold on the sword. Once more that began to warm within my grasp. Slowly I swung it back and forth in the air before me, as if by such a pitiful act I could ward off the maledictions she hurled at me.

It seemed that I could even see those words she did not speak aloud, that they turned into vicious darts seeping through the air to center on my body. Yet the blade of the sword began to glow an even brighter red as once more I must subdue the pain of my flesh where my fingers tightened upon it.

Then I saw Laidan start; her eyes go wide; her gaze follow the swinging of the sword blade, as if for the first time she had seen it.

"No!" She threw her wand as a trained warrior might loose a small spear.

I saw that fly through the air. And, in some odd way, time ceased to exist for a few heartbeats. So that instead of flying at normal speed, it appeared rather to hang transfixed in the air well within my reach. I brought down the blade of the Shadow Sword, fighting the torment that movement caused me, so that it struck full upon the black wand.

Laidan screamed, higher and more terribly than any of the birds of Ninutra. The wand splintered into pieces, shattering into only small needles which hit the ground between us. And from each of these there burst a small black flame and a puff of noxious odor. But Laidan writhed, her body twisting as if she were gripped by great hands which strove to wring her about.

I heard the Gray Ones howl, saw them run madly away. Two blundered into the path marked by the stele and stumbled, falling forward, crawling feebly on, and then lying still.

But Laidan jerked and twisted and screamed—

"Slay!"

Once more came that order, and this time I did not resist it. I threw the sword, even as she had thrown the wand. The misty-edged point entered truly into the hollow of her throat. She crumpled, her body drawing curiously in until—there was nothing.

As the wand had vanished, so was the Shadow Sword

now also gone. I stood with empty hands, staring at what I had wrought at that last order. Then Tsali's hand touched my arm gently:

"She is gone—but they," he pointed with his muzzle toward the silent Gray Ones, "may get their courage back—or rather their fellows will. It is best we go also—"

I shook off his hand with the same gentleness he had used. Rather, now I held both my arms wide and straight out from my body. Down from the leaden sky wheeled and darted the birds of Ninutra. They settled on my arms, my shoulders, silently but as if this was right and seemly.

I thought of Imhar. He was just someone very far away whom I had once known and wished well, but with whom I no longer had even kin-tie. And then, Yonan. In me I realized a little sadly that Yonan had wished me better than well, that I could have put out my hand and he would have taken it eagerly. But no longer could I do that.

Perhaps the gate Ninutra had found was closed past all opening. But in me that other *I* which had been stirring was near fully awake. I could not choose now the road which tradition laid before me, as Imhar's lady. Nor could I accept the richness Yonan wished to offer me. I was myself—alone. As yet I did not know just who or what that self was—or could be. But, even as the Sword of Shadow had burned with its power my hands, so now my spirit burned within me, lighting a hardly endurable fire to learn, to know, to be—

I looked at Tsali, my mind working to fit the proper words together. Before I was sure of them, he nodded.

"So it must be then. You have tasted Power; be very sure it is not tainted."

"It is not!" Of that one thing I was confident; I had been since the defeat of Laidan. So much would not have been allowed me had I been beguiled by the Dark. "Tell them that I must learn—and that I am still—no matter what may happen to change me—kin-bound. I swear this on blood I would not shed!"

I watched him go. Then I turned my back upon the huddled forms of the Gray Ones. And, with the birds still about me, I faced inward to Ninutra's Shrine. Or rather, was it a school for the learning of things not of this time and place? Now it seemed to me that already some of the lines of colored sand were beginning to send forth understandable meanings, even though the Great One who had wrought them was long gone.

There are a lot more
where this one came from!

The MS READ-a-thon needs young readers!

Boys and girls between 6 and 14 can join the MS READ-a-thon and help find a cure for Multiple Sclerosis by reading books. And they get two rewards — the enjoyment of reading, and the great feeling that comes from helping others.

Parents and educators: For complete information call your local MS chapter, or call toll-free (800) 243-6000. Or mail the coupon below.

Kids can help, too!

INSIDE
OUT

INSIDE

OUT

Ann M. Martin

Holiday House / New York

This book is for
FRANKIE, ELLIE, RON, BOBBY,
JIMMY, NICOLE, SCOTT, ARTHUR,
DREW, JILL, ARI, MARK, SANDY,
SUSIE, MICHAEL, MITCHELL, *and*
all the other children who
tried as hard as they could.

The author would like to thank Dr. Barbara Kezur, PhD,
for her sensitive evaluation of the manuscript.

Library of Congress Cataloging in Publication Data
Martin, Ann M.
Inside out.

Summary: Teased at school about his younger brother,
Jonno hopes his life will change when James goes to a
school for autistic children. It does, but not in the
way he expects.
[1. Autism—Fiction.   2. Brothers—Fiction.
3. Schools—Fiction]   I. Title.
PZ7.M3567585In 1984   [Fic]   83-18631
ISBN 0-8234-0512-5

Contents

INSIDE
OUT

1. James

Saturday night I got about three hours of sleep. My mother says this is not natural for an eleven-year-old boy. I'd have to agree with her there. But it wasn't my fault. It was because of James. I could only have gotten more sleep if I'd slept somewhere else—somewhere where there is no boy who screams all night.

The screamer is my brother. James is four. We don't have a nickname for him. You have to know a person pretty well before you can give him a nickname. Like, if we knew him better we could decide if he was a Jamie or a Jim or a Jimmy. But we hardly know James at all. He has a lot of problems.

I have several nicknames myself. My real name is Jonathan Eckhardt Peterson. Most people call me Jon. My parents and sister call me Jonno, which is what I called myself when I was little. And my friends Pete and Termite call me Mac. This is because of my feet. They're sort of large. Actually they're huge. And when Pete and Termite and I were in third grade, a substitute showed us a really dumb movie about a kid named Mac. Mac happened to have huge feet, like mine. So Pete and Termite started calling me Mac. They thought it was hysterical, but the humor in it faded pretty quickly for me. Unfortunately, the name stuck. (How Termite, whose parents call him Charles, got his nickname is another story.)

The morning after the no-sleep night was a Saturday, and I felt rotten. My head ached and my eyes burned. Dad said now I knew what a hangover felt like. I wondered why anyone would want to know that. I was tempted to get back in bed since James was finally quiet, but it was better not to. I'd never get to sleep that night if I slept during the day.

So I sat out on my front porch. That's what I do when I'm bored or tired. I figured Pete or Termite would show up pretty soon. It was only March, but we'd had a few days of warm weather, and it was sunny and about sixty-five degrees. Sure enough, the weather and the sight of me on the porch brought Pete and Termite out in twenty minutes.

Pete came first. He's my oldest friend. We have the same birthday. Our mothers shared a room in the hospital when we were born, and our families have been friends ever since.

"Hi, Mac," Pete said. He sat down beside me on our stoop. He had his new baseball and glove with him.

"Hi," I said.

"Wanna toss a few?"

"Nah."

Pete looked at me. I knew my eyes were bloodshot.

"James again?" he asked. He understands about James.

"Yeah," I said. "From ten-thirty till almost five. Nonstop."

"Whew. That must be some kind of record."

I grinned. "Probably."

Pete likes records and projects and keeping track of things. He's serious about his projects. Once he turned his bookshelves into a real, honest-to-goodness lending library. The books were all categorized and arranged in some kind of order, and they had borrowing cards in flaps on the back, and Pete had figured out this lending system. The library lasted two weeks, and then Pete wanted to set up a wax museum in the garage, but his parents said no. I could see their point, but I like all Pete's projects. Some of them are really wild. You never know what to expect.

We sat in the sun. I was so tired I had to lean up against a post. Pete tossed the ball back and forth from one hand to the other. *Slap, slap. Slap, slap. Slap, slap.* It was putting me to sleep.

Luckily, Termite arrived.

"Hey, everyone," he said with a grin. Termite is just about always happy. He looks a little like a clown with his shock of bright red hair and freckles all across his nose and cheeks.

"Hey, Termite," Pete and I said, grinning back.

In some ways, Termite's different from Pete and me. He usually prefers to keep his ideas to himself and let other people do the thinking. He's kind of like the caboose on a train. But the three of us, he and Pete and I, always hang around together.

Pete filled Termite in on James and last night. Termite nodded. He knows about James, but he doesn't really understand. Not the way Pete does. He may be a little afraid of James, although he's never said so. But sometimes when James is nearby, Termite will disappear.

What with the warmth of the day and me being so tired and all, the three of us just sat around. My parents hate it when we do this, even though we don't do it often, because of Pete and his ideas. Dad says sitting around is unproductive.

After a while, Lizzie came out. She was wearing these Ronald McDonald sunglasses and this old red baseball cap. Lizzie's hair tends to frizz out all over the place, so she hides it under the cap whenever possible. Lizzie is my sister. She's eight going on nine. Her real name is Elizabeth, but nobody, including our grandmother, calls her that. It's because Lizzie is so definitely a Lizzie, and not an Elizabeth. I think an Elizabeth would be a prim, tidy person, and that's just not Lizzie.

Lizzie slumped down next to me. She was as tired as I was.

"Daddy went to the office this morning," she said miserably.

"I know," I answered.

I saw Pete and Termite exchange looks. They know about this, too. We have no secrets.

When things get rough with James, Dad sometimes can't handle it, so he escapes for a while, usually to the office. He's a lawyer. It's not fair that he skips out and leaves us—well, Mom mostly—to handle James, but maybe he can't help himself.

"Come on, you guys," said Pete brightly, "we have to think of something to *do*."

"Yes," I said. "Something quiet."

"Whatever."

We all thought.

"Hey!" Pete cried almost at once. (He's always the first one to get an idea.) "We could have a lemonade stand. Except not just a plain old lemonade stand. It would be more of a snack bar. We could sell lemonade and ice tea and punch. And make Popsicles by freezing Kool-Aid in paper cups with sticks in them. And sell popcorn and frozen bananas, too."

"Yeah!" said Termite.

"Nah," said Lizzie.

"Nah," said I.

We went back to thinking.

"Hey!" cried Pete again. "I know! I've got some caps—"

"I thought your mother confiscated them," I interrupted.

"Only the ones she could find," said Pete. "So we take the caps and get a hammer and find out how high dogs jump when they're scared by exploding caps."

"Yeah!" said Termite.

"Nah," said Lizzie.

"Nah," said I.

Pete leaned back, whistling and thinking. Luckily, he doesn't get upset if you don't like his ideas. Besides, today he knew it was because Lizzie and I were tired.

Finally someone else had an idea. "Well," said Termite. (I knew he was going to suggest making goof calls. I just knew it.) "We could make goof calls," he said.

"Nah," said Pete.

"Nah," said Lizzie.

"Nah," said I.

Termite looked a little hurt.

"I'm sorry," I said. "But you always want to make goof calls, and we've done it so often the fun's running out. Not that we don't enjoy it. But we just made a bunch on Thursday."

Making goof calls was how Termite got his nickname. See, one day he got this terrific idea while we were huddled around the phone in his kitchen. (We make our goof calls from Termite's house because no one's ever there. Termite has two half sisters who are away at college, and both his parents work. Pete's an only child, but his mother works at home, so she's there practically all the time, and she's on the phone a lot, too.)

Termite's terrific idea was to pretend he was a termite exterminator. The idea was a little risky, but it worked often enough to be fun. We'd go through the phone book and pick out a number that sounded like a home phone number. Then Termite would make the call. When someone answered, he'd say, "Hello, this is the Armstrong Exterminating Company. Your husband" (or wife, depending) "just called me from work and told me about the termite problem you're having."

Usually the person wouldn't believe him, but Termite could be pretty convincing.

Then he'd try to set up an appointment to come over with his equipment. That first day he made two actual appointments (both of which he politely canceled later). From then on, as far as Pete and I were concerned, his name was no longer Charles Anthony Armstrong III. It was Termite.

After the goof call suggestion, we were running out of ideas. At last Pete said, "Let's just go shoot a few baskets. Nothing strenuous."

I groaned. "O.K."

"O.K.," said Lizzie.

"Aw, Lizzie," I said.

Now, don't get me wrong. I like Lizzie a lot. So do Pete and Termite. And I don't mind if she wants to hang around with us, but she's not a hot basketball player.

"Please, Jonno," she begged.

It kills me when she does that.

"You need someone to even up your teams," she went on.

"They're already even," Termite joked. "Mac's so tired he doesn't count."

We headed for our driveway where Dad had installed a hoop at the end of the turn-around.

Lizzie ran alongside us, still wanting to play. "Pretty puh-*lease,* with sugar on top."

Pete rolled his eyes.

Before we could even find the basketball, Dad drove up. He looked calm, which was a good sign.

We rushed up to the car and waited for him to get out. "Hi, Daddy," squealed Lizzie.

"Hi, sweetheart," he said, giving her a kiss. "Great glasses."

She touched the Ronalds on the frames and giggled.

"Hi, Dad," I said.

"Hi, son. Hi, Pete, Charles. What are you up to today?"

"Four feet, ten inches," said Termite.

It was an old, old joke between them. We laughed anyway.

Then we heard a terrible screech. We all turned around. James came bolting out of the garage. He was only half dressed (the top half). and he was galloping around and wringing his hands. "Weee-oooh, weee-oooh, weee-oooh," he wailed.

He was really upset, but he wasn't crying tears. He hardly ever does; just wails and groans.

He headed right for us like he couldn't see us, but at the last minute he made a detour.

"For crying out—" my father started to say crossly.

Mom appeared at the garage door holding James's pants. "James!" she shouted.

Everything was happening so fast.

"Weee-oooh," cried James frantically.

He doesn't speak.

Pete and I made a grab for him, catching him by the arms. We carried him back to Mom, who was standing with Dad now. She picked him up and tried to calm him down as they went into the house.

When Pete and I turned around, Lizzie was on the monkey swing under the elm tree where she goes when she's upset. Termite was disappearing through his front door.

Darn old James. Why does he have to ruin everything?

2. A School for James

If anyone had seen my family at dinner that night, they'd have thought we were pretty weird. First of all, we were so tired we were practically falling off our chairs. Second, Lizzie was wearing her baseball cap at the table. Mom and Dad don't make her take it off because they know how she feels about her hair. Third, Mom and Dad and Lizzie and I were eating fried chicken, broccoli, and rice, while James was slowly working his way through a cup of dry Cheerios and half a plain bagel.

This is another thing about James. Eating. The only foods he'll eat without any fuss are Cheerios, bagels, Hawaiian Punch, and milk. At most meals Mom and Dad take turns forcing him to eat normal food. They have to feed him the way you'd feed a baby. Sometimes Lizzie or I give them a break and take over. Then, after you've been feeding him meat and vegetables and stuff for about fifteen minutes, he usually barfs them up. I can't tell you the number of meals that have ended with James puking all over the place. Mom and Dad think it's worth it for the few times he keeps the healthy stuff down. Personally, I think it's revolting.

Also James hardly ever sits still. The doctor's word for this is "hyperactive." James is forever squirming, wiggling, and running around. Meals are especially bad, and so James still eats in a highchair. We have to strap him in. It's the only way to keep him in one spot.

This evening, though, no one was about to force-feed James anything. We just let him go to town on his Cheerios. It was a much pleasanter meal.

"Well, kids," said Dad, "how was everybody's day?" (He'd gone back to the office right after he'd helped Mom get James's pants on.)

"Fine, Daddy," said Lizzie tiredly. "Me and Wendell caught minnows in Harry's Brook."

Lizzie has almost no girlfriends, and no friends her age. Either she hangs around with Pete and Termite and me, or she bugs Wendell to do stuff with her. Wendell is at least fifteen.

"What about you, Jonno?" Dad asked.

"Well, Pete and Termite wanted me to look for golf tees for Mr. Armstrong at the shopping center this afternoon, but I didn't feel like it. I read this book I have to do a report on instead."

Right then James coughed, and we all lunged at him with napkins, positive he was going to throw up, even though he was eating Cheerios. Luckily, it was just a regular cough. James looked up, startled to see us coming at him. Then his eyes glazed over, and he reached for the bagel, as if we weren't even there.

My mother sighed.

"Any word?" asked my father. "I know it's Saturday . . . but you never know."

"No. Maybe next week," said Mom.

They were talking about James's school. This really great

thing had happened. After a couple of years of dragging James around from doctor to doctor and specialist to specialist, they'd found a program, right in the next town, that James could join as soon as there was an opening. The school is only for kids like James. James is autistic.

It took us forever to find that out. See, way back when James was two, this big change came over him. Until then he'd been a pretty normal baby, except that he didn't like to be held or picked up. But he could talk and feed himself, and he was almost toilet-trained, and he liked to play with Lizzie and me. Then (and it happened awfully quickly) he started talking less and less until finally he wasn't talking at all, just making funny sounds like *weee-oooh*. We didn't know *what* had happened. The eating and sleeping problems started, and he stopped wanting to run around after Lizzie and me. Instead he started sitting alone for hours, rocking himself back and forth or waving his hands in front of his eyes or spinning pennies on the bathroom floor. If you touched him or interrupted him, he'd scream.

Now, more than two years later, he's still like that, except when he gets hold of my old Lincoln Logs, or Lizzie's Legos or Tinkertoys. Then he builds these huge, amazing structures. They're really complicated. I don't know how they stand up half the time, but they do. Mom and Dad look at the structures and say James can't be retarded. The buildings are so complex even Pete couldn't make them.

Another reason Mom says James can't be retarded is that he doesn't *look* retarded. When he's not doing something weird, he has this bright, serious look on his face, as if inside his head he's thinking complicated thoughts, as complicated as his buildings. I like to imagine that James doesn't want to have anything to do with us because he's this fantastic genius, and our world is too dull for him, compared with the high-level stuff he's working on in his head. Sometimes I'll come upon him when he's staring—not spinning or waving or wailing—just staring, and I'll watch him sitting with his blond hair falling in his big brown eyes, and I'll think, James, I bet you're smarter than all of us. Then I'll remember about him spinning pennies and only eating Cheerios, and I'll think, No, James, you're just a mystery to me.

Anyway, before we found out James was autistic, Mom and Dad spent months taking him from one doctor to another, trying to find someone who could help him, someone who could tell us what was wrong. Sometimes they'd be gone for a day or two, sometimes for a week or two. Lizzie and I didn't go with them. We'd stay at home, and Granny and Grandpoppy would come take care of us. That was sort of fun, but one time Lizzie got appendicitis while Mom and Dad and James were in Denver, and by the time Mom could fly back here to Massachusetts, the operation was over. Lizzie never forgave her. Or James. I could understand how she felt.

At first, none of the doctors could tell us what was wrong with James. One doctor said he was deaf and we should get a hearing aid for him, but that didn't make sense. Even though he acted like he couldn't hear us talking to him, he could hear the quietest sounds, like a paper rustling in another room. One doctor said he was hopelessly retarded and we should stick him in an institution. But we knew about his fantastic Tinker-toy creations. Another one said (get this) that James was just spoiled and the sooner we stopped treating him like a baby, the faster he'd grow out of his problems. That was stupid. Sandy Macey down the street was as spoiled as rotten eggs, but at least she could talk.

Then, a few months before James's fourth birthday, we

found this doctor in New York who said James seemed autistic, but he was too little for any testing. He suggested Mom and Dad take James home, wait six months, and bring him back for tests. He said our whole family could use a break from doctors. Thank you very, very much, Dr. Lewis, I thought, when Dad told me this.

The next six months were better. With the pressure of the doctors' visits off, James seemed a little more relaxed. You could touch him and he wouldn't scream. He'd let you hold his hand sometimes. But otherwise he was just the same. It was great to have Mom and Dad home, though.

James went back to the doctor in six months and was tested. The doctor said James was autistic, which was the first diagnosis that made sense to my parents. See, autism isn't a disease where your body gets sick and you can say you have a fever and a sore throat or a cough and a runny nose. Instead "autism" describes the way a person behaves. Most autistic kids, like James, act as if other people don't exist. They seem to be lost in their own world. They don't like to be touched, they don't talk, they don't go near people. Usually they get along with *things* better than people, like James spinning his pennies and staring at lights and building with Tinkertoys, and they can do the same things over and over and over again for hours.

Anyway, the doctor helped us find the school over in Weston. Now we were just waiting for them to have room for James. It could be any day, Mom said. We were hoping it would be soon because we couldn't take much more.

"Speaking of school," Dad said, and we all looked at him, wondering if he knew something we didn't, "there's something I've been meaning to say to you kids." Dad nodded at me and Lizzie.

"Us?" asked Lizzie.

I knew she was wondering the same thing I was. What did James's school have to do with us?

"Yes," said Dad. "As you know, having a child like James is expensive," he began.

Lizzie and I knew this. Some of those trips to doctors cost as much as a couple of thousand dollars. Insurance paid for some of it, but not everything. We couldn't take family vacations anymore, and we'd had to sell our cottage at Bayhead Beach.

"When James starts school, we'll have tuition to pay."

Lizzie and I must have looked a little blank, because Dad went on, "The Weston Child Development Institute is a private school. That means we have to pay to send James there. You two go to public school, which is free, but a private school is different."

"Oh," I said.

"What I'm getting at," said Dad as he finished the last of his chicken and pushed his plate away, "is that we're still paying off doctors' bills, and now we'll have tuition payments as well. When James starts school, your mother will have more time for her work" (she's a freelance copywriter), "but money's still going to be tight around here for a while. You'll continue to get your allowances, but if you want extras, you'll probably have to buy them yourselves, so you might want to think about earning some spending money."

"I understand," said Lizzie. She can be so serious.

"Me, too," I said. I wasn't thrilled, but I understood.

Mom and Dad smiled. They used to apologize to us about James, but not anymore. It doesn't do any good, and besides it's kind of mean to James.

Then Lizzie, even though she resents James, managed to

come through. "It will even be fun," she said. "Think of all the things we can do, Jonno. I like earning money."

"Sure, Lizzie," I said, but without quite as much conviction. I was thinking of the Build-Your-Own Starcruiser kit I wanted so badly. It was real expensive—$62.99 at Kaler's Hardware Store downtown. Every now and then Mr. Kaler would have a sale, but even so, that Starcruiser would cost a lot of money. I'd hoped Mom and Dad might pay for half of it if I paid for the other half. They did that sometimes for Lizzie and me. But now I'd just have to earn it all myself. No way could I convince anybody that Starcruiser was a necessity. And my birthday was months away. I tried to look on it as a challenge. I knew just how to start, too. I'd call Pete.

Dad volunteered to clean up dinner since he'd been off the hook with James all day, so as soon as I was excused I dashed into the den and dialed Pete's number.

"Hmmm," said Pete slowly, after I explained the situation. I could tell he was excited that I needed one of his ideas. "Remember that electric belt-buckler I almost invented last year? Maybe we could perfect it and patent it. Then we could round up Termite and Lizzie and mass-produce them and sell them. The belt-bucklers, I mean. Not Termite and Lizzie." Pete is always very precise.

I thought a minute. "Got anything less complicated? I don't want to take too long to earn the money."

"Hmmm," said Pete again.

I tapped my fingers and waited.

"Maybe we could pool all our money and invest it in the stock market."

"*Pete*. You have to have thousands of dollars to do that."

"Oh. Well. Hang on a minute."

I hung.

"Hey!" he cried.

I perked up a little. That sounded like a pretty promising "hey."

"What we need to do is start a business."

"Yeah?" I said excitedly.

"And for it to be profitable, we have to do something people won't have to pay *too* much for. That way they'll be more willing to do business with us."

"Yeah?" I cried. This was getting good.

"And it has to be something that's not too taxing on us. That way it's worth our while."

"Yeah! What do you have in mind? What kind of business?"

"I don't know."

"Oh."

"But I'll come up with something. I'd like to earn some money, too. I've got a long way to go on my mother's birthday present."

Pete and I hung up. He wanted me to come over and watch a horror movie on TV, but I was too tired. I wanted to go right to bed.

I headed for the stairs, but when I got to the living room I came across James and one of his structures. It was made from Tinkertoys. He does his best work with Tinkertoys.

"Hey, James," I said. I always talk to him, even though he won't answer. For all I know, maybe he tunes out human voices. But just in case, I talk to him pretty much. "That's neat, James," I went on. "This is one of your biggest ones. I wish you could tell me what it is. Is it a space station? Or an office building?"

James was standing on tiptoe, concentrating intently on attaching some pieces to the top.

I watched him working. He was straining so hard his arms

were shaking. I could hear him humming under his breath. He was humming a Bach piece he had heard this morning. James has an incredible memory for music. Any song he hears, even just once, he remembers completely. Just the tune, of course, not the words. And it doesn't matter whether it's Stravinsky or REO Speedwagon.

"Want some help, James?" I asked, thinking no four-year-old should work so hard.

He didn't pay any attention. So far he hadn't even looked at me.

I saw what he was trying to do—to get one of the little round pieces on one of the sticks at the very top of the building, but he wasn't quite tall enough to reach.

"Here," I said. I started to take the piece from his hand.

Still without looking at me, he snatched his hand away and sort of danced around to the other side of the building. "Weee-oooh," he said anxiously. It sounded like a warning.

"Well, good night, James," I said finally, and went quietly up the stairs. But when I got to my room, I slammed the door.

I hope James heard it, and I hope he jumped. After all, I was only trying to help him.

3. Edweird

Monday morning.

Pete and Termite and I were sitting in our classroom talking. Mr. Westoff, our teacher, lets us do that when we're not officially in class. Right then we had twelve minutes until the first bell rang.

I was sitting on my desk, Pete was sitting on his desk, and Termite was sitting on Margaret Sesselbaum's desk. Termite's not in our class, but he comes in before the bell to talk sometimes.

It was pretty brave of him to sit on Margaret's desk. Margaret wouldn't like to know that someone as lowly as Termite Armstrong had been sitting on her desk, smelling it up. Even if she didn't come in early enough to see him, she'd hear about it from Louise Werner or Janie Cunningham or Elise Markey. Probably Elise. Elise is the leader of that particular group. They are the in-girls in my classroom. The four of them are pretty and smart, act like they're better than everyone, and do things to impress the in-boys.

Needless to say, Pete and I are not in-boys. The in-boys of the class are David Lowe, Hank Read, Chris Giancossi, and

Alan Steinwick. There is no leader, no Elise, among them. But it doesn't matter. They are just like the in-girls, basically. They are good-looking, smart, and think they're great.

Pete and I aren't exactly shunned by the in-kids, but we hang around on the edge of things. We don't fit in. To them, we're uncool. We're the wrong way around, or upside down, or inside out. Maybe inside out describes us best. We're no good at hiding what's wrong with us. It all shows. The in-kids must have some secret for covering up their feelings when they're dumb or gawky or insecure. The rest of us let everything hang out. Unfortunately.

Termite was talking about how his half sisters would be home from college for spring vacation soon, and Elise and her crew were drifting in. They huddled in a corner, whispering, and didn't even notice Termite on Margaret's desk. Lucky for him.

Then David, Alan, Hank, and Chris sauntered in. Their saunters looked terribly nonchalant. Too nonchalant, if you know what I mean. They seated themselves very, very casually on some desks not too far from the huddle going on in the corner. I noticed that the voice level in the huddle rose just enough so the boys could hear.

There are two girls in the class who are kind of like me and Pete—not in with Elise, but not as far gone as some others. They are Stephanie Kautzmann and Claudia Smith. I happen to like Steph and Claud a lot. For one thing, they don't spend a lot of time poking at their faces in mirrors or whispering about Dave and Hank and Chris and Alan. For another, they're nice to everybody, including the stuck-up in-kids *and* Termite and me and Pete. Sometimes me and Pete and Steph and Claud hang out together. We always try to be a group when group project time rolls around.

The best thing about Steph and Claud is that they don't care much what Elise and everyone thinks of them. I wish I could say the same for myself. I do care. I'm not sure why. I waver between wanting to be one of the in-boys and liking being just myself, goofing around with Pete and Termite.

I was thinking about the little groups that always form in a classroom, when the bell rang. Termite shot off Margaret's desk and charged out the door without saying good-bye. He only had two minutes to get all the way down the hall and around the corner to his classroom before the final bell would ring. He always makes it.

Mr. Westoff usually comes in right after the first bell. Sure enough, in a few seconds the door opened, and in he walked. But he wasn't alone. He held the door open for a very large boy. Well, all right, he was fat. He had his pants hitched up with a belt I could have wrapped three or four times around my waist.

I looked closer. The bottoms of his pants were way above his ankles. A lot of sock showed. And he was wearing a pair of those fancy brown leather shoes with holes punched all over the tops. All the guys wear running shoes. Right away I knew he'd be in for a lot of teasing. I checked over my right shoulder and saw Alan Steinwick laughing uncontrollably into his math book, and David Lowe laughing uncontrollably into his desk, and Chris Giancossi laughing uncontrollably into his lap as he bent over to tie his shoe, supposedly. Hank Read couldn't find anything to laugh uncontrollably into, so he was just turning red from holding it in.

I looked back at the boy. He was about fourteen. Much too old for our class. Just a visitor, thank goodness, so he wouldn't have to endure the laughter too long. I could sympathize. I know what it's like to be laughed at.

The last thing I expected was for Mr. Westoff to face the class, put his arm across the boy's shoulders, and say, "Everybody, this is Edward Jackson. He's going to join our class." Then he added rather pointedly, "I hope you'll make him feel welcome."

Oh, brother. He was a new kid, not a visitor!

Mr. Westoff started to guide Edward to an empty seat over by the door, but Edward continued facing us. "Hi," he said nervously. "I'm glad to meet you. My name is Edward Jackson."

The laughter was spreading. It had contaminated Margaret, Elise, and Janie. It was about to catch up with Louise.

I glanced over at Pete. He just looked surprised. Then I looked at Claud and Steph. Claud was staring intently at her hands. She looked almost sad. Steph was glaring at Elise. It wasn't doing any good.

"Come on, Ed," said Mr. Westoff brightly. "Here's your desk." He led Edward down an aisle.

Edward never stopped talking. "This is a nice school. Where's the water fountain, Mr. Westoff?"

He passed Alan's desk. "Do you like this school? Do you know where the gym is?"

The laughter wasn't silent anymore.

"Where—where's the pencil sharpener, Mr. Westoff? Where's the nurse's office, Mr. Westoff?"

Edward sat at his desk and turned around to Elise, who sat behind him. Unfortunately.

"Where's the—the cafeteria?" he said to her.

I guess it was the thought of Edward adding to his bulk that set everyone off even more. The room was filled with snickers and snorts. Even I was beginning to feel the urge. Not because of poor Edward; just because of all the other laughter. It was rising up in me. I pursed my lips and put my hand over my mouth, managing to laugh silently. I looked over at Pete and saw he was doing the same thing. I felt a little better.

Mr. Westoff was still trying to get Edward settled quietly, helping him put his things in his desk.

Suddenly a note landed in my lap. It didn't come from Pete's direction. I opened it quickly, keeping an eye on Mr. Westoff.

The note said:

> I wonder what planet he comes from?

It was signed *Chris*.

Chris Giancossi?

Sending poor, out-of-it Jonathan E. Peterson a note? Well, I *was* sitting closer to him than any of the in-boys were.

Quickly I scribbled back:

> Planet Fat?
> Planet of the Blimps?
> Planet of the Oven Stuffer Roasters?

I tossed the note to Chris. He read it, scrunched it up, and grinned at me.

I grinned back, feeling ridiculously happy.

Mr. Westoff had finally gotten Edward seated and quiet. As soon as he left him, Edward turned around to Elise, stuck out his hand, and said, "I'm pleased to meet you. My name is Edward Jackson. I'm thirteen-and-a-half-years old."

Elise blushed and busily sorted through her desk. She didn't even look at Edward.

Edward looked hurt and turned around, facing front. He was the most inside-out person I had ever seen.

I was torn between wanting to feel sorry for him and wanting to grin at Chris.

Mr. Westoff took attendance and collected our homework

papers, and we pledged allegiance to the flag.

After the pledge, a messenger appeared at the door.

Mr. Westoff waved her in and said, "O.K. Edward, find your math book, your speller, your reader, and some pencils. This is Sandy Castleman. She'll take you to the Resource Room."

Chris looked over at me and raised an eyebrow. The Resource Room. We all knew what that was. The place for the problem kids.

Everyone watched Edward get his stuff together. He put his math book on top of the pile. It was a *second-grade* book. I looked at Chris and knew he had seen, too.

Just as Sandy was about to lead Edward out the door, he turned around and said loudly, "Good-bye, Mr. Westoff. Good-bye, everybody. I'll be back for lunch."

Snicker, snicker.

Snort, snort.

Chris leaned over and whispered to me. "Hey, his name shouldn't be Edward. It should be Ed*weird.*"

"Yeah!" I said.

Right after Edward left, Mr. Westoff had a little talk with all of us.

Even so, by the end of the day, every kid in the class knew about Edward's new name.

4. "I'll Be Rich!"

"So," I said to Termite, as he and Pete and I walked home from school that afternoon, "Chris says, 'His name shouldn't be Edward. It should be Ed*weird.*'"

"He *is* a little strange," said Termite carefully. He'd seen Edweird on the playground after lunch.

"I'll say," I said.

"I'll say," Pete said.

"It's kind of too bad about him," Termite said.

"Yeah," I said.

"Yeah," Pete said.

Conversation lagged then. Funny how we were embarrassed to talk about Edweird.

We reached our houses and split up. Our parents have this rule. We have to get our homework done before we're allowed to fool around together on weekdays. Since we'd stayed after school for baseball practice today, there wasn't time left to do anything.

"See you tomorrow," we called to each other.

I ran up our front walk. "Hi, I'm home!" I yelled as soon as I walked through the door.

"Shhhh," Lizzie hissed from the living room. She was dust-

23

ing the tables. The house was very quiet.

"What's wrong?" I whispered. "Is someone sick?" I looked closer and saw that Lizzie was crying.

"Hey, Liz," I said. "What's the matter?" I dumped my stuff on the nearest chair and made her sit down on the couch with me.

She began crying so hard she couldn't talk, so I let her sniffle and sob for a while.

Finally I said again, "What's wrong, Lizzie?"

Sniffle. Sob. "It's James," she managed to say.

"Is he hurt?" I asked quickly.

Lizzie shook her head. The crying began to let up.

I straightened her baseball cap.

"I came home," she said, "and Mommy was lying on the couch with a washcloth over her eyes, and she'd been crying. I asked her what was wrong, and she said she'd taken James shopping again."

"Oh," I said.

Taking James shopping is never a good idea. He gets crazy in stores with all the people and all the stuff on the shelves and counters. He starts weee-ooohing after only five or ten minutes. Mom takes him in a stroller so he can't run around, but even so he makes a lot of noise, and people always stare. Sometimes he manages to struggle out of the stroller, and then it's all over. He starts the galloping bit, flinging his hands around. I always want to say to him, "James, it's really O.K. It's just a store. Nothing's going to hurt you." But it wouldn't make any difference.

Recently we've tried to arrange our days so James doesn't have to go shopping. Like, Mom will shop in the afternoons and leave him with me, or shop at night or on the weekends when Dad is home. But she can't do that all the time.

"What happened today?" I asked Lizzie.

"It was worse than usual," she said softly. "They were in the grocery store and Mommy was talking to someone, and before she knew it, James escaped from the stroller and ran away and knocked over a paper towel display. Then the manager yelled at Mommy in front of her friend and said children like James didn't belong in public."

We were both quiet for a while.

"Where are Mom and James now?" I asked after a bit.

"Mommy's taking a nap and...I hope you don't mind, Jonno—I put James in his room."

"That's O.K.," I said, and gave Lizzie a little smile.

I know it sounds mean, but we've fixed James's door so it locks from the outside. That way, when he gets out of control, or when we're too busy to watch him, we have a safe place to put him. There's nothing he can hurt himself on, and he certainly doesn't mind being alone. We don't put him there very often, but I could understand why Lizzie did it today.

"Any reason why you're dusting?" I asked her. "You hate housework."

"I know, but it was the only way I could get Mommy to take a nap. She said she was way, way behind on her job and the chores and the garden because darn old James has been so bad. So I told her I'd clean the living room and weed the front garden and finally she said O.K. But it's not fair, Jonno. It isn't. Why should we have to do all this just because of James? He never does anything around here. And he makes Mommy cry, and he makes Daddy upset."

Even though I agreed with Lizzie, all I said was, "I know. It isn't fair, but James is special. There's nothing we can do about that. So come on. I'll help you with the weeding. We should probably start dinner, too. Is there any spaghetti sauce?"

"Oh," Lizzie said flatly. "That's another thing. Daddy won't be home for dinner."

"He won't?"

"No." Lizzie sounded like she might cry again. "He called a little while ago, and when I said Mommy was taking a nap, he suddenly decided to work late. I guess he figured we were having trouble with James."

I nodded silently.

"Let's just have leftovers," Lizzie said. "Daddy won't be home and Mommy will be tired, and you know James and spaghetti."

I knew.

Disaster.

So Lizzie and I dusted and weeded and started the leftovers heating up, and then I remembered James. He was still locked in his room.

"I better go get James," I said as we finished setting the kitchen table.

Lizzie looked at me and didn't say anything.

I tiptoed upstairs, hoping I wouldn't wake Mom, and turned the lock on James's door.

James was kneeling on the floor in the exact middle of his room. The ceiling light was turned on. I wondered if he had done that himself. He was rocking back and forth, back and forth, gazing at the light and waving his right hand in front of his eyes.

"James," I said softly. I felt funny interrupting him.

He never paused. I don't think he even knew I was in his room.

"James," I said again, a little louder.

This time there was a slight hesitation in the rocking.

"Come on," I said to him. I reached out and took one of his hands very gently.

The rocking stopped.

"Let's go downstairs, James."

He stood up without a sound and let me lead him from his room. He is usually quite calm after he's been up there. I don't know if it's the room or the rocking.

Downstairs I sat James on the floor in the living room and gave him a pile of Legos. He didn't show any interest in them, but he didn't make any noise either.

When Mom came down to the living room a little after six, dinner was all ready, the chores were finished, Lizzie and I were doing our homework, and James was diddling a little red Lego between his fingers and humming a Beatles medley we'd just heard on the radio.

Mom looked bleary-eyed and tired and not really ready to face anything yet. She took the three of us in at a glance and smiled as she sank down on the couch. "How long has it been since I've told you guys how terrific you are? Look at this. You're doing your homework, dinner is cooking away—I can smell it—you've gotten James calmed down..." Her voice trailed off.

We almost always talk about James right in front of him, and lots of times we forget to include him as part of our family. Like right now, all three of us kids were in the living room, and Mom had said "you guys," but she was really only talking to Lizzie and me. It was sad.

"Thanks, Mom," I said, forcing a smile.

Lizzie ran over to her, and Mom gave her a big hug.

In about fifteen minutes we sat down at the kitchen table for dinner. Nobody said anything about Dad not being there. Lizzie had told Mom about the phone call, and that was the end of that.

We ate quietly, hardly talking. James was strapped into the highchair, picking at Cheerios and milk—separately. He won't eat Cheerios like regular cereal, and besides, he hates using a spoon. We had plenty of leftover broccoli and chicken, and some stew from last night, but after Mom's day, nobody was going to make James eat it. We were doing this more and more often recently. It wasn't very healthy for James.

"I guess the school didn't call today," I said foolishly, knowing Mom would have said something if they had.

Mom shook her head. "No. And I should face up to it— the director said they might not have an opening until September."

You'd have thought Mom would have been sad or angry, but she didn't look either way. Just like she was accepting it. I didn't know if that was good or bad.

After dinner Lizzie and I cleaned up while Mom tried to read a story to James. He usually doesn't pay any attention and hardly even sits still, but *sometimes* we think he might be looking at the pictures. So Mom keeps reading to him. Tonight, though, he ran away after three pages, and Mom was too tired to go after him, so that was the end of the story.

I finished my homework and took a pile of magazines up to my room. I closed the door. For some reason I didn't feel like talking to anybody.

I thumbed through the magazines, reading all the sports stories, and then I looked through the ads in back, just in case there was anything you could get free.

There wasn't much, but suddenly something caught my eye. It was an ad in a little box and it said:

MAKE MONEY FAST!

IT'S EASY, IT'S FUN!

You can earn as much as $10 a day—

in your spare time!

The ad went on a bit longer in very tiny letters. It turned out all you had to do was send fifty cents (for postage and handling) to the E-Z Seed Company, and they'd send you three hundred packages of vegetable and flower seeds. Then you were supposed to go from door to door selling the seeds. You got to keep twenty-five percent of whatever you earned. (You sent the other seventy-five percent back to the E-Z Seed Company.) I did some fast calculating and figured out I'd have to sell eighty packages of seeds to earn the ten dollars they were talking about.

Eighty packages a day. It seemed a little high, but who knows? Maybe it was really easy to sell seeds. After all, it was almost spring, and people were starting to plant their gardens.

I figured some more. If I could sell the eighty packages a day, I'd have enough money for the Starcruiser kit in just six and one-third days. That was a whole lot sooner than I'd expected. I'd thought it would take months to earn $62.99, even with Pete's help.

I scrounged around in my underwear drawer until I came up with two quarters. Then I filled out the order blank in the magazine and mailed everything off to the E-Z Seed Company.

At ten dollars a day, I'd be rich! Things were looking up.

5. Time-Savers, Inc.

The next Saturday I got up at eight o'clock after a good sleep. James hadn't made a peep at night since that awful time a week ago.

By eight-thirty I was seated at the kitchen table having breakfast by myself. On Saturday, everyone in my family eats on his own, since we kind of go our separate ways. Right now Lizzie was still asleep, Mom was working on an assignment that was due Monday, and Dad was gardening and keeping an eye on James, who wasn't doing much of anything.

I was digging into a big bowl of Rice Krispies when Pete appeared at the kitchen door. "Come on in," I called.

He came in and closed the door quickly behind him. It was a nice day out, but not as warm as it had been last Saturday.

"Mac, Mac," he cried. "Have I ever got an idea! Listen to this."

"What?" I asked excitedly. I knew it had to be the money-making scheme, and it had to be good. "Want some breakfast?"

"No, thanks," said Pete. "I just ate." But he helped himself to three pieces of toast anyway. He acts like this when he's got an especially fantastic idea.

"O.K.," he began. "I hope you got enough sleep last night

because we have a lot to do today."

"I got plenty," I said. "James has been really good lately."

"Great," said Pete. "O.K., here's the thing. We start an odd job service. You and Termite and I, and Lizzie if she wants. We'll do anything for anybody at a fixed rate of a dollar fifty an hour. We'll wash windows, walk dogs, baby-sit, mow lawns, paint, anything. What do you think?"

I was stuck back on "fixed rate." Pete's always coming up with these things I don't understand. How does he stay so far ahead of everyone?

"It sounds terrific," I said. "What's a fixed rate?"

"It means no matter what we're doing or who we're doing it for, we charge the same. A dollar fifty an hour."

"Oh," I said. "Hey, I think this is super. How do we let people know about us?" Between this and the E-Z Seed Company, I'd have more money than I'd know what do do with.

"I've got that all worked out. You know my old printing press? We'll print up fliers—ads—and stick them in mailboxes."

"Yeah! And we should have a name for us. We're sort of a company."

"Oh, right. Let's see."

We both thought for a minute.

"The Odd Job Service!" I suggested triumphantly.

"Too plain," said Pete. "We need something catchy."

"Time-Savers, Inc.," I said.

"Hey! I like that. That's really good. It's a name people will remember, and it says something they want to hear—we save them time."

"Right," I said, proud of myself for having come up with this particular idea.

"Let's go get Termite," said Pete.

I threw my dishes in the dishwasher and flew out the door

after Pete. "Going to the Armstrongs'," I yelled over my shoulder to Dad.

We collected Termite, who was very enthusiastic about the idea, and headed over to Pete's to use his printing press.

"The ad should tell all the things we'll do," said Pete as we settled ourselves in his room.

"And say we'll do anything else. Any odd job," added Termite.

"And it should have our names and phone numbers," I said.

"And the hours we can be reached."

"And the times we can work."

"And how much we charge."

At first we had trouble setting up all that information on Pete's press, but finally we got it together, and Pete cranked out one flier to see how we'd done.

This is what our ad looked like:

TIME-SAVERS, INC.

We save you time!
Lowest rates!

Do you hate gardening? Cleaning? Mowing your lawn?

Do you want your dog walked?

Do you need a baby-sitter?

Call us! We're here to help.

We'll do any odd job and we charge only $1.50 an hour.

Baby-sitting	Lawn mowing
Pet-sitting	Weed pulling
Cleaning	Painting
Gardening	Dog walking
Window washing	Car washing

And anything else you need done!

Call us now

Peter Wilson	921-5408
Jonathan Peterson	921-4932
Charles Armstrong	921-8611

Call after school or on the weekends.

We can work any afternoon and any Saturday or Sunday.

(We had decided our parents would ease up on the homework rule for something as important as running our business.)

We studied the ad carefully and decided it looked O.K. and that all the spelling was correct. Just to make sure, though, we took it downstairs and had Mrs. Wilson read it. When she finished, she smiled and said it looked fine.

So we trooped back upstairs. Pete was about to crank out a hundred copies of the flier, when I remembered something.

"Wait," I said. "We forgot to ask Lizzie if she wants to be in on this. Let me call her."

"What'd she say?" Termite asked when I came back to Pete's room.

"It was funny. She said no, thanks, she didn't really want to. She sounded awfully...well, sort of smug, like she was hiding something. I wonder what she's up to."

"Oh, well," said Pete.

"Oh, well," said Termite.

Pete began cranking. When his arms gave out, Termite took over. When Termite's arms gave out, I took over. It seemed to take forever, but finally we had one hundred copies.

"I'm starved," I announced after the fliers were divided into three even, neat stacks. "Let's stop for lunch."

Termite and I were just heading out the front door for our

own houses when Mrs. Wilson stopped us and invited us to have sloppy joes with Pete, so of course we stayed.

After that, Termite and I were almost too full to move, but Pete was hopping impatiently around the kitchen. Finally he ran upstairs, got the fliers, brought them back down, and told Termite and me the only way to get over feeling full was to deliver all the fliers. So we groaned and got going.

Out on the sidewalk, Pete handed out the piles of fliers. "For starters," he said, "Mac, you take our street, Termite, you take Random Road, and I'll take Overbrook. Put a flier in every mailbox, O.K.?"

So we did, and it went much faster than I expected. I got rid of all thirty-three of my fliers before I'd finished our street. When the three of us met up, we decided to crank out another hundred. We delivered all those, too. It was almost four o'clock before we finished. We were feeling pretty proud of ourselves.

In fact, we were feeling so good that when we were walking up my driveway and Mom stopped us and said she and Dad wanted to go shopping, we immediately volunteered to take James to the school playground. Well, actually, Pete and I said we'd do it. Termite suddenly decided to go home.

Mom handed James over to us with all sorts of instructions. "Make sure he keeps his mittens on. And his hat. And he's started eating gravel lately, so watch him. He's very subtle about it. We're just going over to the shopping center. I think Lizzie's going with you. If you have any trouble call Mrs. Wilson. She's home, isn't she, Pete?" Pete nodded. "And remember to check James's diaper. I just changed it, but that doesn't mean anything."

James had been toilet-trained before he stopped talking, but he wasn't anymore. He was back in diapers.

"Oh, and Jonno—" my mother started to say.

"Mom," I broke in, "we'll take care of him. Everything will be O.K."

She smiled at me. "I know. O.K. Thanks, kids. Mr. Peterson and I appreciate this."

We waved good-bye, and Dad backed the car out of the driveway.

Pete and I each took one of James's hands, and Lizzie got her red bike out of the garage. We walked slowly down the driveway and turned onto the sidewalk. James was trying to twist his hands out of ours and was weee-ooohing softly.

Lizzie caught up with us and rode slowly ahead while Pete and I struggled along with James. After a while, James calmed down a little. Pete and I discussed Time-Savers, and James hummed to himself and made funny little clucking sounds with his tongue.

"Hurry up!" Lizzie yelled impatiently. She was about four phone poles ahead of us, circling her bike in the street.

"We're trying to," I yelled back. "And get out of the middle of the road."

Lizzie coasted to the curb and rode on so slowly her bike teetered from side to side.

Finally we reached the playground. Even though the weather wasn't too great, a big bunch of kids were playing there, maybe twenty or so from the neighborhood, laughing and shouting, swinging, climbing on the monkey bars, riding the merry-go-round, hanging upside down on the jungle gym.

Lizzie parked her bike in a hurry and ran to the jungle gym, her favorite thing on the whole playground. Pete and I took James over to a swing and sat him on it. Pete pushed him and I stood in front of him, trying to get him to smile each time he swung toward me, but his face was solemn. He wasn't even looking at me. A couple of times he shouted "Weee-oooh!"

and flapped one of his hands vigorously. Three little kids in the sandbox watched him, looked at each other, and began to giggle.

"O.K., James, that's it for now," I said casually, grabbing his feet as he came forward, and easing him to a stop.

We took him to the slide next, pushed him down a few times, then played with him on the seesaw. By the time we sat him on the merry-go-round, he was getting antsy and whiny. When he began squirming tensely, I knew it was time to leave.

"We'd better go home," I said to Pete. "Where's Lizzie?"

We turned to scan the playground—and when we turned back, James was gone.

"Pete!" I shouted. "Where is he?"

We looked around frantically.

"I don't see him!" I said, shouting again, panic rising in me.

"Now just keep cool, Mac. There's Lizzie, still on the jungle gym. I'll go get her, and the three of us will spread out and look for James."

"O.K.," I said.

Pete ran off. The jungle gym was clear on the other side of the playground.

I stood where I was and started searching with my eyes. I climbed up on the merry-go-round for a little added height and looked at all the kids on the swings, the slide, the monkey bars, and in the sandbox.

No James.

Then I noticed a little crowd gathered near the drinking fountain. Something told me to go investigate, even though I knew I was supposed to wait for Pete and Lizzie.

I tore over to the crowd. Before I reached it, I heard one little kid shout gleefully, "Ew! He's eating gravel. Gross!"

Another one giggled and said, "He's taking his pants off!"

James. Darn him.

All the kids were laughing and pointing.

Making fun of James.

I barged through the crowd, not sure what I was going to do.

There was James in the middle of a full-blown temper tantrum. His face was red from screaming, and he was making a funny noise that sounded like a goose honking. But worst of all, he'd somehow taken off his clothes right down to his diaper. Don't ask me how, when he won't dress himself for anything.

I stood glaring at all those giggling, pointing kids and felt I should yell at them—or do something. They were giggling at *me* now, as much as at James. But I couldn't say a thing. I couldn't open my mouth.

Maybe my glaring was enough, though. Suddenly I realized the kids were quiet. Not one of them said a word. They didn't apologize or offer to help me, but they had stopped giggling. They watched me silently. A couple of the kids in back drifted away.

I turned to James, angry at him, angry at the kids, angry at myself, and grabbed his arm, jerking it into the sleeve of his shirt. For just a second he looked surprised and hurt. Then his eyes glazed over and he weee-ooohed softly. It was almost a moan.

I finished dressing him as fast as I could, marched him past the few remaining children, and ran directly into Pete and Lizzie.

"Where were you?" Pete demanded accusingly.

Lizzie looked troubled and began to edge away from us.

"It doesn't matter," I said through clenched teeth. "I found

James, didn't I? Let's get out of here."

Lizzie and Pete knew something was wrong, but they didn't ask any questions. Lizzie just made a beeline for her bike and sped home ahead of us.

Pete and I were silent on the way back, and I was grateful for that. I knew we weren't really mad at each other and that we'd patch things up later.

As for James, I could have clobbered him. I'd never been so embarrassed in my life. But clobbering him wouldn't have done much good.

James didn't understand anything.

6. Monkey-in-the-Middle

On Monday morning, Termite and Pete and I were sitting around on the desks in our classroom as usual. Most of the kids in the class had already arrived. Elise and the gang were in, and so were Steph and Claud. For some odd reason all the in-boys were missing. Edweird hadn't arrived yet, but he didn't usually get in until right before the second bell.

Pete and Termite and I were talking about Time-Savers, trying to figure out what to do if one of us started getting more jobs than the others, when suddenly there was this commotion in the front of the room. Termite stopped talking, and the three of us looked up to see Chris, Alan, Hank, and Dave standing in a row by Mr. Westoff's desk. Alan was holding a piece of paper, and the four of them were reading aloud from it in unison, like they were reciting a poem or something.

"Baby-sitting," they were saying, "pet-sitting, cleaning, gardening, window washing, lawn mowing..."

The list went on and on. Our list.

They had one of our Time-Savers fliers. And they were making it sound really dumb and babyish. Elise, Janie, Louise, and Margaret were practically rolling in the aisles.

The boys started this stupid play.

"Oh, Mr. Giancossi," Hank said, "I'll do anything for you. Anything at all."

"O.K., Jonathan," said Chris to Hank, and I could feel my face burning. "I need someone to clean out our sewer, but I can only pay ten cents an hour."

"Oh, that's fine, sir, just fine," said Hank in this squeaky voice. He made me sound like a girl.

Then they went back to reading the rest of our ad, complete with our names and phone numbers.

Everyone was laughing. Even Steph and Claud looked like they were going to break down any minute. I couldn't blame them.

Just as the boys started reading the last line, Pete jumped off his desk and ran to Alan. "Give me that!" he shouted, grabbing for the paper.

Alan swiped it out of his reach, crumpled it up, and tossed it to Dave, who had run to the other side of the room.

Pete ran to Dave, his face beet-red. "I said give me that!" Dave tossed it to Chris.

It was monkey-in-the-middle, and Pete was the monkey.

"Forget it, Pete," Termite was saying.

I sat down on my chair. I couldn't look at anybody.

Pete gave up and came back to us. None of us said a word. But I felt better when Steph and Claud wandered over and Claud said, "I bet they're just jealous because they didn't have a good idea like that."

I knew it wasn't true, but it was nice of her to say it.

Then suddenly the room went dead-silent. I looked up, expecting to see the vice-principal in the doorway. Instead I saw Edweird. So did everybody else. We were all staring.

Edweird was decked out in a red-and-white checked shirt,

huge blue jeans, a beaded belt, cowboy boots, and a cowboy hat.

For just a few seconds, our whole class was frozen. Nobody spoke or moved.

"Howdy, podners," said Edweird into the silence.

Oh, Edweird, I thought. Now you've done it.

Alan was the first to unfreeze. He snorted. "Howdy," he said sarcastically.

Edweird hooked his thumbs in his jeans pockets. "Flew to a ranch this weekend," he drawled. It was a pretty good drawl, but no one seemed too impressed. "My uncle's," he went on.

"Rope any cows?" asked Chris, with barely concealed hysteria.

The class was ready to explode with laughter. I could feel it. It was like pressure building, but everyone was hanging on longer than usual. I think we were all remembering Mr. West-off's talk last Monday. We knew Chris wasn't supposed to be teasing Edweird, and we knew we shouldn't laugh at him. Mr. Westoff had explained that Edweird wasn't retarded but that he had severe emotional problems. The problems kept him from doing well in school, and they made him act different. He didn't know how to behave around people, and he didn't know how to make friends. So we were supposed to be nice to him. Especially since he'd just moved to our town and this was the first time he was trying out a regular classroom, and the teachers and school officials and especially Edweird wanted it to work.

So we were holding in the laughter. Most of us, at any rate. I heard a few giggles leaking from Janie and Louise.

And then Dave, forgetting everything, came out and said how could Edweird have ridden a horse, he was so fat. The rest of the laughter escaped at last.

Even my own. Even when I saw Edweird's hurt, stunned face as he hung his head and sat down at his desk.

And, I suppose, in order to worm my way back into Chris's good graces after the Time-Savers thing, I said that probably the only horse Edweird could ride was on a merry-go-round.

A couple of minutes later, the first bell rang. Termite made a beeline for his classroom, and Mr. Westoff came in. We weren't much noisier than usual by that time, and he never knew what had happened. He just shot Edweird a curious look when he headed for the Resource Room in his cowboy suit.

All day in school I felt pretty bad about what we'd done to Edweird (and about what the in-kids had done to Termite and Pete and me), but I forgot about everything as soon as I got home.

This was because I heard from the E-Z Seed Company. I opened the letter fast, wondering where the seeds were.

The letter said:

> Dear Mr. Peterson:
> The E-Z Seed Company is pleased that you want to join its nationwide sales force. At the moment we are processing your application. Within several days you will receive 300 packages of vegetable and flower seeds, and complete instructions for proceeding with the venture.
> Congratulations, Mr. Peterson!
> Yours truly,
> Melvin Chamberlain
> President, E-Z Seed Company

I read the letter over a few times.

Wow! *Mr*. Peterson, venture, sales force, nationwise, president. This must be something really big.

I'd just gotten to "proceeding with the venture" for the fourth time when—*CRASH*. A huge thump came from upstairs, followed by the sound of glass breaking, by one of James's more angry shrieks, and by my mother shouting, "James! Bad boy!" She sounded pretty angry herself.

I raced upstairs in time to see James galloping down the hallway toward his room. He was hopping-mad about something. He kept screaming over and over again, not even weee-ooohing, just screaming.

As I reached the top step, Mom bolted out of the bathroom in pursuit of James, hesitated briefly when she saw me, and then continued down the hall.

"What's going on?" I shouted. I tore after them.

I reached James's room and found him throwing a temper tantrum. He was jumping up and down, screaming to beat the band, and hitting his face with his fists.

Mom seemed paralyzed by the whole thing, so I dashed in and grabbed James's fists. The last time he hit himself like this, he left bruises all over his face. He even gave himself a black eye.

James screamed louder when I grabbed him, but I didn't let go. I just stood there and held his hands. Finally he wore himself out. The screaming and jumping stopped and he was still, gazing up at the ceiling light. Very slowly I loosened my grip and let go of his hands. They were limp. He sank down to the floor, lost in his own world.

I turned around to see Mom leaning against the doorjamb, crying silently. The tears were running down her cheeks, and she wasn't trying to stop them. She reminded me of a battery that had worn out. Suddenly she didn't have the energy to react to anything. It was as if James had finally gotten the best of her.

"What happened?" I asked. I was shaking. James scares me

to death when he does that. He acts like a little wild animal.

"Oh," said Mom, tiredly, "he was in the bathroom spinning pennies—don't ask me why; he hasn't done that in weeks, but he's been doing it all day today—and I went in to change his diaper. As soon as I touched him, he got angry. He jumped up, knocked over the wastebasket, grabbed it, and threw it. It broke the mirror."

Mom sounded so tired.

"I really don't know," she said finally, wiping the tears away, "how much more of this I can take."

We tiptoed out of James's room, hoping he'd stay quiet in there for a while.

"Mom;" I said, "why don't you call the school? Maybe they'll have some suggestions or something."

"I guess. All right. Thanks, Jonno," she said. "I'm going to go in the bedroom to make the call, and then I don't want to be disturbed for a while, O.K.?"

"O.K. I'll tell Lizzie when she gets home."

Mom closed the bedroom door softly.

I went back to James's room and looked in. He was sitting cross-legged on the floor where we'd left him. He was rocking back and forth, saying a brand-new sound over and over again. "Oh-*ma,* oh-*ma,* oh-*ma.*"

I wondered if I'd ever know what he meant.

7. Good News

I locked James in his room and considered cleaning up the mess in the bathroom, but decided maybe Dad could do it for once. I didn't see why I should get stuck with so many of James's messes.

Then I went downstairs to start my homework. Mr. Westoff had been pretty easy on us. I only had two pages of math review to do. I finished them just as Lizzie got home.

"Hi," I said as she came in the door. "Where've you been?"

"I stayed late to get some help from my art teacher."

"Art teacher? Help with what?"

"Can't tell you." Lizzie crossed her arms and smiled at me. She was being smug again.

"Come on."

"Nope."

"Well, want to come outside with me? I just finished my homework." Lizzie hardly ever had any.

"Nope," she said again. "I have to go work on something."

I looked at her suspiciously. "Well, be quiet upstairs. Mom's resting. . . . But everything's O.K.," I added quickly.

"Where's James?" she asked.

"In his room. But I think I'll go get him and take him outside."

So I did, and he was much calmer. We fooled around in the front yard. In a little while Pete came over, and we tried to teach James to catch the basketball, but it was hopeless. James darted all over the place, never looking at us or the ball, so of course he couldn't catch it. Finally Pete and I got silly. We were lying on the grass laughing when Mom and Lizzie came out and sat on the front porch.

Mom looked terrific, considering. She was smiling and didn't seem at all tired. That nap or whatever had worked wonders. I guess we all had a little spring fever because suddenly we were in good moods.

Then Dad got home early, which put us in an even better mood. He never comes home early.

"Dad!" I cried as he was parking the car. "What's going on?"

"What do you mean?" he asked cheerfully, easing himself out from behind the steering wheel. "It's a beautiful spring day, that's all." He slammed the door shut.

Mrs. Wilson called Pete in then.

"See you," I yelled to him as he ran home.

Dad strode across the front lawn, kissed Mom and Lizzie, and patted James on the head.

James ducked away from him and squealed, "Oh-*ma.*"

"Where'd *that* come from?" asked my father. "I never heard that before."

"Who knows?" I said. "It's new."

"Funny," said Dad.

"Well, let's all go in and have dinner," suggested Mom.

With everybody (everybody except James, of course) working happily, we threw together a gigantic chef's salad in record time. Mom heated up a quiche in the oven.

We sat at the table and were about to start dishing out the food when Mom said, "Let's say grace."

We don't say grace too often. We're not very religious. We don't even go to church. But every now and then we give thanks for what we have. We have our own way of doing it. First we join hands.

"O.K., Dad, you start," I said. We always start with the oldest in the family.

"I want to give thanks for this beautiful day, and for my family, whom I love very much." He smiled across the table at my mother. "I'm thankful we're here together."

Mom was next. "I want to give thanks for some wonderful news I received this afternoon. I'll tell you about it after grace."

"Oh, no fair!" groaned Lizzie. "I can't wait."

"My lips are sealed," Mom said, grinning. "O.K., Jonno. Now you."

I thought a minute. "I'm thankful for my family and my friends, and I'm thankful it's baseball season."

Lizzie's turn. "I'm thankful for my friends, too," she said. I wondered what she meant, considering she hardly had any friends.

"Oh-*ma*," cried James suddenly. We looked at him almost as if we expected *him* to give thanks.

Mom cleared her throat. "Well," she said, "my good news concerns James."

Dad started serving the quiche and salad and passing around the plates. "James?" he asked Mom. "What is it?"

"Well, we had a little scene with him this afternoon. By-the-way-the-bathroom-mirror-is-broken-and-we'll-have-to-re-place-it," she said in a rush, getting that part over with quickly, before Dad could get angry. "So I called Dr. Wyman, the director of the Weston Child Development Institute, and explained that James was getting out of hand, and guess what he said."

"What?" we all asked, leaning toward her.

"That starting Monday James can go to school for half days—"

"Yay!" I cheered.

"—and that by mid-April they'll have an opening and he can go for full days."

"Hey, that's really something to celebrate," said Dad. "Just a second." He jumped up, went into the kitchen, and came back with a bottle of wine and two wineglasses.

He and Mom toasted each other and James and his future.

During dinner, Mom explained some stuff to us. It turned out we were all going to be involved in James's program. Lizzie didn't look too happy about this.

"How do you mean?" I asked.

"Yeah," said Lizzie, "how do you mean?"

"Now, just a second," said Mom. "I don't like the tone of your voices. I know that having a brother like James makes great demands on you two, but if we want to help him, we're going to have to do our parts. James can't do it alone, or even with just his teacher's help. He's a little boy, and he needs us."

I looked over at James, who, for the moment, was solemnly eating a bagel without ever looking at it. He was peaceful now, but I knew it wouldn't last. He sat and hummed, gazing off somewhere, far away from the dining room. It had been a few days since we'd tried to force anything healthy down him, which I knew wasn't good. We were starting to give up. I knew he needed the school; I just hadn't counted on having much to do with it.

"Of course," my mother continued, "I can't force you to

help James, but the more help he gets, the faster he'll change. So before you decide not to help, why don't I tell you what it will involve."

"O.K.," Lizzie and I said hesitantly.

James screamed suddenly, threw down his bagel, and tried to struggle out of his highchair.

"You might find it interesting," put in Dad, unbuckling James and letting him go. "When your mother and I first spoke to Dr. Wyman, I was concerned about what he expected us to do at home, too, but when I understood how it all worked, I felt differently."

James ran over to a Lincoln Logs project in the living room.

"What we'll be most involved with," began my mother, "is making sure James keeps up at home the things he's learning in school."

"I don't get it," said Lizzie.

"Well, James's school is not like yours. You and Jonno learn reading and writing and math and spelling. But James has a lot to learn before he can ever *begin* those things. He has to learn to eat properly, to use the bathroom, to dress himself, to play, not to have tantrums, and most important, to talk. The school's going to start teaching him those things right away. And James is probably not going to like it one bit. Nobody likes to be asked to change. It would be just as if I got up one morning and said, 'Lizzie, from now on, you have to crawl on your hands and knees instead of walk, and Jonno, you're going to have to learn to eat cabbage three times a day.'"

"Ick," said Lizzie.

"Gross," said I.

"Now, James is going to think he only has to do these new things at school where he's learning them," continued Mom, "but we'll want him to do them at home, right?"

"Right."

"And that's why we'll have to pay close attention to what Dr. Wyman tells us. If we start getting lazy and letting him eat bagels sometimes or wear diapers sometimes, James will be confused. He won't know what we expect of him, and he'll think we're not serious about what we're teaching him—that eventually he can go back to the way he is now."

"Oh, I see," said Lizzie slowly.

"You mean we have to be consistent, right?" I asked.

"Exactly," said my mother, smiling.

We were quiet for a moment, thinking everything over.

"Mom, Dad," I said finally, "I'll help, I guess, but I have one question."

"Shoot," said Dad.

"What if James is happy the way he is now? Why should we decide to change him? Maybe it's not fair. Just like it wouldn't be fair if I did suddenly have to eat cabbage three times a day. I'm happy now. Why should anyone change me? It's my life and nobody else's."

Mom and Dad looked at each other, and at me. Lizzie eyed me from under the baseball cap, frowning.

"That's a very important question, Jonno," Mom said quietly. "And the only answer I have is that maybe it's *not* fair to ask James to change. Maybe we don't have the right. But if we have to continue the way we're living now, I don't think I can handle it. And the alternative would be to put James in an institution, because we can't afford a residential school for him the rest of his life. What it boils down to is either we ask James to change or we put him away."

We were quiet again for a few seconds.

Finally Lizzie let out a long sigh. "I always wanted to be a teacher," she said.

During the rest of dinner, Mom and Dad explained how we would be involved in James's schooling. Family members were encouraged to visit the school and watch James and his teachers as often as possible. Starting Monday, Mom would spend as many mornings there as she could, and Dad would try to get away from the office at least twice a week to do the same. They wanted Lizzie and me to visit, too, but not until our spring vacation, when we'd be out of school and James wouldn't.

Then Mom explained about home visits. "Dr. Wyman and one of James's teachers will come to our house in the evening now and then. They want to meet us—"

"Why?" interrupted Lizzie.

"I guess so they can understand James better. When somebody won't talk, you don't get to know much about him, and it's harder to help him. But if you meet the people in his family and see how he lives, then, well, you know him a little better."

"Also," said Dad, "they'll want to see if James's behavior at school is the same as it is at home. What if James doesn't have tantrums at school? Then Dr. Wyman will have to come here to see them. He can't help us handle them unless he sees them."

"And," said Mom, "when Dr. Wyman visits, we'll have time to ask all the questions we want. You and Lizzie, especially. It'll be a time to speak your minds, to say whether things about James's work are bothering you, or if you've noticed anything new he's doing, or if you want advice about how to handle him. Anything at all."

I was mulling all this over when the phone rang. "I'll get it!" I shouted, jumping up from the table and running into the kitchen.

"Hello?" I said when I'd picked up the receiver.

"Hello, I'd like to speak to Jonathan Peterson," said an unfamiliar voice. It sounded like a grown-up. A woman.

"This is Jonathan."

"Hi Jonathan. My name is Mrs. Rice. I live up on Random Road. I got your Time-Savers ad?" She made it a question.

"Oh, yes," I said. "Can I help you?" I tried to sound calm even though I was so excited, I had a whole fleet of butterflies in my stomach.

"Yes," she said, "I need someone to paint the fence around our garbage cans. It's not a very big fence. I think you could do it in an afternoon. Are you interested?"

"Sure! I can come tomorrow. Is tomorrow O.K.?"

"It's fine."

I got all the details about the time and the address, and then called Pete and gave him the good news. It turned out he'd gotten a Time-Savers call, too—from a very odd-sounding person who wanted him to clean out his sewers for ten cents an hour. It was Chris, of course. We grumbled to each other about it for a while.

By the time I got off the phone, dinner was over, and Dad and Lizzie were cleaning up. I went into the living room, expecting to find Mom reading to James, but James was alone, sitting on the floor. Only when I came in, he looked directly into my eyes. Then he stood up and walked over to me.

"Oh-*ma*," he said, putting his hand on my knee.

"James?" I asked.

I sat down on the couch and James sat next to me all by himself. I put my arm around him and we stayed quietly like that until I realized he was lost to the ceiling light again.

I pulled my arm away and called his name, but he didn't move.

James, I thought, I don't understand you at all.

8. E-Z Seeds

When I got home from school Thursday afternoon, Mom greeted me at the door with a big box. "Look what came in the mail for you today, sweetie. It's from the E-Z Seed Company."

"Oh, wow!" I cried. "That was fast! I can't believe it!"

"What was fast? What is it?" asked Mom.

We sat down at the kitchen table. I could see James in the living room hovering around a half-finished Lincoln Logs project.

"I'm going to sell seeds, Mom," I said. "I've got two ways to earn money now. Time-Savers and seed-selling."

"That's great, Jonno. I'm really proud of you."

On Tuesday I'd earned $3.75 painting Mrs. Rice's garbage can fence, and today I'd earn $10.00 selling eight packages of seeds, and then I'd have $13.75 toward the Starcruiser, which was more than one-fifth of the total price.

"How'd you get those seeds?" asked Mom curiously.

I told her how the E-Z Seed Company worked.

"Hmmm," was all she said.

"What is it? I can tell something's wrong." Sometimes Mom could spoil everything. She was such a worrier.

"Nothing," she said slowly.

"I'm going out right now," I said, leaping up and heading off with my box.

"Don't you want anything to eat?"

"No, thanks, I don't have time."

I took the box up to my room, tore it open, scanned the directions to make certain I knew what I was doing, dumped the seeds in a paper bag, and started off down our street.

The first house I went to was the Marshalls'. They are our next-door neighbors. It wasn't until I was walking up their front path that I began to wonder what I should say when somebody answered the door. Then I began hoping Taylor Marshall wouldn't answer the door. He was sixteen and this neat football player. Maybe he'd think seed-selling was babyish.

I almost turned away to go to another house, but I remembered the Starcruiser. Besides it was only a little after three o'clock. A high school football star would probably be out on the field, practicing dropkicks or something.

So I drew in a big breath and rang the bell.

Taylor answered it.

It never fails.

He must have been home sick, because he was wearing his robe and these old threadbare pajamas.

I'd probably gotten him out of bed for my dumb seeds.

"Hey, sport." He grinned. "What's doing?"

"Hi," I said weakly. "Is—um—is your mother home?"

"Nope. She's off driving Sam's piano lesson car pool. Can I give her a message?"

"Well..." I began. *Now* what was I supposed to do? Obviously I was there for a reason. "Well," I said again, stalling for time.

Taylor began to look a little impatient. "Yeah?"

I took the plunge. "I'm selling these seeds," I said as fast as possible, "and I was wondering if you wanted to buy any. They're from a very respectable place. But I can come back another time."

"That would probably be a good idea," said Taylor, and for some reason I felt relieved. "I don't know what Mom and Dad want to do. About gardens, I mean. Why don't you come back in an hour or so?"

"O.K. No problem." I backed down the steps, shouted "Thanks," and ran across the side lawn to the Franklins' house.

Mr. and Mrs. Franklin are real old and very nice, even if they are a little deaf. I rang the bell and waited forever. Just as I was about to give up, Mr. Franklin opened the door.

"Hi, there!" he said in this loud, hearty voice, but he didn't fool me. I knew perfectly well he didn't have the vaguest idea who I was.

"Hi, Mr. Franklin," I yelled, hoping his hearing aid was connected. *"I'm selling seeds."*

"You're collecting weeds? What is it, a science project or something? Well, my goodness, there are enough weeds out there to eat a horse." (Mr. Franklin sometimes gets his words mixed up.) "Go on. Take whatever you need." He gestured out across his front lawn.

"No, Mr. Franklin," I shouted. *"I'm SELLING SEEDS."* I opened the bag and showed him the packages. *"Do you want to buy any?"*

"Selling them, are you?" he asked.

I nodded.

"Well, let's have a look. Come on inside, son."

I followed him into the living room. It was dark and smelled funny. Sort of like lavender and spices and perfume all mixed up. I wondered how you could live with a smell like that. Maybe the Franklins' hearing wasn't the only thing that was fading. I tried to breathe through my mouth.

Mrs. Franklin was sitting in the living room reading. When she saw me, she took off her glasses and folded them neatly in her lap.

"Hello there, Jonathan," she said in her quiet voice.

"Hi, Mrs. Franklin."

"This young man is selling seeds, Mother," said Mr. Franklin.

"He's felling trees?"

"No, he's *selling seeds*."

I'd tell you the rest of the conversation, but it went on like that forever.

By the time I left the Franklins' it was almost four o'clock, and I'd sold them exactly one package of seeds.

Petunias.

In my pocket was fifty cents.

I got to keep twelve-and-a-half cents of it.

I had a long, long, long way to go before I hit ten dollars.

However, maybe the Franklins were unusual. And after all, I could still go back to the Marshalls'. Later. If felt like it.

The house next door to the Franklins' was the Steinwicks'. As in Alan Steinwick. No way was I going in there. I didn't want to go through the Time-Savers routine again with the in-boys. I didn't even dare to cut across Alan's front lawn. I detoured down to the sidewalk and made my way to the Valentines' house.

I rang the bell. No answer.

I went on to the Cornwalls'. Mrs. Cornwall said that no, thank you, she most certainly did not care to buy any seeds. And that was that.

I checked my watch: 4:10.

I pressed on.

I didn't know the people next to the Cornwalls, but it didn't matter. A woman answered the door and was delighted to see a seed-seller standing on her front stoop.

"This is perfect!" she cried. "I was just planning my vegetable garden. Do you have carrot seeds?"

I nodded.

"Green peppers?"

I nodded.

"Corn?"

I nodded.

I had everything she wanted. In the end she bought ten packets. Five dollars, and I got to keep a dollar twenty-five. That was more like it!

At the next two houses nobody was home.

I'd reached the end of our street. It was time to hit the homes on the other side.

I rang the door at the Phomalonts'. Dr. Phomalont is my doctor. Her husband answered the door.

"Well, Jonathan! Nice to see you!"

"Hi, Mr. Phomalont," I said smiling. I like him a lot.

"I'm selling seeds," I said, suddenly feeling sort of important.

"Well, now, what have you got?"

I showed him. He bought five packages of flower seeds. He was very nice about it, but I had the funny feeling he didn't *really* need them. Not like the lady who wanted the vegetables. I headed next door, to the Jordans.

Since both Mr. and Mrs. Jordan work, a maid comes in to take care of their three children. Her name is Rosa. She doesn't speak a whole lot of English.

When I rang the doorbell, I could hear some yelling going on inside, and a stampede to get to the door.

"I'll get it!" called a high little voice.

"No, I'll get it!"

"No, I'll—"

Thump, crash. I think there was a pile-up on the other side of the door.

Then a very firm voice said, "No, *I* get it." That was Rosa. The door opened about a quarter of an inch.

"Hello?" I said.

"Hello?" said Rosa.

"Hello, my name is Jonathan Eckhardt Peterson, and I'm selling seeds. I was wondering if—"

"Hello?"

I started over again.

"Let *me* see, Rosie," came an impatient voice. The door jerked open a few inches. "What are you selling?" It was Teddy, the oldest of the kids. He was James's age and talking in sentences and everything.

"Seeds, Teddy," I said. "Want to see?"

Teddy squirmed his way between Rosa and the door.

"What? What you sell? You sell something?" asked Rosa suspiciously. She elbowed herself in front of Teddy. Teddy dropped to his hands and knees and tried to crawl out.

I began to feel fidgety. I reached into my bag and pulled out a handful of seed packets, starting in on my little talk again.

But before I got halfway through, Rosa suddenly cried, "No! No selling! No selling! Good-bye!" She slammed the door.

I gave up and went home. It was growing dark anyway.

I must have looked pretty discouraged when I entered our house.

Mom, James, and Lizzie were all sitting around in the living room.

"What hap— How did you do, dear?" asked Mom carefully, as I plopped down on the floor next to Lizzie.

"Well . . . not great and not bad. But I'm already running

out of houses to go to. I mean, there're only a few more streets in this neighborhood, and I didn't make that much money today. Nowhere near the ten dollars I was expecting to earn. I don't know if it's worth it. Plus, I get the feeling some people don't like salesmen at their doors."

"I'll buy some seeds," said Lizzie. Mom must have explained my project to her.

"Thanks," I said, "but you have to save your money. It's O.K., anyway. I think I'm finished with E-Z Seeds."

"Listen, Jonno, before I forget," said Mom. "Pete called a few minutes ago. He wants you to call back. He sounded excited."

"Oh, good," I said without any enthusiasm, and headed for the phone. I dialed his number. "Pete? It's me."

"Mac! Great news! A Time-Saver job. Get this. Mrs. Schwartz on Overbrook Drive called a little while ago, and she needs two baby-sitters for all Saturday afternoon. She'll pay us *each* a dollar fifty an hour. That's seven fifty apiece! Termite's gonna be away this weekend, so do you want to take the job with me?"

"Sure!" I cried.

"Good. We have to be there at one o'clock sharp. Meet me at my house at twelve forty-five and we'll walk over together."

"O.K. . . . . Pete?"

"Yeah?"

"How come the Schwartzes need *two* baby-sitters?"

There was a pause at Pete's end. A loud pause, if you know what I mean.

"Well," he said at last, "because there're going to be eight children to take care of."

I almost dropped the receiver. *"Eight?* But the Schwartzes only have four."

"I know. Their cousins will be visiting."

"Aw, Pete."

"Listen, it's only five hours. And it's seven fifty. You can handle it, can't you?"

"Sure. I guess so."

But I wasn't sure at all.

9. The Baby-sitting Disaster

That Thursday was the end of my E-Z seed-selling. It hadn't been E-Z at all. I figured I earned more money per hour on Time-Savers jobs, and didn't risk angry maids yelling at me either. So I took the 278 leftover seed packs, and the $8.25 the E-Z people earned from the $11.00, and wrapped them up to return to the company.

Mom came into my room as I was finishing. "The seeds?" she asked, watching me write out the label.

"Yeah."

"I wanted to tell you this afternoon that those mail order moneymaking businesses are usually not as profitable or as easy to carry out as they're advertised. But I thought you should have the chance to find out for yourself. Who knows? You might have been a supersalesman."

I smiled at her. "The ad made it sound so terrific. It said you could earn as much as ten dollars a day. They shouldn't be allowed to lie like that."

"Well, unfortunately, they weren't lying. The key words in that ad are *could*—that only means *might*— and *as much as*— that only means anything *up to* ten dollars. You just have to

61

learn to watch out for things like that. Adults get misled by advertisements, too. I'm sorry you had to learn this lesson the hard way, but it wasn't all bad. At least you earned a little money. Now you can forget about the whole thing."

"Yeah," I said again.

Mom watched me finish the label and paste it on the box. "I'll take that to the post office for you tomorrow."

"Thanks," I said. "I don't ever want to see another E-Z seed as long as I live."

Mom grinned at me. "Precisely how I feel about Crack-up Crackers."

"About what?"

"Crack-up Crackers—a joke in every box. I spent all afternoon writing ads for them. You should hear the jokes. They're terrible."

"Like what?"

"What's big and red and eats rocks?"

"I give up."

"A big, red rock-eater."

"Yeah?"

"That's it. A big, red rock-eater."

"That's it? That's the joke?"

"Mm-hmmm." Mom was hiding a smile.

"Sheesh."

We both burst out laughing.

On Saturday I turned up at Pete's at exactly twelve forty-five. He came out the front door before I could even ring the bell.

"Ready?" he asked.

"I hope so."

Mrs. Schwartz seemed awfully glad to see us. We were five

minutes early. "Thank goodness you're here so soon," she exclaimed.

I glanced nervously at Pete. That was not a good sign.

She let us in. The place was a madhouse. People everywhere, but mostly in the living room. There were Mr. and Mrs. Schwartz, their four kids, the four cousins, and their four parents, plus a few more stray aunts and uncles, a grandmother, I think, and Woof, the Schwartz's sheepdog. While Pete and I tried to take all this in, Mrs. Schwartz began the introductions.

"You already know Polly, Andy, Frankie, and Lissa," she said, pointing out the four Schwartzes. Those she could find, at any rate. She couldn't see Andy and Lissa, but it didn't matter because I could. They were wearing pig hats and were tearing up the stairs to the second floor, oinking and grunting and slurping.

Then she pointed out the youngest of the whole crowd—a chubby baby seated on the floor. He didn't look like he could walk yet, thank goodness.

"That's Joey," she said. "And don't worry about him at all. He's due for a nap any minute. He'll sleep all afternoon. He's Mr. Schwartz's brother's baby. The other three, Mr. Schwartz's other brother's children, are Cindy"—she pointed to a little girl about two years old—"Michael"—she pointed to a boy about James's age who had just dumped all the pieces to six jigsaw puzzles in one large heap on the floor—"and Adrienne"—she pointed to a girl Lizzie's age who was playing with little Joey. Adrienne looked like she was the oldest of the passle of kids.

At that moment Woof, who had been hanging around in the kitchen, hiding out from the chaos, came bounding into the living room, whuffling and whining.

"And that's Woof," added Mrs. Schwartz. "He wants his kibbles. I'll feed him before we leave. By the way, Adrienne's cat, Persephone, is here, locked up in Polly and Lissa's room. And Marco Polo, Mrs. Divine's"—here Mrs. Schwartz indicated the grandmother-person—"cocker spaniel, is locked up in the laundry room. All the pets have to be kept separate. They don't know each other and won't get along. Oh, but don't worry about Persephone or Marco Polo. They don't have to be fed or anything. Just don't let them out."

Mrs. Schwartz went on a mile a minute. My head was swimming. Even Pete was looking slightly nervous.

It turned out the adults were going to a wedding. While they were gone we were supposed to:

> Entertain Adrienne (8), Polly (7), Andy (5), Michael (5), Lissa (4), Cindy (2), and Frankie (2).
> Joey, apparently, really was going to nap—but until six o'clock? At any rate he had been put in Frankie's crib and was quiet.
> Keep the pets separated.
> Give the seven older kids a snack at three o'clock.

Mrs. Schwartz had left a long list of emergency numbers and told us the next-door neighbors would be home all afternoon. She'd also left out a can of Hawaiian Punch and a box of Ritz Crackers for the three-o'clock snack.

I breathed a sigh of relief when the wedding posse took off. Even though it meant Pete and I were left alone with all the kids, it cut the number of people in the house down by eleven.

As soon as the adults got out the front door, Cindy and Frankie started crying. Loudly.

"I want Mommy," they wailed in unison.

I looked at Pete. I hadn't encountered too much of this sort of thing. I don't think he had either.

Luckily for us, Adrienne came to the rescue. She carried a big Oscar the Grouch hand puppet over to them.

"Lookit this, Cindy. Look, Frankie. I'm Oscar the Grouch. Here's my garbage can." She stuck her hand in back of a wastebasket.

Cindy and Frankie looked pretty interested. Even so, they let their wails drag on awhile, like they didn't want to let go of them.

I checked out Michael, Polly, Andy, and Lissa on the other side of the living room. They were sitting around trying to straighten out Michael's jigsaw puzzle mess.

Well, was this it? Was this baby-sitting? It seemed so easy. Joey was asleep, four of the kids were entertaining each other, and Adrienne was entertaining two others. There wasn't even anything for Pete and me to do. Taking care of James was harder than this.

So I sat down with Adrienne and the little kids, and Pete sat down with the others, and we all played quietly until almost three o'clock.

Then we trooped into the kitchen for juice and crackers. There were no squabbles. Nobody even spilled anything. I couldn't believe it. Why are adults always complaining about how hard it is to be a parent?

I don't know exactly when Pete and I made our mistake. It may have been when we suggested that everybody play outside. The Schwartzes have a big fenced-in backyard with swings and monkey bars and a jungle gym. Lizzie would have loved it. But when we made the suggestion we got a chorus of no's.

Probably we should've left well enough alone, not pressed our luck. But to be honest, Pete and I were bored stiff with puzzles and Oscar the Grouch stories.

"Oh, come on," said Pete cheerfully. "I'll race everybody. Bet I can beat you all outside."

That did it.

I was almost trampled.

There was this explosion of energy, and seven small bodies, one larger one, and one shaggy, four-footed one scrambled and crashed down a flight of steps and out the back door.

I stood in the empty living room and listened.

Sure enough, Joey began to cry. I tiptoed upstairs, but just as I reached the top step, the crying stopped. I stood still, listening and counting. When I didn't hear a sound for twenty seconds, I turned around and went back downstairs and outside.

In the backyard the kids had gone wild. They were whooping and screeching and chasing each other. Woof was right in the middle of everything, leaping up and down. Pete looked desperate.

"Hey!" I shouted. "Hey!"

Nobody stopped, but Polly yelled back, "What?"

"Come here, everybody!"

"Why?"

"We're going to play Duck, Duck, Goose."

"Are you kidding?" yelped Adrienne. "Yuck. That's for babies."

"What's Duck, Duck, Goose?" asked Lissa.

Pete and I looked at each other and shrugged. I thought kids were born knowing how to play Duck, Duck, Goose.

"Forget it," I said.

They forgot. Cindy and Frankie climbed onto swings, and Pete and I pushed them while the older kids got in a huddle as far away from us as possible.

I nudged Pete. "Hey," I whispered. "Look at that."

Pete glanced over at the huddle and then back at me. "Yeah? So?"

"It looks suspicious. It looks like a plot."

"Geez, Mac, they're only little kids."

I didn't say anything.

In a minute or two, Polly left the huddle and came skipping over to us. "Want to play hide-and-seek?" she asked sweetly. She took Pete's hand. "Please, Pete?"

Pete smiled over at me as if to say, "Now isn't this nice? The children want to play a game after all. And you thought they were plotting. . . ."

I shot Pete this smirk that I save for very rare occasions.

"Sure," Pete said, letting Polly lead him away.

"All right," I said reluctantly. I helped Cindy and Frankie off the swings. "You can play, too," I told them. "You can team up with Adrienne and Polly."

I trotted them over to the rest of the kids. Adrienne was giving directions.

"O.K., the person who's it goes in the toolshed and counts to a hundred." She pointed to a back corner of the yard where a brown wooden shed was partly hidden by some tall grass and a rhododendron bush.

"Why the toolshed?" I asked suspiciously.

Pete kicked my ankle and I kicked him back. He wasn't used to younger kids the way I was. I remembered the day Lizzie was so sweet to me because she'd left a dead garter snake in my bed.

"Why the toolshed?" repeated Adrienne slightly nervously. "Oh, just because . . . because then we don't have to worry about anyone peeking. You can't see out of the shed if the door's closed."

"Oh, all right," I sighed.

Something was going on.

"I'll be first," cried Adrienne.

"Take Cindy with you," I said. "You can be a team. And Polly, you be a team with Frankie."

"I'll count to fifty," Adrienne called, and opened the door.

Cindy just stood there.

"Go on, Cindy," said Adrienne.

Cindy shook her head.

"Yes," insisted Adrienne.

Cindy shook harder. "No. Not in the dark."

"I'll take her," I said. Anything to prevent tears. I wanted everyone to look happy when the mommies and daddies came back.

So Adrienne went in the shed and the rest of us scattered, looking for hiding spots. It wasn't easy finding one I could get Cindy in, as well. The little cousins seemed to know the yard inside out and scrambled up trees, under bushes, behind benches. By the time Adrienne burst through the door, Pete and Cindy and I were still standing around like a bunch of fools.

"You're it!" shouted Adrienne gleefully. "All-y-all-y in free!"

Everybody tumbled out of their hiding places and gathered around Adrienne, who was having a fit of giggles. "Pete and Jon couldn't even find places!" she managed to squeal. "Hee hee hee. They were standing right where I left them. Hee hee hee. Now they're it!"

"O.K., O.K.," I said crossly. "So we don't know the yard too well. Here, Adrienne. Take Cindy. *You* try finding a place big enough for two."

"I know lots," she said maddeningly, still laughing. "O.K., hee hee, now you two go in the shed."

"Sure, sure," said Pete. "Come on, Mac."

"I'll go with you," said Adrienne.

"You don't have to," I said.

But she came anyway, waited until Pete and I were well inside, and closed the door on us.

Then I heard a click. It sounded an awful lot like a lock turning. I rushed over to the door, grabbed the knob, and turned. Nothing. I shook the door. "Adrienne!" I yelled at the top of my lungs. "Open this door!"

"Hee hee hee."

"Geez, Pete, we're locked in. Do you believe it? This is the end of everything—Time-Savers, our reputations, everything. How will we live this down? Wait till Alan and Chris and everyone hear about this."

"Will you shut up?" he hissed. "They'll never hear about it. And Adrienne'll only leave us here longer if she thinks she's upset us. Just be quiet. Then it won't be any fun for her and she'll let us out."

So we waited. And waited. The shed was pitch-black. There was no window, and you couldn't see a thing. It wasn't any too warm either. Pete and I didn't speak. I hoped he'd learned some kind of lesson.

I don't know how long we sat in there, since of course I couldn't see my watch, but it felt like about an hour or so. We couldn't hear a sound. I was positive that by now the kids had let Persephone and Marco Polo out, that Joey was awake and crying, that Frankie and Cindy were playing with the stove, and that all the rest of the kids had been arrested for creating disturbances and had been carted down to the police station and would have to be claimed there by the Schwartzes. I wondered if baby-sitters still got paid when that happened.

At long last I heard another click in the doorknob. I jumped up. "Adrienne, you little—" Suddenly I froze in my tracks.

The door-opener was not Adrienne.

It was Mrs. Schwartz.

I gulped.

Pete jumped to his feet, too. He was standing so close to me I could feel his breath on my neck.

"Well, boys," began Mrs. Schwartz.

I hung my head and began to dream up the most apologetic story possible.

"I see Adrienne has played one of her little tricks on you. My niece has quite a sense of . . . of humor."

Pete and I stepped out of the shed and followed Mrs. Schwartz across the lawn and into the house.

"I hope you're not too upset," she went on.

I wasn't sure what to say, so I didn't say anything. Neither did Pete. I felt awfully uncomfortable. Especially when I heard a muffled "hee hee hee" close by.

"Maybe I should have warned you," Mrs. Schwartz continued. "Adrienne is . . . can be . . ."

At that point all I wanted was to leave. I cleared my throat. "Mrs. Schwartz—"

"Please," she interrupted. "All right. I know you're upset. But look, nothing happened. All the children are fine. They were playing safely indoors when we got home. I'm terribly sorry you were locked in the shed, but how about if I pay you each ten dollars? Will that make up for it?"

She stuffed a ten-dollar bill into each of our jacket pockets and hurried us toward the front door.

"Good-bye," she said as we stumbled onto the porch. "Thank you. I hope you'll come back and sit for us again soon."

"Fat chance," Pete mumbled.

"'Bye, Mrs. Schwartz," I called loudly.

"Sit for her again? Is she crazy?" Pete exploded as soon as we were out of hearing range.

Pete had been very quiet ever since Adrienne locked us in. I guess he'd been building up steam all that time.

"Come on, Pete, it wasn't *so* bad. I mean, look—we earned *ten dollars* each."

"Yeah." He grinned at me.

We walked home slowly. It was growing dark. Front-porch lights and bedroom lights and living-room lights were being flicked on. We passed the Dodsons' house as Mrs. Dodson leaned out the door to whistle Nescafé in. Then we passed the Meiers' house as Mr. Meier came out and called for Cathy and Tommy. Nice evening sounds.

I forgot about being locked in the shed and thought about how I'd earned one-sixth of the Starcruiser.

We reached Pete's house.

"'Night, Pete."

"'Night, Mac."

The baby-sitting adventure was over.

10. Teaching James

"WEEE-OOOH."

Crash. Crash. Splinter.

James's Tinkertoy structure fell to the ground as he kicked and punched at its base.

"Weee-oooh, weee-oooh, weee-oooh."

James was good and mad. It was Wednesday evening. He'd been in school for three mornings, and the only result I could see was that he was angry all the time at home. He ran around the house, hands fluttering, weee-ooohing, and crying his no-tears cry. When we could get him to keep still long enough to build something, he'd build in a frenzy, fast and furious, with his hands trembling, and then he'd send his creation smashing to the floor.

A couple of times he'd punched himself. Last night when I tried to stop him, he bit my wrist and made it bleed. *Darn* him. So of course in school this morning, Alan asked what happened to my arm, and I forgot myself for a second and told the truth—my brother bit me—and now the whole class thinks I've got the weirdest brother in the world. They think James is crazy.

But what on earth was happening to James in his new school? What were the teachers doing to make him angry? It'd taken so long to get him into the Weston Child Development Institute, and for *this?*

Mom had been observing James at school—Dad, too, a couple of times—and she said he was very good there and that nothing awful happened to him. So I wanted to know what was going on. And I'd find out soon. In twenty minutes Dr. Wyman, the director of the WCDI, and Ms. Rinehart, James's speech teacher, were coming over.

I couldn't wait to meet them, but Lizzie was hiding out in her room. She was jealous. She said *her* teachers never took the trouble to come over for coffee and talk about *her* school-work. What was so special about James? I knew how she felt, but I did want to meet Dr. Wyman and Ms. Rinehart. Anything to make James calm down.

When the doorbell rang I was torn between wanting to answer it and wanting to go get Lizzie. But Dad answered the bell while Mom got hold of James, who'd gone dancing and weee-ooohing off toward the den. I went up to Lizzie's room and knocked on her door.

"They're here, Lizzie," I said.

"So what."

"Come on. You know you're supposed to come downstairs."

"No way."

"Liz-*zeee*. I thought you said you wanted to help teach James."

No answer.

"Lizzie? Will you let me in?"

"The door's open."

I walked in. Lizzie was sitting cross-legged on her bed, sorting through Dad's old baseball card collection. Her red cap was pulled down about as far as it would go.

"You said you'd teach, you know. We all did," I reminded her.

"Well, what do those two people have to do with anything?"

"They're James's teachers. They'll show us how they teach James so we can teach him the same way. Mom and Dad already explained that."

"What are you being such a big shot for, Jonno?" Lizzie's lower lip was trembling. "You were madder than anything at James for biting you."

"And I'm still mad. But aren't you even curious? I want to see what these people think they can teach him."

"Then go ahead."

That did it. I yanked Lizzie's baseball cap off her head and shouted, "Your hair stinks!" Then I slammed her door and stomped down the hall, feeling like a rat. But I wasn't going to apologize. If Lizzie wanted James to stay like he was, then she could suffer for it.

Downstairs Mom and Dad were serving coffee to a man and a woman seated on the couch.

Dad introduced us. "How do you do?" I said as I shook their hands.

They smiled at me. "Please call us Bill and Edie," said the director.

"And this is Lizzie," my father went on.

I whirled around, surprised to see her coming slowly down the stairs. Her eyes were a little red and her baseball cap was on crooked, but otherwise she looked O.K. She gave me a half smile, and I held up my pinkie finger, our secret signal meaning everything was all right.

"What we'd like to do this evening," said Bill, after we were all seated comfortably, "is simply talk with you a bit, observe James here in his home, and then show you some things you can work on with him."

"O.K.," said Dad.

Mom smiled.

"Where *is* James?" asked Lizzie.

He hadn't stayed around long after Mom caught him. He was never thrilled when we had visitors. Usually, he hid out in the den.

"I'll go get him," I said.

I walked into our den, which is at the back of the house, and switched on the ceiling light. There was James on the couch, sitting in the dark, for pete's sake.

"Geez, James," I said, totally exasperated. I took him by the hand and led him back to the living room.

"Weee-oooh, weee-oooh, weee-oooh." He howled all the way. As soon as he saw Bill and Edie, he looked particularly pained.

"Hey, I think he recognizes you!" I exclaimed.

I sat James by the collapsed Tinkertoy tower, hoping he'd start building. Otherwise, he'd leave again.

He gave a few whimpery weee-ooohs, then took the sticks I handed him and began to build listlessly. Bill watched him closely.

Nobody was talking, so I spoke up.

"I, um, have a question," I said, feeling a little scared. I hoped Bill and Edie wouldn't be offended when I asked it.

"Shoot, Jon," said Bill.

"Well," I began carefully, "ever since James started school on Monday, he's been . . . he's been sort of horrible at home." I held up my wrist as proof. "I thought school was going to *help* him."

"Oh, it is," said Bill, "at least, we think so. Nothing is ever a sure bet. But what James is going through now is pretty normal. It's a reaction."

"A reaction?" I asked. "Like an allergic reaction?"

"In a way," said Edie. "See, we're putting a lot of pressure on James in school. We're making demands on him. We're asking him to do things he's never had to do before, like hang up his jacket, wash his hands, put away his toys. He's used to having those things done for him. Since he's not sure about us or the school, and doesn't know how we'll react if he gets mad, he's doing all his getting mad at home. It's hard for children like James to trust people, so he's not taking any chances with the new faces at school. But he trusts you a little more and probably thinks it's O.K. to get mad around you."

"Oh," I said slowly, thinking this over. "Will he stop?"

"He will," said Bill, "if you'll help him."

I glanced at Lizzie. She knew I was looking at her, but she wouldn't look back.

"How do we help?" asked Dad. "What do we do?"

"Well, this is something I wanted to talk to you about tonight," said Bill.

Then Mom and Dad and Bill and Edie started talking. They talked for almost forty-five minutes. I listened carefully and tried to follow everything they were saying but I got lost quite a few times. The main thing I understood was that we were supposed to reward James for doing things we wanted him to do, and punish him for doing things we didn't want him to do. The rewards would be feeding him Cheerios, or saying "Good boy, James!" with a big smile, or hugging him (if he'd let us). The punishments would be not giving him Cheerios, or saying "No, James," without any smile.

At first I thought it sounded pretty easy, but it turned out you had to do this all the time—for practically *everything*. We were supposed to do it at meals to get him to try new foods and not barf. We were supposed to sit him on the toilet a few times a day and reward him if he happened to go. We were supposed to reward him for building nicely or coming to us for a hug or trying to put his clothes on, and we were supposed to punish him for weee-ooohing or punching himself or biting me or fluttering his hands.

My head was a total jumble, but Edie said, "It's not as hard as it sounds. I'll demonstrate something to you. Have you noticed how hard it is to get James to look you in the eye?"

We all nodded. It was almost impossible. He'd look anywhere but in your eyes.

"Well," said Edie, "this is typical of autistic children. It's scary for them. It means they have to come out of their own world and open themselves up to other people. Looking someone in the eye is a sign of trust or intimacy, and James doesn't want that." She glanced at Lizzie to see if Lizzie was following her, which was very nice. I liked Edie and Bill more and more.

"What I mean," Edie continued, seeing Lizzie's frustrated face, "is that most autistic children feel threatened by making eye contact. But that's the first thing we teach them. It's important because when a child is making eye contact we know he or she is paying attention. I'll show you. Could I have some Cheerios for James?"

"Sure," said Lizzie, wondering what was going to happen. It was kind of like a magic show.

In a few minutes, Lizzie came out of the kitchen with a dish of Cheerios.

James zeroed in on them immediately, but Lizzie was pretty quick and handed them right to Edie. James stood in the middle of the room with his eyes on those Cheerios.

Edie held the dish out to him. "James?" she asked. "Do you want Cheerios?"

James took a step closer.

"Do you want Cheerios?" Edie asked again.

James walked all the way over to Edie and stood next to

her, never taking his eyes off the cereal.

Edie took a few Cheerios out of the dish and held them up by her face. "James, look at me," she said.

James looked a little confused. He wanted those Cheerios *so* badly.

"James, look at me."

James's eyes flickered to Edie's for just a fraction of a second. I think it was just by accident.

"Good boy!" Edie cried as she popped some Cheerios in his mouth and gave him a hug.

Immediately she tried it again, holding the Cheerios up to her face. "James, look at me."

"Weee-oooh!" shrieked James, and flapped out of the room, crunching a couple of Tinkertoy pieces on the way.

In a flash, Bill was after him. He picked James up in one swift movement, carried him back into the living room, and plopped him on the couch next to Edie.

Edie tried again, but James gazed stubbornly off into space. Boy, was he surprised when Edie hid the cereal behind her back and said sternly, "No, James."

Before he could get too upset, Edie put the dish back in her lap and started working again. James looked at her once more.

"Wow!" I couldn't help shouting after the last time. "James learned something! He really did!"

"Why don't you try it now?" suggested Bill. "James has to learn to look at other people besides Edie. We have to be sure he knows what 'look at me' means."

"*Me* try it?" I asked.

"Sure," said Edie. She leaned over and gave me the Cheerios.

"Should I sit on the couch like you?"

"No, stay there. Let's make the game a little different and see if James understands."

"O.K.," I said nervously. I was sitting on the floor by the Tinkertoys. "James?" I asked, just like Edie had done. "Do you want Cheerios?"

He sure did. He might not have wanted to look at me, but he wanted his Cheerios all right.

He walked right over to me and stood in front of me. I left the cereal on the floor and said, "James, look at me." He waited a few seconds, then glanced uncertainly at me. I gave him some Cheerios and a gigantic hug. James, you really can learn, I thought. If only the in-kids could see this. They wouldn't think you're crazy.

After that, everyone including Lizzie, tried the look-at-me game, but James had had enough. Or maybe he was full of Cheerios. Anyway, he wouldn't look at anyone else. Edie said progress would be slow. Still, James had looked at Edie and me, even if it was just for a second, so I knew one thing for sure. We *could* teach James. He was going to be O.K. after all.

It wasn't until I was in bed that night and almost asleep that I remembered Noodle. Noodle was Termite's sisters' dachshund. He was at college with one of the sisters now, but what I remembered was two summers ago when Pete and Termite and I taught Noodle to beg and roll over. We did it exactly the way Edie and Bill were teaching James to look-at-me. One of us would hold a dog biscuit out to Noodle and say, "Roll over, Noodle." If he did it right, he got the biscuit. If he didn't, no biscuit, and maybe a little scolding.

Great. Was James becoming a trained dog, just like Noodle? Look at me, James, and you'll get your Cheerios. Hang up your jacket and you'll get a reward. Here, James, here, boy. Good James, good dog.

It was a long time before I fell asleep that night. I had a lot to think about.

11. My Brilliant Idea

March is supposed to come in like a lion and go out like a lamb. But this March was backward. It had come in like a lamb with warm, sunny weather the first week or so, then had become more and more lionish, with cold air and gray days and a few little snowstorms. And on the night of March 31 we had an honest-to-goodness blizzard, which meant April came in like a lion.

Now it was the middle of April, and after all the blizzards and stuff, spring was finally here. I wondered if James noticed. I knew spring was not a terribly cool thing to think about; I was sure Alan and Chris and the others didn't care about chirping birdies or blooming flowers, but I did. And I had an idea Pete and Termite and Stephanie and Claudia did, too. Or maybe everyone did and the difference between the in-kids and the rest of us was that we would admit it and they wouldn't. It was hard to tell.

This is what I was thinking over one warm April afternoon as I sat on our front porch after school. I wasn't exactly bored, but I couldn't think of anything to do, either. So I sat and dreamed.

80

After a little while a blue VW van pulled up our driveway. The driver got out, jogged around to the back door, and opened it. Slowly, very slowly, James eased himself and his Flintstones lunchbox off the seat and down the step. The step was pretty high, but the driver let James alone, and James managed everything fine.

He'd been going to school full days for a week now. He didn't get home until three-thirty or four in the afternoon. It seemed like a long day for a four-year-old. On the other hand, James wasn't any ordinary four-year-old.

The driver slammed the door shut and said good-bye to James. James flapped his free hand in front of his eyes and galloped over to me.

"Hi, James," I said with a smile.

"Oh-*ma,*" he answered.

I sighed.

A piece of white paper was pinned to James's jacket. It didn't say who it was for, so I unfastened it and read it.

Dear Petersons,

Please send in separate photographs of every member of your family. If possible, they should be fairly recent so James can recognize them. I need them for speech sessions. Thanks!

Edie

That was strange. Edie and the other teachers had done a few unusual things with James, like encouraging him to roll around on a mat so he could start learning to laugh and play, but what was she going to do with photographs?

I took James and the note in the house. I wondered if this was important enough to interrupt Mom for. She was working in her study. Now that James was settled in school, she and

Dad observed there only a couple of hours every week, which meant Mom had a lot more time for copywriting. She'd taken on more projects in the last month than she had in the past two years. I was afraid all the work might make her tired, but she seemed really happy instead.

James and I were hesitating at the study door just as Mom opened it and came out.

"Well, hello, you two!" she exclaimed. "James, you're home." She kissed his cheek. "How was school?"

He didn't answer, of course, but Edie had said it was important to talk to him like he was a regular kid.

"Mom, look at this note from Edie." I held it out.

Mom scanned it. "That's funny. I wonder...oh, well. James, come on and we'll find the pictures for Edie." She led him off toward the den and the family photograph albums.

I wandered back out to the porch. After a while Termite came over.

"Hey!" I greeted him.

"Hey," he answered. "I saw James come home. How's he doing?"

"Pretty well. He ate a whole serving of peas last night because Dad gave him a Cheerio after every bite. He didn't even barf. And sometimes he repeats words if you tell him to. He can say *hi* and *'bye.*"

"That's really great, Mac," said Termite, but he didn't sound all that impressed.

"Had any Time-Savers calls?" I asked after a while.

"The last one was two weeks ago. How about you?"

"Mr. Phomalont called yesterday. He needs their first-floor windows washed. Other than him, no one's called in about a week and a half."

"Business is slacking off," said Termite dejectedly.

"Yeah. I've only earned twenty-seven dollars and nineteen cents toward the Starcruiser. I've got a long way to go."

"We better do something."

"Like what?"

"Like get Pete. He'll know what to do!"

We ran over to Pete's house, hoping he didn't have any homework so he could come out.

Pete, it turned out, didn't have any homework left, but he didn't want to come out either, so we went up to his room.

"We have to have a conference," I said as we sprawled out on his floor. "A business conference."

"Right," said Termite. "Time-Savers is failing."

"What?" shouted Pete.

"Well, when was the last time you got a call?" I asked him.

Pete was silent, thinking.

"That long, huh?" said Termite.

"Just a second, just a second..."

"Never mind, Pete. We get a call every now and then, but not like before," I said. "People are forgetting about us."

"Yeah, they've probably lost our fliers." Termite toyed with Pete's printing press.

"That's it!" cried Pete. The old idea glint was in his eyes. I'd been hoping to see that glint. "It's simple. What we have to do is *revamp* Time-Savers!"

Termite and I glanced at each other. "Do what?" asked Termite.

"Revamp it," repeated Pete. "You know, spruce it up."

"Yeah," I said. "We could make up a new flier. Hey, maybe even put an ad in the newspaper!"

"Yeah!" Pete and Termite shouted. "Who gets the paper?"

"We do," I said. "It should be delivered any minute now. That is..."

"What?"

"Oh, just that it hasn't come the last two days for some reason, but let's go wait anyway."

We charged back over to my porch.

"I think I'll give Lizzie another chance to be part of the business," I said while we waited. "She should be home soon."

"Where is she?" asked Termite.

"At a Brownie meeting."

"At a Brownie meeting! What's she doing going to Brownies? She's never done anything like that before. Sheesh," exclaimed Termite.

"She just joined a few weeks ago. She really seems to like it. She hardly ever hangs around with Wendell anymore."

At that moment Lizzie ran up the front lawn in her brown dress and brown sweater and brown socks and brown shoes and red baseball cap. A little brown beanie was supposed to be part of the uniform, but Lizzie refused to wear it. She said she preferred her cap. It did more for her hair. Her troop leader called my mother one evening to find out about the cap, and after Mom explained, Lizzie was allowed to wear it to meetings, as long as she promised to wear the brown beanie in the Memorial Day Parade.

"Lizzie," I said, "we're... we're *revamping* Time-Savers. Do you want to be part of it now? We could put your name on the new fliers."

"Thanks, Jonno, but I've got other things to do. I have to go now."

"Where are you going?"

"Up to my room. And don't come in unless you knock first. 'Bye, Pete, 'bye, Termite."

She dashed off.

"Lizzie has sure been spending a lot of time in her room lately," commented Pete.

"I know," I said. "I wish I knew what she was up to."

"Maybe it's so she can hide out from James," said Termite.

He would think that.

"Geez, Termite," said Pete, which was just what I wanted to say.

There was an embarrassing silence.

"Well," I said, "anyway, James is much better."

And as if to prove it, Mom and James came out to take a walk.

"See?" I said as they moved slowly down the driveway. "James's hands aren't fluttering as much. He only said weee-oooh a few times this morning. And he's almost looking straight ahead."

I knew it didn't sound like much.

"For heaven's sake, where's the paper?" burst out Pete.

"I don't know. This is the third day in a row it hasn't been delivered. Last night Mom had to go out and buy it.... *Hey!*"

"What?" cried Pete and Termite.

"I just thought of something. I've got to go make a phone call. This could be really important!"

12. The Newspaper Disaster

Three days later I rolled out of bed at five A.M. I looked outside. Still dark. I got dressed as quietly as I could, ran downstairs, and hopped on my bike. It was kind of exciting.

I rode through the shadowy, silent streets, looking at the dark windows of the houses and thinking about all the people asleep inside.

It was the first morning of my paper route. What I'd found out from my phone call was that our paper hadn't been delivered for three days because our paperboy had quit without even telling anybody. And sure enough, they needed somebody to take over his route. I'd felt pretty proud of myself after I made the call. I mean, I'd felt really nervous on the phone, but I'd just tried to be polite and calm. When someone answered the phone at the newspaper office, I'd said, "Hello, my name is Jonathan Peterson. I live on Napanee Road, and our paper hasn't been delivered for three days."

"Yes," said the woman on the other end, "we're sorry. We're not charging you for it, but the newsboy who usually takes your route has ... left. ..."

That was my chance. I hoped I wouldn't blow it. "I—you're

not—are you looking for anybody to take over his route?" I managed to ask.

"Well, as a matter of fact... Do you know of anyone who might be interested?"

"Yes, ma'am," I said, trying to sound enthusiastic and polite and responsible and grown up. "I do. I'd be interested."

"How old are you?" she asked.

"Eleven," I said. "Almost twelve." (I only had five-and-a-half months to go.)

"Could you come to our office tomorrow so we can meet you?"

"Sure," I said. If Mom couldn't drive me, I'd ride my bike.

"Fine," she said. "Four o'clock?"

"Four o'clock," I repeated. "I'll see you tomorrow."

She told me her name and we hung up.

When I got off the phone, I was so excited I let out a whoop and went cheering and jumping outside to tell Pete and Termite.

The next day, Mom drove me to the newspaper office. She said she might have to sign papers or something, you never know. But she didn't come in with me. I wouldn't let her. I made her stay in the car. For one thing, James was with her, and I wanted to make a good impression. Which would be hard to do if James weee-ooohed or hit himself or started yelling and fluttering.

The interview was really easy. I talked to two people, and they just wanted to know what school I went to and what grade I was in. Stuff like that. Then they told me what I'd have to do to keep up the paper route, and asked me if I honestly thought I could handle it. They reminded me about how the last boy had quit. The job didn't sound easy, that was for sure, but I said I thought I could do it. It paid pretty well.

So the next afternoon, I followed this girl, Maureen, around on her paper route to make sure I knew the procedure, and this morning I was on my own. The *Tribune* came out every weekday afternoon and on Tuesday, Friday, and Sunday mornings—the Coupon Clippers Club Morning Special.

I reached the corner of Random Road and Swing Lane as the sky was beginning to lighten a little. Nobody was on the corner. I parked my bike and stood there, fingering the canvas *Tribune* sack that was tied around my middle.

After about five minutes, Maureen rode up. "Hi!" she called, swinging expertly off her bike before it even stopped. She parked it next to mine.

"Hi," I answered.

"You all ready?" she asked.

"I guess so," I said. "All I really have to learn is who's on the route so I don't have to look at the addresses so much." I took the plastic-covered piece of paper with my route listed on it out of the *Tribune* bag and studied it.

"You'll know the whole thing by heart in four or five days," said Maureen. "You'll be surprised."

"The other thing I'm not sure about is collecting the money. I wonder what morning I should do that."

Maureen started laughing.

"What's so funny?" I asked.

"Are you kidding?" she spluttered, trying to get back in control. "You can't collect the money in the morning. Your customers would kill you." She looked at her watch. "It's five thirty, for pete's sake. You have to collect after school."

I blushed furiously. "Oh. Right."

Luckily, the newspaper van drove up just then, and three more kids arrived, two on bikes, one with a wagon. A man wearing a brown *Tribune* uniform swung himself out of the front and slid open the doors on the side. "Morning, everybody," he shouted cheerfully.

"Good morning, Max," the rest of the kids called back.

Max started to unload stacks of papers.

Two more boys arrived.

"What do we have here?" asked Max as he dumped a pile of papers in front of me. "Oh, you're the new kid, right?"

I nodded.

"Well, good luck." He grinned at me.

"Thanks," I said. I counted out thirty Coupon Clippers Club Morning Specials, one for everybody on my route, and began stuffing them in my bag. I had this feeling all the kids were watching me. I hate being the new anything. I hoped I was doing everything right. Was I supposed to be folding the papers or something? Was everyone watching me be a total foul-up?

Finally I glanced up. Most of the kids were getting ready to ride off. Max had gotten back in the truck and was starting the motor. He flashed me the thumbs-up sign. I waved to him. Nobody said anything to me, so I jumped on my bike and pedaled toward Vandeventer.

My route was not a really long one, which was O.K. with me. It meant I didn't get paid quite as much, of course, since you get paid according to how many papers you deliver, but I decided it was just as well to have a short route at first. There was an awful lot to remember. The people on my route were on Vandeventer, a short street that intersected with mine; Poe Road, another short street; and Napanee.

I decided to start with Vandeventer. I rode to the corner, checked my chart to see the first address on the route, and walked my bike to the driveway. Then I folded the paper the way Maureen had shown me the day before, and threw it, aiming for the front porch. It landed smack on the doormat. I smiled to myself and coasted down the sidewalk to the next address. Again I folded the paper and tossed it. Another bull's-eye.

I was feeling pretty proud of myself by the time I reached the third house. I couldn't see the front porch too well because there were all these overgrown bushes around it, but I aimed and tossed the paper anyway.

Thud.

"Grrrowooooof!"

This gigantic dog tore off the front porch. I must have hit him. He gallumphed right at me, barking and snarling. A window shade snapped up in a second-floor window, but I didn't stick around to see what would happen. I just jumped on my bicycle and lit down the street as fast as my legs could pump.

I overshot the next house on the route, but I didn't care. The important thing was to lose that incredible hulk of a dog. Finally I put on the brakes and turned to look behind me. Superdog was sauntering home. He had this air about him that said, "I guess I showed *him*." He looked suave and cool, like one of the in-boys after he's been teasing Edweird.

I stopped my bike, turned around, and went back to the house I'd missed. The front porch was all clear. I tossed the paper.

It landed on the roof.

I guess my shooting was a little off after the last experience. What the heck was I supposed to do *now?*

I had exactly twenty-six Coupon Clippers Specials left, and exactly twenty-six more houses to deliver them to. One of the houses was my own. I wondered if Mom and Dad could do without their coupons for one morning. But that wouldn't make me look so hot.

I sighed and got off my bicycle. Then I stood on the sidewalk, scratching my head. Who's house was this, anyway? I wondered. I got out the list of addresses. 42 Vandeventer. Giancossi.

Oh, no, I groaned, smacking the palm of my hand to my forehead. Of all houses, this was *Chris Giancossi's.*

Oh, no, I groaned again.

I looked at my watch. Almost six. I'd promised Mom I'd be back by six forty-five every morning. On the dot.

So.

I could forget about the Giancossis' paper, or give them ours, or try to figure out some way to get the paper off the roof. Three choices. None of them very inspiring.

I looked the house over. One part of it was one story high; another part was two stories high. The paper had landed near the edge of the lower roof just above the front door and right under a bedroom window on the second story. The Giancossis' backyard was closed in by a stockade fence. I think they had a pool back there.

I was still standing by my bike, thinking. The papers were getting pretty heavy, so I put them down.

Then I checked out that fence again. It looked like it went right up to the edge of the roof in back of the house. Maybe if I could climb up the fence, I could get on the roof, crawl over the top, and drop the paper down onto the porch. Actually, it wouldn't be hard to do, but I sure didn't want anyone to see me. And it was pretty light out by now. You could probably get arrested for what I was doing. What was it—trespassing? Sneaking around? Unlawful paper removal? On the other hand, I was just doing my job.

I propped my bike against a phone pole and left it leaning there with the nearly full *Tribune* bag next to it. Watch, everything would probably be stolen before I got back.

I looked up and down the street, saw that no cars were coming, and made sure the Giancossis' window shades were drawn on the second floor. Then I dashed around the side of the house.

After looking over the fence for a few seconds, I grabbed the top of one stockade, or whatever all those wooden things are called, slapped my sneakers up against the fence, and did a pretty good Spiderman imitation right up the side. When I reached the top, I was all bunched up, hands and feet together. I looked like Pete's old cat, Kiki, who used to sleep with his feet and his tail slung together in one pile near his head.

I grabbed for the edge of the roof, lost my balance, teetered, and righted myself just in time. A good thing, too. The Giancossis would have been pretty surprised to find a body by their stockade fence when they woke up that morning.

Shaking a little from the near miss, I clutched the gutter and crawled onto the roof. Luckily, the gutter held.

SKRITCH.

I moved my left knee forward.

SKRITCH.

I moved my left hand forward.

SKRITCH.

Every move I made sounded like a whole army of newspaper thieves on the Giancossis' roof.

Oh, well. I couldn't do a thing about it.

I crawled to the peak, by the wall of the higher roof. At least I wasn't so out in the open. I looked over the roof and checked on my bike and newspapers. Still there.

Gingerly, leaning against the wall for support, I eased myself over the peak.

SKREEETCH.

Suddenly I started sliding and didn't stop till I was halfway down the other side of the roof. Somebody must have heard it. I was right under that bedroom window. I lay still, trying to make myself very small.

I didn't hear a sound.

I took a huge breath.

The newspaper was about six inches away from my right foot. I sat up, slid forward, and kicked the paper over the edge.

I had made it. Almost.

Just then a head poked out of the window. It was Chris.

"Nice work, Peterson," he called.

Oh, no.

I would never ever ever live this down. But I didn't want to appear too upset. "Thanks!" I called.

I began the climb back to the fence.

Five minutes later I was dusting myself off and then jogging around to the front yard.

I hopped on my bike and rode off to deliver the rest of the Coupon Clippers Club Morning Specials, but all the excitement was gone from the job. Chris wouldn't let something like this go by. I knew I'd hear about it in school.

Boy, would I hear about it.

13. Getting Better

A couple of hours after that wonderful newspaper experience, I was sitting in our classroom with Pete and Termite. Mr. Westoff had recently arranged our desks in groups of four. Our group was Pete and me and Claudia and Stephanie.

I watched the kids trickle in.

Edweird arrived earlier than usual. He was wearing white shoes and baggy tan pants that were held up with suspenders, if you can believe it. Brother. I was almost glad. I was anticipating a little trouble from Chris, but I figured Edweird's outfit would be good competition for the razzing.

Edweird flumped onto a chair, huffing and all out of breath. He must have been running or something. Edweird hardly ever participates in gym. Our teacher lets him sit on the bench a lot.

Pete nudged me and pointed at Edweird. He had just caught sight of the white shoes and suspenders.

"I know," I said. "Too weird. Too-weird Edweird."

Pete grinned.

Edweird's huffing was slowing down. He looked around the room and caught us staring at him. "Hi, Jonathan!" he

called. "Hi, Peter! Hi..." He didn't know Termite's name.
"Hi, there!"

"Hi," we mumbled.

Then Edweird did something new. He heaved himself out
of his seat and lumbered over to us.

"Oh, *no*," whispered Termite, sounding panicky the way
he does when he sees James get out of control. "What's he
doing?"

I rolled my eyes. "I don't know."

"Aw, geez," said Pete under his breath. "Aw, geez."

Edweird was standing by our group. He struggled to sit on
one of the desks, like we were doing. It took him a few tries.
He kept slipping back.

I hoped really hard that I'd never get as fat as Edweird.

"Good morning, boys," Edweird said, when he finally managed to get his bulk arranged on Stephanie's desk. "How are
you today?"

Why did Edweird sound as if he'd learned to speak from
one of those foreign-language records?

"Fine, Edwei—Edward," I muttered.

Chris and Hank came in just at that moment. They *would*.
They didn't even try to hide their laughter.

Hee, hee, hee. Very funny.

They stood in a corner snorting and snickering and pointing
at us.

Termite had had enough. "See ya," he said disgustedly, and
marched out of the room.

I watched him. It was worth it. As he got out the door, he
turned so he was facing Chris's and Hank's backs. He twisted
his mouth and rolled his eyes so his pupils were up inside his
head and all you could see were the whites. Then he pointed
at Chris and Hank, bobbing his head and letting his tongue

hang out. He waited until he knew he had Pete and me smiling before he ran down the hall.

Elise and Janie came in.

"Hello," they said sweetly to Chris and Hank.

"Hi," said the boys. "Hey, come here."

"What?"

The boys pulled them into the corner and started whispering and snickering and pointing at us again. Janie and Elise began giggling.

I hate it when they giggle. They sound so fake.

"How are your parents?" asked Edweird suddenly.

Pete and I didn't even bother to answer.

"I hope they're well."

"Come on," I said. Pete and I hopped off the desks and headed for the coat closet. If Edweird followed, it would take him a few minutes to catch up.

"Hey, Jon," yelled Chris from the front of the room, "how's your paper route?"

I scowled.

"Are you deaf?" shouted Hank. He raised his voice as much as he could without letting the vice-principal overhear us. "CHRIS ASKED YOU HOW YOUR PAPER ROUTE IS."

"FINE," I hollered back.

"*I'm* not deaf," said Hank maddeningly. "You don't have to yell at *me*."

"Then why are you—" I started to shout back, but Pete put his hand on my shoulder. "Cool out," he muttered. "Forget it."

"Hey, Jon," called Chris again. "Do you deliver all your papers on the roof, or is that just a special favor for us?"

"It was no favor," I said loudly. "I don't do favors for jerks."

The class fell silent, sensing trouble. The bell was about to ring, and almost everyone had arrived. Except Mr. Westoff, of course.

"Jon—" Claudia started to say.

She was standing next to me, but I wasn't looking at her. My eyes were glued to Chris. He looked like a bull getting ready to charge. You could practically see smoke coming out of his ears. I'd never been in a fight at school (or anywhere else, for that matter). It looked like now was going to be my first time.

I tensed up, getting ready to defend myself if Chris charged. But he didn't charge. Suddenly his whole face changed—softened, sort of. I still didn't trust him, though.

He positioned himself in the middle of the classroom and said, "I saw that dopey little brother of Jon's riding on the retarded bus yesterday."

The class snickered appreciatively.

"I think you're the dopey one, Chris," Stephanie said, which surprised me because usually she's pretty quiet. "Buses can't be retarded."

The class snickered again. Even Elise and the other in-girls laughed.

I flashed Steph a grateful smile.

"No," said Chris uncomfortably, "but Jon's brother can be. Man, is he weird. A real retardo." Chris started fluttering his hands around.

More laughter.

"And," he went on, "he's not the only weird one." He glared meaningfully at Edweird, who flushed and then stumbled, trying to get off Steph's desk.

Part of me wanted to crawl into a hole and hide there forever. Another part of me wanted to give Chris and the others just what they deserved. I started forming words in my head and opened my mouth to let the in-boys have it—for once, just for *once*—when Mr. Westoff hurried into the room.

Immediately everyone scattered, clambering for their desks. Saved again.

That night, after the newspaper disaster and the rotten morning at school, I was really beat. All I could think of was going to bed. The sooner the better. But at dinner, Mom reminded everybody that Bill and Edie were coming over. I had to stay up for that. It was important.

When dinner was over, Mom and Dad cleaned up the kitchen while Lizzie got to watch TV and I had to read James his story. How come I always got stuck with him? I sat him on the living-room couch next to me and opened up this baby book called *Pat the Bunny*. James sat quietly for about three seconds. Then he jumped up suddenly and exclaimed, "Oh-ma!"

"Come on, James," I said tiredly, pulling him back down on the couch.

"Weee-oooh!" he cried. He leaped up again.

Maybe he didn't like the book. Or maybe he had a stomachache. Or maybe he suddenly remembered something bad that happened two or three years ago. How could you tell *any*thing with James?

"Ja-ames," I scolded. I sat him down roughly. I was too tired to fool around with whatever his problem was.

"Weee-oooh, weee-oooh, weee-oooh," he whined nervously.

He started to flap his hands. I knew he wasn't supposed to do it.

"No, James," I said sharply.

He flapped harder.

"No, James." I slapped his hand and turned my back on him. When I turned around to look at him a few seconds later, his hands were almost still. Wow, that worked pretty well, I told myself. "Good boy, James!" I praised him.

Pat the Bunny had fallen on the floor. I picked it up and started in on page three.

Without warning, James snatched the book out of my hands, bending the cover. "Weeeeee!" he shrieked. He was trembling with rage.

"Mom!" I called. "Dad!"

Dad ran into the living room.

James had careened off the couch and was standing on the floor, stamping his feet and hitting his face.

"You handle him," I said crossly to Dad, and marched into the den to watch TV with Lizzie.

After a few minutes, though, I began to feel guilty. Just as I was about to head back into the living room to apologize, the doorbell rang. I ran to answer it, but Dad beat me to it.

As Bill and Edie were hanging up their coats, I said to Dad, "I'm really sorry." I'd have spent the whole evening worrying if I hadn't apologized.

"That's O.K., son," he said quietly. "You were angry." He patted me on the back.

I smiled up at him.

"Problems?" asked Bill.

"James is a little upset," said Dad as we found chairs in the living room. "Jonno's been handling him very well, but he's had a hard day today."

In the back of the house I could hear Mom calling Lizzie. Then she came into the living room with James. Dad must have handed him over to her.

James skirted tensely around Bill and Edie. He almost danced right back out of the room, but Lizzie caught him on her way in.

"Come on," she said. She sat on the floor and pulled James into her lap, where he squirmed and struggled.

"Well," said Edie. "How are things?"

Everyone began talking at once.

We laughed and started over.

After a few minutes, Edie said, "James, come here."

James stayed put until Lizzie heaved him upright and pushed him toward Edie.

On the way his eyes darted to hers briefly. It looked like an accident, but Edie exclaimed, "Good boy!" and gave him a hug.

James accepted it stiffly.

Edie checked the table next to her and saw that a bowl of Cheerios had been placed on it.

It was funny. We did that automatically now before Bill and Edie came over, the way you'd put out nuts or potato chips before a cocktail party.

Edie took a few Cheerios. "Hi, James," she said clearly.

"Ha!" he answered.

"Good boy!" Edie gave him Cheerios and a smile. Then she pulled an envelope out of her purse. From the envelope she took five photographs. They were the photos of our family that Mom had found for James the other day.

"This is really something," said Edie to all of us. "James has been working very hard on it. His progress is slow, but still, it's progress. . . . Come here, big guy," she said as she hoisted James up on the couch and sat him so he was facing her. Then she spread out three of the photos—Mom, me, and Lizzie. "James," Edie said, to get his attention.

He appeared not to hear her.

"James," she said again.

He looked at her reluctantly.

"Touch Mommy," said Edie.

James looked down at the pictures and considered. "Weee-oooh," he moaned. Finally he stuck his finger out hesitantly in the direction of the picture of Mom.

"Oh, *good* boy!" cried Edie. She rewarded him quickly, before he could make a mistake or get upset.

"Wow!" I shouted.

"Yeah," said Lizzie.

Mom and Dad were grinning.

Edie mixed up the five photos and laid down a different group. "James, touch Lizzie," she said.

But James squirmed off the couch like a frightened rabbit. Edie let him go. "That's enough for now," she said. "He's been working hard. This is difficult and a little scary for him."

I could feel this seed of excitement growing in my stomach. James was going to get well. I just knew it. Even if we did have to train him like a circus dog. He was smart after all.

I left the room to find James, and when I brought him back, Dad took him upstairs to bed. I was getting more tired by the minute, but I stuck around to hear whatever else Bill and Edie might have to say.

We talked about James for a bit, and then Bill mentioned that the Weston Child Development Institute was having a fund-raiser the next weekend.

"What's a fund-raiser?" asked Lizzie.

"It's a project to raise money for something," said Bill. "WCDI is very expensive to run, and we need money for new equipment. So next Saturday, if you come to Palmer Square in Weston, you'll find tables set up and people selling brownies and cakes and cookies and handmade things. The money we earn will go toward some playground toys and teaching materials for James and the other kids."

"Yum," said Lizzie dreamily. "Brownies..."

"Could we help out?" asked Mom. "We make mean fudge around here."

"We need all the help we can get," said Edie earnestly. "The chairman of the fund-raising committee should be calling you any day now. It sometimes takes him a while to contact the families of new students, but once he does, the whole family is usually involved."

Dad came back downstairs and sat down near Mom.

"Can I ask something?" I said.

"Always." Bill smiled.

"Well, I was just thinking. We pay...we pay...tuition, right? To send James to WCDI? The other kids must, too. So how come you need more money? What's James's tuition for?"

"Good question," said Bill. "It's for lots of things—the teachers' salaries, equipment, food, renting the rooms we use for the school. The state *gives* all that money to towns to run public schools, but special schools like WCDI don't usually get much help from the government. So we have to depend on the families of the students. And some of them don't have much money at all. Then we let them pay less money. We'd hate to turn a child away from school just because the family was having trouble making ends meet. But then *we* don't have enough money to run the school."

"Oh," I said. "I see." It was complicated. Was it fair that we paid more tuition than some families? And what if Bill and Edie couldn't raise enough money to keep WCDI going? What would happen to James?

I decided not to worry, though. I decided to think about James getting better.

* * *

Later that night, after Bill and Edie had left and Lizzie had gone to sleep, and I was falling asleep myself even though I was still down in the living room with Mom and Dad, I said groggily, "Old James is pretty neat."

"Neat," repeated Dad, with a smile. "I guess he is at that, Jonno."

"I'm really proud of him," I said. "He recognized your picture, Mom."

"We're proud, too." Mom grinned.

"He's going to get well now, isn't he?" I said. I was hardly expecting an answer; I was so sure Mom and Dad would be thinking the same thing.

They glanced at each other.

"Jonno," said Mom slowly, "with James, you take things one step at a time and just see how they go. You don't predict or plan where he's concerned."

"But he's *talk*ing, Mom."

"Honey, he's beginning to learn a couple of words, which he uses only when you ask him a question or when you tell him to say one of them. . . . Do you know how big your vocabulary was when you were almost five?"

"No."

"It must have been hundreds of words. It was so big, Daddy and I had stopped counting when you were three. You talked a blue streak. So did Lizzie; so do most other almost-five-year-olds."

I stared uncomfortably at the floor.

"You talked about cars and trucks and books and TV shows. You made up long stories and told them to Lizzie. You sang songs and memorized commercials and—"

"All right, all right," I said.

"Jonno, we're pleased with James's progress," Dad put in.

"It's just that it's *so* slow. We thought school would make more of a difference with James—that he'd change faster."

I nodded.

"But Edie and Bill have told us several times to be patient. They said progress is sometimes painfully slow," added Dad.

"They did?" I asked.

"Yes," said Dad. "I guess we just wanted to believe that somehow James wouldn't be like other autistic children. He'd be an exception. We want...so much for him."

I nodded again. I knew what he meant. "But," I added, "James is really trying, I think. He's trying as hard as he can."

"Yes," said Mom. "I think he is trying."

Dad didn't say anything.

14. Spring Vacation

Vacation at last! There's nothing I like better than vacation—
day after day of sleeping late, and catching all the TV shows
you miss when you're in school, and no homework, and endless time to do whatever you want.

It was Easter vacation, only the school called it spring vacation. We had a weekend, a whole week, and another weekend off. Nine straight days of freedom, including three special
events. One was Easter, which would fall on the first Sunday
of the vacation; one was James's birthday, which we were
going to celebrate the following Saturday, even though his
birthday was on Thursday; and one wasn't very exciting but
was pretty interesting—Lizzie and I were going to visit James
at his school for the first time. (James didn't get a spring
vacation.)

On Easter morning I had to get up at five A.M. to deliver
the paper. It had to be delivered even on Easter Sunday. I was
pretty good with the paper now. I could fold it up really fast,
and when I threw it, it almost always landed on the front porch.
Except for that one house—the one where Superdog lived.
Usually I left Superdog's paper somewhere in the middle of

his front lawn. So far, his owners hadn't complained.

I had collection worked out, too. I collected every other Tuesday afternoon. If any of my customers weren't home that day, I'd check back the next afternoon and the next and the next until I found them at home. My customers were all good about paying, and it was beginning to look like that Starcruiser could be mine after all.

In fact, it looked so possible that now I wasn't sure whether I wanted the $62.99 Starcruiser, or this $85.98 automatic baseball pitcher that was also at Kaler's. Pete had pointed out that if I bought the baseball pitcher, we could open up a baseball training institute in my backyard this summer and earn money training the neighborhood kids for Little League. He said that in no time at all I'd earn back the money spent on the pitcher, and then I could buy the Starcruiser, too. I said I'd have to think it over.

Easter morning I got home right at the dot of six forty-five and delivered my thirtieth paper to the kitchen table. Everyone was still asleep. I headed upstairs, thinking I might catch a few more Z's myself, but I heard an odd thumping sound coming from James's room, so I unlocked his door to check on him. (We latch his door at night because once he started getting up really early in the morning, like around three or four, and wandering through the house weee-ooohing. We were afraid he'd hurt himself or accidentally catch the house on fire or something.)

I eased his door open. James was standing by his bed. He was staring at me. Not into my eyes, just at my body.

"James?" I asked softly. I was trying to figure out what the thumping sound had been.

He continued staring at me. It was as if he could see right through me. I shivered. James scares me sometimes.

I looked around his room. It was very neat, since there was hardly anything in it. His bed was unmade, of course. (Bill had promised that James would learn bed-making at WCDI when he got older.) A Tinkertoy structure stood in one corner. It had been there for weeks.

Then I spotted something red behind James's feet.

"Hey, James, what are you up to? What are you hiding?"

"Ha."

"James, come here," I said, just the way Edie always said it.

He stepped forward.

Behind him was my old red superball. How had James gotten it? It had been out in the garage for months.

"You want to play ball!" I exclaimed. "Is that it?" James had never been interested in anything like that. But the ball must have made the thumping sound.

"Oh-*ma*."

"Well, hey, terrific." So the Z's could wait. "Come on, let's get you dressed." I pulled James's jeans and a faded N.Y. Mets T-shirt out of his dresser and helped him into them.

"Hmm-hmm-hmm," he hummed softly. It was the theme from some TV show.

"Mom'll probably make you change later if she wants us to go to church," I told him, trying to make conversation, "but these'll do for now."

"Hmm-hmm-hmm." He switched to classical.

When he was dressed, I tiptoed over to his door. James followed me. And without my saying anything, he slipped his hand into mine. A peaceful moment. It was so un-James-like. I hoped it would last awhile.

We walked quietly downstairs, and I put our jackets on us.

"You bring the ball, James," I said, just to see what he'd

do. And like any regular almost-five-year-old, he ran into the living room where we'd left the ball while we put on our jackets, grabbed it off the couch, ran to me, and tried to open the front door. I was amazed.

"Do you want to go *out?*" I asked him.

"At," he repeated.

"Good boy!" I cried. Then I had an idea. I touched the superball. "James, *ball,*" I said. "Say ball."

"Ba!"

"Good boy!" I touched the front door. "Door. Say door."

"Doe."

I touched my hat. "Hat."

"Hah."

What did my parents know? James was getting better practically in front of our eyes. *See, I told you so,* I'd say when they got up.

I opened the door, letting the morning sun stream in.

James stood in it, looking dazed.

"Come on," I said, closing the inside door behind us and holding the screen door open.

James just stood there.

"Come *on.* Bring the ball. You've got the ball." I gave him a little shove onto the porch and ran past him down the steps. "O.K., toss it to me," I cried, turning to face him.

James wasn't listening. He wasn't even looking at me. He was gazing into that sun.

"Hey, it's Jonno, remember? Throw me the ball."

"Weee-oooh, weee-oooh, weee-oooh," he whispered.

"Aw, *James,*" I said angrily.

He let me lead him onto the lawn, but it was no good. He wouldn't do a thing. He was way off in outer space or somewhere.

What *hap*pened? I wanted to shout at him. What *hap*pened?

And that was the end of Easter, as far as I was concerned. Oh, Lizzie got an Easter basket and I got two new baseballs and about a pound of bubblegum, and James got a special Lego kit, and then I helped Lizzie and James hunt for Easter eggs, and we did go to church, but I was mad at James all day long. What was he trying to pull? I didn't even tell Mom and Dad how he'd almost said *out* and *ball* and *door* and *hat*.

On Wednesday, Lizzie and I visited James at his school. In fact, our whole family went. We got there around eleven o'clock. James had left on his school bus at eight-thirty.

From the outside, WCDI didn't look like much. It was in the middle of downtown Weston, which is a nice enough little town, but the school just didn't look like a school. We drove along Ashton Avenue, the main street, passing by Woolworth's and Kentucky Fried Chicken and Jane Read's Lingerie and a few real estate offices and beauty parlors. Finally Mom parked the car in front of a flower shop. We all piled out.

"This way, kids," Dad said.

We walked a little farther until we came to a glass door sandwiched between Russo's Hobby Shop and the Shoe Tree. The door was very small and simply had a *12* on it.

Inside, a long, dark hallway led to the back of the building, and a flight of stairs led the way to the second floor.

"Upstairs," said Mom.

We followed her.

I glanced back at Lizzie once as if to say, *"This* is a school?" She shrugged.

But things were different upstairs. Mom opened a door that said *WCDI* on it and had a picture of a huge helping hand reaching out to a very small boy and girl, and suddenly we

could hear school sounds—teachers talking and paper rustling
and a few little voices and somewhere a piano playing.

We stepped into what was sort of a combination hall and
reception area. A long row of cubbies stuffed with jackets
lined the left side of the room. Across from them, a friendly
looking young man was seated at a desk surrounded by stacks
of paper.

"Hi," he said cheerfully to my parents.

"Hi, Tom," said my mother. "Meet Jon and Lizzie. Kids,
this is Tom. He's WCDI's secretary. I think the school would
be lost without him."

"Lost in a blizzard," grinned Tom, indicating all the paper.
Lizzie giggled.

"Well," said Tom, "you're here to see James, and right now
he's in..." Tom checked a huge chart hanging on the wall
over his desk. "He's in Self-Help Skills. With Andrea. Take
a right, go in the fourth door on your left, and be very quiet.
You know what to do. Why don't you leave your coats here?
I'll hang them up for you."

"Thanks," said Dad.

We gave our coats to Tom and turned down the hall.

"Hey, this place is *big!*" exclaimed Lizzie.

"Shh," said Dad. "School, remember, Lizzie? Yes, it is big.
It's the whole top floor of two buildings. There are eight
classrooms, an office, and a large room used for lunch and
group activities."

"Where do they go for recess?" whispered Lizzie.

"Back down the stairs and through that long hallway. There's
a small playground in the middle of the block."

"Oh."

We walked slowly through the hall, peeking in a few doors.
The rooms looked pretty much like regular school classrooms

except for the kids. There were usually no more than five in each room, and some of them, like James, looked much too little to be in school, while others looked much too big. Bigger than Edweird, even. One class had only two kids—and two teachers!

We reached the fourth door on our right, and Dad said, "When we go inside, we'll be in a small, dim room. We can't turn the lights up because the walls of the room are two-way mirrors, and if the room becomes too bright—"

"What're two-way mirrors?" interrupted Lizzie.

"Oh, sorry, honey," said Dad, "I thought you knew."

Lizzie shook her head, putting on that frustrated look she sometimes gets because of James. She pulled her baseball cap tighter over her ears.

"It's O.K.," said Dad. "A two-way mirror looks like a regular mirror on one side, but from the other side you can see *through* it, like a window. Now, this little room we're going into is between two classrooms. The side wall of each classroom looks like a mirror to the children, but when we're in the little room, we can see right into the classrooms. In other words, we can see the kids, but they can't see us. Get it?"

"Yup," said Lizzie.

I nodded.

"Now, the mirror works best for us if we keep the lights dim, so you'll just have to let your eyes adjust to the darkness. Also, we have to be very quiet, because even though the children can't see us, they can hear us."

We stepped into the room. It was lit with a funny yellow-brown light. There were a lot of chairs in the room, and a woman was seated in one, pulled up to the window, gazing intently into the classroom on the right. She glanced at us when we came in, but then went back to looking.

"Which is James's classroom, Mommy?" whispered Lizzie.

"I'm not sure. Let's see..."

"I see him!" I hissed. "He's over there." I pointed to the class across from where the lady was. We all pulled up chairs to the other window.

"Not too close," cautioned Dad. Lizzie was practically pressed into the glass. She leaned back a little.

James was in a room with three other kids and two teachers. Two of the kids, a boy and a girl, looked just a little older than James. Another boy looked as if he were about my age. They were sitting in a row in small wooden chairs.

And they were all in their underwear. The kids, I mean. Not the teachers. "Mo-om," I yelped when I saw this.

"Shh. Just watch," she whispered.

The teachers, who were also sitting on little wooden chairs, were facing the kids. The kids' clothes were in piles in front of them. "O.K.," one teacher said. "James and Nicole, put your *pants* on."

The little girl leaned forward, found her pants, and started to put them on.

James did nothing.

"James, put your *pants* on." The teacher guided James's hand to his blue jeans.

It was a slow process that took almost five minutes and a lot of prompting, but James did get his pants on. He was rewarded with Cheerios an a gigantic hug.

We watched for half an hour while the four kids worked on getting dressed. James was the slowest, but then he was probably the newest, too. The little girl, Nicole, was pretty good, and the big boy could even button his shirt. It would probably take a long, long time to teach James how to button, I thought.

After Self-Help, we watched James have a speech lesson with Edie. She was trying to teach him his name—both parts—because what would happen if he ever got lost and couldn't even say his name? But James was having a lot of trouble saying his name.

In fact, he spent most of the time fidgeting and jumping out of his chair. Each time he jumped up, Edie patiently sat him back down, saying, "No, James," firmly. The few times he did sit still, Edie made sure he got plenty of hugs and Cheerios. Then she'd start in with the speech lesson again.

"James, what's your name? Say 'James.'"

A couple of times James looked at her, and looked like he might be thinking about repeating his name, but he never did. Instead he'd stand up or squirm or weee-oooh.

I was amazed at how patient Edie was.

When Speech was over, it was lunchtime at WCDI. All the kids and teachers went to the big room and spread out their lunches on two long tables.

Bill called us into his office.

"Nice to see you," he said as we were sitting down.

Lizzie smiled. She really likes Bill. "How's the fund-lifting going?" she asked.

"Fund-raising," corrected Bill gently. "Not too badly, Lizzie. We made about three hundred dollars at the sale on Palmer Square, but we have a long way to go."

Oh, no. I had hoped for better news. James needed all the help he could get. "What's next?" I asked anxiously.

"With the fund-raising?" asked Bill.

"Yeah."

"Actually, Mr. Holtz—he's the chairman of the fund-raising committee—has a clearer idea than I do. But I think a big dinner is coming up."

"A dinner with songs and speeches?" asked Lizzie.

"Exactly like that."

Mom and Dad and Bill began discussing James then. He was making progress, Bill said. Good progress in some areas, slow progress in others.

What's *really* going to happen to him? I wanted to ask. Is he going to be normal? But I didn't say anything. I knew nobody had the answers to those questions.

On Saturday evening we celebrated James's fifth birthday. We had dinner first, and James ate some hamburger and carrots with just about no complaints. Then Lizzie and I cleared the table, and when we were seated again, Mom carried in a big chocolate cake and set it in front of James. It said HAPPY BIRTHDAY, JAMES in yellow frosting and was decorated with candy circus clowns. Five blue candles (plus one to grow on) were stuck in it, but they weren't lit because James isn't always too good with fire, and he wouldn't know how to blow them out, anyway. But we sang to him, and James gazed at the ceiling with a funny half smile. Then Mom served up the cake, and James discovered he liked chocolate. But after a couple of mouthfuls he got wiggly. When he began smearing chocolate in his hair and on the tablecloth, Mom decided dessert was over.

Presents came next. We sat around in the living room. Lizzie had insisted on wrapping all the gifts. "You *have* to. It's a *birth*day," she'd said.

But she got mad when James wouldn't open them. He didn't know what "open" meant or how to tear off the paper or anything. So he sat there with the first present in his lap and diddled the ribbon between his fingers.

"Open it," commanded Lizzie.

James let the present slide to the floor.

In the end we opened all his presents for him. James sat solemnly, sometimes looking on, sometimes humming softly.

At last all the gifts were spread on the floor in front of him. Mom and Dad had gotten him a fancy set of new building materials called Construx, two new shirts, a pair of Snoopy bathing trunks because he was going to have swimming lessons at WCDI this summer, an easy wooden puzzle, and a tricycle. Lizzie had made him a storybook called "Bruno, the Big Bad Bear," and I had gotten him his very own red superball, just in case.

James reached out, and we all leaned forward, eager to see what new toy he wanted first. I watched his hand close over a fistful of shiny blue wrapping paper. With his other hand, he grabbed for some yellow paper. Then, giggling and squealing and calling out "oh-*ma*," he scrambled around the room, crinkling the paper and tearing it and flinging it in the air. His presents sat ignored in the middle of the floor.

Lizzie disappeared. A few minutes later I saw her outside, swinging alone on her monkey swing in the falling darkness.

Happy birthday, James, I thought.

15. Getting Even

The day after James's birthday party was the last day of spring vacation. A good thing, too. Pete and Termite and I were bored practically out of our skulls. A little freedom goes a long way.

I was really glad when Pete called me that morning.

"Hey, Mac," he said. "Want to go to the roller rink? Termite and I are going."

"Yeah!" I said. "That sounds good." I'd delivered my papers and didn't have any plans for the rest of the day. "Would you mind if I asked Lizzie? She might want to get out of the house." I was remembering her after the party last night. "I mean, she wouldn't have to skate with us or anything. She can find her own friends when she gets there." I hoped.

"O.K.," said Pete. I could tell he was shrugging.

"Who's driving?" I asked.

"My mom. Come over at noon."

"O.K. Thanks. See you."

I ran upstairs. "Lizzie!" I yelled. Her darn door was shut again. It couldn't be James. Dad had taken him to the playground while Mom worked on a writing project.

"Lizzie?" I knocked on her door.

"Just a minute," she called. She opened the door a crack and peered out.

"Um, can I come in?"

"We-ell." She eased herself through the door, closing it behind her as she stepped into the hall. "We—we can talk out here."

"What are you doing?" I demanded.

"None of your business, Jonathan Eckhardt Peterson."

"Hey, O.K. Do you want to come to the roller rink with Pete and Termite and me?"

"Today?"

"No, Memorial Day."

"Come *on.*"

"Of course today, Lizzie. Around noon. Mrs. Wilson's driving."

"Oh, thanks, but I can't." She started to squeeze herself back into her room.

"Lizzie, what *are* you doing? Why can't you come with us?"

She paused. "I'm busy."

"With what?"

Another pause. "All right, you might as well see now. You're going to find out sooner or later. I was going to start today, anyway."

"Start?"

She opened her door all the way, and I looked into her room. It was the hugest mess I'd ever seen. Junk everywhere. Scraps of felt and pieces of yarn clinging to the rug and the bedspread. The wastebasket overflowing with stuff, spilling out onto the floor.

"Mom is going to kill you," I said flatly.

Lizzie nodded. "That's one reason the door was closed."

"Well, what on earth *is* all this?"

"It's a project. I learned some of it in Brownies, and then my art teacher helped me."

"What *kind* of a project? Come on, Lizzie. Just tell me."

"It's easier to show you," she said. She tiptoed over to her bureau, picking her way through the junk. Then she opened the bottom drawer and removed a layer of neatly folded shirts. "These shirts are camouflage," she said. "When Mom sees a drawer looking so neat, she always leaves it alone." Lizzie laid the shirts on her bed. "Come here, Jonno."

I stumbled to the bureau.

"Look," she said.

I looked. In the drawer were stacks of pretty felt things. "Those are really nice. . . . What are they?"

"This pile here is eyeglass cases." She took one out. "See?" The letter *M* was on it.

"What's that *M* sewn on for?" I asked.

"It's not sewn on; it's embroidered. I can do any letter of the alphabet. These are *monogrammed* eyeglass cases."

I could tell she was proud of the word. "Hey, wow! Good idea, Lizzie. What else have you got?"

"This pile's monogrammed bookmarks, and this pile's monogrammed change purses, and this pile's monogrammed handkerchiefs, only there aren't too many of them yet, because you have to buy plain handkerchiefs first, and they're a little expensive. For me."

"This is pretty terrific, Lizzie. Really."

"Thanks."

"What are you going to do with it all?"

"Sell it. Door to door. I know it didn't work with your seeds, Jonno, but maybe this would be different. People might buy them as gifts or something. Also, I get to keep *all* the money I earn."

"And you're going to start selling today?"

"Yup."

"Wow."

"I better get back to work. I've got to clean all this stuff up before Mom sees."

"Yeah.... Hey, Lizzie, how come you kept this such a big secret?"

Lizzie contemplated me from under her red cap. "I was afraid you'd laugh," she said at last.

"Laugh? Why would we laugh? When have we ever laughed?"

"Not really too often, I guess. It's just that you and Pete and Termite always think up such great ideas. I didn't think I could come up with one as good as yours."

"Oh. Well...you did."

Lizzie grinned.

"Good luck today," I said, closing her door behind me.

"Thanks!" she called.

"O.K., boys," Mrs. Wilson said as she dropped us in front of the roller rink. "Just give me a call when you're ready to come home."

"Oh, I almost forgot!" I cried. I slammed the car door shut and leaned in the front window toward Pete's mother. "My mom said she'd pick us up this afternoon since you drove us here. So we'll call her, O.K.?"

"Oh, that's fine, Jon. See you later, boys."

We waved and ran through the big double doors to the rink. We headed straight for the skate rental booth, paid our money, and then sat down on the benches by the rink to lace up.

I hadn't gotten further than about two laceholes when Pete elbowed me. "Hey, look over there!"

I looked across the rink in the direction he was pointing,

but didn't see anything. "What?"

"There. It's Edweird. And some woman."

"You're kidding!" I jumped up, forgetting my skates, and my feet almost shot out from under me. I regained my balance and craned my neck around.

Suddenly I spotted them on the other side of the rink, moving slowly along, clinging to each other and hugging the railing at the side. Edweird looked like he was dressed for a roller derby or something. He was in these bright blue-and-gold shorts and a bright blue-and-gold tank top with a *24* on the back. And his fat was showing everywhere.

I sat down, gawking.

"Geez," said Pete, "where does he think he is? The Olympics for the Fat?"

I smiled uneasily.

Edweird and the woman inched their way around the rink. By this time, Pete and Termite and I had pretty much given up on our skates and were just staring.

The woman looked a lot like Edweird. She was heavy, with dark wavy hair and brown eyes. And while she wasn't dressed like Edweird, she didn't look like she belonged in a roller rink. I mean, she still had her coat on, and it wasn't like the rink was freezing cold or something.

"I bet that's Edweird's mother," I hissed.

"Yeah," smirked Pete. "Mrs. Edweird."

I couldn't figure out what they were doing here. Obviously they didn't skate well; they could barely stand up. They didn't look like they were having any fun. Maybe Edweird thought it was the thing to do. The kids from our class came skating here a lot. But why had he come with his mother? Then again, who else would have gone with him?

The three of us watched their progress around the rink with interest. Finally we turned back to our skates. Termite finished lacing his first. He stood up, and just as he did so a bunch of kids whizzed by him and snatched his Mets cap off his head.

"Hey!" he shouted angrily.

I heard familiar laughter. Four figures crashed to a halt at the side of the rink. David, Alan, Hank, and Chris.

"Give it!" yelled Termite, ready to fight.

"O.K., O.K.," Hank came back, even though everyone was supposed to be going around the rink in one direction and he had to skate against the flow. He handed Termite the cap.

"Did you see?" asked David, skating back to us, too.

"Edweird?" I asked.

"Yeah," laughed David. "What a jerk. With his *mother*."

We all laughed, only my heart wasn't in it for some reason.

Suddenly the in-boys took off. "Watch this!" Chris shouted to us. The four of them charged around the rink, skates flying, doing about eighty miles an hour. They skated right up to Edweird, then darted around him and turned to face him, skating backward while Edweird and his mother crept forward. Edweird's mother looked annoyed. She was saying something to the boys. She shook her finger at Chris.

The boys took off again, doing another turn around the rink, then slowing down as they caught up to Edweird and his mother. This time, they dogged along behind them, talking to them, teasing them. "Who's your girlfriend, Ed*weird?*" I heard Alan jeer as they neared us.

"Boys," Edweird's mother admonished, but she sounded nervous as well as mad. Just then she lost her balance and fell down with a thud. Edweird, startled, gave her his hand and tried to pull her up, but he fell, too. With shouts of laughter, the in-boys left Edweird and his mom struggling on the floor of the rink.

And suddenly I remembered the day not so long ago when Pete and Lizzie and I had taken James to the school playground.

I remembered the horrible feeling, like a kick in the stomach, when I heard the kids laughing at James, teasing him, making fun of him for eating gravel and taking his clothes off and weee-ooohing and flapping his hands. How dared they?

And now I felt the rage all over again, only this time I wasn't angry at a bunch of neighborhood kids for teasing James; I was angry at the in-boys for what they were doing to Edweird. Edweird couldn't help being the way he was any more than James could help being the way *he* was.

Without thinking, I leaped out of my seat and sped around the rink, Pete and Termite right behind me, until I caught up with Chris, and grabbed him by his shirt collar.

Chris's feet shot out from under him, but he clambered for the railing and managed to stay upright. "Hey!" he yelled in surprise. He turned to face me. "What do you think you're doing?"

"Leave Edwei—Edward alone," I panted.

Chris looked at me as if I were crazy.

The rest of the in-boys and Pete and Termite gathered around us, watching uneasily. Edward and his mother, who had managed to get up and start skating again, stopped a few yards away and were watching, looking both interested and confused.

"Leave . . . him . . . alone," I repeated slowly.

"Since when do I take orders from you?" yelled Chris.

Alan, Hank, and David moved closer to us.

Pete and Termite moved closer to them.

Edward's mother, looking like an angry hornet, started to stomp over to us, only she was too unsteady on her skates.

"I'm tired of your being such a big shot," I said to Chris.

"Oh, yeah?" he threatened.

At that point, Mrs. Jackson grabbed Edward by the wrist

and pulled him off the rink. Edward kept stumbling because he was watching me over his shoulder. His eyes were wide and staring, as if he couldn't believe what was happening. I didn't blame him. *I* used to tease him.

Chris inched his face closer to mine.

"Yeah!" I yelled back.

Chris jumped in surprise, then raised his fist to sock me one.

"Run!" hissed David just then. "Here comes the manager."

I turned, and over my left shoulder I could see a big man striding toward us. He was wearing a red blazer with an emblem on the pocket, and was followed by a couple of the guys who worked at the refreshment stand. Mrs. Jackson must have warned them about us. I thanked her silently.

The seven of us scattered, and melted into the crowd before the manager could catch us.

"Let's go," I said raggedly to Pete and Termite when we reached the bench we'd left our jackets on. My breath was coming in gasps, my chest heaving, from fear as much as from the fast skating. With shaking fingers, we unlaced our skates, yanked them off, and left them on the floor.

Ten minutes later we were outside, and my fear was fading away. I'd done it! I'd really done it! I'd stood up to Christopher Giancossi. I'd fought with him—sort of—and I'd said what I felt about Edward. Maybe I'd never be one of the in-boys, but at least I was being honest, and that would mean a lot to the kids I liked best—Pete and Termite, Steph and Claud.

I realized I didn't care one bit what Chris or Hank or Alan or David thought.

16. Pete's Brilliant Idea

"Hey, Mac! Hey, I swear—I swear on a stack of Bibles—I've just had the most brilliant idea in the whole world!"

I turned around, almost falling off my bike.

It was Sunday, a week after the afternoon we'd spent at the roller rink, and it was only six forty-five in the morning. I was just finishing up my paper route, and out of the blue, Pete had appeared, pounding along the sidewalk behind me.

"Pete, geez, what are you doing? You nearly scared me to death. Nobody's up at this hour, except the other paper route kids." I put on the brakes and stopped at the end of our driveway.

Pete dropped down on the grass near me. I parked my bike and flopped next to him.

"Who can sleep?" asked Pete. "It was about six this morning and I woke up with a jolt, thinking this great idea. I don't know where it came from. Maybe a dream or something."

"So what is this great idea?"

"That we give a carnival!" cried Pete. "Wouldn't it be terrific? You and Termite and me. It would really be fun, and we'd probably earn a ton of money. We can have games with

124

prizes and a refreshment stand and a raffle and *every*thing!"

"Yeah..."

"We can make up signs and post them all over the place, maybe even put an ad in the paper, so everyone will know about it. Think—lots of little kids will come, and we'll charge like twenty-five cents or something for each game. We could make a fortune, and the kids will have fun, of course. After it's over, we'll divide all the money three ways. You'll probably have enough to get the automatic baseball pitcher—and maybe more left over—and then we can start planning the training institute for the sum—"

"Wait, Pete. I can't think that far ahead," I complained.

"Well, what about the carnival?"

I chewed on a piece of grass. "I think it's a good idea," I said finally.

"Good. Now, first we have to make lists. Lots of lists."

"Unh-unh."

"Unh-unh?"

"First I have to have breakfast. And I promised Lizzie I'd help her with something this morning. But how about right after lunch?"

Pete looked disappointed.

"You can tell Termite about it this morning."

"O.K.," said Pete. He leaped up and charged across the lawn to Termite's house.

"I'd wait'll they're all up," I yelled after him.

Pete turned and waved, and I headed into my house. There was no one quite like Pete when he was starting up a project, I thought. There was no one quite like Pete, period.

That afternoon, Pete and Termite and I finished our weekend homework in a big hurry and met at Termite's house for a carnival meeting. We chose his house because no parents were around.

"What first?" asked Termite.

We were slumped around the floor in Termite's rec room, drinking Cokes and eating potato chips out of the bag.

"Lists," replied Pete definitely.

"Lists?" asked Termite.

"Yeah. A list of booths we'll have at the carnival, a list of things we have to do, a list of things we have to buy—"

"Like what? I mean, what do we have to buy?" asked Termite.

"Oh, lots of stuff. Oak tag so we can make signs, ad space in the *Tribune*, prizes for the games, junk to sell at the refreshment stand..."

"And where are we going to get all this—this advance money?" I asked skeptically, although I was pleased with myself for coming up with one of those fancy terms Pete always uses.

Pete cleared his throat. I could tell he was going to hedge.

"Be honest," I said firmly.

He cleared his throat again. "We could borrow it."

"From the bank?" I asked, knowing darn well that wasn't what he meant. I crossed my arms and glared at him.

"We're too young to borrow from the bank," put in Termite, looking from Pete to me and back again. "To borrow from the bank you have to be able to put up Uncle Latimer. My dad said."

"Collateral," I corrected him. "But Pete didn't mean borrow from the bank. He meant borrow from me....Didn't you?" I accused him.

"Aw, come on, Mac. You've got more money than you know what to do with. This'll put you right over the top for the pitcher or the Starcruiser or anything. You loan us some bucks for the carnival; then when it's all over, we pay you back first, and divide the rest three ways. You can't lose."

"Yes, I can. What if I put up more money than we earn back?"

Pete paused.

"I'm the only one who's got anything to lose here," I persisted.

"So you risk it. It's like buying a lottery ticket. Only you have a better chance of earning money with the carnival than of winning the jackpot."

"I'll have to think about it," I said. "I'll let you know. And another thing. What about Chris and those guys?"

"What about them?" countered Pete.

"You know." Ever since the incident at the roller skating rink, the in-boys and Pete and I had been at a standoff. I had won something, but I wasn't sure what. They didn't speak to us, and we didn't speak to them. Not a word had been said about what had happened. They just ignored us—and Edward. Pete and I had tried to be nicer to Edward whenever we saw him. For one thing, we never called him Edweird, even behind his back. And we said hi to him at least twice a day. Edward always seemed really glad to see us, but he also seemed scared of the in-boys, especially Chris. He must have been more scared than he was glad, because he steered clear of our class whenever possible, coming in late and eating lunch with other kids from the Resource Room. I guess he felt safer with them.

But about the in-boys—I knew things weren't really settled between us, and the carnival might stir something up. They were going to think it was a really jerky idea, just like Time-Savers. They'd probably start in with the cracks and teasing again.

"Let's talk about this tomorrow," I said at last, as uncertain about Chris as I was about letting go of my money. "Meeting adjourned."

We didn't get to have a carnival meeting the next day, though. We all had baseball practice after school, and then I had to deliver the Monday *Tribune,* and then I had homework. All during everything—school, baseball, paper delivering, and homework—I kept thinking about whether to invest some of my money in the carnival. I just couldn't decide. I sure didn't want to put a whole lot of work into the carnival, and then lose half the money I'd earned getting up at five to deliver papers and battle Superdog. On the other hand, a carnival could be a lot of fun, if the in-boys would let us alone, and Pete was right—it could bring in a lot of money, too.

Finally I made my decision and called another carnival meeting. "I've decided," I announced, "to put up the money and ignore the dumb in-boys. The carnival's going to be fun, and we're not going to let anyone spoil it for us."

"All *right!*" shouted Pete and Termite, and we started making plans.

We decided to hold the carnival at Pete's house. He had the biggest backyard. The posters we'd make up would say:

COME TO A CARNIVAL!
Games! Prizes! Food!
Place: 320 Napanee Road
Date: Saturday, May 27th
Time: 10 A.M. to 4 P.M.
Come one, come all!
Don't miss it!

We planned to collect big cardboard boxes to use as stands for our booths, and to spend fifteen dollars of my money on little toys at the dime store to use for prizes, on lemonade mix and popcorn and other stuff to sell at the refreshment stand, and on an ad that would appear in the *Tribune* the week before the carnival.

We also had a big discussion because Pete had said people were more apt to come spend money at a carnival if the carnival was for a good cause.

"What do you mean?" Termite asked.

"You know, like if we were going to donate the money we earn to the Red Cross or something."

"Oh. Well, we aren't," said Termite simply.

"Yeah..."

There was this huge pause.

"Pete," I snapped, "you're not thinking of *say*ing the money is for a good cause and then keeping it, are you? That's lying."

"Well, no, but what about saying the money is for a good cause, and then donating some of what we earn to the good cause, and keeping the rest for ourselves?"

"That doesn't sound quite right, either," said Termite.

It wasn't, of course. And in the end we decided the carnival would not be called a charity event or a fund-raiser or anything. But all the talk had given me a good idea. I wouldn't know if it would work out until after the carnival, though.

It's funny how fast things can go from good to bad or from happy to sad. After that carnival meeting, I went home feeling excited. I had a million ideas, and everything seemed terrific.

Later, Bill and Edie came over, and James showed off his stuff. He repeated the words *hi* and *'bye,* and looked at Edie once. It wasn't much, but it was an improvement.

A couple of hours later, things went bad. Bill and Edie had left, and James and Lizzie and I were in bed, only I wasn't asleep yet. I was too excited about the carnival. I lay awake for what seemed like a year, and finally got up for a drink of water.

I tiptoed down the dark hallway, listening to Mom and Dad, who were talking in the living room. Something about their voices made me stop and listen, even though I knew it was eavesdropping.

"I still think we should prepare ourselves for it," Dad was saying.

"I agree with you," answered Mom. "I'm just pointing out that it could be several years from now. We can't give up on him."

Give up on who?

"I'm *not* giving up on him," hissed Dad. He sounded as if he wished he were shouting. "But we can't live in a dream world. We'll make ourselves crazy, too."

Crazy, too. They were talking about James. And they were calling him crazy.

"Well, putting him in an institution will make *me* crazy. He's only a little boy."

An *institution*. What was happening?

I couldn't keep it inside. I ran downstairs and stood glaring at Mom and Dad.

"Jonno?" asked Dad tentatively.

"What?" I was trying very hard not to cry, trying so hard my throat was aching.

"What's wrong?" asked Mom. "Are you sick?"

I shook my head. "I heard."

"Oh." She and Dad looked at each other.

"Come here, son."

Mom and Dad made space for me on the couch, and I sat down between them. Dad put his arm around me.

"It's not for right away," said Mom, "and it's still only maybe."

"But I thought all that changed when we got James into WCDI."

"Honey, James has a *chance* now. But he's still a very slow, very handicapped child."

"But he's smart," I protested. I couldn't let this thing go.

"He may be smart, but he can't dress himself—" began Dad.

"Yet," I interrupted.

"—he rarely speaks, he's not toilet-trained, he'll probably never learn to read, he can't take care of himself, and he barely knows who his family is," continued Dad.

"But he's *learn*ing," I said angrily.

"Jonno, I'm not going to argue with you," replied Dad. "I know it sounds cruel, but institutionalizing James is still a possibility. That's all there is to it."

"How about—" I began.

"No 'how abouts.'"

I glanced at Mom, who was rubbing her forehead, looking very tired. "We're giving James a chance in school," she said, staring out the bay window at the streetlights. "We're watching him, we're helping him, we're loving him. He's just not moving along very fast."

"Are you saying—"

"We're not saying anything right now," broke in Dad. "Come on, it's been a long day. Everybody to bed.... And Jonno, I'd appreciate it if you wouldn't mention this to Lizzie."

"O.K.," I said. I trudged up the stairs without saying good night. When I reached James's room, I unlatched his door, flicked on the hall light, and peeked in at him.

He was sleeping curled up in a little ball, his blond hair spread across his pillow.

Silently I latched his door again, turned off the light, and crept back into my own bed.

17. The Carnival

The morning of the carnival was warm and sunny. I was relieved, since we hadn't decided what we'd do if it rained. By seven-thirty, Pete and Termite and I had eaten breakfast and were rushing around Pete's backyard, setting everything up.

First we put up the big card table. That was for Pete. He was in charge of the refreshment stand. Then we set out six cardboard boxes. Those were for the game booths. Termite was in charge of two of them, I was in charge of two of them, and Dad had volunteered to be in charge of two of them, after I'd told him about my secret idea.

On each box, we hung a sign with the name of the game printed on it: RING TOSS, GRAB BAG (that was for little kids), SPIN & WIN (another easy game), TENNIS TOSS (that was a hard one), BALLOON BURST, and PENNY PITCH. Then we put all the equipment we'd need for each game on top of the boxes so we could set them up later.

Around eight-thirty, Lizzie lugged over one of our old card tables. She was setting up a booth to sell her felt things. She'd had pretty good luck selling door to door, but she had some stuff left over, and besides, she said this would give her an opportunity to take special orders. Of course, she got to keep the money she earned—she didn't have to give any to us—

but I thought her booth might bring more people to the carnival. We figured we were doing each other a favor.

Lizzie wasn't the only one who decided to get in on the act. Her friend Wendell had some special equipment for inflating helium balloons, so he was going to walk around selling a big bunch of them at the carnival, and also on the street, where he might attract customers. Pete's mom was going to sell plant cuttings taken from the jungle she called her living room, and Termite's mom was going to sell secondhand stuff since the Armstrongs had cleaned out all their closets recently. We thought the mothers would be good for getting other mothers (and hopefully their kids) to the carnival. (My mom couldn't help out because she had to watch James. I sort of hoped she wouldn't bring him over. You never knew what he'd do.)

By ten o'clock we were all set up and ready to go. Pete was behind the refreshment stand with big pitchers of lemonade and Kool-Aid, bags of popcorn, and some trays of cookies and brownies. He was also selling Goody Bags for the little kids to carry all their food and prizes in. We'd spent about two hours yesterday decorating those Goody Bags with magic markers, drawing clown faces and animals and cars on them.

On one corner of the refreshment stand sat a stack of tickets and a bowl full of slips of paper. That was for the raffle, and Pete was selling the tickets as well as everything else. The prize we were raffling off was a radio Termite had gotten for his birthday from his grandparents. He already had two radios and didn't know what to do with this one, so it was just sitting in a box in his room, all brand-new and unused. It was a really nice radio, too. We looked in Kaler's and saw one just like it for $29.99. So we were selling tickets for $1.00. We thought it was a pretty good deal. In front of the bowl of tickets we had stood up a sign that read:

WIN A RADIO!!!
• VALUED AT $29.99 •
• TICKETS FOR JUST $1.00 •
• INCREDIBLE BARGAIN •
TRY YOUR LUCK!!!

I looked around at all the booths, all the people ready and waiting. Mrs. Wilson and Mrs. Armstrong were standing behind their tables, arms folded, chatting quietly. My dad and Termite were checking out the prize situation and making sure they had enough change. Pete was counting cups and napkins for the ten millionth time, Lizzie was pulling at her hair, looking worried, and Wendell was out on the sidewalk, hawking balloons and announcing the carnival. I was slouched between my two booths, the Balloon Burst and the Penny Pitch, surveying the scene.

Everything seemed to be under control.

So why did my stomach suddenly turn over? It was nerves, and I felt awful. Really pukey.

Then it hit me. The in-boys. What if they showed up? And what if Mom brought James over?

My stomach was really going crazy. Very slowly, I took five deep breaths and concentrated on counting to ten with each one. When I was finished I felt a lot better.

Which was lucky, because just then our first customers arrived. They were Rosa, from my seed-selling disaster, and the three little Jordan kids. Teddy was proudly showing off a big yellow balloon he'd bought from Wendell, which Rosa had tied around his wrist.

He ran up to me. "Hi, Jon!" he called. "Look what I got." He held out his wrist.

"That's neat," I said.

"I have one dollar and fifty cents left," he said carefully.

Teddy and James were the same age. Teddy could count money and James couldn't even say his own name.

"Would you like to play Spin and Win?" I asked him. "It's just twenty-five cents, and you get a prize no matter what."

"Really? Yeah!"

All the Jordan kids ran over to try Termite's Spin & Win.

"Hi, Jon," said a voice at my elbow.

I turned around.

Oh my gosh. It was *Adrienne*. Adrienne with the sense of . . . humor. And right behind her were Polly, Andy, Michael, Lissa, and Cindy. Bringing up the rear was Mrs. Divine, the grandmother-person. She was trying to watch the kids, but they all scattered. Adrienne headed for me and the Penny Pitch. She would.

And suddenly everything was very busy. More and more people wandered into Pete's backyard. Wendell must have been doing something awfully good or noisy in the street. At any rate, all I could think of was making change, handing out pennies and darts, blowing up balloons, and keeping little kids from getting frustrated or impatient. When I finally had a chance to look at my watch, it was almost noon. I couldn't believe it.

I looked in the cigar box on the Penny Pitch stand. It was full of money. This was great!

"Jon! Pete!" called two breathless voices.

I looked up and saw Steph and Claud parking their bicycles in the driveway and then running over to us.

"Hey, this is excellent!" Steph cried.

"Yeah," agreed Claud. She trotted back across the yard toward Pete.

I handed five pennies to a little boy in blue overalls, and he began tossing them very seriously.

"Listen," whispered Steph. "We thought we should warn you."

"What?" I asked, my stomach sinking.

"The *boys* are on their way over. We passed Alan, Hank, and David on their bicycles at the Giancossi's, waiting for Chris to come out."

"Oh, *no*," I groaned.

"Did I win? Did I win?" asked the little boy suddenly.

"You sure did," I said, checking the board he'd tossed the pennies on. "Come choose your prize."

He selected an eraser that looked like a piece of bubble gum, and moved over to the Ring Toss.

"Steph," I said urgently. "Would you do me a big favor?"

She nodded. "Sure."

"Would you take over for me here while I go talk to Pete and Termite?"

"O.K."

I showed her what to do, and ran to the refreshment stand. "Pete," I said, "I just wanted to warn you. All the in-boys are on their way over. Steph told me."

"Well, O.K. I'll be on the alert."

I gave Termite the news, too, and he nodded, looking scared.

Then I went back to Steph, who needed another pair of hands. So many kids wanted to play both games now that it was too much for one person.

"Here, Jon. You handle the Balloon Burst, and I'll take the Penny Pitch for a while," she suggested.

"Thanks, Steph," I said, flashing her a grateful smile.

For ten minutes everything went smoothly.

Then, just as I was beginning to relax a little, two boys showed up. Not Chris or Alan or Hank or David, but Edward (with his mother) and James (with my mother).

I could have died.

Edward huffed over to me.

"Hi," he grinned.

"Hi," I said trying to sound friendly. I really *wanted* to be friendly, especially after trying so long to make up with him about the business at the roller skating rink. But why did he have to choose this particular time to show up?

"This is a really good idea," he said, still grinning and looking around at the people and booths.

His mother smiled hopefully at me.

"Thanks, Edward," I said. "Do you want to play a game or something?" I checked the driveway to see if the in-boys had arrived yet.

"Sure," he said.

While he was deciding what to play, I heard a sudden explosion of "Weee-oooh, weee-oooh, weee-oooh, weee-oooh, weee-oooh," and some screaming.

James had had it.

Two minutes in the crowd was too much for him. He was squirming and yelling and flapping his hands while my mother tried to pick him up.

Chris, Hank, David, and Alan, of course, showed up in the middle of this. Smirking, they watched as Mom tried to calm James down. She took him to a quiet corner of the yard and held him, talking quietly to him.

Then the boys sidled up behind me and watched Edward, who had decided to throw darts, and had already hit two balloons.

"I want to play," said Chris, shoving a dirty dollar bill in my face.

"Well, you'll have to wait your turn," I said. Edward had two darts to go.

"Well, you'll have to wait your turn," mimicked Chris. "Did you hear that, Alan? He sounds like a stupid teacher."

"How's it going, son?" my father yelled over to me just then. I think he was watching what was going on.

"Fine. Fine, thanks," I shouted back.

Edward threw his last dart. He'd hit three balloons, which was hard to do, and he chose a pencil sharpener as his prize. He showed it proudly to his mother.

"Idiot," muttered Chris, watching him.

"Come on, let's see you do that," I challenged him as I fastened new balloons on the board.

Chris snorted. "A moron could do better."

"Well, in that case, maybe you'd better not play."

Angrily, Chris snatched the first dart out of my hand and aimed at the big bulletin board that was propped up on a chair with five little balloons pinned to it. He threw the dart as if the target were about a mile away. It smashed into the board, just barely hitting a balloon.

Chris glared triumphantly at me, aimed the next dart, and threw it, but not quite as hard as last time.

The dart landed in a big patch of bulletin board.

Steph, Claud, Alan, Hank, and David, who had also gathered to watch, all laughed nervously.

Chris looked as if he wanted to aim the third dart at me instead of the bulletin board.

"Come on. Any moron can do it," I goaded him.

Famous last words. The dart sailed into the center balloon, bursting it with a small pop. I half expected the boys to clap, but everyone was silent.

Chris took the fourth dart from me wordlessly, but managed to give me a look that could have stopped Superdog in mid-growl.

"Last chance, pro," I told him. "You've got to hit one more balloon to tie Edward."

Chris faced the target and closed one eye, aiming carefully. He pulled his arm back and let the dart go.

He didn't even hit the target. The dart landed in the grass.

"Way to go," I said. "Want to play another round?"

Everyone laughed again, and this time the laughter didn't sound the least bit nervous. Even Edward joined in. Chris looked as if he were about to say something, but he kept quiet. He and the other boys turned to leave—and almost bumped into my mother, holding James, who was quiet now. He was smiling slightly and looked pretty normal.

The boys stared for a few seconds, then headed back to their bikes and rode off.

I felt relieved. And pleased. Very pleased.

I signaled over to Pete and then to Termite that everything was O.K.

Four hours later the carnival was over, and everyone was cleaning up. At four o'clock we had held the drawing for the raffle. Rosa had won the radio! She'd been thrilled, and had talked on and on so fast we couldn't understand a word she was saying.

Lizzie had sold everything she'd set up on her table and had taken special orders for six eyeglass cases and two change purses.

By five-thirty Pete, Termite, and I had the Wilsons' backyard pretty well cleaned up. Then the fun began. We took all our boxes full of money up to Pete's room, dumped them out in one gigantic pile on his floor, and started counting.

I couldn't believe it! Even after we paid me back the fifteen dollars I'd lent us to start the carnival, we had each earned over twenty-five dollars. I had enough for the automatic baseball pitcher, *and* enough for my surprise.

I couldn't wait to tell Mom and Dad and Lizzie.

If only I could tell James.

After all, I was doing this for him.

18. Celebrities

On Monday morning, Mom, Dad, Lizzie, and I piled into our car. We were going to school—James's school. (James had left earlier on his bus, as usual. It was better not to disturb his routine.)

I was feeling pretty excited because I was going to get to carry out my surprise. I was going to present fifteen dollars of my carnival money to WCDI for their fund-raising. If the school had more money, then they could help James better, and if they could help James better, maybe he wouldn't have to go to an institution. Of course, I knew fifteen dollars wasn't a lot compared to the thousands Bill said they needed, but I figured every little bit helped. You put enough fifteens together and eventually they'd add up to a thousand or so.

Also, of course, I hadn't told anybody *why* I was giving fifteen dollars to WCDI. There were two reasons for this. One, when I thought about it, I realized I was donating the money more to help James then to help the other kids in his school. That was sort of selfish. And two, I wasn't supposed to talk about James and the institution anyway. So I kept my mouth shut and let everyone think I was being a wonderful, generous

140

person. And who knows, if they all thought so, maybe I was.

But no matter how wonderful and generous I was being, I was a little surprised when Mom and Dad took Lizzie and me out of school to go to WCDI. I mean, fifteen dollars wasn't *that* big a deal.

But on Saturday night, right before I started reading James his story, Mom had said to me, "Jonno, I just got off the phone with Bill. I told him you had something to present to him, and he suggested we all go to WCDI on Monday."

"After school?" I asked, trying to control James, who was getting squirmy.

"No," replied Mom, "in the morning, while WCDI is in session."

"Oh," was all I said. I should have known then that something was going on. But I was too happy realizing I'd miss a math test on Monday.

Monday morning when Mom woke me up, she spent about five minutes rummaging around in my closet.

"Mom," I croaked. "What are you doing?" I don't always sound too polite early in the morning.

"I'm laying out the clothes I want you to wear."

Laying out my clothes? I swear, she hadn't done that in at least four years. "Why?" I asked.

"Never mind. Just wear them."

"Why?" I asked again. They had to be pretty awful if Mom was being so firm at seven in the morning.

I managed to sit up, and sure enough, she'd laid out my gray suit—and a necktie. Those were the worst clothes I could think of. "Mo-om," I complained, "those—"

"No arguments, Jonno."

"Are you laying out Lizzie's clothes, too?"

"Yes, I am. Now get a move on."

"Does Lizzie get to argue with you?"

"No. And if you don't stop, I'm going to...going to..."

I grinned. Mom can never think up threats.

She grinned back. "Put them on. Breakfast will be ready in twenty minutes."

"O.K."

Those clothes should have been another clue that something was up. But at that hour my mind wasn't operating fast enough to solve any mysteries.

We arrived at WCDI around eleven o'clock. This time Lizzie and I knew where we were going, and trooped right up the stairs to greet Tom.

"Well," he said, "here's Jon, our—"

He broke off as Mom came in behind us. I turned around and saw her shake her head frantically at him.

Before he could say anything else, Bill joined us.

"Hello, everybody! Jonno, Lizzie, don't you two look nice."

This came as a surprise to me, since I felt hot and stuffy and itchy.

"James is having a speech session with Edie. Why don't you go watch?"

So we did for a while, spying from a dimly lit room, watching James struggle over his name. He wasn't saying anything yet, but he looked like he might be concentrating better. He was sitting still longer, and looking at Edie more often.

I smiled and glanced at Dad to see him smiling, too. He couldn't possibly put a five-year-old in an institution...could he?

When James's class was over, Edie led him to the music room and then directed Mom, Dad, Lizzie, and me to Bill's office. I was going to present Bill with the money now, and even though there was no reason for it, I began to feel a little nervous—hotter and stuffier and itchier than I did already. My face was probably the color of a pomegranate.

I patted my pocket where I had tucked the envelope for Bill. A crisp, new ten-dollar bill and a crisp, new five-dollar bill were inside. At first I had had nine ratty one-dollar bills, twelve quarters, nineteen dimes, sixteen nickels, and thirty pennies, but Dad had traded me the ten and the five so I could be neater.

We stepped into Bill's office—and to my surprise, Bill wasn't the only one in it. Two men with pencils stuck behind their ears and pads of paper in their hands, and a woman holding a camera with this huge flash attachment, were crowded in as well.

"Surprise, Jonno!" said my mother. "These are some of your co-workers from the *Tribune*."

For a minute, it didn't register. What did WCDI have to do with my paper route?

I guess I looked pretty confused, because Bill stood up and said, "The *Tribune* wants to do a story on you, Jon. It's not every day someone your age donates his money to a school. You're news!"

"Wow!" I said, ignoring the reference to my age. It was not the moment to be insulted.

Then one of the reporters started asking me all these questions: how old I was, where I lived, where I went to school, how I earned the money, and then a bunch of questions about James and the rest of my family.

Mom and Dad and Lizzie lined up along the back wall of the office, watching me and grinning like crazy. I guess they'd all known about the newspaper story.

I answered the questions as best I could. Then the lady with the camera took some pictures of me, and some pictures of me with Mom and Dad and Lizzie. Finally another teacher brought James into the office. He weee-ooohed nervously (James, of course, not the teacher), but even so, the lady got a few pictures of James and me, James and me and Lizzie, James and Edie, and a few other combinations of people. Finally James went back to his music class.

Then one of the reporters said, "O.K., Jon. Now present Bill with the money and we'll take a shot of the actual ceremony."

What ceremony? I was beginning to feel embarrassed. Was I supposed to make a speech? I thought of all the attention I was getting and decided I better live up to it.

I slipped the envelope out of my pocket and handed it to Bill. The camera started flashing. I was seeing spots before my eyes.

"This money," I said proudly, "is for WCDI so you can help James and all the other kids like him." I realized I really meant it.

I glanced across the room and saw Mom sniffling and wiping her eyes, and Dad smiling, and Lizzie giving me our pinkie signal.

Bill took the envelope and said solemnly, "On behalf of WCDI, thank you very much, Jon."

Flash, flash. Flash.

And it was over. What a morning! I'd been shocked at first, but now that everything had had time to sink in, I was pretty excited. I'd never had my picture in the paper, or even my name, except for when I was born, and once when I was one of fifty-eight kids who volunteered to pick up trash on our school playground and the paper printed all fifty-eight of our names.

The reporters and the photographer left, and Bill and Edie thanked me again for the money. "You two are pretty special," said Bill to Lizzie and me. I could tell Lizzie was flattered that Bill thought she was special, too.

"James can be a pain," she said, "but we...we..."

She trailed off and we all looked at her questioningly. She didn't finish, though.

A few minutes later we left, and as we were getting in the car, Dad popped a surprise on us. I didn't know if I could take many more surprises.

"Let's all go out to lunch," he said.

Out to lunch, instead of back to school?

"Really?" Lizzie and I cried at the same time.

"What about school?" Lizzie asked.

"And what about saving money?" I asked.

"I think the four of us deserve a vacation *and* a treat," said Mom.

"All *right!*" I shouted.

So we drove to Howie's Hamburger Haunt and gorged ourselves. And right in the middle of everything, Lizzie said, "Mom, can I have a friend over after school tomorrow?"

I could tell Mom was so surprised she was about ready to shoot out of her seat, but she just said calmly, "Of course, dear. Who is it?"

"Tammy," answered Lizzie casually, as if that cleared everything up.

"Tammy?" asked Mom.

"Yeah, she's in my Brownie troop....I *told* her about James and she said, 'So what?'"

"Very reasonable of her," smiled Dad.

Lizzie went back to her french fries, and that was the end of that discussion.

My thoughts drifted to the newspaper article. I could hardly wait to see it!

19. James Again

The article appeared the very next day, in the Tuesday afternoon edition of the *Tribune*. Those newspaper guys must have
worked pretty fast, I thought, but then, that's what a newspaper
is all about: getting the news out fast.

On my paper route I proudly delivered all those stories about
me, and then tore home with the last *Tribune* tucked safely in
my bag.

"Mom!" I yelled as I threw my bike in the garage and banged
my way into the house. "Mom!"

"Jonno, what is it?"

I found Mom in the kitchen with James. These days, she
usually stopped her copywriting when James got home, and
then worked with him on the things he was learning in school.
I knew I'd probably just destroyed their work session. James
looked up at me, said, "Oh-*ma,*" and started to get off of his
chair.

"Sorry, Mom," I said breathlessly, "but, look."

I spread the newspaper open to page two, and James escaped
to the living room.

"Right on the second page!" exclaimed Mom.

146

"Yeah," I said.

There was a big picture of me presenting the envelope to Bill, and under that were three smaller pictures: one of me, one of James and Lizzie and me, and one of Edie holding James. James wasn't looking at the camera in either picture, but he was smiling in one, and all in all he looked pretty good.

To the left of all the photos was a paragraph describing them. It read:

> *Top:* Young Jonathan Peterson presents his donation to Dr. William Wyman, director of the Weston Child Development Institute. *Bottom, left to right:* Jonathan Peterson. Jonathan with his sister, Elizabeth, and their brother, James, a student at WCDI. James Peterson with Edith Rinehart, his speech therapist.

Under the photos was a fairly long article. It started out by telling about me and the carnival. I had very carefully told the reporters Pete's and Termite's full names, and sure enough, they were in the paper, too! Then the article told about our family, and about James and the problems we'd had with him—trying to find out what was wrong with him, then trying to find a school for him. Finally, the article said, we'd placed James in WCDI. Then there was some stuff about Bill and the teaching methods at WCDI, and the progress James was making. It was a little off the subject of the carnival and the money, but that didn't matter. Much. Besides, Mom said with all the publicity for WCDI, people would probably make donations, and that would be wonderful.

Mom and I read the article through twice. Then Mom turned to me and said, "Oh, Jonno, I'm *so* proud of you! You know that, don't you?"

I nodded.

Mom hugged me, and then held me away from her, looking into my eyes. "Dad and I give so much attention to James, sometimes I worry about you and Lizzie."

"Well," I admitted, "it's not always easy. It really isn't. The kids tease me in school. They call James crazy and retardo, and make me feel like *I'm* weird just because James has problems. And Termite's still scared of him. And sometimes James makes me so frustrated I could kill him, but, well, you know . . ."

"Just like Lizzie yesterday," said Mom thoughtfully.

She looked like she might cry, so I was really glad that Lizzie burst into the kitchen just then. Tammy was right behind her. They were wearing their Brownie outfits. Lizzie even had the beanie on, instead of her baseball cap. She didn't seem to care that her hair looked like a Brillo pad.

"Well, hi," smiled Mom. "Hi, Tammy. Nice to see you again."

"Hi," said Tammy shyly.

"See you, Mom. Tammy and I have stuff to do," shouted Lizzie, and she and her friend took off upstairs.

"I guess they didn't want a snack," said Mom.

"I guess not."

We looked at the article once more, and Mom called Dad to ask him to stop in at Cox's on the way home and buy five extra papers so we could send the article to our relatives. I was just about beaming. My teeth would drop out if I smiled any more.

I walked into school the next day feeling awfully proud. I knew the in-boys would probably think the newspaper article was jerky (I mean, it was about my crazy brother and me), but I really didn't care. Steph and Claud wouldn't think it was jerky, and Pete and Termite were so puffed up with pride they were almost exploding. I decided that if this was where being inside out got us, then inside out was O.K.

Just then Steph and Claud charged into the room. "Hey, you guys, this is fantastic!" they were exclaiming.

Claud shoved a copy of the article on my desk. "I brought this in so everyone could see!"

"I can't believe it!" Steph cried. "I've never been in the paper. I never even knew anyone who had an article written about him—except you. Hey, Pete, Charlie, you're mentioned in it, too. Did you know?"

Pete and Termite nodded, grinning.

The next thing that happened shocked me practically out of my shoes. Janie and Elise came into the room, followed by Margaret and Louise. They marched right over to us. Elise had a copy of the article, too.

"Oh, Jon," she exclaimed in this high, false voice. "I think this is just wonderful!"

I glanced at Claud, who rolled her eyes.

"Do you want to sit with us at lunch today?" Elise asked.

"Well," I said, blushing right to the tips of my ears, "um...why don't you eat lunch with Pete and Charlie and Steph and Claud and me?"

Before she could answer, a couple of other kids came over to our group, and then a few more, Edward among them. They all wanted to talk to us. Some of them hadn't read the article yet, but Claud passed her copy around.

Everybody was saying things like, "Neat," and "Great," and "Good idea." I even heard Janie look at the pictures of James and say, "He doesn't look crazy. Are you sure he's the weird one?"

"Well, if it isn't young Jonathan Peterson," said a sarcastic voice all of a sudden.

I looked away from a conversation with Steph and Louise to see that Chris had come in, surrounded, of course, by Hank, David, and Alan.

I decided to ignore him.

So did everybody else, except for Elise who said, "Oh, shut up."

Chris, surprised, did shut up. He looked at a copy of the article, and then at me. Finally, with a sidelong glance at Elise, he said "Nice going, Jon."

"Thanks," I said. I wondered if he might say something nice to Edward then since he seemed to be trying to make up, but he didn't, of course. I guess that was asking too much. Why had I ever wanted to be like the in-boys?

That night at dinner, Mom said, "Edie's coming over tonight for a few minutes."

"Why?" asked Lizzie. "She and Bill were just here."

"I know. I think she has something to show us."

"Hi!" called James from across the table. He wasn't talking to anyone in particular. He was just making noise, but it was a nice change from "weee-oooh."

Lizzie giggled.

I saw Mom and Dad hide smiles.

Edie arrived when I was in the middle of reading to James. When James saw her, he wiggled out of my lap and ran over to give her a hug around her legs.

"Hey, tough stuff," she greeted him.

James leaned back to look at her, giggled, and said, "Oh-ma."

When Mom, Dad, Edie, Lizzie, James, a bowl of Cheerios, and I had all gathered in the living room, Edie said, "O.K., everybody hang on to your hats."

We looked at each other curiously.

Edie sat on the floor facing James, the Cheerios beside her. She made sure she had his attention. When he was sitting quietly and looking at her, Edie said slowly and clearly, "What's your name? Say 'James.'"

James hesitated. "Ja—" he managed to say. "Ja..." He flapped his hands nervously and stood up.

"That's about as far as he gets," said Edie, "but it's a fantastic beginning."

"Hey, I think he just gave himself a nickname!" exclaimed Lizzie. "Jay-Jay! He's Jay-Jay. Now he doesn't have to be James all the time."

Edie was showing us some other things when the phone rang. I ran to answer it.

"Hi, Mac," said Pete's voice.

"Hi. What's up?"

"I've got this amazing idea!" Pete was so excited the receiver was practically jumping out of my hand. "It's for a fund-raiser. For James's school. See, we..."

And Pete was off again. I sat there and listened to his idea and thought about Jay-Jay and WCDI and the carnival. "Don't forget," I said when he stopped for a breath. "This weekend I'm going to go to Kaler's to buy the baseball pitcher. Then we can plan the training institute."

"Right," said Pete.

I heard voices in the front hall then and knew Edie was leaving.

"Pete, I gotta go. I'll see you in school tomorrow. O.K.?" I hung up the phone and ran out in time to yell good-bye to Edie.

Mom and Dad took off for the den to watch TV, and Lizzie decided to call Tammy.

I led James into the living room, thinking it would be hard to start calling him Jay-Jay after all these years. He pulled me over to a Lego building, and tugged on my hand to make me sit down. Then he sat down, too, and began building. He was humming the theme song from *The Flintstones*.

"Do you want help, Jay-Jay?" I asked.

He hummed some more.

I picked up a few Legos and started to put them on the building. James stopped humming and watched me. Then he smiled and went back to work.